Paul Day Chronicles – Goo
The complete

It is 1992.
Paul Day is entering the final year of]
same pressures as every other 16 year olc
His all important exams are fast approacinng ionowcu ωy ω.ω ω..ω
further education and/or those vital career choices.
Monumental decisions that pretty much shape the rest of your life.
But Paul isn't interested in any of that.
He is a 16 year old boy!
He wants to have sex!
Preferably with a girl!
He wants to know what falling in love feels like – preferably with a girl!
He wants to go into a pub for the first time, and to pass his driving test when the time comes.
But, as they say, be careful what you wish for!
Because, unfortunately for Paul, all the events of his life come with an unwanted side order – his own unique brand of *life chaos*!
Experiences that are ordinary events for *normal people*, somehow always turn into extraordinary dramas...

Goodbye B.M.X. Hello S.E.X. is a comedy epic that proves that youthful enthusiasm, when mixed with brutal fate and *exceptional stupidity,* can be an explosive cocktail!
But, beyond the wild rollercoaster of a teenagers' hopes and aspirations and desires and *urges!,* could there be even greater treasures in life than you could possibly dream of?

Goodbye B.M.X. Hello S.E.X.

By Gary Locke:

The complete days of 1992 –
Paul Day Chronicles – Goodbye B.M.X., *Hello S.E.X.*

Short Stories from 1992 –
Paul Day Chronicles – Love for the Very First Time.
Paul Day Chronicles – Dead Legs, Exam Dreads and Fun Behind the Bike Sheds.

The complete days of 2006 –
Paul Day Chronicles – Happily After *Ever*!

Short Stories from 2006 –
Paul Day Chronicles – Love Is Like Fireworks!
Paul Day Chronicles – The Stag Do.
Paul Day Chronicles – Football Is Like Sex!
Paul Day Chronicles – Fate… Bloody Fate!

Cling and Grow Publishing

Copyright © Gary Locke 2013

Cover Design by Andy Tiplady – Freelance Graphic Designer

www.pauldaychronicles.com

First published in Great Britain in 2013 by Cling and Grow Publishing

This Createspace edition published in 2013 by Cling and Grow Publishing

The rights of Gary Locke to be identified as the author of this work have been asserted in accordance with Copyright, Designs and Patents Act 1988.

All rights reserved. No part of this publication may be reproduced, stored in a retrieval system, or transmitted in any form or by any means, electronic, mechanical, photocopying, recording or otherwise, without the prior permission of the publisher.

All characters in this publication are fictitious and any resemblance to real persons, living or dead is purely coincidental.

ISBN 978 1 494 36775 6

Paul Day Chronicles – Goodbye B.M.X. Hello S.E.X.
the complete days of 1992

Gary Locke

Chapters

Author's Note…..*page 6*

Prologue…..*page 7*
Chapter One – *Saturday, 25th July 1992 at 20.33!*…..*page 9*
Chapter Two – *SEX!*…..*page 17*
January 1992…..*page 25*
Chapter Three – *this could be the best day of your life don't let it pass you by*…..*page 25*
Chapter Four – *Yates' Wine Bar*…..*page 30*
Chapter Five - *Louise*…..*page 39*
February 1992…..*page 50*
Chapter Six – *bathroom dash*…..*page 51*
Chapter Seven – *a matter of principle*…..*page 58*
Chapter Eight – *Valentines Day*…..*page 64*
March 1992…..*page 72*
Chapter Nine – *Poetry Club*…..*page 73*
You Are…..*page 80*
Today…..*page 81*
Chapter Ten – *earliest memories*…..*page 83*
I Miss My B.M.X.…..*page 89*
April 1992…..*page 90*
Chapter Eleven – *Love?*…..*page 90*
Chapter Twelve – *the parents*…..*page 98*
Chapter Thirteen – *work experience*…..*page 109*
Chapter Fourteen – *motorbikes and tits*…..*page 117*
May 1992…..*page 124*
Chapter Fifteen – *the corridor*…..*page 126*
Chapter Sixteen – *Science and Sex Education*…..*page 134*
Chapter Seventeen – *sports day*…..*page 143*
June 1992…..*page 152*
Chapter Eighteen - *exams*…..*page 153*
Chapter Nineteen – *Father Christmas and the Tooth Fairy*…..*page 160*
HD…..*page 166*
Chapter Twenty – *en-suite hostage*…..*page 167*
Chapter Twenty One – *the woman with the Dragonfly tattoo*…..*page 174*
July 1992…..*page 183*
Chapter Twenty Two – *my moment*…..*page 186*

Chapter Twenty Three – *Love!*.....*page 195*
Always.....*page 199*
Something Worth.....*page 202*
August 1992.....*page 203*
Chapter Twenty Four – *the day will come*.....*page 203*
Chapter Twenty Five – *exam results*.....*page 209*
September 1992.....*page 220*
Chapter Twenty Six – *the driving test*.....*page 222*
Chapter Twenty Seven – *if I could turn back time*.....*page 230*
Mirror, Mirror.....*page 236*
Chapter Twenty Eight - *Lynsey*.....*page 237*
October 1992.....*page 242*
Chapter Twenty Nine – *view from the hill*.....*page 243*
Chapter Thirty - ~~Love~~.....*page 252*
Just A Beautiful Dream.....*page 256*
November 1992.....*page 257*
Chapter Thirty One – *box of memories*.....*page 257*
Chapter Thirty Two – *the Birds, the Bees and Snooker*.....*page 265*
December 1992.....*page 272*
Chapter Thirty Three – *when Angels scream out loud*.....*page 273*
Now.....*page 279*
Chapter Thirty Four – *the great tapestry*.....*page 280*
To Really Have It All.....*page 282*
Chapter Thirty Five – *New Years Eve*.....*page 285*
To Be Alive.....*page 294*
Acknowledgments.....*page 296*

Goodbye B.M.X. Hello S.E.X.

Author's Note

Gary Locke – author of the Paul Day Chronicles series'

I was born, raised and continue to reside in Hazel Grove, a bustling village just outside of the town of Stockport, near to Manchester – with my wife and two daughters.

Paul Day was born, raised and resides in the bustling, fictional village of Holly Grove, just outside the fictional town of Stoneport, near to Manchester.

Any similarities between Hazel Grove and Holly Grove, especially Hazel Grove High School and Holly Grove High School are purely coincidental!

In fact, any similarities between *any* places, events or people within this book are also purely coincidental!

Paul Day is an ordinary, young man who somehow turns ordinary events into extraordinary and humorous dramas.

Goodbye B.M.X. Hello S.E.X. chronicles Paul's final School year (1992) and describes events that will hopefully amuse and entertain you.

Thank you to all my family and friends and to everyone I've known and loved past, present and future.

As always, this book is dedicated to my three girls – *Sharon*, *Ella-Louise* and *Hazel*.

You are my everything.

xxx

Prologue

Paul Day Chronicles - Goodbye B.M.X., Hello S.E.X.

SEX!

Everyone remembers their *first time*!

Who it was with! - Your childhood sweetheart? The girl next door? A one night stand? A very quiet girl named Lorna Latex??

Where it happened! – The bedroom? The Bathroom? In the back of a car? At the back of the cinema where, unfortunately, it wasn't quite as dark as you thought it was??

What it was like! – Good? Bad? Fast? Slow? Missionary? Doggy? Paid for in cash??

And, maybe most importantly for young men, *When* it happened -

For some it was in the 80's.
The decade of pop music, keyboards, the synthesizer and endless "power ballads".
The fashion faux-pas era when the New Romantics looked normal and there were more shoulder pads than at an American Football boot camp!
Cans and cans of hairspray created *big, big* hair - and a gigantic hole in the ozone layer! And the majority of men wore skin tight, testicle-crushing, stone wash jeans - probably the main reason for the huge reduction in pregnancies!

For others it was the 70's.
Vietnam, Flower-Power, Disco, Feminism, Punk Rock.
Sex, Drugs and Rock 'n' Roll. Preferably in that order, because sex *after* drugs was dangerous. Depending on your narcotic of choice, you could sometimes be *so* relaxed that performance was impossible, or be *so* paranoid that you thought that you were shagging Margaret Thatcher!

There were those for which it happened in the 60's.
When the Beatles ruled the Earth! (Not one of those tacky B movies - the four lads from Liverpool!)
There was the Space Race, JFK, and Martin Luther King's - *"I have a dream"* - which was very different to ABBA's *"I have a dream"*, which came much later!

For some it was the 50's.
My history gets a bit blurred this far back, but I'm pretty sure the 1950's was

Goodbye B.M.X. Hello S.E.X.

all about Teddy Boys and Greasers.
   The World was still in black and white; and there were two World Wars, the Industrial Revolution and the Roman Empire!

   For me, it happened in the 90's.
   It was the last decade of the 20th Century; the pathway to the new Millennium.
   The 90's was famous for………………..The Spice Girls?
   Was that it? Was that all a whole *decade* had to offer?
   Not for me!
   The 90's was my coming of age. The transformation from boy to man.
   The metamorphosis from ugly duckling to……….well, ugly duck!
   The time when I could hopefully say "Goodbye B.M.X., Hello S.E.X.!"
   And it all began one particular night in 1992…..

Chapter One - "...Saturday, 25th July 1992 at 20.33!...."

Do Woodpeckers get splinters in their beaks?

And what do they take for their inevitable headaches? And that's not even mentioning.....

What the Hell was I doing?

The most important moment in my life was only seconds away, and I was thinking about bloody Woodpeckers?

I took a deep breath.

Was I ready for what was about to happen?

Was I prepared?

Was I confident?

Was I *up to it*?

No, no, no, *no*!

But none of that *really* mattered.

The important question was:

Was I excited?

Yes!

In fact – yes, yes, yes, *yes*!

I was about to, God willing, make that monumental step from boy to man!

The kind of step that only Neil Armstrong's words seemed appropriate for!

I would be handing in my virgin card and replacing it with............do you get a card that proves that you've had sex?

You know, another card to clog up your wallet, like an id or donor card, but something that would give real proof that you'd got your leg over!

Something like a Barclay card or a Master card – anything to replace your *Mastur-bator* card!

Maybe it's good there's no such card. I'd probably be getting it out to show everyone all the time. I might even be tempted to have a hat made with a rim for it to sit on!

But I was getting ahead of myself.

I was sitting alone in my bedroom waiting for my girlfriend, Louise, to come back in from the bathroom.

We had been seeing each other for nearly six months which, after sixteen years in this big, bright World, represented my longest relationship by quite some distance.

In truth, the *relationship stakes* was pretty much a one Horse race!

But Louise and I had decided that tonight would be *our night*.

The physical side of our relationship had progressed over time and, recently, our "petting" had rapidly become heavier and heavier. (Is *petting* still the right word for snogging and a bit of "finger pie" etc.? I'd been to petting *zoos* and there didn't appear to be *any* of that sort of thing going on!)

We hadn't pre-planned *it* before this night but, after a good half an hour of vigorous, busy-handed snogging, we had agreed to make this our *special night*.

Goodbye B.M.X. Hello S.E.X.

Louise had whispered into my ear four words that couldn't have sounded more beautiful if they'd been sung by a dozen Angels, or even Aled Jones in a snowstorm!

"Do you *want to?*"

"Hell yes!" I had rather casually answered!

Well, that was after making sure she actually meant what I thought she meant.

A similar incident a couple of months earlier, and a hasty answer to what turned out to be a *completely different* question, had led me to an *after-School* club that I wouldn't normally be seen dead at. (But that's another story!)

But <u>this time</u> we *were* on the same wavelength.

Which was also a bit of a relief and meant that Louise wasn't totally put off me by the rather embarrassing incident during an end of School *Sex Education* class! (Again, *another* story! Wow – all these *other* stories you've got to look forward to!!)

I began to panic about how long Louise had actually been in the bathroom.

She had said she would just be a minute while she "slipped into something more comfortable".

When she said it I was initially worried and hoped that she meant something sexy, and not that she was going to put her slippers on!

Now though, I had two *further* worries.

1...If she was much longer I would have to send out a search party. She may have changed her mind and slipped out of the bathroom window or, worse still, banged her head on the sink after slipping on a wet floor caused by Dad's, yet again, poor aim whilst having a piss!

2...The more time she was away from me, the more time I had to think about what was going to happen!

And the older I get the more I realise that having time to think, about *anything*, was extremely dangerous for me.

My mind was becoming so negative of late I was thinking of nicknaming it Arsenal!

(I know 1-0 is a *win*, and constantly passing the ball back to the goalkeeper is a legitimate tactic – but what happened to *entertainment?*)

The first thing my *Gooner* brain had me worrying about was – was I <u>clean</u> enough?

Especially, you know, around the area that was nervously waiting for his debut!

I *think* so.

I had been paying particularly extra attention to that area anyway since I'd been seeing Louise – and had come to some conclusions.

Using Mum's (*Lavender Explosion*) body oil wash may clean ok, but didn't leave the *manly* fragrance any self-respecting hetero-male aims for!

The family sized bottle of Mint and Tea Tree body wash smelt ok, and probably left you nice and clean, but produced the kind of stinging sensation to sensitive areas best left for torture sessions!

As it was, I had settled for copious amounts of my Brothers' (better known as *Brother Simon*) Lynx Marine shower gel. Hopefully it cleaned ok and, even if it did smell a little Macho-American, anything was better than the potential specialist cheese board aroma that may have otherwise festered down there!

My paranoia had even made me consider using a splash of bleach, but I had decided that would probably be going too far.

It would definitely result in the level of cleanliness I was looking for – but I certainly didn't want a *blonde* bell-end!

So, after coming to the conclusion that I probably *was* clean enough, there was only one other thing to worry about.

Yep, that one word that actors, sports cars and nervous pre-sex males absolutely dread – *performance*!

Maybe if this was just going to be a one night stand kind of debut then it wouldn't matter so much.

But seeing as it was with Louise, by far the most important person I'd ever known in my whole life, I needed to make sure that I was at least *half decent*.

Luckily for me – I had taken some advice!

Oh no!

Scrub that!

Unluckily for me – I had taken advice off Brother Simon!

He had been my only choice really.

None of my closest friends, Little Si, Mark or John, had been fortunate enough to have had sex – their combined experience with girls could be summed up by one word: "_____"!

And asking Dad about sex would be like, well, *asking your Dad about sex!!*

So I was stuck with Brother Simon.

In fairness he did seem to have had an unfathomably high amount of success with the opposite sex, and so it was worth giving him a go.

First, he blessed me with his observation that *all women are different!*

I had the feeling there and then that his advice wasn't going to be ground breaking!

But he explained what he meant in spectacular detail.

All women like different things.

All women like different things *doing* to them.

All women kiss different.

All women like to *fuck* different.

All women smell different.

All women *taste* different!

I stopped him there.

Although a bit uncomfortable about him using the f-word (something he did, at least, another twenty times! – it's not big *or* clever!) he was obviously talking about *going down*, and it was something I felt I needed to know about.

"No matter how subtle it may be – they all have different tasting fannies! I think I could actually go on You Bet and pick out each different girl I've been with – by tasting her pussy juice!"

Oh my God!

This is what it must be like to talk to Hugh Hefner!

Did I really want to hear this?

He carried on.

"The key thing about eating pussy..."

I shuddered more than a piano falling down a huge flight of stairs!

"...is to work through the tongue ache! It will be difficult, and it will be a struggle – but the rewards you will get, if you do it right, will be well worth the effort! Actually, a good way to exercise you tongue is to spend a good ten minutes a day trying, as hard as you can, to touch your nose with it!"

What was he going on about?

Was this complete Horse shit, or real golden advice?

Do all men who are *going down* experts do, at least, ten minutes tongue exercising *every day*?

Brother Simon gave me a further ten minutes worth of *women wisdom*.

Most importantly, he said, was making your way "South" *only* when the time was right.

And don't force it – work your way in slowly and gently.

Uhh?

Then there was a whole section about *bases* during which he told me, in no uncertain terms, that I was *"well behind schedule!"*

My explanation of *"Me and Louise are just going at our own pace and enjoying it very much, thank you!"* brought out a response of "GAY!" from him.

Following this, there was a good three or four minutes of random sporting analogies.

Why on Earth does he, like most men, insist on using these weird sporting references?

My mind became a confusion of those *bases*, and then *holes being goals* and *slam dunks* and *jumps* and *leg before wickets* or *leg over wickets* or something random to do with cricket!

And that's not mentioning *all* the "G"'s.

G-strings and *G-spots* and *G-forces* and, probably, *G-whizzes*!

Whatever he was talking about, he may as well have been speaking a foreign language.

He apologised that there wasn't enough time to talk properly about positions, but suggested that I try to get Louise to *go on top!* (Which I had always thought was a bunk-bed reference!)

The last thing he told me, before he thankfully left me alone, was his, *very important*, "Three step - fail safe guide".

"Slow, Steady, Strong."

Nice and <u>slow</u> to start with - there's no second chance for false starts!

Then <u>steady</u> for a few laps.

Then, when everyone's in the home straight, good <u>strong</u> finish.

What the hell had he been talking about?
My confusion was greater than before I had foolishly approached him.
What should I do?
I suppose I only really had two options.

1...I could try and incorporate what I did actually *know*. Which, in reality, meant trying to emulate something from *Wildlife on One*! You know, the episodes in which David Attenborough excitedly watches mating rituals, like he's got some kind of weird animal porn fetish! In reality though, the only episode I could clearly remember was two *Spiders* going for it. And I'm not really sure that I could recreate what can be achieved with eight limbs! I will make sure though that I get off Louise pretty damn quickly afterwards – in case she tries to eat me!
2...I could try and go with the flow and hope that everything comes to me *naturally*. As far as I'm aware our Dog has never had any kind of advice off anyone (even dodgy Brotherly advice!) – but that doesn't stop him giving things a good go with every other Dog we come across on the field! (Probably male and female!) Although, in fairness, I'm not sure how much Louise would appreciate having her leg humped, as my tongue hung out of my mouth and drooled all over her - while I howled at the top of my voice!

It was too late to worry about anything anymore because, thankfully, I could hear gentle footsteps coming out of the bathroom and heading towards my room.
I glanced at my alarm clock.
In bright red LED lighting it read "20.33".
So this was it.
The most important moment in my life was about to begin on *Saturday, 25th July 1992 at 20.33!*
The door opened and Louise slipped into the room – thankfully *not* wearing slippers!
What she was wearing though was a rather sexy, silk-looking negligee.
Her dark hair hung down on her shoulders and she looked at me with a pouty look on her face, and seriously smoldering eyes.
She looked hotter than hot!
She sat beside me on the bed and, without a word, launched headfirst into a full-on, passionate kiss.
I instinctively put my hands on her shoulders.
As I did, I couldn't help but feel that her negligee seemed slightly too big for her.
We continued kissing but I couldn't help but wonder whether the silky garment may actually belong to her mother.
Maybe she had borrowed it for the evening – possibly known or unbeknown to her mother?
I tried to stop it, but once my mind starts to wander, it likes to go for a *full*

Goodbye B.M.X. Hello S.E.X.

walkabout!

I began to actually picture Louise's Mum wearing the negligee. It would probably have fitted better as she was certainly *curvier* than Louise. (Polite way of saying heavier / chunkier!)

But, for a mother of her age, she was certainly still very attractive!

In fact, I'd go as far as saying she's one of those Mum's you'd quite like to (in Brother Simon's potty-mouthed words) *fuck*!

Why isn't there a word for such women?

Mother I'd like to fuck?

You could call them MILTF's!

Or maybe MILF would sound better?

That's good.

I should write that down before someone else thinks of it!

I pulled my mind back to where it should be.

I wasn't interested in MILF's I had a girlfriend, or a *GILF*, to focus on.

Although GILF maybe sounds a bit close to that "sport" for people who can't, or can't be arsed, running – so, instead, they try to hit tiny balls into tiny holes!

I opened my eyes as Louise pulled away from the kiss.

"Are you ready?" she asked in a sexy, almost whispered voice.

Despite, during the lengthy time in which she was in the bathroom, I'd had my worst fears confirmed that no, I was most certainly *not* ready; I lied.

"Yes!" I whispered back, unfortunately missing the aim of also sounding sexy and coming across more like an asthmatic Snooker commentator!

I stood up and turned the light out.

I then reached over to turn off the lamp on my computer desk but Louise grabbed my arm.

"Leave the lamp on." She said. "I want to be able to look into your eyes!"

I did what she said and, as I looked back round, she slipped under my bed sheets.

She held the corner up and said,

"Take your clothes off, and come in!"

First I put some music system on.

I had prepared a loop of Bryan Adams' *"Heaven"* – which was "our song". It seemed like it should be playing for our special moment.

I took my jumper and jeans off, followed by my socks, whilst being grateful that my case of Athletes Foot had cleared up.

I sniggered to myself as I contemplated why some body ailments were described the way they were. You know, like *Athletes Foot* or *Tennis Elbow* or *Cauliflower Ear*.

As I did I hoped, for mine and Louise's sake, that I didn't suffer from any kind of *Knob of Butter*!

I left my boxer shorts on, slipped under the sheet, and pulled Louise close to me.

She smelt good.

Gary Locke

Thankfully her citrusy perfume was easily overpowering my naval warfare Lynx smell!

In fact, maybe too good, I could almost *taste* her perfume – it was like someone was using my teeth as an orange squeezer!

I ignored my taste buds and concentrated on my sense of touch.

The feel of the silk against my body as we, again, pressed our lips against each other gave me a feeling to suggest that, so far, I didn't need to worry about any potential buttery knob!

After a couple of minutes of kissing I decided to take the initiative.

I reached to the bottom of Louise's negligee and pulled it up over her head. I threw it to the floor, leaving her completely naked.

As usual, I instinctively reached for her breasts. They were smooth and firm and, even though I was no Peter Shilton, they were a good handful for me!

As I gently caressed them though I realised that, what was usually the *main course*, would tonight be merely an aperitif!

I moved over Louise and put my head over her left breast and gently put my lips around her nipple.

I'd found during this particular move "gently" needed to be the operative word. In the past Louise had complained about my <u>excessive</u> sucking, explaining that her nipples were *not Lockets Lozenges!*

As this was purely first course tonight, I didn't linger there too long. Instead I traced my tongue slowly down her stomach towards her belly button.

I didn't have a compass but was pretty sure "south" was *down*!

After tongue circling her belly button (thankfully she doesn't have one of those weird *outies*!) several times, like some unfortunate National Lampoon-esque roundabout driver – I headed further down.

Louise was nicely trimmed and Brother Simon's teeth-flossing tales of woe would not be happening to me!

I thrust my tongue into her and got ready to experience Louise's "unique taste".

It was hard to get it fully from the first tongue full. It tasted like nothing I'd tasted before and my sense of taste still seem to be influenced by Louise's orange-tinged perfume.

KNOCK! KNOCK! KNOCK!

I snapped my head up faster than the hind legs of that Mule in *Buckaroo*!

Louise and I looked at each other but remained silent.

Someone had clearly just knocked on my door but it's as if we both thought if we were silent it might actually *not* have happened.

KNOCK! KNOCK! KNOCK! KNOCK! KNOCK!

The knock was back – and, this time, included an *extra* knock.

"Paul, can I have a quick word please?"

Shit, it was Dad!

What was he doing <u>upstairs</u>?

He only ever made the effort to ascend the stairs if he was going to bed or needed a long shit! (The heating in the downstairs loo wasn't working – it was

Goodbye B.M.X. Hello S.E.X.

like shitting in an Igloo!)
 What did he want?
 Did he know what me and Louise were up to, and maybe objected, and so wanted to stop us?
 Was *our night* just about to end, before it had even begun…?

Chapter Two - "...SEX!..."

Ok, despite *Dad's Armys'* Corporal Jones constantly reminding us to "Don't Panic!", there are certain times in life in which you are left with no option *but* to panic!

Those times are probably various and widespread but I'm pretty sure that top of the list of *acceptable panicking* is when you are in bed with your girlfriend, all but naked, and your Dad is knocking on your bedroom door!

This was supposed to be mine and Louise's special night but, right now, seemed like it was going to be our special *nightmare*!

I looked at Louise who, thankfully, looked every bit as panic-stricken as I felt.

"What do you want?" I shouted through the door at Dad.

"Come out here, please!" he replied.

Something was seriously wrong.

I'd never heard Dad use the word "please" in a sentence aimed at me, and he'd just used it twice in about ten seconds.

I got out of bed and wondered how quickly I could get all my clothes back on.

It was too late!

The door was opening!!

Dad was coming in!!!

I desperately grabbed my jumper and threw my head and right shoulder into two of the holes.

Luckily I'd guessed the right hole for my head and it wasn't stuck tight in a long sleeve that would require some kind of escapology to get free!

I jumped over to the door and popped my head out before Dad could pop *his* head in.

Behind me I could sense Louise burrowing under the bed sheets, probably hoping like mad that Dad couldn't break through my last line of defence.

"Yes?" I said to Dad, with hopefully only the clothed shoulder and arm part of my body on show.

"Have you had some of my Chocolate Orange?" he asked me.

Despite the, seemingly, ridiculous nature of his question, I could tell by his deadpan expression that he was being deadly serious.

Dad had his *own shelf* in the fridge – a shelf that contained goods that were *forbidden* to be even *looked at* by anyone else.

He often had chocolate in there.

Bars that he would savour over weeks, even months, and know *exactly* how many pieces he had left at *all times*.

He was very serious about anyone taking his stuff.

He even once hid a Mousetrap in an empty Galaxy wrapper!

Brother Simon's two broken fingers were a "good lesson about stealing"!

Especially as it all but ended his dream of playing the guitar!

Goodbye B.M.X. Hello S.E.X.

"No, I haven't had any of your Chocolate Orange" I said. "Not since that time you had one and said, in case anyone was thinking of taking some, that every now and again you would be swapping it for a wrapper on a Tarantula!"

He looked at me with suspicion.

"If there's any missing, it must have been Brother Simon!" I added.

"Probably," said Dad. "But seeing as he's out, I can't check with him!"

I thought that may be the end of the conversation and so went to push the door shut.

It didn't move – Dad's foot was in the way.

"Let me smell your breath!" Dad said.

"What!?!" I said, in protest.

"Now!" Dad said, in his not-to-be-messed-with tone.

Oh shit!

It would just turn out to be my luck if Louise's "unique taste" turned out to be pretty damn close to Chocolate Orange!

I moved my mouth closer to Dad's nose and nervously breathed out like a motorist who'd had two pints and was being breathalised!

Dad paused for a moment with his head held back, like his was savouring the scent of a fine wine.

"Nope!" he eventually said. "Whatever you've been eating, it certainly isn't Chocolate Orange!"

He patted me on my one-clothed arm and headed back down the landing, as I felt a bit nauseous that he may have smelt some of Louise's unique taste!

I heard him reach the bottom of the stairs muttering something like, "Damn, I should have had a shit while I was up there!"

I closed the door and quickly re-joined Louise under the bed covers.

"That was kind of exciting, wasn't it?" said Louise grinning.

"What?" I asked, confused about what was even *remotely* exciting about any of it.

"You know, us nearly getting caught!" she added.

Her grin turned into a Devilish smile.

"Let's do it!" she said. "Let's do it *now*!"

I reached into the bottom drawer of my bedside cabinet and pulled out my three pack of Extra Safe Condoms.

I had taken a long time weighing up the pro's and con's of the different types of "johnnies" and had come to the conclusion that, as the main purpose in the life of the rubber ones is to prevent any tadpoles performing their own "Escape to Victory", frankly, the *safer* the better!

We could experiment with *Ribbed* (apparently more pleasure), *Featherlites* (apparently more feeling) or *Glow in the Darks* (gimmick if ever there is one!) in the future.

"Let me!" said Louise as she saw my fumbling attempts to unsheathe one from its foil captor!

"It'll be sexy!" she added as way of explaining why she wanted to do it.

I wasn't fooled though.

Her main reason was probably something to do with my failure to successfully apply a condom to a *banana* in the Sex Education class – and Mr Upsons' *trapped condom* horror story that followed!

(I had erased all traces of what happened in the class *following that* from my mind!)

It didn't matter, though, because as Louise began to roll the condom over my, thankfully not blonde bell-end!, it felt pretty damn good.

About half way down (I'm not giving measurements!) the condom seemed to snag and not want to unroll any further.

Was my girth *too big*?

Fantastic!

Wait until I told everyone about this!

Louise tried to stretch it a little away from my skin in an attempt to get it moving again.

What happened next couldn't have been more painful had Louise flicked the World's biggest elastic band at my cock from two inches away!

Or taken a swing at it with a giant axe!

The condom had split in two and slapped me right across the middle of my little man – accompanied by a rather unpleasant THWACK! sound.

I would have screamed if my vocal chords, along with every other part of my body, hadn't rushed to my genital area to check whether my dick had been chopped in half!

Tears formed in my eyes every bit as huge and uncontrollable as they had when I lost the tiny plastic, green lightsaber from my Luke Skywalker action figure – Christmas 1985!

What a lousy, lousy Christmas that was!

"Oops!" said Louise as if she'd just snapped a shoelace!

Oops?

What about "oh no!" or "sorry" or, even better, "do you want me to kiss it better?"!

I looked down and, sure enough, even through tear-blurred eyes, I instantly looked like I was wearing a mini, red penis-scarf!

I wondered whether I should say anything to Louise or just get dressed and head straight for A&E!

Louise seemed to be oblivious to the seriousness of the situation. She was reaching for the box of condoms – no doubt about to begin a second attempt.

Could we just carry on, like it seemed she was intending to do?

I did what any other self respecting man would do in my position.

I ignored the pain.

I scrunched my eyes tight together and freed them of most of the water that had just formed there.

I refocused my mind and got myself back into the zone.

And I asked myself the question – was it remotely possible that I *could* carry on?

I wasn't sure!

Goodbye B.M.X. Hello S.E.X.

It certainly wasn't in my character to do *any* of the "self respecting, manly" things mentioned above!

But wasn't that why I was here?

To take that monumental step towards *becoming* a fully-fledged man?

You know - goodbye B.M.X., hello S.E.X.!

I was going for it!

I was, though, hit straight away by a bout of pessimism.

There were now only *two* condoms left!

We were in that precarious position, like when a football team is 2-0 up.

Everything feels nice and easy and comfortable, but you let another goal in and it's panic stations. Suddenly everyone's a headless Chicken knowing that one more goal against you and you're not winning anymore.

One more split condom and we would be down to last-chance-Johnnie!

There wasn't time to worry too much as Louise had broken through the foil and was, again, attempting to apply the rubber armour!

I decided not to watch this time. If there was to be any repeat THWACKING I didn't want to see it coming.

As I stared at the wall, thinking that a lick of paint was probably eight or nine years overdue!, my mind comforted me with a back up plan.

If Louise did, unfortunately, subject me to the *slight discomfort!* of another two snapped condoms, we could always try Clingfilm!

It would probably be easier to apply, and Mum had rolls and rolls of it in the kitchen.

She liked to strangle the life out of sandwiches with it by wrapping it round so much that sometimes getting at the bread could take up most of your lunch break!

But, fair play, I'd never seen any *mayonnaise* escape from a well Clingfilm-ed sandwich!

Mmm, I could just eat a nice Chicken and mayonnaise sandwich right....

What the hell was I doing?

Was I *seriously* thinking of butties at a time like this?

I turned away from the *graying*-white wall just in time to see Louise finishing her condom application.

"There you go, big boy!" she said, tapping me on the end of my uber-insulated penis!

Big boy?

Was she referring to what I was hoping she was referring to, or perhaps passing comment on seeing my belly properly for the first time?

I glanced down at myself and wasn't sure whether it looked big or not. I certainly didn't linger in the shower rooms at School trying to measure up how I compared to everyone else!

There were more than enough *teachers* doing that!

I could still clearly see the red, THWACK ring around the centre of my dick, despite me now wearing the *extra safe* rubber that felt like it was, at least, as thick as a wetsuit!

"Come on, get on top of me!" Louise continued.

I wasn't sure whether I was put off or turned on by Louise pretty much directing every aspect of proceedings. It certainly didn't seem, for now, that I would be able to get her *on top* as Brother Simon had advised.

I went with the flow and straddled over her.

She opened her legs wide and gave me a beautiful smile.

This was it!

Bryan sang his heart out in the background as I wiggled my hips and tried to guide my shining knight into the mouth of the cave where he was going to slay the Dragon!

(*Slay the Dragon?* Was I *really* ready and mature enough for this??)

"A little higher!" said Louise, in the irritated voice of someone being poked at by a stick!

"Lower!"

"Left!"

"Too far!"

"A bit to the right!!"

"Up again!!!"

She was clearly getting frustrated but, in reality, it was like I was being asked to play a game of naked Blindman's Buff!

I needed to strap a torch to my cock to have any chance of seeing where I was going!

Or maybe wear one of those *Glow in the Dark* condoms? (Ohhh! *That's* what they're for!)

Ahhhh!

Louise gasped, and it seemed my *buffing* had ended in success.

I was in!

Well, part way in!

I presumed this was the part that Brother Simon said needed to be worked in "slowly and gently."

Louise groaned a little *argh!* each time I tried to move out and push back in a little further.

"I'm alright!" she snapped a little, after the fourth time I asked her whether she was, well, alright.

As I slowly made my way further inside I began to feel Louise's warmth.

It was like someone was wrapping a warm flannel around my rubber protected Dragon Slayer!

And it felt nice!

Once in fully, I remembered Brother Simons "very important three-step fail safe guide"

Slow. Steady, Fast.

I started up a *slow* rhythm.

After a few hours (ok seconds!) Louise's groaning changed.

The *argh!*'s started to become *ohh!*'s and then *mmm!*'s.

When they transformed into, moderately loud, *yes!*'s I felt like things might be going to plan.

As for me, everything felt good but also felt like it could be better.

I didn't *feel* like I was *feeling* everything as much as I could.

It was almost like I was trying to read Braille – whilst wearing oven gloves!

Glow in the Dark Featherlites next time?

I think so!

Louise had also now opened her eyes and they were sparkling at me just as much as her huge, happy smile.

Everything felt perfect.

I took it all as a sign that I could step up the pace to level two.

Steady.

I concentrated on maintaining a good thrusting pace whilst my body painfully pointed out to me that I was using muscles that previously had never been called upon.

My heart also began to pump a little faster, confused as to why I had used more energy in the last few seconds than I normally would in a fortnight!

Louise's *yes's* and *mmm's* got louder and more frequent and, seeing as Bryan was nearing the chorus of *Heaven,* I decided to slip up to third gear!

Fast!

Whilst probably not 100% prepared for such a physical workout, I was soon pumping my hips as fast as a determined Woodpecker!

(Bloody Woodpeckers *again*! What's wrong with me?)

It was now hard to tell if Louise was enjoying the experience or not.

The sounds she was making now were just as you'd expect from someone who had a really bad and fast case of hiccups!

Bryan was in the home straight.

It isn't too hard to see, we're in Heaven...!

I was in the home straight too.

I could feel the liquid slowly building; slowly climbing its way up the centre of my penis.

All those enthusiastic Tadpoles that were imminently going to be disappointingly crashing into that double-thick sheet of non-penetrative rubber!

CRASH!

There they go!

I let out a loud, euphoric groan.

"OHHHHHHH!"

Louise did the same.

After a minute of looking into her eyes from above, my muscles achingly refusing to move, Louise put her arms around me and pulled me down tight to her.

"That was fantastic!" she whispered. "I'm so glad my *first time* was with *you*. I love you so much, Paul Day!"

Whist ignoring the undertone of her comment, that implied there would be *other* times with *other* men!, I said back to her.

"Me too! I love *you*!"
I held her tight as I continued to breath heavily; my heart still pounding. This was *perfect*.
It couldn't have gone any better.
My already fantastic relationship with Louise had found a new level.
The excitement in my stomach that had previously, with Louise, felt like wriggly Worms had reached a whole new height. Those Worms were now doing somersaults and high jumps and back flips!
And, to top everything off, my mind decided to dispense with the usual celebratory party poppers and, instead, let a New Years Eve amount of fireworks off in my head.
Yep, I'd just had SEX!

Goodbye B.M.X. Hello S.E.X.

So, there it was.
When it happened.
How it happened.
Who it happened with.
But I suppose that's only part of the story.
What were the events that lead me to that spectacular night in my bedroom?
And what happened after that?
Where is it best to start?
Probably where it's always best to start – at the *beginning*.
And it all began at the start of 1992.....

January 1992

Chapter Three - *"...this could be the best day of your life, don't let it pass you by..."*

January is a strange time of year.

The rest of the year is geared up for the advertising hype before Christmas and New Year; then all of a sudden, as soon as the main events have begun, they're all over.

As quick as a flash they are gone; kind of "blink and you'll miss it" events, like Halley's Comet or Frank Bruno Title Fights!

All that's left then is the realisation that the country has been struck by the sudden coldness, which until then had been somehow hidden by the giddy excitement that comes with presents, over-cooked Turkey and the latest *Only Fools and Horses* Christmas special!

At least in Holly Grove it was cold all the time.

Therefore January was just *colder*, and when you already need to dress like Eskimos, you don't tend to notice too much!

Recently, January seems to have been reinvented as the time for new beginnings.

New opportunities.

What that really means for most people, is the "opportunity" to go back to work after the holidays.

Usually several pounds heavier, many, many pounds less wealthy and numerous pairs of socks richer.

Mum, would be going back to work. She was a part-time lollipop lady at the nearby St. Paul's Infant School - which may seem like a trivial job, but it isn't.

When she was handed her lollipop by the retiring "lollipop master", in some strange mystical, Red-Indian Chief-like succession ceremony (which in my mind took place in a smoke-filled wig-wam at midnight, on a full Moon!), she was told quite clearly that her job was to safeguard a whole generation of the country's future.

Not only that, she had to wear a uniform that made her look like a giant milk bottle, and also had to think of a different flavour for her lollipop every day.

Although I had heard her at work a couple of times, snapping at some poor infant School child.

"I *know* it was Strawberry yesterday, but it's Strawberry *again* today! Now stop asking silly questions and just cross the road!" followed by, under her breath, *"you little shit!"*

Dad wouldn't be going back to work because he was "between jobs"; which was a phrase he had used for the last *eight years*!

He had a "bad back" and was also apparently waiting for the "right opportunity".

Goodbye B.M.X. Hello S.E.X.

He had said that his "ideal job" would be to become the next manager of Manchester City Football Club, stating that he "couldn't do any worse than any of the idiots from the last ten years!"

While this may be true, I'm not sure it was the greatest way of staking your claim for any job.

Seeing as this position had never been offered to him, he had obviously decided not to take any position at all.

He had told the job centre, on numerous occasions over the years, that he was unable to do any lifting - which I assumed included his own feet!

My Brother, Simon, (or *Brother Simon* as I now referred to him) was a member of the working World.

"Brother Simon" was a new nickname that had only come about during the Christmas holidays.

I had mentioned something to Mum about "Simon" and, because she didn't know if I was maybe talking about my mate, "Little Si", she asked *"Which Simon - friend or Brother?"*

When I replied "Brother Simon", Brother Simon went mad, and said

"I'm not a bloody monk, you know!"

The last time I had seen him that angry was a couple of years earlier when Mum had washed his only white School shirt with a pair of red socks, and he had to spend a humiliating week looking very similar to a young Larry Grayson!

It seemed wherever he went in the School someone would shout *"shut that door"* at him! Brilliant!

The fact that it annoys him so much is perfect - definitely what I will always call him from now on!

And *forever*!

He would be returning to work in a somewhat *miffed* mood though.

His "lads' holiday" over the festive period hadn't quite gone to plan. Him and his mates had excitedly booked a three day break in *Lapland*, thinking it was the description for some kind of lap dancing paradise! I suppose when you're expecting, scantily-dressed, hot women to be sitting on *your* lap, actually having to sit on a fat, grey-bearded mans lap, *yourself*, was something of a let down!

Since leaving School, *Brother Simon* (I love it!), had become a YTS (Youth Training Scheme) at Uncle Geoff's garage.

Although YMTS (Youth Mickey Taking Scheme) would be more appropriate.

There was a hardware store next to the garage and it seemed like Uncle Geoff liked to entertain their staff by sending his apprentices round with "humorous" tasks.

Every day Brother Simon would come home and tell tales of near misses, after being given jobs like "go to the hardware store for some tartan paint", or "fetch me a bucket of steam".

But for nearly every near miss, there was a direct hit.

Just the Thursday before Christmas he had spent an hour in the hardware store after being asked to "go next door and get a long stand."

The day after he had caused hilarious uproar by going in and asking for "a box of sparks for our spark plugs".

He seemed to spend half his working life being laughed at by people in the hardware shop. I think members of the public used to go in for a good chuckle, regardless of whether they needed any hardware supplies or not - it was like a comedy hotspot!

Mum had pestered Dad to have a word with Geoff, to ask him to lay off the practical jokes. Dad had refused, saying that they were "character building", and that Simon should be thankful he had a job in "these difficult employment times".

Secretly though, I think he used to enjoy having a good laugh most nights as Brother Simon re-told his embarrassing incidents.

That was the ways things were in our house.

If there was an opportunity to laugh at someone's humiliation, then you were encouraged to take it.

Cruel it may be at times; but I suppose it was the "Days'" sense of humour.

For me though, this working wonderland was just something to look forward to; because January meant going back to School.

And this was the last year.

Or last *half-year* to be accurate.

I was a fifth year. Top of the Tree. King of the Jungle. Top Dog.

Which in reality only meant, if you gave out the right kind of tough-guy bluff, it was likely that you wouldn't get your dinner money stolen anymore.

It was important to make the most of these next six months because, as everyone keeps reminding you, School days are the "happiest days of your life".

Strict lessons, excessive homework, unlimited female rejection, exam pressures, awkward body changes?

If these really were the happiest days, and it was all down hill after this, then I wasn't ruling out a post-School trip to Switzerland for a euthanasia jab!

Still, I was determined to start the year off in a positive frame of mind.

Before breaking up for the School holidays I had found inspiration in the most unexpected of places - the School toilet.

It was not somewhere I made a habit of going, because it was a haven for sneaky cigarettes and first year head flushings; and I'm pretty sure that none of the cleaners knew where it was!

But on an unfortunate Wednesday afternoon, following an evening of eating a few (obviously too many) apricots, I had a stomach movement that could only be justifiably described as an "extreme emergency".

While reading some of the graffiti, including things like; on one wall: "how to play toilet tennis - see opposite wall", on opposite wall: "how to play toilet tennis - see opposite wall" (which left me shaking my head like Ozzy Osbourne for a few seconds), or "Paul Day is a cross dresser" (a blatant lie); I came across

Goodbye B.M.X. Hello S.E.X.

fifteen words that struck a real cord with me.

"This could be the best day of your life - don't let it pass you by."

I'm not sure if there was some make believe phone-sex telephone line number underneath, (which, usually, I would have tried to call!) but it didn't matter.

I was mesmerized by the words.

You don't expect to find wisdom in a place so grim.

Anyhow, I decided it would be my new motto in life.

My old motto, which I had retained from my days in the Cubs, of "Be Prepared", seemed a bit outdated, and didn't really work for me anyway.

A good example being that, after reading the graffiti and "dispensing my emergency package", I realised that there was no toilet paper.

Did I have tissues or equivalently useful paper on me?

No.

I was certainly: *Not Prepared!*

So, after drastic measures, and a damn good hand wash!, I decided that I would adopt this new motto; and I would seize every moment and live each day *to the full*.

And maybe there was another sign. The first pop charts number one of 1992 was Queen - *"These are the Days of Our Lives"*.

Admittedly it was a double A-side with the re-release of a little known song called *"Bohemian Rhapsody"*, but it must be more than just a coincidence.

I decided not to supplement my new attitude with any New-Years resolutions.

Mainly because I don't really believe in them.

In fact, I had never known anyone who had ever kept one.

On a few occasions, Mum had "resolved" to cut down on food and give up smoking and drinking. Each time though, less than a fortnight later, after finishing a takeaway pizza; she would sit there, fag in one hand, Babycham in the other saying

"I would rather die than carry on like that!"

No, it was clear that resolutions couldn't work.

The main problem is that you have reached your aim straight away, and all that is left, is to try and maintain it for as long as possible.

And the people around you are no real help.

It's a bit like tightrope walking.

And those people around you, just like anyone who watches tight rope walking – are only really hoping that you fall as quickly and as spectacularly as possible!

No, I worked out that, not resolutions, but *aspirations* were the way forward.

Aspirations are like Mountain climbing - and you can chart your progress as you climb.

You are aiming *up* to something, not just waiting for the inevitable fall towards the safety net or (as those nasty onlookers would prefer) concrete floor!

As this was a pivotal year for me, one that would shape my whole future, I

Gary Locke

decided I would set myself some important targets.

1...I would get a tattoo.
2...When I turned seventeen (in September), I would have driving lessons, pass my test, and buy myself a car. (In the meantime I would have to find a lot of money from somewhere to pay for this.)
3...I would find myself a ~~nice~~ girlfriend (Shouldn't start off too picky!)
4...I, with my friends, would gain access to a real public house. (Not just to compare it to the Youth Club Disco, but to also drink some hand pulled lager.)

As some of these aspirations were already looking a bit far-fetched, I decided I would also win the Pools and climb Mount Everest!

With this being my final year I realised later that I should have added something about passing some exams - D'oh!

I may have set the bar a little high but, unlike every other year of my life, I had a plan. And an inspirational motto to work to.

I would make every day count!

On returning to School on January 6th, after comparing worst Christmas presents (my Thundercats hot water bottle won at a canter!), me and my buddies decided to address one of my targets as soon as possible.

Mark Hayes, John Tate, the aforementioned Little Si (Hadden) and I, would attempt to crack the public house entry.

Which surely couldn't be too tricky.....

Goodbye B.M.X. Hello S.E.X.

Chapter Four - "...Yates' Wine Bar..."

The message was the same as the one we had been given at the last six pubs we had tried.

"No id?, Sorry lads - not tonight."

The two impossibly wide Yates' doormen may have shown a level of civility we had not previously witnessed in the bouncer community this evening, but the outcome was the same - we were not going to be allowed in.

"Ok, cheers mate!" said Little Si in his high pitched voice that showed not even the slightest hint that it would ever break.

The four of us turned away and walked back along the row of people that we had just queued in for twenty minutes. I couldn't help but look over my shoulder at the three guys who had been waiting behind us. They were now approaching the doormen who inexplicably stepped aside and let them in without so much as a look, let alone a growl or even a question.

How could it be? They were obviously much younger than us. Probably by a couple of months at least!

I couldn't help but hear the sniggers coming from the queue as we headed back towards the town square where we had retreated after each of our six previous rejections.

We had tried all our pre-planned venues, even plan G, the fail-safe option of Yates' Wine Bar. You didn't even need to wear shoes to get in, and we had been told that the only chance of being turned away was if we were wearing short pants, eating lollipops and carrying a bag of marbles!

Even Andy Hickling had boasted about going to Yates' regularly on a Friday night, and he was so baby faced that he made the milky bar kid look like a chain smoking OAP!

"So back to Holly Grove, try to get some Diamond White from the boulevard and off to Tatty Park?"

Mark said the words that had been forming in all our minds. The subconscious "Plan H". The admission of failure. The retreat back to the known.

As we caught the bus back to Holly Grove, the irony of us all paying children's fares, without the bus driver even raising an eyebrow, seemed to be lost on everyone but me.

But where had we gone wrong?

The bus journey was quiet, so I contemplated the possibilities.

On Brother Simons' advice I had been shaving since the age of twelve in preparation for smooth public house entry.

And I had definitely developed a *hint* of stubble. Maybe it wasn't the Clint Eastwood grade that you could light a match on; and it arguably couldn't be seen in *all* lights, but there definitely was a hint of stubble.

Coupled with one of Brother Simons finest chequered blazers, it was hard to see why *I* had been turned away.

And Mark was wearing a suit!

Not trousers and a jacket, but a fully fledged three piece suit!

It may have belonged to his Brother, Daz, been bright blue and three or four sizes too big, but it was a real suit.

How many under eighteen year olds even *owned* a suit?

He had a tight belt on and, with his jacket sleeves rolled up, he looked exactly like a business man who had come to the pub straight from work.

It was also difficult to see how John had been refused - he had a moustache that was almost fully formed. Granted it was 100% bum-fluff, so there was no chance of him being mistaken for Magnum! It was also the exclusive area on his face that had any hair, but it did make him look older than the average sixteen year old.

Perhaps the clothes he had borrowed from *his* Brother had been an unfortunate choice. In association with his "tache", the long fake leather jacket and pink Pringle jumper meant he probably wouldn't have looked out of place in a cheap German porno movie!

But surely, at the very least, the pub doormen would have thought that he was an eccentric European art student.

No, through my musings I confirmed that the three of us were flawless in our preparation. Unfortunately, the reason for the nights' failure was as clear as Maggie Thatcher's Christmas card mantelpiece!

It was Little Si!

He was probably hindered by the fact that, unlike us, he had an older Sister rather than an older Brother, and therefore had no clothes to borrow. Having said that, surely anything that *she* had leant him would have been better than the Parker coat and *Dennis the Menace* t-shirt he had inexplicitly chosen to wear!

It was also unfortunate that he was at least a foot smaller in height than the rest of us and was extremely clumsy on his tip-toes. (We had, after the failures of Plans A & B, encouraged him to try and tippy-toedly enhance his height for the subsequent Pubs. It had turned out that he had the balance of a one-legged tight rope walker!)

Harsh as it sounded, there was only one way forward.

If we wanted to sample the inside of a Pub, within the next ten years!, we would have to do it *without* Little Si.

At School on Monday, despite neither of them being heartless enough to say it outright, I could tell that Mark and John had come to the same conclusion.

When talking about our Friday night failure, the conversations took two very different forms.

When we were with Little Si, we spoke about trying a new approach the following week; including "more mature clothing", "stacked shoes" and "possible ways to deepen high-pitched voices".

When Little Si was in a different class, facts were eventually faced.

Mark was the first to approach it out loud.

"Do you think, next week, maybe just for one Pub, we should try just the *three of us* getting in? Just to see what would happen?"

Goodbye B.M.X. Hello S.E.X.

"Yeah," added John "We could see if the three of us would be able to get in. If we were allowed in, we could still just come straight back out."

I joined in.

"Yeah. We wouldn't be *deserting* Little Si - we would just be finding out if he was the reason we weren't allowed in. *We* probably wouldn't get in anyway!"

It was out there.

The uncomfortable thoughts that we'd all had, were now shared; and things felt better.

The three of us nodded contently, not unlike us being members of the A-Team having just heard Hannibal muttering those famous words *"I love it when a plan comes together!"*

Only we didn't have a plan yet.

Little Si was obviously our weakest link, but could we really be heartless enough to tell him?

He may have been holding us back, but he just wanted to sample the same simple things as us - to see what a night out in the Pub was all about, to have a cool refreshing beer in a social environment and, most of all, to be able to boast to everyone that he had successfully broken the law!

That all being said, we realised that we would *have* to tell Little Si.

I decided it would probably be easiest, and cause the least embarrassment, if just one of us spoke to him, one-on-one.

I told the other two.

"I think one of us should tell Little Si what we've been talking about, make sure he's ok with it."

The way John and Mark both focused their toothy grins squarely at me, it didn't take anything like a genius to work out that they wanted *me* to talk to Little Si.

Not being anything like a genius I double checked!

"You want *me* to talk to him?"

They both nodded steadily like enthusiastic, aging rock fans at a Status Quo concert.

The honour was to be mine.

It made sense, I suppose, because I had known him the longest.

In fact, I had known him since his was plain and simple "Simon Haddon".

We had been in the same class at School since 2nd year infants, when we had both shared Ronnie Corbett's perspective on life!

Little Si's main problem was that he still had that point of view, because he hadn't seemed to have grown a single inch since!

That was why the "Little" nickname was born. It had started as "Little Simon", but as much time had passed without any noticeable height increase, it had been generally accepted he no longer warranted a full Christian name!

How could I go about telling him?

After mulling over the options (or more accurately avoiding the issue) until Thursdays C.D.T. lesson, I decided to tell him straight.

There would be no sugar coating, no punches pulled, I would go straight in with the brutal truth.

"No-ones going out tomorrow night!"

My brain unexpectedly changed the plan at the last minute without telling me. It was a surprise at the time, but probably for the best.

How could I really have told him the truth?

It would almost have been like he was being dismissed from the gang.

I think he had always seen us as the four musketeers. How could I tell him that we were breaking away as the three musketeers?

And that he couldn't be D'Artagnan!

In fact, he couldn't even be *Dogtanan*!

As soon as I said the words, I could see Little Si's mind working.

As he stared into my eyes the reality of the situation hit me. I had just told my best friend a lie. A big, fat, stinky lie!

I had betrayed him totally with my dishonest, forked tongue.

And I knew Little Si had worked it out. It couldn't have been more obvious even if I had been sat there with my pants on fire!

As the silence between us stretched into it's third second, I knew I had to find reasons why all three of us would not be going out on Friday - when we had gone out *every* Friday night for the last three years.

Instead of working on excuses my brain decided to work out how many Friday nights there were in three years.

There was one Friday a week, fifty-two weeks a year, and there were three years in, well, three years.

So that was 1 x 52 x 3. I could eliminate the 1, so it would just be 52 x 3. This was the same as (50 x 3) + (2 x 3), which was 150 + 6.

So there was one hundred and fifty-six Fridays in three years.

I spent a couple of seconds congratulating myself on a tricky calculation; comfortable that is was correct that I was in set one for maths, and wondering what we could possibly have been doing on one hundred and fifty-six nights at Tattington Park.

Before I got too involved wondering whether I should take a few numbers off 156 to take into account holidays and potential Christmas clashes, I concentrated again back to where I was - the C.D.T. class.

Despite the unspecified duration of my mental absence, the class was still going, Little Si was still uncomfortably staring at me and I had no excuses ready.

I called upon my brain to use the same kind of speedy processing, that it had just shown in the Friday night calculation, to produce three plausible "non-going out" reasons.

Thankfully something popped into my mind immediately, surely something that would ease my uncomfortable squirming.

Unfortunately, it wasn't quite what I was hoping for.

The only suggestion it could offer was that I should run out of the classroom as quickly as I could.

I prepared my legs for "springing up" mode, put the "run like a girl" setting

Goodbye B.M.X. Hello S.E.X.

on standby and readied myself for a speedy getaway.

Little Si negated my need to activate them with a dignified interjection.

"Actually, I couldn't have come out tomorrow anyway." he said. "It's my Grandad's 60th birthday. My Mum's organised a surprise party at the Labour club."

Something didn't sit right.

I was sure that his Grandad was older than sixty already. There was also no way he would ever go to the labour club - he was a diehard conservative support. I had unfortunately once seen him wearing a string vest, and he had a rather grotesque tattoo of Maggie Thatcher on his left shoulder!

Imagine the tattoo artists reaction to *that* request!

"I didn't spend four years at tattoo school to produce shit images like that!"

As I contemplated whether tattoo artists were actually as melodramatic as actors, I soaked in the emotion of the moment.

Little Si had engineered a story to help us both out of the awkward situation.

He had found a way of us both retaining at least a hint of dignity with his selfless and generous sacrifice.

Then it occurred to me.

He had just told me an unequivocal, blatant, outrageous lie!

Whose underwear was on fire now?

I know that everyone says that two wrongs don't make a right, but I've always totally disagreed with that sentiment.

Little Si's untruthfulness had cancelled mine out totally. I was happy to believe that we had both just told little white lies in the best spirit possible.

However dubiously it happened didn't matter - my conscience was now clear.

Onwards and upwards towards Friday night.....

Standing in the queue, I was supremely confident.

The three of us had upped our game even further - there was nothing that could stop us this time.

We had changed our tactics and gone straight to Yates'. If it was fairly quiet, surely we would have more chance of being let in.

Mark, again sporting the big, blue suit, had furthered the authenticity of his look by "borrowing" his fathers briefcase. It was unfortunate that he hadn't removed the uneaten apple inside, meaning that it sounded like a bass drum if he moved it too quickly!, but it definitely enhanced his business man-like look.

John had brought a golfing umbrella with him. How sensible and "mature" would someone have to be to take a large, cumbersome, luminous, fabric pole into the Pub?

Genius!

And I had a cigarette lodged behind my ear!

(I had tried smoking one, but my uncontrollable, asthmatic coughing didn't assist with the look I was trying to achieve!)

The queue moved quickly and we were soon faced with the bouncer barricade. Instead of allowing us to pass, as they had everyone else, one of the giants held up a huge hand, indicating that we should stop.

Why was he stopping us?

Little Si wasn't with us!

Had he remembered that we were with Little Si last week?

The brutal truth of the situation slapped my face like an oversized wet kipper!

It wasn't Little Si's fault after all.

I had savagely betrayed my best friend for no reason. We obviously *all* looked too young to be allowed entry.

We had failed again.

The bouncer lowered his hand and indicated that we could enter.

He had just been holding us up whilst those in front had got through the door.

I never doubted it for one second!

As the two doormen stepped aside, one to each side of the door, it was a monumental moment and seemed to happen in slow motion.

I had seen *The Ten Commandments* several times and so was familiar with the miraculous spectacle that was the parting of The Red Sea.

But that had nothing compared to what was happening right now.

As the two steroid-swelled Goliath's parted, they didn't offer a miraculous passage to freedom, but rather a miraculous passage to life!

As we walked on through, into the entrance lobby, the atmosphere of the main room hit us fully in the face.

Smack!

There was a fantastically unique aroma that welcomed us to our new World. In retrospect it was a rather unpleasant blend of stale beer, cheap perfume and strong body odour!, but it was *new and exciting*.

Music was booming out loud; the heavy bass rattling through our adolescent rib cages like the wild wind through brittle tree branches.

There was also the muffled, microphone enhanced voice of a DJ making announcements.

We picked up our stride.

We couldn't wait to be part of it.

As we stepped into the main room we paused for a second trying to take it all in.

There were tables everywhere, spread over three levels; a large dance-floor took up most of the ground floor over which flashing lights winked and dazzled away.

The DJ was on a platform next to the door - wearing sunglasses.

He was inside, and it was nearly pitch-black - and he was wearing sunglasses!

How cool can you get?

Best of all, the place was packed with people, and there were young, attractive women – everywhere!

Goodbye B.M.X. Hello S.E.X.

We had made it.
We had found where we needed to be.
And it felt right!
I instantly felt comfortable and a part of it.
It was like we were standing on stilts, ten feet tall, ready to begin this new chapter in our *mature* lives.

At that very moment the music volume lowered as a record came to it's end, and the DJ's voice announced itself again - only this time crystal clear.

"Alright lads?" he said directing his gaze over to where we were standing. We all instinctively smiled, nodded and gave him thumbs up before he added,

"Finished your homework have you?"

It was as if he had fired up a chainsaw and cut our stilts down to size with one horizontal slash!

Logic later told me that a couple of nearby people sniggered slightly at his comment - one he probably used several times a night. But at that moment, in my paranoid mind, every single person in Yates' Wine Bar stopped what they were doing, looked around and began pointing at us while laughing uncontrollably.

I felt my shoulders arch as if I had just aged sixty years in the space of one devastating second!

I could see the same thing had happened to Mark and John, and the three of us stood there like members of an OAP bowling club, waiting to be told it was our turn on the green.

"Let's get a drink." I whispered and, after the other two nodded, we made our way out of our humiliating spotlight, like three hunchbacked, Ninja Turtles!

On our way towards the bar we spotted a small, unoccupied table in the far corner, underneath the open staircase to the mezzanine floor.

It was obviously not taken because it was cramped and dark and, as we found out later, a target-zone for people dropping chunks of ice from upstairs, but it seemed perfect for us. We would be able to have a drink whilst "blending into the background".

I agreed to "save" the table while the other two went to the bar - obviously none of us had hands big enough to attempt carrying three glasses at once.

I waited in my dark corner for what seemed like forever. After about two hours (maybe ten minutes) of being bombarded from above by ice cubes, plastic straws and various liquids, whose origins I decided were best not to speculate on!, there was still no sign of Mark and John.

Had they left the pub?
Perhaps they'd been thrown out for some reason?
Perhaps they had forgotten where I was and now couldn't see me. The table was so badly lit it was probably reserved for any drug deals "going down"!

I began to panic and my breathing picked up pace, escalating quickly as I realised that I hadn't brought my brown paper bag out with me!

I soon developed an unhealthy, heavy pant that didn't go unnoticed.

A couple of nearby faces turned and squinted into the darkness, probably expecting to witness some kind of lewd sexual activity.

This increased my agitation, which exploded out of control as I noticed two figures approaching rapidly, no doubt coming to challenge me about what I was doing.

To my relief it was John and Mark.

I didn't react to their surprised, inquisitive looks, deciding I didn't need to explain why I was out of breath, sweating profusely, had wet hair and probably several pink straws sitting on my head!

Mark sat down, pint in hand, sporting a grin that would have made the Cheshire Cat look miserable in comparison.

John approached his chair with a pint in both hands. With a satisfied look he carefully placed one in front of me as he took his seat.

I felt like someone had just put the World Cup in front of me.

The Pub surrounding disappeared and was replaced by Wembley Stadium.

There was an anticipation building in the crowd as I slowly reached out to lift it up.

It was a truly historic moment.

I raised the World Cup slightly into the air and the whole crowd went completely wild.

I quickly returned to the dark Yates' table because John had loudly cleared his throat - obviously concerned by the fact that I was singing out loud.

"We're playing for England….ENG-ER-LAND…….."

I stopped abruptly, and focused on the task at hand.

As I raised the glass towards my lips, I could almost taste the amber nectar before it got there.

We had made it into the pub. We had been served no problem.

We were living the dream, and fitting in seamlessly.

I let the lager kiss my lips, and prepared for the cool, refreshing liquid to lovingly, lubricate my throat.

There was just one problem - it actually tasted like warm Cat piss!

And that was not a loose statement. Unfortunately I was well qualified to make the comparison because of a rather elaborate apple juice-switching prank, courtesy of Brother Simon!

The looks on both John's and Mark's faces confirmed that they were both "enjoying" their lager as much as I was. They both wore expressions somewhere in between disappointment and disgust.

In fact, so much so, that they wouldn't have looked out of place on Centre Court watching a Jeremy Bates match!

"This cost four times as much as beer from the boulevard" said a disgruntled John.

It was the only thing that any of us said over the next ten minutes as we sat in silence and drank our beers as quickly as we could.

With three empty glasses on the table Mark said

"Shall we go back to the Grove?"

We all bounced up as if we had spring loaded trampolines under our chairs.

Goodbye B.M.X. Hello S.E.X.

We made our way out of the Pub, sneaking past the DJ as inconspicuously as possible.

As we passed a lot of nervous looking young faces waiting in the queue outside, we gave each other smirky, knowing looks - we remembered how it used to feel when we couldn't get into Pubs!

The bus ride home (once more for just 20 pence each!) was filled with excited chat about how good it was in the Pub, and how cool it would be on Monday to tell everyone at School about it.

Any thoughts about keeping it to ourselves to spare "Little Si - the liar's" embarrassment were dismissed out of hand.

We had spent the night in a real Pub!

And we had each "liberated" a Yates' Wine Bar beer-mat as evidence.

It was the first time ever that I couldn't wait for Monday morning, so much so that I cursed the fact that I had to first face two full days away from School.

As our bus pulled into Holly Grove a thought struck me.

"Now we've done the whole Pub thing," I suggested to Mark and John "Do you think we should try a nightclub next week?"

The month had got off to the perfect start.

I was no longer a young, wet behind the ears, just out of short pants, fresh faced, naïve, jammy-dodger eating adolescent!

I was a man.

I had escaped from my tree-house den and walked into the first room of the big house known as adulthood.

With my friends, I had stood shoulder to shoulder with those aged eighteen and over, and we had been equals.

It was like the next phase of my life had begun. I saw what the post-School World may be like, and it wasn't dark and scary.

It was bright and…………..well, not scary!

It suddenly felt like some of my other start of year targets were achievable.

They no longer felt like they were "as likely as me winning an ice sculpture competition in the Sahara Desert", as my mind had "encouragingly" told me on several occasions!

They seemed *almost* reachable.

Little did I know that, on the twenty-fourth day of the month, something amazing was about to happen…..

Chapter Five - "...Louise..."

It was the same long, arrow-straight road that we walked each week day on our way to School. So it was strange how, on a Friday night, when headed in the opposite direction towards Tattington Park, it suddenly seemed to meander left and right like a great river.

It's funny how your viewpoint changes totally after three bottles of Diamond White cider!

Tattington Park, otherwise known as "Tatty Park" (a more appropriate abbreviation and description rolled into one, you would be unlikely to find!), was where we had spent our Friday nights for years.

The night had begun in the same way as usual; with me meeting John and Little Si at Marks house, for the four of us to have a few drinks before we went out.

With the exception of the two Friday nights in which Mark, John and I had flirted with public house entry, this was pretty much how we always did things.

We had decided to go back to the old routine because we were becoming increasingly uncomfortable telling Little Si lies about what we were doing on Friday nights. (We had tried taking Little Si with us at first; but soon discovered he had more chance getting into Fort Knox than a pub!)

We had come to realise that, despite the charms the pub had to offer, being deceitful to Little Si each week was wrong.

We were a "team" of four friends, and so should stick together.

The A-Team would never leave one of their own behind - they would even put sleeping pills in BA's burger or milk if they needed to get him on an aeroplane. Just so they could always stick together.

I'm not sure how BA fell for it every week, and yet still had the audacity to call everyone else "Fool"!

So we were going to act like *real* friends again, and forsake the pub - just for Little Si.

Besides it wasn't very pleasant in Yates' the previous week when Mark, John and I had attempted to talk to a group of attractive girls, and one of them had asked us if our "baby sitters knew we were out"!

So back to the old routine it would be - which included meeting up with girls of our own age. Which had to be a good thing, because it was clear that older girls were just rude and mean!

As usual, we had met up at Marks house at 6pm - which we did for two reasons.

One - both his parents were always out.

His Dad *always* seemed to work late - apparently Friday night was his best chance to "catch up on his admin with his secretary"!

And his Mum always went "jogging" on a Friday with her personal trainer – Enrique!

Goodbye B.M.X. Hello S.E.X.

And Two - Marks older Brother, Daz, was happy to go to the off-licence for us.

This did however mean that there was a fairly hefty commission, or "D.A.T." (Daz's added tax!) added to the price of our alcohol.

Marks Brother was the only person I knew who made the Chancellor of the Exchequer look like an honest and fair man!

We had tried on a few occasions to get served ourselves at Patels mini-mart at the boulevard but, despite rumours that it was easier to get alcohol in there than it was at a Scottish wedding, they had always refused to serve us.

Although I'm pretty sure that a good lawyer would successfully argue our claim that advertising lager in the fridge as "*Child Beer*" should mean that, by the trade descriptions act, they should have to sell us, well children, with the advertised beer!

There really is no excuse for bad Englishyness!

Diamond White was usually our drink of choice. It was lethally strong, but still had the hint of the taste of apples, which helped because, in honesty, we were not too fond of the taste of lager.

We had, for a brief period, experimented with Carlsberg Special Brew, but it was so hideously harsh that you could practically feel the lining of your throat flaking off with each swig!

It's a mystery to me why no-one has come up with some alcoholic drink that tastes like pop - I am sure they would make a killing. They could call them "Pop-ohol's" or something!

As usual, Daz had got us a four pack each; which was the perfect amount. We had found that four bottles nicely negotiated the fine line between being nicely fuzzy, confident and funny - and being violently sick!

We had been through too many nights when that line had been regrettably and messily crossed!

As was routine, we had two bottles at Marks house, drank one during our meandering journey, and saved one for our arrival at the park.

In reality, most of the kids who hung out in the park had been drinking, (it wasn't unusual to have an older sibling who would buy you some alcohol - most of whom probably didn't charge loan shark rates for the service) but we thought we looked cool entering the park with a full bottle of cider each.

So, here we were, at the entrance to Tatty park.

As we swaggered in, with the last glow of daylight disappearing behind us, like four bad John Wayne impressionists, Mark pointed out a group of girls from our year at School, hanging around the swings.

Tattington Park was a *strange* place.

By day it was a hive of recreational activities for all ages. There was a playing area with swings and climbing frames, tennis courts (only actually used during Wimbledon fortnight!), bowling greens and football pitches.

By night it was something very different; and just as socially varied and dangerous as the Star Wars Cantina!

I'm pretty sure that I've seen Greedo wandering around a few times –

Gary Locke

waiting for someone to shoot at him – *first*!

With the park being, at best, a hazardous place, it was important to be careful about which group you were approaching. As well as numerous, small collections of School kids, the park was also inhabited by older youths - probably taking hard drugs or, worse still, strange adults hanging around the car park - watching other adults "getting it on" in cars.

Weird!

I think these people are known as "Doggers" - even though they never seem to have Dogs with them!

Very weird!

Either way, a wide birth from these groups was more than recommended.

As we neared the girls by the swings, Mark said,

"I think I'll have Kim tonight!"

I smiled to myself at his cider-fuelled, mis-guided confidence.

By *"have Kim tonight"*, I knew what he was saying was, he would work up the nerve to *talk* to Kim Bell, before saying something ridiculous and being laughed away from the group.

As we got closer, I could make out the faces around the swings. Kim was with Alison Starr, Zoë Pott, Gemma Wilson, Joanne Powell, Janine Pearson and Vicky Barlow - all friends of ours who we knew from a variety of shared School lessons.

They all always wore very similar long, beige coats that had earned them the nickname around School as the *Beige Brigade*!

Which was probably an upgrade on their nickname from the previous year when, after all having their hair permed around about the same time, they were known as the *Poodle Pack*!

Standing a few metres behind them, looking like they were trying to appear like part of the same group, were two other girls I didn't recognise at first. A couple more steps and I saw that it was two girls from my maths class - Lisa Bell and Louise Knight.

My walking slowed.

I couldn't believe it!

Just before leaving my house tonight, me and Brother Simon had been talking about Louise Knight.

He had asked me whether she was in my year at School. I had said she was in my maths class; and that she sat at the front near the teacher, because she was a bit swotty.

A real geek!

He had said "Geek or not, she's pretty hot!"

Like most things he said, I had dismissed it out of hand. Struggling to picture her clearly in my mind, I thought, at best, she was possibly an above average looking nerd.

Besides, Brother Simons taste was questionable to say the least. Non of the girls I had ever seen him with could hardly be described at Beauty Queens.

In fact, most of them looked more like Drag Queens!

Goodbye B.M.X. Hello S.E.X.

But I couldn't believe the coincidence - after just talking about her, Louise Knight was actually here.

And Brother Simon was right - she was pretty hot.

In fact, very hot!

Tall, slim - but curvy, long brown hair and beautiful blue eyes.

Why had I not noticed her before?

And why was she at the park *tonight* - where I had never seen her before. Was this fate?

I thought fate only existed in movies, and some episodes of Neighbours!

I carried on walking with the lads and, before we were within sound range of the girls, Little Si said,

"I'm going for Vicky!"

After laughing, and saying something about flying pigs, John said,

"I'm going to try for Zoë.........again."

"That's the way," I said "You'll catch her off guard one day!"

"What about you?" asked Mark, turning to me as he took a far too energetic swig from his bottle. After sniggering as I watched his Diamond White fizz out of control and reappear through his nose, I said,

"I think I'm going to go for Louise."

Three shocked and confused faces stared at me, like I had said something weird, like I was wearing womens underwear.

"Louise Knight!" I said, trying to clear things up, before watching their expressions turn from confusion to horror, as if I had just dropped my trousers and shown them the underwear!

"Are you joking?" asked Mark.

"No, look at her - she's well fit." I said looking over at Louise.

As I did she glanced up and noticed me staring.

Her eyes sparkled and she flashed a smile that instantly lit up the darkening evening sky.

With my new "seize the moment" philosophy, I would have considered approaching Louise and speaking to her straight away.

But I didn't have that choice to make.

My feet were travelling towards her without me having any say in the matter.

It was like I was hypnotised - so much so that I was somewhat concerned that I may begin a Chicken impression at any second!

"I'll see you later" I said as I walked towards Louise, leaving the guys as open mouthed as three Hungry Hippos!

I passed Kim, Claire, Zoë, Janine and Vicky without even glancing at them; which was probably a shock to them, but also a relief, as I usually tried it on with all of them on a Friday night!

I arrived in front of Louise and Lisa and said,

"Hello!"

"Hi!" they both said in unison.

It was now that I realised that I had no idea what to say.

Gary Locke

Despite the fuzzy thickness of my mind, I couldn't help but wonder what to say to a girl who was obviously more intelligent than me. She was also certainly a lot more clever than the girls who were always unimpressed with my usual lines - most of whom for which the phrase "dumb blonde" was a more than adequate description!

So I said nothing.

Thankfully, just before the silence threatened to leave embarrassing and enter excruciating, Louise spoke.

"Is that cider?" She asked, indicating the bottle I was holding.

Still unable to speak I nodded.

"Do you mind if I have some?"

My voice suddenly made a comeback.

"Course not." I said handing her the Diamond White.

She sparkled another smile before taking the bottle and throwing it back in harmony with her head.

My heart skipped a little.

She was readily drinking strong cider - this was not the actions of a swotty geek.

She was ok!

Added to that, she had taken a drink without first wiping the top of the bottle.

We were practically kissing!

"That's nice." She said, returning the bottle to a vertical position.

She didn't even shudder from the initial shock of the first taste of strong alcohol - like some people do. (Luckily, usually in the privacy of Marks house!)

I couldn't help but smile at her - which she reflected with another Sun-shine bright grin.

We had a connection.

It was a perfect moment.

She was beautiful.

She certainly wasn't a geek.

She seemed to like me.

She was perfect!

She was taking another swig!

Who the hell did she think she was?

My eyebrows instinctively moved into frown mode, as my mouth geared up for a verbal attack.

Before I let it out though, I tried to calm down.

Perhaps, because of my smiling, she had read some kind of authorisation for a second mouthful.

Another reason why smiling too much was dangerous - as well as being the inevitable path to, above eyebrow, wrinkles!

"Thanks" Louise said, thankfully passing the bottle back to me.

"It's ok" I said through clenched teeth, trying hard not to make it obvious I was checking for the cider level, to see how much she had consumed.

Goodbye B.M.X. Hello S.E.X.

It wasn't too bad - there was plenty left.
Lisa stepped forward and began to talk.
"Is it ok…"
I knew she was also going to ask if *she* could try some cider and had to quickly decide what to do. Should I try to say "no" as politely as possible?, or just hit her with the bottle?
"…..if I go and find Abbey Trueman?"
It was alright, she was talking to Louise.
I stopped holding the bottle like a baseball bat and watched Louise as she responded to Lisa.
"No that should be fine…." she said before reaching out and gently holding my hand.
"…..I'll be safe here with you Paul, won't I?"
For a split second, the blatant flirting left me feeling like a Rabbit, who had mastered crossing the road by letting cars pass directly overhead - caught in the headlights of an approaching Reliant Robin!
Fortunately, the alcohol fuelled confidence quickly took over and I said,
"You sure will!" while at the same time attempting an awkward wink.
I have found that there were only certain groups of people who can get away with winking - Grandad's, some Uncles, the super cool - and homosexuals!
So far in my life, despite a couple of accusations, I wasn't in any of these groups.
I agreed with myself that it would be best if I didn't try to wink again.
Louise and Lisa gave each other a giggly little grin before Lisa turned and walked away towards the field.
"Don't go too near the car park!" I shouted after her, before turning to face Louise.
"You know," I said "I don't think we've ever really spoken to each other."
"Maybe that's because you always ignore me at School!" Louise replied a little curtly.
She had me. She was right.
In fact, the only contact with her that I could remember was one lesson when I had thrown a maths text book at Daniel Wilkes, and had struck her on the head by accident.
But there was no need to remind anyone of that right now!
"Well, let's make up for that." I said, pointing towards the roundabout, shifting myself into "smooth mode".
"Tell me everything there is to know about you."
She blushed slightly and smiled as I walked her slowly towards the brightly painted wooden mini-carousel - smooth mode up to full power.
We sat on the roundabout and talked.
And laughed.
And talked, and laughed………for hours.
The sky above us darkened, and Stars slowly grew brighter, before sparkling

Gary Locke

intensely like randomly arranged Cats eyes.

It felt natural being with her.

I learnt *everything* about her.

The things she liked, and disliked.

Things about her past (her first kiss was with a boy called Dave Barlow) and her future ambitions (she wanted to be a Vet when she was older).

Everything about *her*, Louise, the girl that had been right in front of me for years, but I had been too stupid to see.

I realised this was a special moment.

She was beautiful, she was intelligent, she was funny and, most importantly, really fun just to be around.

Everything you could possibly put on a "perfect girl" checklist.

After what seemed like forever, and yet no time at all, there was a break in our conversation. Not the kind of awkward silence that usually followed when a teacher would ask me a question; but rather us both stopping talking so we could look into each others eyes.

Within Louise's eyes I could see a real flicker.

A dancing flame.

A window to a soul erupting with life.

We slowly moved towards each other and our lips gently met.

But it was more than a kiss, it was something special - a connection.

I had kissed my fair share of girls, (if my fair share was three!) but this was something more.

It was soft and sensual, tender and meaningful.

Totally different from any kiss I'd ever had.

I had experienced some bad kisses in the past - including some that had been wetter than eating a peach!

But there was certainly no need for a bib with Louise; because this was perfect.

As we pulled away from each other our eyes opened at the same time and we both instinctively smiled.

This was something *truly* special.

I felt a wriggling sensation in my stomach, similar to the time when I was nine years old and Brother Simon had tricked me into eating a Worm!

It was possible that he had done it again - we had eaten noodles for tea and he could have hidden a Worm amongst them - but could it be because I had found someone I could be falling for?

As we shared our beautiful moment, Lisa Bell and Abbey Trueman approached.

I noticed Abbey noticing that Lisa had noticed that Louise had my jacket tenderly draped around her shoulders.

That same excited giggly grin from earlier returned, this time bouncing between Louise, Lisa and Abbey.

It must have been catching because I couldn't stop myself joining in.

It was disgusting.

Goodbye B.M.X. Hello S.E.X.

I felt like slapping myself!

"We're going now, if you're ready?" Lisa said to Louise, when all the sickening smiling had ended.

"Erm, Ok yes." said Louise looking at me.

"I'll walk you home if you want?" I said, gazing intently into her eyes, as if I may never see them again if I looked away.

Louise nodded intently.

"Looks like it's just you and me, Abbey" Lisa said.

The three girls again grinned at each other in that kind of "Annie the Musical" way. This time I held firm, threatening never speak to myself ever again if I joined in for a second time!

"I'll speak to you tomorrow" said Lisa, leaning in and kissing Louise on the cheek.

For an awkward, split second Lisa looked like she may kiss me, but pulled away and contented herself with instead saying,

"See you later, Paul."

"See ya!" I said as her and Abbey turned and faded into the darkness as they walked away from us.

Mark, John and Little Si had left about half an hour earlier - on their own obviously!

They were excited, and convinced, that they had seen Stan Collymore walking through the park, headed towards the car park!

They were being ridiculous - what would he be doing at Tatty Park?

I looked back at Louise.

"So, I suppose I best get you home."

"In a minute." she said before slowly leaning in and gently attaching her lips to mine.

My stomach jiggled around again causing that unusual, but pleasant, funfair Pirate Ship sensation. I couldn't help but wonder if somehow Brother Simon had managed to substitute every single one of my noodles for Worms!

It was some time later that we embarked on a slow stroll towards Louise's house. As we walked, she linked my arm; the kind of way that only old, married couples or footballers in a free-kick wall did.

But it felt comfortable.

We continued talking and laughing, interrupted by the odd kissing / tingling tummy moment, all the way back to Louise's house.

And what a house it was.....

It was huge, with the biggest satellite dish in the World attached to the massive double garage.

There was a long driveway with not a car, but three cars parked there - and one was a Sierra Cosworth!

My mind reopened the girlfriend checklist and wrote the words "absolutely loaded" and underlined them twice.

Things, that were already perfect, were getting better and better.

At her front door Louise whispered

"Wait there and be quiet. I'm over an hour late."

She slipped her key into the door and opened it in complete silence like some kind of professional bank vault thief.

She disappeared into the hall that, even in the darkness, I was pretty sure was bigger than our entire house!

She returned straight away armed with a pen. She took my left hand and gently wrote out a number on my palm.

"Ring me tomorrow." She said before grabbing my head with both hands and kissing me passionately.

"Thanks for a great night." She said as she winked and re-entered the house, silently closing the door behind her.

And it was a more than passable wink. So there was another group that I could add to the winking list: Sexy Girlfriends.

As I turned and began walking back down Louise's drive a pleasant question entered my mind.

Did I have a girlfriend?

My steps felt all light and springy - like I was walking in a freshly pumped up pair of Nike Airs!

It was the most wonderful feeling ever.

For some reason my spoil sport brain decided to ruin the moment by recommending I check the time.

Shit - I was late!

And it wasn't the kind of "late" where I could turn my watch back fifteen minutes and pretend it was running a bit slow - I was over 45 minutes late.

I was in trouble.

I began to run.

Like my life depended on it.

Which in reality it did!

Mum and Dad were really strict when it came to curfews. And punishments ranged from months worth of washing up duties to reductions in pocket money (which was way under minimum wage as it was!) to complete groundings.

I couldn't afford to get grounded – especially as it looked like I may have miraculously just landed a girlfriend.

The aftermath of four bottles of Diamond White (or more like *three and a half* - but I have nearly forgiven Louise for her mischievous, unauthorised drinking!) made running a little unwise.

At best it meant that I was a little uncoordinated - not too dissimilar to a Gloucestershire downhill cheese chaser!

At worst, it meant the uncontrolled running may end in a head first trip into the pavement, or the unwanted reappearance of semi digested strong cider.

Luckily, after running for several minutes, I turned the corner into our street with neither a broken nose or a cider / carrot stained t-shirt.

Why *does* all sick always have carrots in it?

I slowed and began to walk the last few steps trying to catch my breath before I reached our drive. (Which, after seeing Louise's, appeared more like a

Goodbye B.M.X. Hello S.E.X.

tight parking space than an actual driveway!)

I approached my house just in time to see Dad reversing the Volvo out into the road - no doubt coming to find me.

I was in *real* trouble.

I tapped the car window to let Dad know I was home.

Instead of waiting for him though, I ran towards the front door. It was a bit like a suicidal knock and run!

Despite trying to repeat Louise's stealthy house entry, my key turn and door open was rather louder - closer to a police raid than the silent entrance I was aiming for.

I walked into the living room, where Mum was standing, with her hands on her hips.

"WHERE THE HELL HAVE YOU BEEN?" she shouted in her angry voice - the voice she saved for special occasions like this.

I decided not to answer straight away. I thought I would probably be best phoning a lawyer, because the seriousness of the situation suddenly struck me - the television wasn't even on!

Someone must have turned it off!

Which meant that someone would have had to look for the off switch!

"I'm just getting some crisps." I said giving Mum a wide birth, well out of striking range.

I found that a packet of pickled onion crisps usually hid the smell of most alcohol; and surely the best way to face my situation would be to try and at least *appear* sober.

I entered the kitchen and shuffled through the multi-pack of crisps in the cupboard. To my horror I couldn't find any pickled onion - they must have all been eaten.

I searched for an alternative.

Ready Salted? - No Good.

Salt 'n' Vinegar? - Not Much Better.

Cheese 'n' Onion? - Would have to do because I could hear the kitchen door opening behind me.

I quickly opened the packet and stuffed a handful of crisps into my mouth.

I slowly looked round, trying to make some kind of cute Puppy-Dog eyes, only to find it was Brother Simon who had entered the room.

"Where have you been?" he asked "Mum and Dad are going mental!"

I showed him the numbers on my left palm.

"Whose number's that?" he asked.

"Louise Knight's" I said, spitting half a mouthful of cheese 'n' onion crisps across the kitchen!

A slow smile grew on his face, until he looked almost proud of me.

It was a beautiful couple of seconds.

"Nice work!" he said, offering me his hand for shaking.

I couldn't help it - as I reached out to shake it, a giggly grin burst out of my face.

Gary Locke

I am now officially never going to talk to myself, ever again!

"WHERE IS HE?"

Dad had entered the living room - every bit as terrifying as a Darth Vader entrance.

Brother Simon obviously spotted (or smelt) my panic.

"I'll handle this." he said, before leaving the kitchen and closing the door behind him.

I could hear his muffled voice saying something to Mum and Dad. After about a minute it stopped, and there was just silence.

I decided to face the music - which would quite probably be the funeral march!

I opened the door slowly and slightly, weary of potential poison arrows being blown my way; but only saw three smiling faces.

"So, you've met a girl have you?" asked Mum beaming, all traces of her angry voice long gone.

"Good on you, son!" said Dad, walking over to me and patting me on the head; ignoring my nervous flinch.

"Tell us all about her." continued Mum, indicating I should sit down in the central armchair.

Dad's armchair!

The chair that no-one but Dad was ever allowed to sit in!

Dad even nodded to suggest it was ok.

I tentatively sat down, as Mum, Dad and Brother Simon sat down on the chairs / sofa around me.

Although I was relieved that it seemed I was going to escape any punishment for my curfew break; this over-the-top family euphoria because I had met a girl was a little extreme, and some what insulting.

I gave them a couple of minutes of censored evenings events (the non-alcoholic edit), and then headed off to bed with a huge smile on my face.

Even Dad's attempted whispered comment of "It's a relief to be sure he's batting for the right team!" as I ascended the stairs, couldn't dampen my spirits.

I copied Louise's number down into my diary; and onto any surface in my room that would take ink - it would be a catastrophe to lose it, before turning the light out and getting under my bed sheets.

I smiled gently as I closed my eyes and pictured Louise's face leaning into mine.

And a thousand worms began to wriggle all over again.......

Goodbye B.M.X. Hello S.E.X.

February 1992

February arrived in its own undeniable way.
It was always like an extreme January - Darker, Colder, Bleaker.
And yet there was something of beauty to recognise each morning when I looked out of the window.
The freshness and cleanliness of the light dusting of white that covered everything; the evidence of Mother Nature going about her Winter deep clean.
Yes that immaculate and spotless, almost sanitised, layer on the ground that you know will make you fall arse-over-tit the first minute you step on it!
The month began with the continuation of Wet Wet Wet's *"Goodnight Girl"* topping the pop charts. It was a slow, sickly, over-sentimental ballad.
I loved it!
It was strange how my appreciation and tastes were changing.
Maybe it was because of my new positive attitude.
Maybe because I was experiencing a relationship that had lasted longer than one night at the youth club.
Maybe it was because, just a few weeks into the year, I had successfully achieved some of the, seemingly improbable, targets I had set myself.
In fact, I was ticking them off quicker than a veteran bingo go-er, playing six cards at once!
Whatever the reasons, things were going well; and February wasn't going to stop my progress.
There are events in history that dictate a date becoming synonymous with them.
21/10/1805 - Nelson was victorious at Trafalgar.
15/09/1928 - Sir Alexander Fleming discovers Penicillin.
08/05/1945 - VE Day.
11/02/1991 - The inaugural day of the first annual British Chip Week!
For me, a day was about to arrive, 14/02/1992, that, for several reasons, would be every bit as historically important.....

Gary Locke

Chapter Six – *"...bathroom dash..."*

It was a Friday and, as such, started as any other Friday; which was the same as any other weekday - it started with a race.

A race between me and Brother Simon.

And not a friendly, meaningless encounter; it was the daily, no-holds-barred, winner-takes-it-all, *bathroom dash!*

Of late, things had become more tactical.

Brother Simon had been getting the better of me with a fairly simple, but effective approach. He had begun, each evening, to subtly tell Mum what time he would be getting up for breakfast the following morning. He would do it in a whispered voice, not unlike an anonymous telephone pest, (a voice he had a lot of experience with!) that made me believe that he was trying to ensure that I didn't hear him.

It is now clear that he wanted me to hear him; because each following morning he would be in the bathroom anywhere between ten and fifteen minutes earlier than the time he told Mum.

He had been playing me as easily as a pair of maracas!

If he wanted to be tactical though, then so be it.

I had not been infant School chess champion for two whole months, without knowing a cunning plan or two.

I would have to raise my game.

I did just that by setting my alarm clock on Thursday night for midnight. After it woke me, I carefully sneaked into Brother Simon's room - quieter than a rubber-soled, slippers wearing Mouse!

I checked his alarm, which (surprise, surprise) was set for ten minutes earlier than the 7.25am he had "whispered" to Mum, in that seedy voice!

After returning to my room, and also setting my clock for 7.15am, I settled into my bed.

As my room was closer to the bathroom than Brother Simons, as long as I got up as soon as I heard my alarm, I couldn't fail to win the race.

It was brilliant!

And one of the many things I did that made me wonder why MENSA weren't begging me to join their society.

The comfort of knowing that I would be first to the bathroom assisted my sleeping.

Whereas, for the past few nights, I had been anxious; trying to hear if there was any sign of movement from Brother Simon's room, now I was totally calm.

I don't think my state of relaxation could even have been heightened by a dozen aromatherapy candles, and a double album of Whale songs!

I was so settled that I even began to dream again.

And not my usual childish dreams about slaying dragons or piloting Airwolf!; but real, grown up visions of beautiful women.

Well about *one*, beautiful, young woman.

Goodbye B.M.X. Hello S.E.X.

Louise.

She always seemed to be on my mind, whether awake or dreaming; which was the way I liked it.

I slept right through until my alarm went off. As it did, I was turning slowly with Louise on the roundabout in Tattington Park. The thick, dark blanket sky was draped over us, punctuated only by glistening, diamond stars; as I once again relived our perfect, first kiss.

I slapped the snooze button on my clock and, still semi-sleeping, remained in the beautiful moment.

As our lips tenderly caressed, it was like we were the only people in the whole World - the exquisite silence wrapped around us, like a huge, luxury duvet.

In fact the only sound at all was coming from an opening door, followed by heavy footsteps running across a stair landing.

My eyes opened wide, as if I'd had a hot poker inserted somewhere unpleasant!

I leapt out of bed and was quickly at my door but, as I opened it, the flashing blur of Brother Simon passed right in front of my eyes.

I made it to the landing just in time to see his smug face, and two-fingered victory salute, as he entered the bathroom.

I walked back into my room and sat down on the bed muttering one of Dads favourite lines,

"Bridesmaid again!"

I took a deep breath and resigned myself to the fact that I would probably have to use the bathroom *after* breakfast.

I got my trousers and shirt out of my wardrobe and placed them on the comfy chair next to the computer desk. I left my blazer hanging on the rail.

I think I had only ever worn the black, HGHS-badged blazer twice. Once, on my first ever day at the School, and the second because the headmaster, Mr Langden, had insisted on it one day when the education auditors were due to visit the School.

All other times, I think Langden was happy about blazer-wearing being used as a way of identifying the geeks!

I got dressed and headed out of my door towards the stairs.

Miraculously, Brother Simon was emerging already from the bathroom as I passed. Usually he was in there long enough to read the newspaper cover to cover - at least three or four times!

"It's all yours" he said smiling, surprisingly graceful as he headed off back towards his bedroom.

I wasn't fooled.

I had seen that triumphant grin before.

It was natures equivalent of a Poison Arrow Frog being brightly coloured - it was a clear signal that no-one should go within twenty metres of the bathroom for quite some time.

It appeared he had been so quick because he had managed to even stink

Gary Locke

himself out!

I resigned myself to the fact that I would now probably have to use the bathroom after *School!*

I headed downstairs, entered the kitchen, and took my seat at the table.

As usual, Dad was nowhere to be seen, but Mum was standing at the window, cradling a cup of tea.

"Morning." I said, surveying the breakfast spread in front of me.

"Morning, love." Mum said, continuing to gaze out into the back garden, as if almost in a daydream.

She even started humming, which was something she rarely did; mainly because when she did, she sounded very similar to someone gargling TCP!

She had outdone herself this morning and the choice was extensive. Not only Cornflakes, but also Rice Crispies *and* Shredded Wheat.

I was determined not to agonise over the choice for too long, and so just quickly filled my bowl with Cornflakes.

I checked the milk to make sure that Brother Simon had not tampered with it.

This was an essential part of breakfast.

I had found that there were not many more unpleasant ways to start a day, than to pour three lumps of last weeks milk all over your cereal!

Thankfully the milk was fresh but, on taking my third mouthful of cornflakes, I realised that I didn't really like cereal at all!

In fact, at the moment, it was hit or miss whether I even felt like having *any* breakfast at all. It seemed that since I'd been seeing Louise my appetite for food was very often missing – and was regularly replaced by that feeling of wriggling Worms in my stomach!

I think the real problem with cereal is that it almost *symbolises* breakfast, and is therefore the last meal before the "psychological-execution" known as School.

Or maybe it's just that soggy, cold, flakes "sweetened" by *one* click of Sweetex actually tastes quite disgusting!

There was no sugar because Mum was on *another* diet.

We were also on a tight shopping budget, so we were each limited to just three clicks of Sweetex each day, and so had to be careful not to waste them.

This was one of the more workable "budget restrictions" that was in operation. It was far easier than "2 minutes maxiMum in the shower" (I was a teenage boy!!) or "2 toilet paper squares per visit." (Which I'm not sure how Brother Simon adhered to, given his explosive deposits!)

"Can I have some toast?" I asked Mum. (Luckily there was no bread restriction in place as yet - but only because we were buying lots of "No Frills" products, including bread at 9p a loaf. It wasn't the nicest bread I had tasted, but it was multi purpose - you could also use the loaves as house bricks!)

Mum ignored my request; miles away in her own little World - a World that obviously accepted out-of-tune humming.

At least she wasn't signing. She was the only person in the World who made Hilda Ogden sound like an opera singer!

Goodbye B.M.X. Hello S.E.X.

I got up and walked towards the bread bin. I opened it and found one piece of *green* bread, that probably (hopefully) started life as a piece of *white* bread. (You could never really be sure though with "No Frills"!)

Although disappointed I wouldn't be having any toast, I comforted myself with the fact that if Brother Simon had been able to, he would have happily toasted the green piece for me.

As I stood there, wondering whether perhaps a packet of Wagon Wheels would be an acceptable and nutritional breakfast choice, Brother Simon entered the kitchen.

"What's that?" he asked Mum, pointing at a card that sat face down on the worktop in front of her.

"It's a Valentines Day card." she said tentatively, after ceasing her toneless hum.

"Oh yeah, it's Valentines Day." said Brother Simon "Has the postman been already?"

"No" said Mum "This is one that your Father sent me."

Me and Brother Simon instinctively looked at one another in a state of shock. The only time we'd known Dad to do anything, even remotely, romantic was when he once ran a bubble bath for Mum, forgot about it – and ended up flooding the bathroom! The first anyone knew about it was when the ceiling cracked, and a torrent of lavender and rosemary scented liquid rained down onto the dining table!

"I suppose the postman will be late today; what with all the cards that my birds will have sent me!" said Brother Simon in a cocky, kind of Men Behaving Badly way.

I looked at Mum's card.

"Oh lovely," I said, sounding a little soppy, even for me in my current loved-up state."Let me see."

I picked up the card but Mum's hand moved faster than a Frogs tongue, catching an unsuspecting fly.

"It's private" she said, snatching it back. She left the kitchen straight away with her cheeks reddening quickly.

Brother Simon sat down at the table and began to pour himself some cereal.

"Fancy a piece of toast?" I asked.

"No, thanks" he said, examining the two pieces of Shredded Wheat that he had removed from the box. They do look uncannily like slices of our bathroom loofah; a loofah that was getting shorter and shorter by the week!

I think two Shredded Wheat's was his limit. He had often boasted about having three, but I had never seen it!

He next shook and smelt the milk (two can play that game!) before gently covering his wheat with it.

Finally he checked two pieces of Sweetex into his hand, before letting them drop into his bowl.

He had been less than impressed last week when he had ruined a cup of coffee by "sweetening" it with two mint tic-tacs!

Oh what fun we have!

As he took his first spoonful of cereal, the unmistakable sound of mail coming through the letterbox could be heard.

Brother Simon looked up sharply, but quickly accepted defeat, as he was sitting at the table and I was standing by the door.

I tried my best to mimic the smug face he had shown me earlier after the bathroom dash, before slipping through the door like a warm knife through margarine. (We weren't getting butter anymore- we were on a budget!)

I barely had time to flick through the four items - two bills for Dad, a political campaign leaflet from the Liberal Democrats, and a pink-enveloped card for me (Yippee!) - when Brother Simon appeared at my shoulder.

"Nothing for me?" he asked in a slightly dejected voice, all traces of cockiness gone.

On realising his disappointment and sadness, I responded in the only sympathetic, Brotherly way possible.

"Absolutely nothing at all!" I said; smile mode at 100%.

"Nobody loves you. Loser!" I added, waving my card in his face; not unlike you would smelling salts on somebody who was semi-conscious.

Just as his bottom lip threatened to slightly quake, he regained some dignity, or rather some of his usual cockiness, and said,

"I suppose there'll be a full sack load for me. They may have to put another postman on, probably on the second delivery. Yeah, mine must be coming later."

With my best sarcastic voice and face combination, I said,

"Yeah - that must be it! Your sack load will be coming later!"

I wanted to make the most of the moment, because deep down I thought that he would get some cards.

He did have an, unfathomably, good record with the female species. Especially now he was working, had more money and his own car. Although I'm not sure how anyone would be that impressed by a cream/rust coloured Peugeot 205.

I placed the Liberal campaign leaflet in Brother Simon's hand, and ran upstairs with my card.

I entered my bedroom and, after shutting the door behind me, lay down stomach first on my bed.

I held the card in front of my face and stared at my name written on the envelope. It was in the same neat handwriting that I had seen for the first time in the form of a telephone number just two weeks earlier.

There was a heart with an arrow through it drawn in the corner with PD4LK written underneath it.

I wondered for a split second whether that was a character from Star Wars, before realising that they were mine and Louise's initials.

I turned the envelope over and saw the word SWALK written over the flap.

Despite it sounding like the noise a Parrot with a lisp would make!, there was something beautifully romantic about it.

Goodbye B.M.X. Hello S.E.X.

Sealed With A Loving Kiss!

I pictured Louise gently kissing the envelope after licking the flap and sealing it together.

Thankfully she hadn't left a really obvious bright red lipstick mark under the word - that was so *tacky*.

On closer inspection she had - the outline shape was there, it was just that most of it must have smudged off.

I changed my mind - lipstick marks aren't tacky, but actually quite sexy really!

I gently opened the envelope, trying not to tear it at all (this was definitely something I would be keeping in my box of memories), and removed the snugly fitting card.

The picture on the front was of two fluffy penguins embracing on a heart-shaped children's roundabout. (How appropriate - our first kiss was on a roundabout. Not really sure about the relevance of the Penguins though!)

There were four lines of printed words underneath the picture that I read slowly in my mind.

Come hail or sleet, rain or shine,
You always are, on my mind,
Please by mine, 'til the end of time,
My one and only, Valentine.

I slowly opened the card and, through my slightly glazed eyes (caused by unseasonably early hay-fever!) I saw the neatly handwritten words

"Paul, I Love You, x ?"

My hay-fever intensified and liquid rolled quickly down my cheeks.

I had never felt so happy.

I quickly opened one eye just to check that the card was definitely for me! It was!

I checked again to make sure that it was from Louise: my girlfriend! It was!

Wow - she loves me!

She had never said that before.

It had only been two weeks, but everything felt *so* perfect.

I couldn't wait to get to School and see her.

Maybe I should buy a pack of Rolo's and give her my last one.

No, that would be a step too far!

And you don't really get that many Rolo's in each tube; so if I did buy some it would need careful consideration!

I wondered if she had received my Valentines card to her yet. I hadn't been quite as cool as her, and had actually written: "Love from Paul" at the bottom; just so she was sure it was from me.

I wasn't totally un-cool though. I had resisted the urge to write "Love from Paul *Day*"!

Gary Locke

I wiped my eyes on what I thought was a handkerchief on my bedroom floor, but soon realised was a pair of boxer shorts that must have missed an attempted throw towards my laundry basket.

Better wash my face then!

I foolishly opened the bathroom door without a care for my own safety.

BOOM!

The "atmosphere" that had been contained by the closed door and <u>not</u> opened window!, hit me like the back-draft in a towering inferno!

Although my body stayed where it was, my senses were thrown backwards and crashed against the wall opposite, like they had just been fired from a canon.

For several seconds I had no idea where I was.

When my mind made sense of the situation, I felt sick; no doubt having taken several mouthfuls of the less-than-pure air.

Only the fearful thought of perhaps having accidentally transferred a small "skid" onto my face made me enter the bathroom.

I held my breath and walked forward.

I splashed soap and water onto my face as quickly as I would have if I had been standing in Crocodile infested waters.

I didn't bother drying, as my eyes were beginning to sting, and just quickly left the room.

I fell to my knees as I made it back out onto the landing, as though I had just about made it into a fallout shelter following a nuclear bomb detonation.

Brother Simon passed me in my Pope-like kneeling position; the expression of control returning to his face.

"Good, God" he said, just as Mum was coming out of her bedroom.

"Close that door after yourself!" he finished, adding a mischievous smirk to his triumphant face.

"PAUL!" Mum shouted. "How many times have I told you to open the bathroom window?"

Still unable to breathe sufficiently well enough to believe I would live beyond this moment, I didn't have the energy to plead my innocence.

Instead, I could only stare at Brother Simon as he smugly walked into his bedroom.

It seemed, for now, he had got over the fact that I had received a Valentines Day Card and he hadn't.

He should have enjoyed that feeling, because it wouldn't last for long.....

Goodbye B.M.X. Hello S.E.X.

Chapter Seven - *"...a matter of principle..."*

There were very many things that you could accuse Dad of.
Maybe sponging off society because of his "bad back".
Possibly that he had a bed mattress that was sponsored by UHU!
Certainly that he had been selfish enough to take me and Brother Simon to Maine Road enough times to expose us to the bad addiction, and perpetual disappointment, that was supporting Manchester City!
And he was one of those weird people that *insisted* that his own shits actually smelt *nice*!
But the one thing you couldn't say about him was that he didn't have *principles*.
He was definitely a man who *lived by* principles.
Not just things like pointing out to the pub landlord that he had rung the bell for the end of last orders at 10.59 and 30 seconds, and that he should still get served!
No, also things like - if he gave you his word on something, it was set in stone.
He stood up for what he believed in; even if some of his "beliefs" were "a little out there" at times.
Who else would lead a sit down protest in a *McDonalds*, because they claimed to be a "restaurant" but didn't have any real knives and forks?
But it was something he believed in, so he argued his point of view - even later when he was taken to the Police station!
Despite the, sometimes odd, application, he always stuck to his principles; and encouraged Brother Simon and I to do the same.
It was a valuable lesson - and so, I too, tried to live by my beliefs.
And that is why it started that morning in the English Literature classroom.
Maybe I was buoyed on a little more than usual by that "Friday Feeling" - even if I hadn't eaten a Crunchie!
Perhaps I was a little over-excited by my first Valentines Day card, and the fact that I was meeting Louise for a *special lunch*.
It was probably a combination of these things; along with the fact that I was sitting next to Mark - and we had a reputation to uphold.
We hadn't earned the nicknames "Stadler and Waldorf" (a.k.a. the two old men from the Muppets Show) for nothing.
You only get those kind of accolades through moaning a lot.
And by "a lot", I mean "a Hell of a lot"!
In truth, I had many nicknames, due to my "Day" surname. Many of the School kids would call me "Birth" or "Christmas"; and I did quite like any new and inventive names, such as "St. Georges" or "Boxing".
As long as no-one called me "Darren", I rather liked the attention a nickname encouraging surname brought.
Mark's surname was "Hayes" and so, apart from sometimes having "Hey,

Gary Locke

Hey" shouted at him; he had to make do, solely, with the "Stadler and Waldorf" joint nickname.

I'm not sure whether anyone had decided which one of us was which.

I suppose they were both pretty similar; they both lived to moan - as did Mark and I in the English Literature classroom.

I mean, come on. Who in their right mind enjoys *reading books*?!?

And not just any books, books that were so old that most of them had numerous black and white films made about them!

Why does everything that's supposedly "classic", have to be so damn old?

So, by rights, we had every reason for moaning each lesson.

But what better cause for grumbling is a principle that's worth fighting for?

Our stand started when it was revealed it was going to come down to a class vote.

It was unbelievable!

Miss Wilder couldn't have been clearer at the start of the year: If you handed any piece of coursework in late, it would not be accepted and would not count towards your final exam result.

She could not have been any clearer.

Her rules were clearer than a freshly Mr Sheened window!

I suppose she could have been less aggressive when presenting the regulations, but that was her style. She thrived on playing the Sergeant Major; upholding a controlled and disciplined environment.

Like all teachers she was subject to rumours; her main one was that she was a hardcore feminist who was part of a TA select group that performed strategic exercises each weekend on the Yorkshire moors!

I think it was born from the day that she came to class wearing camouflage dungarees, but it did fit her well.

She was an ice Queen. She was kick ass.

She was a 20th century Joan of Arc!

Her aggressive attitude had earned her the number three spot in my "league table of most dangerous teachers".

It was a league made up of eight teachers (as I was being taught by eight teachers!) and the number three spot was not given lightly; on a whim!

After this though, perhaps I need to re-evaluate where her position should be.

League of most Dangerous Teachers -

Position – 1st
Teacher – Mr Jones *(C.D.T.)*
Comments –
Crazy, old, buffoon - can "flip out" at any given moment. Should have probably retired 20 years ago - looks like an older version of Montgomery Burns!
<u>Danger Rating</u> *- Lethal - Be on best behaviour.*

Goodbye B.M.X. Hello S.E.X.

Position – 2nd
Teacher – Mr Winters *(P.E.)*
Comments –
Insists on every Student having shower after lesson - and watches / checks. Either OCD about cleanliness or something rather unpleasantly worrying!
<u>Danger Rating</u> *- Potentially Very Dangerous - Be sure <u>not</u> to be last in shower!*

Position – 3rd
Teacher – Miss Wilder *(English)*
Comments –
Military woman. Most likely has loaded gun hidden under desk for outspoken Students.
<u>Danger Rating</u> *- Dangerous - Keep a low profile.*

Position – 4th
Teacher – Mr Martin *(French)*
Comments –
Scottish teacher in an English School, teaching French! Have no idea what he says in <u>any</u> language!
<u>Danger Rating</u> *- Be careful. Has never shown real aggression, but he <u>is</u> Scottish!*

Position – 5th
Teacher – Mr Rivers *(Geography)*
Comments –
With his name, I suppose he had to be a Geography teacher or a Canoe instructor! It's just my luck he chose teaching!
Arrogant and confrontational.
<u>Danger Rating</u> *- Medium. Could be a threat if (in his own words) he "gave a shit!"*

Position – 6th
Teacher – Mr Boland *(Science)*
Comments –
Handled me accidentally "damaging" the Science Labs in a reasonable way. "Threatened" to kill me, but didn't follow it through.
Banished me to "isolated" work; but I do have a telescope with which I can zoom in and watch whatever I want around the School.
<u>Danger Rating</u> *- Fairly Low - All talk; no action (thankfully!)*

Position – 7th
Teacher – Mr Gillard *(Maths)*
Comments –
Subject - Boring. Lessons - Boring. Voice - Boring.
Duller than a cloudy day in Scunthorpe!
<u>Danger Rating</u> *- Very Low - Although watch out for being bored to death!*

Position – 8th

Gary Locke

Teacher – Mrs Wright *(Music)*
Comments –
Despite her nervousness to allow me to use the class instruments (how authentic would my "rockstar" performance have been without smashing the guitar and "stage diving" onto the desks in front of me?) she is mild and good natured.
<u>Danger Rating</u> - *Nil - Less aggression than War-time France!*

Of course, there were other dangerous teachers in the School, none more so than our crazy, nut job Headmaster Langden, but if I didn't have daily contact with them, they didn't need to be in the league table.

But despite being number three in the "Dangerous League", here was Miss "Joan of Arc" Wilder, putting down her sword, and allowing us to overrule one of her *laws* with a class vote.

Melanie Crawford and Debbie McCloy had missed the deadline for handing in their essays and were asking for more time.

It was Friday and more time, even the *least amount* of time, would mean that they would hand their work in on Monday, giving them *two* whole days more than the rest of the class.

How can this be fair, when the rest of us had busted our arses for the last week (or crammed it all into one hour last night!) to finish our work, *on time*?

Why was Miss Wilder even asking for a vote?

It was a formality.

There was no way they would be allowed to hand their essays in late.

"If you think that Debbie and Melanie should have a second chance, and be allowed to present their work on Monday, put your hand up now." said the fake ice Queen.

I couldn't believe my eyes - hands were shooting up everywhere like rockets on bonfire night. Had everyone gone mad?

Miss Wilder looked around the room and gave a little contented nod. The class had shown the mercy she had in mind, without her totally having to expose her image for the fraud that it obviously was.

"If you *don't* think that Debbie and Melanie should have a second chance, put your hand up now." she added, as an after thought.

I'm not sure that she noticed at first that me and Mark had put our hands up more vigorously than everyone had for the previous question. You could forgive her slightly because we did always insist on sitting on the desk right at the back of the room. It was at least 10 metres further back than the next desk, and symbolised our status in the class.

We were the rebels, the top Dogs, the bad boys………or maybe we were the disliked, stinky loners. (I suppose it depended on your point of view, really!)

Whatever way, the desk position served a purpose.

We were so far back that we blended into the background. Any essential power-nap needed during an especially tedious Shakespeare sonnet would go unnoticed. Also, paper projectiles catapulted by ruler power would strike their

Goodbye B.M.X. Hello S.E.X.

skull targets from an undetected launch site.

From way back there, it was classroom "shock and awe."!

But today we *wanted* to be noticed.

It took a fairly vigorous throat clearing harmony that, the longer it went on, began to vaguely resemble a rough, but pleasant, acappella version of *"Blue Suede Shoes"*, to catch her attention.

It was so good, it seemed almost a shame when Miss Wilder recognised our vertical reaching arms and encouraged us to stop the noise.

From the front of the classroom she began to approach our desk, moving in her trademark bouncy, military march. It was an energetic walk that made her big, curly, bouncy, black hair wobble up and down and left and right, uncannily like a frenzied, dancing Fraggle!

All the eyes in the classroom followed her as she arrived at our desk.

"So.....you two.....you are sticking to your principles are you? You think that I shouldn't accept their essays late?"

Despite the fact that she had either forgotten our names or perhaps wondered whether, sitting that far back, we were actually part of her class; it felt good that she had endorsed our principles and was championing our stance.

We both leaned back and nodded energetically while muttering phrases like "It would be unfair on the rest of us!" and "The rules were very clear!" in grumpy low tones.

It was exactly those types of moments that gave credence to those comparisons to the veteran Muppet moaners.

Moments we could be truly proud of!

I was beginning to think that our stance was going to result in Miss Wilder raising us up onto an imaginary lofty moral podium, when she began to wander around the classroom sporting a pensive look.

Suddenly, at the far side of the room, her look changed alarmingly and she arrived back at our desk faster than Linford Christie.

"So, while everyone else is prepared to give Melanie and Debbie a second chance, you two don't believe in second chances? You don't think people should be allowed to make mistakes without society punishing and condemning them?"

Again, I couldn't believe it.

This wasn't something like juvenile shoplifting, an ill advised petty crime that arguably required guidance rather than punishment; this was two girls who couldn't be arsed doing their homework!

"I'll tell you what I'm going to do." she carried on. "I'm going to agree with the vast majority. The *compassionate* majority. Debbie and Melanie *will* have a second chance and can hand their work in on Monday. And everyone else in the class will have a second chance should they ever need it. As for you two, you may want to re-think your attitudes!..........you'll get chance to start in detention after School on Monday!"

I felt the rage instantly - Miss Wilders detentions always involved tidying her bookshelves! (No, that isn't a metaphor for anything!)

After a sinister smile, she bounced off back towards the front of the class.

My angriness was temporarily postponed as my mind played the Fraggle Rock theme tune as I watched her crazy, dancing hair.

"Dance your cares away, Worries for another day, Let the music play, Down at Fraggle Rock."

As she reached the blackboard, the music in my mind stopped although I continued to rock my head ridiculously from left to right for no apparent reason. I stopped and briefly told myself off, before contemplating what had just happened.

Miss Wilder had spinelessly turned her back on her own rules, and criticised us for making the stand that *she* should have made.

She had instantly transformed from a Churchill inspired hard-line leader, to a creature with less backbone than an Octopus!

It crossed my mind that this incident may have a bigger consequence than the detention that we would have to face the following week.

Would Miss Wilder dissect mine and Marks future essays and mark us down because of our "attitudes"?

I comforted myself with the fact that she would have to know our names to be able to match up our writing to her dreaded red pen.

We would maybe have to temper our napping and paper flicking for a while, in case Miss Wilder kept a closer eye on us.

I felt fairly confident though that there would be no long-term harm done. I was sure we would soon be able to catch up with any lack of sleep and ruler rustiness, as again we blended into the background.

The bad boys *would* be back in town!

This was a curious outcome though, and maybe it should be taken as a valuable lesson in life.

I may need to choose my battles more carefully; and know when and where to make stands.

Principles are nice to have; and were certainly a good option for women's clothing!, but executed at the wrong times, against the wrong people in authority, they can also lead to consequences and book-sorting detentions.

Goodbye B.M.X. Hello S.E.X.

Chapter Eight - "...Valentines Day..."

My first Valentines Day in a (real) relationship (flesh and blood girlfriends were turning out to be much more fun than imaginary ones!), was a truly memorable one.

I had quickly forgotten my stand against Miss Wilder by the time Louise and I had enjoyed a romantic, but highly risky, lunchtime blanket picnic in a secluded corner of the School field.

It meant that I wouldn't be playing football on the Tennis Courts, as usual. But thankfully that, in turn, meant I wasn't at risk of the dead legs that usually accompanied the, often brutal, lunch-time kick abouts!

It also meant that it was another clear sign to Helen Dunbar that I had a girlfriend!

I had kissed Helen once, a couple of years earlier, at the Tuesday night Youth Club and she had been almost stalking me ever since!

And whilst having a stalker when you're single and desperate is acceptable, having one when you have a girlfriend is a bit like the Liberal Democrats – pointless and annoying!

Due to her clinginess, I would have given her the nickname "Velcro" if I hadn't, fairly cruelly, already lumbered her with the label of "Dumbo"!

It was a play on words regarding her surname which fitted well because of her ears that were of similar size to Disney's most famous Elephant!

Thankfully her regular "bumping into me" and "casual" question of *"going Youth Club next week?"* didn't seem to happen as much when I was with Louise!

Eating outside was dangerous.

It had been banned by bonkers headmaster "Crazed-eyed Langden", but the air of danger only added to the sense of occasion.

It was hardly Champagne and Caviar, but our amalgamated packed lunches - tuna-mayo on a granary barm, apple, banana and natural yoghurt; along with wafer thin ham on no-frills white (thankfully not green), orange Club biscuit, a hand full of roasted peanuts and a packet of ready salted crisps (no prizes for guessing which half was mine!) - made for a more-than-adequate banquet.

We were even ten minutes late for afternoon lessons after "losing track of time" in our secluded dining haven.

The perfect School day had ended after walking Louise home.

Before entering her house, she said,

"I meant it, you know?..........I love you! You're the best thing that has ever happened to me."

I wasn't sure what I should say.

It would have been a bit cliché for me just to say "I love you too!", and seeing as I had decided not to buy any Rolo's, I just said nothing.

I'm not sure if she was hoping I would say something, but she didn't look too disappointed after we had kissed and said goodbye.

I returned home, just before Brother Simon returned from work; his face

Gary Locke

shining with hopeful anticipation.

He was soon wearing a mask of disappointment, though, as Mum explained to him that the second post had only yielded an advert for the Scouts' latest paper recycling collection, and therefore not a single Valentines Day card for him.

His mood wasn't helped by me placing my card on the window sill next to where he was sitting. Moving it to the top of the TV, when Mum later closed the curtains, also didn't result in his spirits being raised.

I pushed things too far later on by putting my card on the cabinet next to his bed. He kindly returned it to my room as soon as he noticed it, and perhaps I needed to be thankful that it was just two pieces that he had turned it into!

I was annoyed but had to accept my actions had been somewhat similar to rubbing his nasal organ in some Canine waste product!

A little sellotape and I was able to put the card back together and stand it up in it's new pride of place: on my computer desk, where it would stand forever - or at least until the next time I could use it to take the piss out of Brother Simon!

Following a night out with the lads to Tatty Park where, to their annoyance, Louise "coincidently" was; Saturday came with more bad news for Brother Simon.

Postman came and went - no late Valentines card(s) left behind.

I spent most of the day thinking up clever lines to say to him, rather than just use the "no one loves you" insult again.

I must have been having an uninspired day, because the best I could come up with were - in response to one of his jokes - "Oh, you are a *card*", "Fancy a game of *cards*?" and "Well it was always on the *cards*, wasn't it?"

After saying those, I resorted to saying things like,

"Was that the postman?" at random times, whether there was a letterbox-like sound or not.

Most of the time he took these lame little mocking lines on the chin, but every now and again he would snap viscously - like a hungry Alligator.

He even once shouted,

"Shut up you blonde haired little freak!", which came as a shock, as they were words normally used by Dad, not Brother Simon.

(Dad had always mocked me for being tall and fair haired, when the rest of the family were short and dark haired.)

But despite his occasional outburst, I kept going.

By early evening, just when I was beginning to get bored with it all, Dad joined in.

And there was no thoughtful, subtlety from him.

His idea of tip toeing around was the equivalent of ballet dancing in Doc Martin boots!

"You know you are the only person in this family who hasn't had a Valentines Day card don't you?" he asked, as Brother Simon shrank into the chair he was sitting in.

"Well you and the Dog anyway!"

Goodbye B.M.X. Hello S.E.X.

I couldn't help but laugh out loud, but Dad wasn't finished; he was just warming up.

"It must be a grooming issue with you two!............or a breath freshness problem!"

He kept going for twenty minutes, encouraged by me and my relentless cackling. The result was that Brother Simon went to bed earlier than I can ever remember, and it was a Saturday night!

He cut a lonely and forlorn figure as he traipsed up the stairs; his usual David Hasselhoff swagger conspicuous by its absence.

It was almost like there was a chink in his armour.

I felt sorry for him.

So much so, that I even went to bed not exclusively thinking about Louise - because I was planning how I could be nicer to Brother Simon the following morning.

Something to try and make him feel better.

Of course, as I rose on Sunday morning, my mind was empty of nice thoughts and, instead, was refreshed with new ways to humiliate him further.

I had no choice really.

I had played enough arcade beat-em-ups to know what you have to do when you have your man down: "FINISH HIM!"

Mum shouted at me the following morning for taking one of the blank envelopes out of the "emergency" budget birthday card pack.

I think she was equally annoyed at the fact that I had ruined a perfectly useful envelope, as well as being angry that I was, again, poking fun at Brother Simon.

I had written his name on the envelope and drawn a few hearts; all in pink felt tip. It was priceless seeing his "I told you so" face (when he had found it in the hall) change into desperate despair, when he opened it only to find my patched up card from Louise inside!

It's amazing how well a taped up Valentines card, with no further modifications, can fly like a paper aeroplane!

Luckily for me, my cat-like reflexes didn't let me down, and the card missed me and crashed harmlessly into one of Mum's mantelpiece ornaments.

Judging by her angry reaction, she would much have preferred me to have been struck than her precious glass Tortoise!

Nothing like good old fashioned motherly love!

When Dad got up later, crashing around and shouting,

"Has anyone seen my cheque guarantee CARD?" I knew it was going to be a good day.

Our fun at Brother Simon's expense continued through to the afternoon, and only really subsided when preparations began for the Sunday night card School.

The Sunday night card School was a tradition that had run for as long as I could remember.

Mum would put some green baize on the dining room table; Dad would put on his dealing visor, and various members of the family would descend on our house for an evening of "friendly" gambling.

I say friendly because, although all games did require an entry stake, 2p each time was hardly going to encourage a Police raid!

Although I did have my suspicions that things got slightly more serious after me and Brother Simon had gone to bed.

I had been woken up on a few occasions by Dads booming voice shouting things like,

"YOU HAD THAT UP YOUR SLEEVE!" or,

"THERE'S NO WAY YOU HAD TWO ACES, I DEALT YOU TWO FOURS!" - Which I think is what you would call an accusation and a confession rolled into one!

There had even been one Monday morning when I woke up to find that our car was mysteriously missing.

It probably wasn't a coincidence that Uncle Geoff seemed to be driving it around for the next few weeks; before it turned up again one Monday morning, when Dad also seemed to have a "new" Rolex watch - very similar to one that Uncle Geoff had worn for as long as I could remember.

This week we had a near full compliment. Joining Me, Brother Simon, Mum and Dad; were Grandma and Grandad, Auntie Miriam, Uncle Geoff, Auntie Lynda, Uncle Mel and our cousins Violet and Angus.

We didn't really see much of Angus - he was older than both me and Brother Simon and didn't come round much.

When he did attend the Sunday card School, Dad liked to question him about his "social life".

Dad was convinced he was gay!

I think it was because he seemed to often wear pink or yellow shirts. (A dead give away in Dads World!)

He also had small peg-like teeth and Dad would say "I'd put money on him being gay - you don't get teeth like that unless you're used to excessive pillow biting!"

(It hadn't occurred to him that his teeth had always been like that - because they were that way naturally.)

Because of the high number, it would be one of the occasions when Mum would have to extend the dining table. There were two leaves to rotate up, plus an extra piece of wood that slotted into the middle of the table - after the rest had been pulled apart.

The "extra piece" was stored in the garden shed and became a little more warped each year. At least it didn't have as many scuffs and scratches as the rest of the table.

Under the green baize the bowing piece didn't look so bad. It actually helped the games because the cards, when placed in the centre of the table, were somewhat raised and helped all players to see them more clearly.

As usual, Grandma and Grandad arrived first.

Grandma liked to be early so that she could watch *Songs of Praise* and "sing"

Goodbye B.M.X. Hello S.E.X.

along to the hymns. We used to enjoy listening and mocking, because she had the unique gift of making singing sound like a chorus of wailing Cats.

But despite any comments about *"Top Cat the Musical"* or *"Sylvester's' Symphony"*, she was never deterred - she just loved to sing.

Their arrival couldn't have been more perfect.

Grandma had brought an invitation <u>card</u> with her. It was an invite for the four of us to Grandma and Grandad's Golden Wedding Anniversary in July.

Of course, they could just have verbally invited us; and Mum was actually organising most of the party details, but Grandma liked the formality of written invitations.

She was also proud of the fact that, despite her advancing years and some arthritis in her hands, she was still able to write her own cards and letters.

You wouldn't mistake her for a professional calligrapher however - most of the cards she sent looked like they had been written during an Earthquake!

I saw Mum looking at the card and a small tear seemed to form in her eye, which was strange for a simple anniversary invitation.

When I looked later I realised why. Grandma had inserted a copy of a poem that Grandad had written, entitled "You Are…"

He had sent it to Grandma, after writing it while away with the army during the war.

It always made Mum emotional. She often said it was the most beautiful and romantic thing she had ever read - which was saying something given the number of Mills and Boon books she got through!

I remember, a couple of years earlier, she had even typed copies for me and Brother Simon, in case we wanted to put them up on our bedroom walls!

Yeah Mum! I'll just take down my Sam Fox poster to make way for – a poem!!!!

I just put my copy in my School bag, telling her that I wanted to show it to my friends at School.

She had fallen for it; but she could be quite gullible at times. She had never twigged why Brother Simon and I wouldn't eat our sprouts when she was with us in the kitchen, but managed quite quickly when she left the room. Maybe she just thought the Dogs' sprout-like farting a couple of hours later was just "coincidence"!

Anyway, the presence of Grandma's invitation card was the catalyst for a brand new assault on Brother Simon.

Dad started things,

"You best give Simon the card - we don't want him sulking around again because he's been left out. We don't want him thinking no one loves him again!"

Grandma soon realised what was happening, and she sprang to Brother Simon's defence, like a comic book hero fighting injustice.

Dad and I soon had to stop and concede defeat - we were no match for Supergran!

There was no more talk of cards for the rest of the evening - crossing an angry Grandma was like openly flirting with a death wish!

By the time Brother Simon and I went to bed on Sunday evening, wondering what essential family item Dad may gamble away as we slept, the whole Valentines Day card thing was long forgotten.

And it probably would have stayed forgotten forever, if something strange hadn't happened the following Tuesday.

The morning started in an unusual way to begin with.

For one, after a surprisingly successful performance by myself in the bathroom dash, Dad was with us at the breakfast table, which was odd because he was hardly a "morning person". In fact his presence at the kitchen table could only mean one of three things.

1...His bad back was playing up,
2...He hadn't actually been to bed, or,
3...Joanna Lumley was a guest on breakfast TV!

Whatever the reason, it meant conversation, and sound in general, was kept to a minimum - so we didn't aggravate Dad. You didn't disturb him if he was in pain, was really tired or was thinking about the "wonderful Joanna"!

(Apparently, "they don't make women like that anymore, you know"!)

Mum was doing the "early shift" on the lollipop.

After several minutes of painful silence, which included trying to eat cornflakes without making any hint of a crunch, the letterbox swung open and shut, announcing the arrival of the morning post.

Unlike Friday, there wasn't a flicker of movement from either me or Brother Simon.

Dad rolled his eyes and said,

"I'll go shall I? There's no point in you two getting your youthful legs tired is there?"

As Dad left the room, Brother Simon broke the silence.

Not with any intelligent conversation, but with a long, low motorbike-like sound, that made me wish I hadn't beaten him in the morning bathroom race.

I took a deep intake of air, wondering if I could hold my breath long enough to avoid the aroma that would be joining us imminently.

Dad returned to the kitchen holding two letters.

"Looks like the postman's been on the whisky again" he said before throwing one, a pink envelope, onto the table.

He began opening the other, a brown envelope, before quickly heading back into the living room. He was either occupied with his letter, or appalled by the kitchen atmosphere; that I had still not sampled, despite my lack of air turning my face a somewhat lobster colour.

Dad didn't care much for the postman. He had always blamed him for the damage of a limited edition Shawaddywaddy LP he ordered through the post.

How the postman could have possibly scratched a sealed record was something that Dad hadn't seemed to take into consideration.

Goodbye B.M.X. Hello S.E.X.

I suppose, however, the postman should think himself lucky, because the dislike Dad held for him, was nothing compared to the pure hatred he had for the milkman.

He often shouted names at him - whether we had been delivered the wrong milk or not.

"Lanky, blonde idiot", "Blonde, lanky idiot", and "Idiotic, lanky blonde" were his three favourite insults - although I was uncomfortable with the way he would often study my face when he shouted at him!

Brother Simon and I both looked at the pink envelope on the table.

I let out the trapped air in my lungs, realising that a foul smell would be better than death, as I read the writing on the envelope.

"Sexy Simon" it said in big, black, wavy writing, above our address.

Just above it, in smaller red, but also slightly shaky letters, like it may have been written by someone three or four pints on the wrong side of sober, it said,

"*Sorry for the delay. Card misplaced. Postman.*"

Brother Simon looked up at me, suspecting another potential prank. My confused face obviously reassured him there was no foul play this time.

A smile ten miles wide exploded through his face, as he triumphantly lifted his pink envelope. He opened it and produced a card that said in big pink letters "Be My Valentine".

He read the inside message to himself, but quickly relayed it out loud to me.

"*Simon you are the sexiest young man in the World.*
Please be mine, from your secret Valentine."

He aggressively held it high, like he was a football referee producing a red card.

"What do you think about that, then?" he said, throwing the card in my direction. "I bet there's loads more like that one; that have got lost."

He stood up from his chair and began a bizarre dance that made him look like a crazy Chicken!

I felt a little light glow inside me.

Despite his over-the-top celebration, I was actually pleased for him. The last couple of days, he had not only lost some swagger but also some energy and confidence, perhaps even a little life spirit.

I looked at the card and had a strange sense of déjà-vu.

The writing looked familiar.

Where had I seen it before?

It occurred to me.

No!

I wasn't right was I?

I walked into the living room and picked up Grandma's invitation from the mantelpiece.

The writing was identical!

We wouldn't need Columbo to crack this case!

Grandma had sent Brother Simon the card!

I returned to the kitchen carrying both the Valentines card and the invitation; just in time to see Brother Simon stopping the flapping of his arms and performing a pretty impressive headstand.

I turned both cards upside down and placed them in front of his face.

His eyes made the connection between the writing.

He quickly lost his balance, and came crashing to the floor - in more ways than one.

The new look on his face reflected the state of his heart and soul.

He was broken.

He looked lower than I had ever seen anyone look.

I couldn't help it, it was like a pre-set impulse.

I laughed out loud!

I couldn't help it: Grandma had sent him his one and only Valentines Day card.

It was hilarious.

I called out to Dad and told him of the revelation.

He shouted something about being quiet, because Joanna was talking, but I couldn't help but laugh on.

This felt like sweet revenge for some of the (numerous) times that he had humiliated me.

And it was definitely funnier than the time when I had accidentally wet myself "a little", laughing hysterically during my tenth birthday party!

The next time Brother Simon told *that* story - I could tell *this* one.

The one about Grandma sending him a Valentines Day card!

My laughing subsided slightly for two reasons.

One - I didn't want a repeat of my birthday "accident"!

Two - I felt a little uncomfortable and slightly sickened as I pictured Grandma writing the words "Simon, you are the sexiest young man in the world"!

I wasn't sure how I would be able to look her in the eye the next Sunday!

I shrugged off the weirdness of the details and focused on Brother Simon.

He hadn't moved from the prostrate position in which he had landed after his headstand collapse. If it wasn't for his tearful eyes and slow head shaking, I may have been concerned that he had injured himself.

I looked at him and smiled.

Brother Simon was no longer invincible.

I had received a Valentines Day card and he hadn't - because I had a girlfriend and he didn't.

I was no longer the obvious and easy target for his and Dads mocking.

Things were becoming more equal.

Times were changing.....

Goodbye B.M.X. Hello S.E.X.

March 1992

If, in the simplest terms, the four seasons are each made up of three whole months, then March is the beginning of Spring.
As such there was a change in the Holly Grove weather.
The crisp mornings, icy pavements and blizzard filled skies were replaced by - crisp mornings, icy pavements and blizzard filled skies!
Something I used to wonder every year around this time was whether the Sun had enjoyed its Winter holiday so much, that it had decided to permanently emigrate!
Maybe Holly Grove should consider a new twin town scheme and strike up a relationship with Siberia!
Nationally, the Country was presented with the news that Prince Andrew was to split from Fergie. (Apparently he wanted to concentrate solely on Manchester Utd!)
No, not *that* Fergie - Sarah Ferguson - the Princess that the nation were indifferent about. Why did we need *her*, when we had *Diana*?
"*Goodnight Girl*" had been replaced at number one by Shakespear's Sisters' "*Stay*". (Possibly a bit ironic in the wake of the Royal split!)
How the hell the pretty good, but also pretty morbid, *Stay* kept Def Leppard's brilliant "*Let's Get Rocked*" off the top spot, only God will ever know.
Do the people who buy chart singles actually have ears?
Despite Holly Groves unmistakably Russian cold front, things with Louise were continuing to hot up.
Not only were we still an "item", we were spending more and more time together.
It wasn't pleasing John, Mark and Little Si, as they believed I was going out with them less and less - which I couldn't argue with, because I was.
This had even included a couple of Friday nights - which was breaking a rule that we had always lived by.
"Girls would never be put before friends - especially on Friday nights!"
Of course this was a directive that had been previously easy to live by, seeing as none of us had ever had a girlfriend before!
Nevertheless, it was difficult to imagine my "abandoning" them prompting a more hostile reaction if I had murdered all their Mothers!
After having shagged them all!
My continued relationship with Louise wasn't really pleasing Dad either - he was loosing a fortune on his "when will she dump him" book. He had taken a real hammering after offering odds of 100-1 that we would "still be together in March!"
But we *were* still together in March; and, as we continued to get closer, things were approaching another level.....

Chapter Nine - *"...Poetry Club..."*

For the last few weeks, I hadn't only been seeing Louise at School, but also on some evenings.

It was always at my house, where we would watch TV, listen to some music and, most importantly, practice our kissing.

We had discussed maybe going to Louise's house, but because her Dad was apparently a "little protective" (Louise had said he may want to cross examine or possibly shoot me before letting me enter the house!), we had decided it would be best to have a formal meeting with her parents before any "casual visits".

At my house Mum and Dad were much more relaxed about Louise coming round. I think they still liked getting proof now and again that I did *actually* have a girlfriend.

Louise was a little nervous about coming to the house on her own; which was understandable - Dad had that affect on most people!

The Pools man was often a gibbering wreck if he ever had to listen to Dad's opinions on politics, or sport, or the weather, or the news, or.......pretty much *everything*!

As a result, when seeing Louise, I would walk out from my house to meet her. (Yes *walk*! It was probably the first time in my life that I was leaving the house by foot – and not on my B.M.X.!)

We would both leave at exactly 7pm, after making sure that our watches were perfectly synchronised. (I was like a soppy, loved-up, teenage James Bond!)

After meeting about halfway between our houses we would walk, often holding hands, back to mine together. Often, if it was *extra* cold, I would have to wrap my coat around her shoulders which, despite leaving me feeling chilly made me feel warm inside.

It was one of those things that guys in *real* relationships do!

So here we were in my bedroom, on a Wednesday night, not wasting time on watching Coronation Street or doing homework, but smooching on my bed.

Louise was hotter than ever.

She was wearing some blue jeans and a tight fitting red vest top that enhanced her slim, but curvy torso. Her brown hair was down, cascading over her shoulders; and she was wearing dangerously sizzling red lipstick.

She wouldn't have looked out of place running in slow motion on a beach next to David Hasselhoff!

But she wasn't on my TV in an episode of Baywatch (whilst I watched, sitting next to a king-size box of tissues!) - she was lying next to me, on my bed, *kissing me*.

She had brought round a mix tape of pop and cheesy rock songs; including a ballad we had called "our song" - Bryan Adams' *"Heaven"*.

It was the sort of song that, if my ears hadn't been distorted by the feelings

Goodbye B.M.X. Hello S.E.X.

of growing affection, I would usually have hated.

I had adopted *Rock* music as my "thing", mainly as an antidote to Brother Simons "*Five Star*"-style pop obsession.

Heavy guitars, stage diving and head banging - anything to be *different* from him.

This hadn't included soppy power ballads though - until now.

In my current mood I loved anything slow and emotional, and I now realised that "*Heaven*" was quite possibly the greatest song ever recorded!

It was certainly right up there with another one of Bryans' songs - "*Everything I Do, I Do It For You*"; which mystifyingly bored me to death for *sixteen bloody weeks* the previous year!

If it wasn't Bryan we were listening to then it was *Richie Sambora's* beautiful "*One Light Burning*" or *Bad English* - "*When I See You Smile*" or *Robin Beck's* "*First Time*" – another song I'd mistakenly dismissed as being shit when it blasted out of those *Coca Cola* adverts every time there was a break in *The A-Team*!

Or, Roxette's entire "*Joyride*" album!

Who knew that *Roxette* were actually really good?!?

It's strange how different moods can change your perspective on, not only music, but pretty much most things.

It was only during the last couple of weeks, during ITV re-runs, that I realised how good "*The Love Boat*" was!

As time had passed, mine and Louise's kissing had become more "hands on". Although we hadn't reached the taking clothes off stage yet (although Louise did now usually take her coat off when she came round!), it was normal to caress each other quite suggestively when we kissed.

Brother Simon had given me some advice about how to take our relationship a bit further. His gentle "cupping" stroke was working well (especially tonight over that tight top!), but I hadn't yet found the confidence to attempt his suggested "one-handed belt removal".

I certainly wasn't comfortable with his advice to "slap her on the arse and say "let's get naked"!"

I assumed it was far too soon in our relationship to do that.

But perhaps I was mistaken.

As Bryans gravel-like voice quietened at the end of another perfect "*Heaven*" performance, Louise whispered something into my ear.

"Do you want to do something that will bring us *closer together*?"

I attempted a silent gulp.

Unfortunately it sounded like I had just twanged a large rubber band!

Thoughts buzzed around my head like frantic Bluebottles trapped inside a car on a hot Summers day.

This was what I wanted - but was I ready?

I was dreadfully unprepared.

I had tried to speak to Mark, Little Si and John, hopefully to get some advice about what to do in these situations; but it had been a complete waste of time. None of them had any experience whatsoever.

It was like asking Maggie Thatcher for advice on the nutritional benefits of milk to School children!

I needed to find *someone* who could assist me, but who?

For now, I had to face facts.

No matter how much I pretended to be, or how much I wanted to be, I wasn't ready.

I wondered what was the best way to tell Louise this.

My voice, inspired by something other than doubt, found some words to say.

"Hell, yes! I'd love to do something to bring us closer together!"

I shrugged the uncertainty aside. Even if I would just be making it up as I went along, I would give it a damn good try.

Louise smiled.

"Great", she said "Do you want to come to Poetry Club with me, after School tomorrow?"

I remained still; confusion painted all over my face.

I'm not sure why, but I felt like I had been cheated somehow.

"How will that bring us closer together?" I snapped like an angry Jack Russell.

Louise, not put off by my show of diminutive Canine aggression, spoke enthusiastically, with that familiar sparkle in her eyes.

"Poetry is so romantic. We have learnt about all the classic love songs - they really are beautiful. We are encouraged to write our own - I really love it. I think we could have a good time doing it together. Writing poems to each other!"

I listened to her words and let them soak in.

I had spent the best part of seven weeks convincing myself that Louise wasn't the geek that I thought she was before I had got to know her.

She had spoilt all that in just two words.

Poetry Club!

Who, in their right mind, stays behind *after* School has finished, to read and learn more about *poetry*?

I couldn't believe she was actually asking me.

Who the Hell did she think I was?

I had a reputation to uphold. One that had taken to best part of five years to build. In what crazy, alternative universe did she think I would throw all that away by agreeing to this?

"Go on say you will" she whispered, looking deep into my eyes. "It will be brilliant, I promise you."

She leant in and kissed me, while at the same time gently running her hand all the way up the inside of my leg.

"Of course I will" I said, powerless to say anything different! "I'm looking forward to it."

There is a well known saying - "The way to a mans heart is through his *stomach*", but right at that moment, I could have thought of an even more

Goodbye B.M.X. Hello S.E.X.

appropriate one, involving a different area of the body!

Our "touchy" kissing continued, and became more intimate as the night continued (as much as it can be fully clothed). I even tentatively attempted the "belt release"; but after a bit of fumbling around, realised it would take a more skilled hand than mine. It was like the belt had it's own combination lock, and *I* certainly didn't have the code number!

After walking Louise home, ending another romantic evening with just the three of us - me, Louise and *Bryan*; I began to contemplate what going to Poetry Club would really mean.

How would I live it down?

I would have to find a legitimate and compelling argument that would support and justify why I was attending, possibly the most ridiculous, after-School club.

I came up with a plan.

I would do whatever it took to keep it a complete secret - lie, fight, deceive and even *kill* if necessary!

My first lie was the next day, and was to convince Little Si and Mark that I wasn't walking home with them from School, because I had a detention.

I thought it was quite cool to tell them it was because Louise and I had been caught snogging behind the bike sheds by the Fraggle herself, Miss Wilder.

Judging by their pretend vomiting, they possibly didn't find it as cool as I thought they would.

It didn't matter, I was in the clear; and I was pretty sure that there wouldn't be anyone at Poetry Club who would ever speak to anyone I even *remotely* knew.

And I was right.

What a bunch of mis-fits!

There were blazers, national health specs, teeth braces, bad acne and ginger hair everywhere!

It was like a School bully's dream come true!

Even so, I couldn't help but question why they were all here. A quick count told me there were (about) fifteen people here (I didn't want to take too long looking at any of them to count properly, in case they thought I was letting on to them.)

But why were they all in this club?

If you had to stay late at School then there were a variety of "Sports Clubs" going on. If you didn't want to be too active, you could always watch the Cheerleaders Club as they did their practising and "stretching". (Something I hadn't done since I had been in a relationship!)

I entered the classroom and sat next to Louise - a little nearer the front of the room than I was either used to, or was comfortable with.

I glanced around the room again, and gauged that there was a fifty/fifty split of looks on the fifteen or so faces. Half looked surprised that I was there; the others seemed to have utter contempt at my presence.

Not surprising really, if they thought I was as out of place as I felt.

Gary Locke

A fish out of water.
A black sheep.
A normal person in a room full of super-nerds!
And these weren't even the brainy super-nerds - they were all at *Science Club*. These were the soppy, romantic-wannabe super-nerds!

I uncomfortably shuffled in my chair as the teacher entered the room; mad, curly hair bouncing up and down - it was only Miss Wilder!

I tried not to make any kind of eye contact with her; but I could sense that she was confusingly staring at me.

"Are you here thinking this is a detention class?" she asked as she got to the blackboard; obviously recognising my face but, unsurprisingly, not able to recall my name.

"Yes" I said instinctively, sticking to my own cover story.

Louise elbowed me in the ribs.

"No" I said, correcting myself, as best I could with the wind knocked out of my lungs. "I'm here for the club, Miss"

After a couple of seconds of glancing around the room, that I can only assume was her checking for Jeremy Beadle, Miss Wilder said,

"Excellent, a newbie!..........ok class, let's welcome our new member."

A less than enthusiastic round of applause followed, that wouldn't have sounded out of place during a Man City end of season "lap of honour"!

Miss Wilder leant forward on the desk in front of her, her voice taking on a slightly sinister tone.

"Ok, as is usual for a newbie.......lets have the *initiation*."

I began to panic.

I had a vision of the class surrounding me, stripping me naked and then carrying me to, and throwing me into, the School pond.

"Recite for us your favourite poem" continued Miss Wilder.

I shouldn't have been worried - it obviously wasn't *that* kind of club!

There was a problem though, I didn't know any poems.

Who, in there right mind, goes around taking up valuable memory space with bloody poems?

The class began to stare at me.

"I know it's difficult" said Miss Wilder "There are so many to choose from.........just pick one, and speak it out loud.........after introducing yourself to the club.........by telling them your name!"

A couple more seconds passed; but my good old brain came to the rescue.

I did know a poem.

I cleared my throat.

"Hi, everyone. Mr name is Paul Day. Here's the poem.
There once was a man called Rick,
Who had an affair with a chick,
It angered his wife,
Who took a sharp knife,
And with one slash, cut off his...."

Goodbye B.M.X. Hello S.E.X.

"OK, OK, OK.....I think that will do!" interrupted Miss Wilder.

There were a couple of sniggers around the room; a lot of students looking disgruntled, and a teacher wearing an expression that looked like she was contemplating sending me to that detention class.

"Ok, I think we'll skip the rest of the initiation" said Miss Wilder in a low voice. "I'm not sure hearing your *second* favourite poem is anything any of us need to experience!"

Miss Wilder then handed out some books and said she was going to go through a couple of the "timeless" classics with us.

I could tell by Louise's face that she was somewhat disappointed with me. She looked slightly embarrassed and her eyes, that usually sparkled when she looked at me, now looked more like laser beams that were intent on decapitating me!

I asserted that she wouldn't want me to come to Poetry Club with her again.

A party popper went off in my mind - it was the perfect scenario.

I didn't want to be here; so if Louise *also* didn't want me to be here as well, wasn't that something that business guru's would call a "win:win" situation?

As the gun powder from the popper explosion began to clear in my head, I realised this wasn't true.

I had let Louise down.

She had invited me to a part of her World that was important to her, and not only had I not taken it seriously, I had also embarrassed her.

I sat up in my chair.

I needed to concentrate. Surely I would have something to offer the club. Something to clear Louise's embarrassment, and make her proud of me.

"In front of you," began Miss Wilder, referring to the books she had just handed out. "Are a collection of poems by William Blake. He is one of the country's best loved poets and has written many memorable poems. He was actually also a painter and a print maker, something that not many people know. Can anyone tell me what he is probably best remembered for?"

A few hands shot up around the class like Snakes responding to the hypnotic playing of a pipe song.

I wracked my brain.

Blake? Blake? Blake?

Ping!

It was there. Miraculously the answer had come to me; arriving like the satisfying announcement of a readied Microwave meal!

I outstretched my index finger and thrust my arm into the air like an enthusiastic Cricket Umpire.

I noticed the dilemma in Miss Wilder's eyes. Should she take the gamble of allowing me to answer, or take the safe option of (probably) *any* of the other raised arms.

Luckily for me, she obviously enjoyed a flutter.

"Ok......Paul?"

Here was my chance.

"He was the illustrator for most of the Roald Dahl books!"

Despite the sniggering that was breaking out around the room again, Miss Wilders deadpan expression didn't alter - by even a millimetre.

"That wasn't *William* Blake, it was *Quentin* Blake!" she said. "And we are not here to talk about children's books; we are here to talk about poetry!"

The undercurrent of laughing continued around the room after Miss Wilder's comments.

None was coming from Louise though - she was too busy holding her head in her hands.

Although I was fairly confident that something as trivial as this wouldn't bring our relationship to an end; I also had to accept that it couldn't help things.

Louise didn't even look at me once for the next ten minutes, as Miss Wilder spoke about this bloke - "*William* Blake" (I wasn't *that* far out with *Quentin*, was I?), and about "Innocence" and "Experience", and about little boys that were lost and then found. (Come on Blake - make your bloody mind up!)

Miss Wilder asked a further five questions, each time ignoring my raised hand - raised in a desperate attempt to redeem myself in Louise's eyes.

It was just as well that she ignored me, because each time I would have given an answer as ridiculous as my previous response. (What were the chances of there being a *poet* named *Kipling* as well as the guy who makes cakes?)

Despite still being desperate to get involved, there were twenty minutes of club discussion, including Louise getting involved, that may well have been spoken in a different language.

It was like watching a European Art Film - dull and unfathomable!

It came as a welcome relief when Miss Wilder looked at her watch and brought the debate to an end.

"Ok, we're coming up to the end of the session" she said. "We'll finish as usual. Does anyone have a poem written by themselves or a member of their family, that they want to share with the group?"

This was it - "end of session" - it was last chance saloon.

I was aware of a couple of hands slowly rising, when my brain came up with a MENSA moment.

I had Grandad's poem sitting in the front compartment of my School bag.

Would the class like that one?

It was definitely worth a try.

I added my arm to the five that were already in the air.

Miss Wilder's eyes were drawn to my movement, but she instinctively and quickly looked away - like someone who had accidentally looked at a woman breast feeding!

She focused on a girl with shortly cropped ginger hair sitting at the back of the class. She was wearing national health glasses, a pink neck scarf and an "*I Love Bros*" badge. Surely Poetry Club is the only place you could see such fashion. (I had no idea who this girl was - in fact I was wondering whether most of the kids in here even attended our School!)

Goodbye B.M.X. Hello S.E.X.

Miss Wilder made her choice.
"Ok, Jessica. Can….."
"*MISS WILDER!*"
I loudly and rudely cut her off mid-sentence.
A few shocked gasps, that sounded like well-shaken Coca-Cola bottles being opened, hissed out loud.
"I have a poem that my Grandfather wrote for my Grandmother. He was away during the War, and wrote it while alone and missing her in Germany. He sent it back to her in the post."
Despite my interruption, Miss Wilder looked intrigued.
After a couple of seconds, she gave in to her gambling spirit.
"Ok, Paul. I'm not sure what to expect, but off you go."
I got the poem out of my bag whilst wondering whether Miss Wilder should consider attending gamblers anonymous!
I composed myself by running over the first couple of lines in my mind; ignoring the loud spoilt-brat like tutting that was coming from the direction of the girl I now knew was called Jessica.
I began reading slowly and clearly.
"*You Are…*" by my Grandad, Howard Fry, written on Tuesday, 05th December, 1944.

<u>*You Are*</u>

Your picture is the last thing that I touch at night, and each morning the first thing I see,
And you are everything I dream about, for the few hours in between.

You are as gentle as a new born lamb, and yet a tiger that cannot be tamed,
You are the scent of a rose, the touch of pure silk, the taste of the sweetest champagne.

On cold, rainy days when gun fire flashes, and bomb blasts echo out loud,
You are the warmest clothes, the biggest umbrella, the sunshine that breaks through the cloud.

When the weight of the world pins my shoulders down, and it feels hard just to go on,
You are the clown with the song and the dance and the jokes, the one who makes life so much fun.

And when the first light arrives on a perfect spring morning, you are always the first bird to sing,
You are beauty, you are love, you are all I think of, you are my everything.

Throughout the reading, I was conscious that more and more eyes were fixing on me; and wasn't sure if that was a good thing or not.

Despite the discomfort I felt, I read Grandad's poem perfectly from start to finish.

As I looked up, following the final word, I noticed that many of the staring eyes were a little glazed. Even Miss Wilder seemed to be wiping a tear away with her handkerchief - although she was trying to disguise it by a fog horn-esque blow of the nose. (She'll do anything to try and maintain that "false" ice queen image!)

I looked across at Louise.

Her eyes were wide and, once more, were sparkling as brilliantly as ever. She was almost melting into her seat.

Good old Grandad - he never lets me down!

"That was beautiful." said Miss Wilder, now her nose had been well and truly emptied. "Thank you very much for sharing it with us."

She looked at her watch again.

"Wow, we are over time now; so I'll end this week with a really short poem.

"Today", by T. Summerfield.

Just waiting for your moment?
Until then just passing your time?
But that's killing time, and it's murder,
and murder is the worst crime.

Because you'll wake up one day,
And tomorrow will be yesterday,
And there's nothing you can change,
Because everything's too late.

Tomorrow will always happen,
Don't wish this day away,
Don't waste another second,
Live your life today!

I listened to every word and soaked them right in. They were like a, well poetic, version of my new motto in life.

"Ok, think about the words in this poem, and we'll talk about it at the beginning of the next session. See you all next week." said Miss Wilder, picking up her things from off the desk.

"Well done Paul......Well done!" she said patting me on the shoulder as she bounced past, towards the door.

As I stood up and reached for my bag, about half a dozen of the class deliberately passed my way on their way out of the room.

"Beautiful poem" said Jessica, obviously now over her earlier snub.

"That was a cool poem, Paul. See you next week." said a dark haired boy in

Goodbye B.M.X. Hello S.E.X.

a blazer - who I now thought *may* have been in my French class. Name?..........no, idea!

He sounded a little awkward; as if it was perhaps the first time he had ever used the word "cool" in a sentence.

The others smiled at me as they walked past.

It was nice to know that I had been accepted by the club. In fact, the response I had received made me feel like a mini-celebrity.

Louise grabbed my hand tightly and, once more, she looked pleased that I was with her.

"Did you enjoy that?" she asked.

"Yes, I did." I said, instinctively lying.

Then I realised, I *had* actually enjoyed myself.

Maybe this Poetry Club wasn't just for sad losers. We had learnt about "*Tigers burning bright*", and "*Forests of the night*".

My whole perception of poets was beginning to change.

Maybe they weren't just a community of romantic fools with too much time and too many pens on their hands!

Some of them were *Rock Stars* - they just didn't have electric guitars back then!

It was suddenly feeling like Poetry Club maybe wasn't the most uncool thing in the World.

It was possible I would come again.....

Chapter Ten - "...earliest memories..."

By the end of March, I had secured a curious hat-trick. I had attended the after School, Thursday night Poetry Club for three weeks on the trot. And I was not only enjoying it; but had also found it an uplifting and insightful experience on each occasion.

So much so, that it was important to pose some serious questions to myself.

Had I been wrong about what Poetry Club was and what it represented?

Had I realised now what it really meant, and so had therefore changed my perception?

Or, was my willingness to now accept it, a simple indication that perhaps it was actually me that had changed?

Was I now just a shadow of the man I wanted to be?

Perhaps just the shadow of *any* man?

Even just the shadow of a man like Julian Clary?

I decided not to dwell on it too much. My new philosophy had shown me to embrace everything that was enjoyable in life - and it was certainly working so far.

So this was how I saw Poetry Club - it was *interesting* and *enjoyable*, and I was also learning something. (Which couldn't harm my fast approaching exams.)

I was also spending more time with Louise, which was the main aim anyway, and as a result, our relationship was definitely developing.

I had also, so far, been able to keep it secret from my friends and family - which was extremely important because that information would be grade-A mocking material.

So, there was really no downside to be concerned about.

If I found myself becoming over-sensitive, or developing an attraction towards *men*, that would be the time to start to be alarmed!

As it was, my post Poetry Club routine of listening to heavy metal music, whilst burping and farting for at least an hour, seemed to be maintaining my masculinity nicely!

The last club of the month had included Miss Wilder encouraging us to talk about our earliest memories.

Louise had spoken out loud about her first memory. She told a cute story about her going on holiday with her Mum, Dad, Brother and both sets of Grandparents.

For a month they had soaked up the sun in Portugal - for the first of what turned out to be annual visits to the area.

She told of the excitement of travelling by aeroplane for the first time.

Apparently they had flown first class - Louise's Dad insists on it, saying "What's the point of working hard and being well off, if you don't reap the rewards of it?" (I had never met him, but was quite sure that he was probably my all time hero!)

Goodbye B.M.X. Hello S.E.X.

Louise spoke about realising that other families were also on holiday - and what being part of a family was all about.

So her earliest memory was one that taught her about the love and respect that keeps a family close.

There were a few stories from some of the other members of the club, although none were anywhere near as sickly-and-sugary-American as Louise's!

They were mainly tales of first days at School or Christmas's or Birthdays.

Jessica told of her 3rd birthday party, during which she had got too close to one of the candles on her cake during the *"Happy Birthday"* song - setting her hair on fire!

The situation wasn't helped by her Father, who apparently grabbed her Mothers' glass of "water" and threw it over Jessica's head to put the flames out. Unfortunately it turned out not to be water, and was in fact *vodka*!

The scene, apparently, quickly took on the feel of a bad chip pan fire.

So, Jessica's earliest memory included a night in hospital being treated for severe burns, the revelation that her Mum was an alcoholic, and her having her long auburn hair flambéed so badly, she had to have it all shaved off. (A style she had maintained, because "long hair is just a fire-hazard and a painful reminder of that day!")

I think it is safe to say that Jessica's story represented a low point of the poetry club evening.

Despite my new found stardom in the club, I had kept fairly quiet; allowing these others to talk. It wouldn't be right for me to always hog the limelight - even the lead singer in a Rock band vacates the stage and allows a little time for guitar and drum solo's!

Besides, I couldn't actually put my finger on a *single* earliest memory.

I just seemed to have multiple memories that blended into a similar kind of time period.

Like Louise, one of these included a family holiday.

Not eight people jetting off, first class, to the Sun; but rather me, Mum, Dad and Brother Simon cramped into a small caravan at a Wales campsite.

All I can remember is being stuck inside because of a week of torrential rain - which sounded like someone with a pneumatic drill trying to break in through our roof!

Being trapped inside, what is effectively a large Sardine can, with no ventilation, with Brother Simon and Dad should not, by law, be allowed to be called a holiday!

Although we did learn the intricacies of Monopoly hustling, as Dad slowly won all our holiday spending money!

But as well as *wet* holidays, I remember *hot* Summers.

Summers that involved playing football everyday in the park, and water fights in the early evenings.

Some kids had genuine water fight "Power Blasters", while me and Brother Simon had to make do with used washing up liquid bottles. They did have their benefits though - our targets often got the remains of "no-frills" washing up liquid in their eyes, rendering them blind for a few seconds, and vulnerable to a damn good soaking.

There was also a large group of us who would ride our BMX's around with attitude, like some sort of juvenile Hells Angels group; crushed cans stuck into our wheel spokes, so we sounded like we were riding real, meaty motorbikes!

If we weren't riding around, we were making ramps out of bricks and planks of wood.

Many a time, Dad had to run out of our house, after spotting me lying at the back of the row of kids to be jumped, out behind the back of the ramp.

He probably saved my life on numerous occasions, or at the very least stopped me from receiving a permanent Chopper wheel print on my chest!

As well as all the fun in the Sun, I also clearly remember my best friend, Paul Dale, moving away because his Dad had got a new job.

Before he moved, we were *inseparable*.

Because we were both called Paul, people used to refer to us as "the two Paul's". This sometimes got abbreviated to "the two P's" or "two Peas in a pod".

On cold days, which obviously covered most of the year in Holly Grove, Dad liked to call us "the two frozen peas"!

Paul Dale was in most of my earliest memories.

We were Tom Sawyer and Huckleberry Finn, Han and Luke, Robin Hood and Little John and, on stranger days, Kermit and Miss Piggy!

We were best friends forever - until his family moved to Birmingham.

At the time it felt like Birmingham was the other side of the World.

After visiting a few times, it felt like Birmingham was a different planet!

We did visit each other on a few occasions and, in reality, the distance wasn't that great. But we would have to commit to a full weekend, and we were relying on parents driving us there and back.

Sometimes the effort can seem like a big price, when surely the prize would be more than worth it.

So visits became phone calls, and phone calls became Christmas and Birthday cards; and then everything just became memories.

And Tom and Huckleberry, who'd had a friendship that deserved a full novel, would just be confined to a first chapter.

They would then go their separate ways – and the rest of the book would have to be about something else!

These earliest times were also dominated by believing that Mum and Dad, and probably adults in general, were always right - no matter *what* they said.

I remember Mum threatening me on several occasions that I would be left with certain facial expressions (usually grumpy frowns!) "if the wind changes"!

I was scared to death - I always assumed that a particularly unpleasant wind change must have struck Peter Beardsley!

I didn't want to be caught out by a similar, unforgiving breeze.

Grandma used to promise me and Brother Simon "thick, curly" hair if we ate all our sandwich crusts up. We didn't really twig that it was just a saying

Goodbye B.M.X. Hello S.E.X.

designed to encourage us to eat more.

It now seems ridiculous we even entertained what she said.

At Grandma's, we would eat our sandwiches sitting opposite Grandad, who always ate his crusts, yet he was balder than an entire flock of coots!

I also remember a very informative conversation with Auntie Lynda on the subject of Father Christmas. Because we had no chimney, I was confused about how Santa would deliver our presents on Christmas day. Auntie Lynda explained that for every house without a chimney, Father Christmas would use the front door - because he had a "magic" key that could open every front door in the World.

It seemed like a reasonable explanation.

Later though, when I had gone to bed, I couldn't help wondering - what if someone else somehow got hold of this key?

Not a good person, delivering presents for children, but a <u>bad</u> person - maybe a *burglar* or a *murderer*.

I didn't sleep for weeks worrying about the whereabouts of that key!

Maybe it was part of the job of being an Auntie to dispense these "pieces of wisdom" that caused distress; because I also remember one from Dads Sister, Auntie Miriam.

She had warned me to be careful when eating an Apple once, saying that if I swallowed any of the pips, I would end up having an Apple tree growing inside me!

That was a scary thought - I certainly didn't want to be shitting Apples or pissing Cider. (Although that may come in useful now I've developed a liking for Cider!).

This situation wasn't helped by, what I suppose could have been, Brother Simon's "earliest prank" on me.

He confessed, years later, to sneaking into my bedroom one night, and putting an apple under my duvet as I slept.

I assumed Auntie Miriam's frightening tree-growing warning had come true!

For ages, I took hours over eating any seed based crops - meticulous not to swallow any further pips.

My diligence included not going anywhere near certain fruits. Imagine the damage that could be caused by accidentally swallowing a Melon pip?

I didn't want to be the only male in the World who could genuinely empathise with women about the pain of giving birth!

A more serious adult-delivered answer, that seemed to come from around the same period of time, was when I asked Grandad about what happens when someone dies.

He told me that good people went to Heaven and met up with everyone they had ever loved.

He also said that, the close loved ones left behind hear the sound of the Angels screaming out loud.

Screaming in agony and pain.

Gary Locke

Screaming for the loss and the loneliness.
But, he also said, if you listen further, you can also hear them singing.
Singing as the gates to Heaven opened.
Singing as Souls are reunited.
And within these songs are the echoes of happy memories, and the feelings you need to also celebrate the life that was lived, rather than just mourn the passing.

I had thankfully never experienced the *screams* or the *songs*, but I had always remembered Grandad's words clearly - whether he's right or not, maybe I'll never know.

And there was also the chance he was just like every other adult in the World - constantly having a laugh at children's expenses, or blatantly lying or just being ridiculously stupid!

It obviously came later than these earliest memories, but I remember the first time I began to question some "adult wisdom".

Perhaps unsurprisingly, it was an incident involving Dad that brought this first doubt about grown-ups.

He would often used the phrases -
"Early to bed, early to rise,
Makes a man healthy, wealthy and wise!" <u>and</u>
"The early bird catches the worm!"

They were two of his favourite sayings, and he would use one, or both, of them every time there was the hint of an argument when the "bedtime" call came.

Like any point he wanted to emphasise, he would say them with raised eyebrows, accompanied by an outstretched, pointed finger that wiggled up and down, like he was tapping the ash off an imaginary cigar!

Both phrases seemed reasonable, and they were words that me and Brother Simon accepted without question.

For a time anyway.

Then one day it suddenly struck me. Although Dad regularly spoke these words, *he* certainly didn't adhere to his own advice.

I had never known him to go to bed early, and there was certainly never any sign of him each morning as Mum force-fed us our Cornflakes, before throwing us out of the house - roughly in the direction of School!

In fact, given the actual hours that he spent awake, it wasn't so far-fetched to wonder if Dad had some kind of Sun allergy!

So, one day I questioned him about the flaw in his advice.

His face was full of disappointment - not too unlike the time when he had bought Frosties instead of Cornflakes, because the box had a 3-D scene on the back - only to find there were no red and green-lensed glasses inside!

He shook his head.

"There are two types of people in this World." he said. "There are the *Birds*, and there are the *Worms*. Everyone wants to be a Bird, to be able to fly high in the sky. But not everyone can be. *You've* still got a chance, but *for me* it's too

Goodbye B.M.X. Hello S.E.X.

late."

The confusion on my face must have been shining brighter than a lighthouse beacon.

He explained what he meant by using another rhyming piece of wisdom.

"There are the birds and the worms; the hunters and the prey,
You need to know the one you are, just to survive each day.
Because if you don't have feathers, the best thing you can learn,
Is that the early bird catches, the early bloody worm!"

I couldn't argue, because it seemed to make good sense!
But so did his other sayings.
So, when you thought about them together, there was only one thing that was clear - a blatant contradiction.
And before I knew it, they were everywhere!
Like, how could *"many hands make light work"*, while at the same time *"too many cooks spoil the broth"*?
I began to wonder about all sorts of things.
Just before Christmas each year, Dad always seemed to phone Santa. He would ask him to keep a close eye on me and Brother Simon - and if he saw us mis-behaving, not to deliver us any Christmas presents that year.
Each time they would chat away, as if him and Santa were *best mates*. He used to ask all about Rudolph and Mother Christmas. (In fact sometimes Mother Christmas would answer - and Dad seemed to know her very well also!)
It was like Dad and Santa were old School chums, just catching up with each other.
But why did he never phone him any other time of the year?
Surely someone you were that close to, you would want to speak to more than once a year?
It didn't make sense.
At least while they were on the phone, Dad could (at my request) get Santa to check that he hadn't misplaced his magic key!
Perhaps things weren't meant to make any sense though.
Maybe that's the point of being a child - you are just learning about life. It doesn't help that, most of the time, that process is complicated by all the confusing, contradictory and down right preposterous things you are told by adults!
So that was it - my "earliest memories".
A mix of friendship and *lost friendship*, discovery, confusion and fear, and, perhaps more than anything else, a sense of innocence and of carefree times.
Surely I could find a poem in there somewhere.....

Gary Locke

I Miss My B.M.X.

I miss riding really, really fast, down the big hill by the bank,
And doing Evil Knievel Jumps, over ramps made of old wooden planks.

I miss playing footy on the field, with fifty lads until it gets dark
And slides and swings and climbing frame things, when we'd spend all day at the park.

I miss space hoppers, scooters and frisbee's, and glow in the dark yo-yo's,
And clear starry nights, sleeping in tents, with never ending fights with pillows.

I miss marbles on the landing, and top trumps in the car,
And butterflies in fishing nets, and spiders caught in jam-jars.

I miss baking conkers for weeks and weeks, thinking they would bring me real fame,
Only to string them up and take them to School, where they'd all crack in their first game.

I miss Airwolf and The A-Team, and Knight Rider on the box,
I miss James and the Giant Peach, and Fantastic Mr Fox

I miss waiting all day by the radio, to tape my new favourite song,
Or going round to Grandma's house, where you could never do anything wrong.

I miss Summer days so baking hot, they could only be cooled by water fights,
Followed by barbecues on the lawn, on those endless balmy June nights.

I miss wheelies and riding non-handed, backies and bunny-hops,
Or the chance of the chequered flag, when we'd race back home from the shops.

I miss my B.M.X.

Goodbye B.M.X. Hello S.E.X.

April 1992

Chapter Eleven - *"...Love?..."*

As April arrived I was able to tick off another of my 1992 targets - I had got a tattoo!

A black, Scorpion on my left shoulder!

Well, I suppose it could be technically described as more of a "transfer" than an actual "tattoo", (apparently real ones can sometimes last forever!) but it gave the same effect.

Louise hated it – and said it looked "tacky".

Although I didn't want to appear to be doing *everything* she said, it was more than possible that I wouldn't now get one done for real!

The radio soundtrack was still dominated by Shakespear's Sister remaining at number one.

The longer "Stay" continued at the chart pinnacle, the more haunting and bleak a song I realised it was.

What happened to good, old, soppy love songs?

Where was Cliff Richards when you needed him?

Dad was saddened by a news announcement reporting that Neil Kinnock was going to resign as leader of the Labour party.

Not because he liked him, or supported Labour or anything like that; but because he had put twenty pounds on him being the next Prime Minister!

Although Dad seemed to like a flutter on most things, I think he had an ulterior motive on betting on Parliamentarian outcomes. It put some weight behind him claiming he "kept his finger on the pulse" if he ever felt like joining in any political arguments!

April usually saw a slight thawing of the great freeze; and, during the first week of the month, I do think I saw a glimpse of the Sun.

I couldn't be 100% sure, because it could equally have been a shiny UFO.

And wouldn't that be my bloody luck!

After wishing, almost forever, for a close encounter; (preferably without any anal probing!) I didn't want some Extra Terrestrials turning up now; messing everything up just when my life was going well!

Whether it was the Sun or a Flying Saucer; one thing was for sure - "April Fools" Day had arrived.

April Fools Day was always a *big event* in our house.

Practical jokes were an all year round hobby, but April the 1st was the "official" day and, as such, everyone usually tried to "up their game."

In the past we had almost kept the local charity shop in business, with donations of things like fake flies in ice cubes, whoopee cushions and plastic Dog turds - all bought specially for April Fools Day.

My favourite "joke" of recent years was one that Dad had played on Mum.

For a while he had been reading out the "Daily Mirror Mega Bingo" numbers out each day for Mum - who marked them off her card.

On April Fools Day, he had made a note of the numbers Mum still wanted for her "full house", then read those to her instead of the real numbers.

Mum marked them off one by one and Dad, worthy of an Oscar winner, kept cool then understatedly surprised, as Mum danced around the room thinking she had won 20 grand!

He perhaps should have owned up before Mum told the headmaster at St. Paul's to "shove his lollipop where the Sun doesn't shine"!

I can't think of anything much more humiliating than having to beg for your job as a lollipop lady back - but it was a classic moment watching Mum repeatedly shouting "House" as she jumped up and down in our living room that morning!

This year though, the day surprisingly passed without event.

Dad hadn't bothered getting up before the 12 o'clock deadline; and Brother Simon, although slowly peeking up a bit after his Valentines Day low, evidently hadn't fully regained his mojo.

I hadn't even noticed April Fools Day approaching - even though Dad had begun to call me "a fool in love" - whatever that actually meant.

Whether I was actually "in love" or not; Louise and I had, again, entered a new phase.

We were now going shopping for clothes together - which was a good thing because Louise's taste was so much better than Mum's.

I had not been trusted to shop for my own clothes since the occasion I was sent out to buy some new School trousers, and had returned with some tie-dye jeans! (It was in the eighties - and wearing jeans at School *would* have been cool!)

The result of this had seen Mum buying me and Brother Simon everything. She used to say that she bought us clothes that "looked good and would last us".

In reality, we had to wonder if she was just shopping as quickly as she could; because the results were, mostly, "hit and miss".

And she often bought us "similar" things.

At best, this may be the same trousers and jumpers - but in different colours and sizes.

When we weren't so lucky, it was the same trousers and jumpers - in the same colour *and* size!

This would mean Brother Simon would have something way too small for him - and look like his clothes had either badly shrunk or he was auditioning to be a backing dancer for a Wham tribute band!

Either that, or I would have something way too big for me - and look like I was wearing someone else's clothes or I had been struck by a particularly nasty weight-sapping illness!

Whichever way, we both looked ridiculous wherever we went, because we were wearing the same clothes.

I think, since we were little, Mum liked to dress us the same so she could

Goodbye B.M.X. Hello S.E.X.

easily spot us if either of us ever went missing in the supermarket!

Anyway the fashion nightmares were behind me. Mum now trusted me (or, more accurately, she trusted Louise) to choose my clothes.

As such, I was now one of the best dressed men in the country - certainly right up there with the likes of Nigel Havers!

Mum seemed to like Louise, and they often chatted when she came to our house - which frustratingly ate into valuable "snogging time"!

I think Mum probably liked the company of another female after having to put up with a house full of males all the time. Grandma did come round often, but I suppose there are only so many conversations you can stand about bunions and piles!

My shopping expeditions with Louise would take place on Saturday afternoons, and usually lead us to the Shopping Centre in Stoneport.

It wasn't the greatest place to hang out, but it just about shaded watching Dad studying the horse racing and waiting for the BBC vidi-printer to announce the football results - which always ended with much cursing and the ripping of betting and pools slips! Quickly followed by him manically rocking in his arm chair muttering "one day, one day....!"

So, on an early April Saturday afternoon, Louise and I walked hand in hand along the pedestrianised street in Stoneport Shopping Centre.

As we passed Worthington's jewellers and discussed the merits of either a Greggs pasty or a McDonald's burger for lunch, I couldn't help but notice a couple of guys walking towards us.

They looked of similar age to us, maybe slightly older, and they stood out like two sore thumbs at an Arthur Fonzarelli tribute night!

Here we were in the middle of the annual Stoneport area Ice Age - and they were both wearing nothing, on the top halves of their bodies, other than tight fitting *vests!*

For a split second I felt sorry for them, wondering if their Mothers had bought them clothes that were too small for them - in the same way Mum did for Brother Simon.

I soon realised though, that this was not another sad case of parental fashion faux pas!

They both had arms that were thicker than both of my legs put together - it was like they were auditioning to be Yates' doormen.

They were obviously gym enthusiasts; body builders wanting to show off their physiques.

By the orangey tint to their skin, they were also wearing fake tan - no one around these parts got to naturally look like Des O'Connor!

They were walking in the centre of the street with a slow motion-like swagger that, in body language terms, through a full-volumed megaphone, shouted: "LOOK AT US!"

I laughed to myself and shook my head.

I turned to Louise to say "Look at these two arseholes!"

Luckily, Louise spoke before me.

Gary Locke

"There's my cousin, Steve!"

She changed direction quickly, and headed towards them, pulling me sharply with her, like a Dog on a lead.

I had no time to wonder if I may have a slight whiplash injury, because we were soon standing in front of the two Mr Universe wannabes.

"Hi Steve." said Louise, addressing the slightly smaller of the two Hulk-like teenagers.

"Louise……Hi, nice to see you!"

Steve leant in and kissed Louise on the cheek.

"You remember Dave, don't you?" he asked as he returned to an upright position.

Louise didn't answer and, instead, the three of them laughed out loud like it was a joke I didn't get.

Dave stepped forward and kissed Louise on both cheeks, like he was some kind of cool European stud.

"Nice to see you again…..you look great!" said Dave, his attempted smoothness easily passing cringing level.

Louise didn't seem to be put off at all by his sickly, smarminess.

"So do you!" she replied, gripping her hand around one of his freakishly, abnormal Popeye-like arms.

I was uncomfortable with the way that they were looking at each other, so decided to clear my throat to catch their attention.

I was hoping for a deep, Harley Davidson like rumble; but had to make do with a high-pitched 50cc Kawasaki junior training bike!

I wish my voice would hurry up and bloody break properly!

It did the trick though, and Louise finally remembered that I was there.

"Oh, let me introduce you all." she said. "Paul, this is Steve Fairclough - my cousin; and this is Dave Barlow - ……..Steve's friend! You two, this is Paul Day - my boyfriend!"

As the three of us acknowledged each other, and I withstood a couple of meaty handshakes (thankfully without squealing!), I felt the warmth that came with Louise's words: *Paul Day - my boyfriend!*

No sooner had I started to bathe in the heat of those beautiful four words, than I was chilled by a thought that struck me like an ice cold bucket of water.

I had heard the name "Dave Barlow" before.

He was the *first guy* that Louise had ever kissed!

My heckles were immediately up.

I felt like Dave was an open and imminent threat on me and Louise - and I would fight to protect us if needed.

I decided to try and stay calm at first - which, perhaps unsurprisingly, was relatively easy when confronted by someone twice my size!

I listened as the two human boulders spoke to Louise about what they had been doing recently.

Bungee Jumping, Kick Boxing, Sky Diving, Rock Climbing, White Water Rafting - were they seriously thinking that anyone was impressed by this

Goodbye B.M.X. Hello S.E.X.

mindless, suicidal thrill-seeking?

Given Louise's wide-eyed wonder at their stories, there was a good chance that *she* was.

"Wow, you're so brave to do those things. They sound exciting, but I'd be too scared to try them!" Louise said, worryingly focusing more on Dave than Steve as she spoke.

"You'd be ok - you would just need someone there to hold your hand and help you through!" replied Dave, going well beyond the mild hint of flirting that I was willing to accept.

Did he not see that there was someone already holding her hand - *right here, right now!*

Me!

He had gone too far.

I decided I needed to do something. I ruled out a physical or verbal attack – that would seem ridiculously stupid following the Kick Boxing story they had just told!

Instead, I decided to join in the conversation.

"I've always fancied something like paragliding or sky diving!"

Louise looked at me, half surprised, half shocked, which was not so astonishing seeing as I had surprised myself, but it was not the "impressed look" I was hoping for.

"I know someone who runs a sky-diving club. I could get you on a course if you fancy it?" said Steve, trying to be nice.

What a Prick!

"Great," I said through clenched teeth.

"I'd really love that!" I continued, while at the same time shaking my head - hoping that it would cancel out my words!

"I'll speak to him and let you know." said Steve.

"Thanks" I whispered, a slight panic creeping into my voice as I imagined sitting by the open door of an aeroplane, being encouraged to jump.

The floor just a blur, a million miles below.

Nothing but a flimsy piece of fabric stuffed into an oversized rucksack, strapped to my back.

Prepared by a complete stranger!

Newspaper headlines of *Parachute Failure Tragedy* and *Pancake Paul Day* flashed through my head!

"Have you met Louise's Mum and Dad yet?" asked Dave, thankfully pulling me out of my sweat-inducing nightmare vision.

I shook my damp forehead.

"Actually, forget that. I meant to ask whether you had met her *Dad* yet?"

Again I shook my head.

What an *idiot*. If I hadn't met Louise's Mum <u>and</u> Dad yet, how could I have met her Dad?

How stupid <u>was</u> this guy?

"Well good luck when you do," Dave chuckled. "It will be scarier than any sky-diving course!"

He and Steve laughed, as Steve glanced at his watch.

"Ok, we've got to go - get to the gym before it closes!" he said.

"Nice to see you again, Louise" said Dave, again as if I wasn't there.

"Take care!"

He turned towards me.

"Good to meet you………?"

"Paul!" I said, getting us all out of an awkward situation.

"Paul!" said Dave, as he turned away and began walking with Steve.

Louise squeezed my hand and smiled, and we began walking in the opposite direction.

I was just about to say "What a pair of Arseholes!", when a voice from behind sounded first.

"Louise!"

We both looked round to see Dave walking back towards us.

"Steve just told me you're thinking about going to Stoneport College when you leave School?"

"Yes." she said smiling.

"That's where I go. I'll be a second year when you come. I'll be able to show you all the cool places to go, and get you introduced to all the cool people. I could even be like your mentor - you know, look after you!"

Louise didn't say anything, but the smile she was wearing was hardly the "piss off" message I was hoping she would give!

"See you there in September, then!" said Dave, before awkwardly turning his freakish, post-David Banner transformed body, and stomping back towards Steve.

I had always kept my future options open; but I made a clear decision that very second.

After School, I was going to Stoneport College!

Even if I didn't pass enough exams; I would just hang out there and keep an eye on Louise, and protect her from Dave and any other like minded Vultures.

Where could I get my hands on some steroids?

When Louise and I started walking again, my mood could only be described as: *Stroppy Teenager!*

Louise hadn't actually done anything wrong; but I felt annoyed that she hadn't at least slapped Dave for his blatant flirting.

As such, I only spoke when Louise asked me a question - and then only gave her curt, one word answers.

I even said "Yes" when she offered to pay for our lunch at McDonalds - and then ordered a Super Size Meal *and* a hot Apple Pie!

Instead of mentioning my change in attitude, Louise decided to ignore it.

She tried to keep talking to me, but soon got bored by my lack of response.

By the time we were at the bus stop, waiting to come home, she had stopped making the effort, and we had been through about fifteen minutes of complete silence.

Goodbye B.M.X. Hello S.E.X.

It was a full on stand-off; waiting to see which one of us would be the weakest and crack first.

Of course, it was me!

"How come Dave Barlow knows your Mum and Dad?" I asked quickly, being very careful not to look at Louise.

"He's a family friend." said Louise.

"I don't know them, and I'm your <u>boyfriend</u>!" I said, a little more dramatically than I meant to.

Louise grabbed my right hand.

"Mum's been asking about you all the time. She wants to meet you. How about next Friday? Come round for a meal?"

"Ok, great. I will" I said.

Louise gave me a big smile and we hugged.

Damn, I thought.

Little Si, Mark and John will be less than happy again. We had arranged to go bowling, and then stay over at Mark's house - his Dad was away on business and his Mum was going away with a friend.

We were going to have a crazy drunken night - not a "girly slumber party" like Brother Simon had called it!

Surely they would understand though - this was an important step for me.

Despite the proposed meal, I couldn't get Dave "arsehole" Barlow out of my mind. I needed to find out more about him.

"So what happened with you and Dave ars.... Barlow then?" I asked, deciding at the last second to leave out the middle name I had thought up for him.

Louise sighed a little as if bored by me mentioning him again.

"We just kissed once at a party." she said matter-of-factly.

"But it was your *first ever kiss*, wasn't it? It must have meant something to you?" I asked.

"Of course it meant something - it was my first kiss! It also only lasted about five seconds!"

In my mind I laughed out loud.

Five seconds!

Ha!

Dave "arsehole" Barlow didn't have my kissing stamina, did he?

Even if he seemed to be a little underwhelming with his lips, I was still a little uncomfortable with how flirty Louise had been with him.

"You like him, don't you?" I asked.

Louise rolled her eyes before looking directly at me.

"I don't want to talk about Dave "bloody" Barlow anymore."

I wondered whether I should tell her I had already given him a middle name, and that it wasn't "bloody"; but she produced a big smile and continued talking.

"I do like him, but don't be jealous. I *like* him........but I *love* you!"

As she stared into my eyes, I said it automatically without thinking.

"I love you, too!"

Louise leant into my face and we kissed - and it was as warm and passionate as always.

And it lasted a lot longer than five seconds!

We continued to wait for the bus, again without speaking.

This time though, it was a comfortable silence; with our arms around each other.

As our 192 appeared at the top of the hill, I began to wonder about love.

Did I love Louise?

I thought I did; and it certainly felt natural to say the words to her.

But how do you *really* know for sure?

Was it something you needed to see the Doctor about?

Whatever, I certainly felt a lot better.

That <u>tiny</u> bit of jealousy had passed, and I knew I had nothing to be worried about.

Except maybe going to Louise's house the following Friday and meeting her Mum and, especially, Dad for the first time.

I smiled to myself and shrugged off any doubt.

I was a charming guy.

What could possibly go wrong?

No, meeting Louise's parents would be a piece of cake.....

Chapter Twelve - "...the parents..."

So here it was, the imposing black door of number 2 St. Anne's Road.

I had seen it many times before, but not up this close and within reaching distance to knock.

This was the door to Louise's house.

I say house, but it was more like a mini-mansion.

The Queen wouldn't have looked out of place, performing her limp wave from one of the windows!

In fact, as I stood before it, the door didn't look too dissimilar to the grand, black door that leads into number ten Downing Street!

Well, apart from it having a number 2 instead of a number 10.

And it having a fairly humungous drive leading up to it.

And it probably not being quite *as* black as number ten Downing Street.

And...

Ok, it was *nothing* like number ten Downing Street!

It was just a big, black door!

Louise and I had been seeing each other for three months. That was exactly one sixty-fourth of my whole life, so this wasn't a casual, fly by night thing - this was serious.

I wasn't just snogging her once a week at youth club, like I had previous "girlfriends". I was leaving lunch-break footy on the tennis courts ten minutes early for "daily snogging" behind the bike sheds!

How much more serious than that does it get?

I clenched my hand into a fist in preparation for knocking, while acutely aware that I was feeling differently to how I had at any point in my whole life.

My body was shaking uncontrollably.

I was producing more sweat than a slimming world coach trip to the sauna! And my stomach was threatening to throw up everything I had eaten – ever!

If I had not heard my Mum talking about similar symptoms, I would have been petrified about what was happening to me.

I contented myself that I was going through nothing more than something called the "menopause"!, and reached out to knock on the door.

"Rat-a-tat-tat!"

I stepped back and took a deep breath.

Suddenly questions began to flash through my mind uncontrollably.

Had I knocked *too hard*?

Would Louise's parents think I was destined to become a Policeman?

Had I knocked *too softly*?

Would Louise's parents think that I was the owner of a weak, limp wrist?

Had I waited *too long* before knocking?

Maybe someone had seen me lingering outside the house and had mistaken me for someone casing the place. Maybe the police would come to arrest me before anyone even opened the door!

Gary Locke

The questions ceased instantly as I heard the inside door lock being turned.

I swallowed as hard as I could to clear my throat. The puberty process was playing havoc with many of my bodily functions, (the full details of some were not pleasant!) including sometimes distorting my voice, if my throat wasn't totally clear.

I had prepared an opening conversation exchange and certainly didn't want it spoiling by one of my Joe Pasquale moments!

"Hello Mr/Mrs Knight, nice to meet you. Thank you for inviting me to dinner."

The door opened fully, and I was relieved not to have to deliver my words, as it wasn't the parents standing there to greet me, it was Louise.

The familiar huge smile and sparkling eyes put me at ease instantly, (it seems the menopause was easily curable!) and we shared a little kiss as she beckoned me in out of the Sunshine.

As I entered the hall, the sheer size of it took me by surprise.

An immense staircase led up to a gallery balcony, all of which was canopied by a huge chandelier. It was as if I had stumbled onto the set of Dynasty!

There were doors leading off in infinite seeming directions.

Louise had told me that the house had an intercom system so the family could speak to each other from any room. I had assumed that the Knight family were a bunch of lazy arses - but could now see why they would need such a system.

I wondered whether there would be a map for me to find my way to the toilet and back.

I began to feel a little underdressed, even in my smartest clothes - a checked shirt and a pair of black corduroy trousers. (Probably the first C&A clothes to have ever entered *this* house!)

Louise led me through the second door on the right, into a sitting room that was even bigger than the hallway.

It was as big as, I assumed, an aircraft hanger would be - maybe Mr Knight had has his own 747?

In this room you would need a telescope just to see the television - that is if the TV in this room wasn't the biggest one in the whole World!

I had seen smaller cinema screens.

"Do you want some water?" Louise asked me.

"Yes please." I replied and she disappeared through a door at the far end of the room. (One of five doors in the room!)

I looked briefly around the room and realised that it would probably take several days to explore it fully.

One thing I spotted straight away though was a ball of string that was sitting perfectly in the centre of the room.

What a good idea, I thought, as I picked up the string and put it in my pocket - a way for new visitors to find their way through this house-disguised labyrinth.

There would be no danger of me getting lost and stranded with the

Goodbye B.M.X. Hello S.E.X.

Minotaur!

I sat down on the sofa, in front of a large window, and tried to relax.

As I began to contemplate whether there would be an echo if I began yodeling!, the door on the left wall as I looked began to open.

A tall man with dark hair entered the room. It must be Louise's Dad.

He began a slow stroll through the sitting room, towards a facing door on the right wall.

Despite my best attempt to smile at him, I could not break what could only be described as an "icy stare".

After a cross-room journey, that's duration felt as lengthy as a Captain Cook expedition, he vanished through the door on the right wall.

I wondered whether perhaps he hadn't seen me.

Yes, I contented myself with that thought, even though he would probably have needed to have been guided by a Labrador not to have seen me, because his piercing eyes were aimed right at me!

As I checked to make sure that the daggers he was throwing hadn't fatally wounded me, the door on the right opened again.

He must have been coming back in - hopefully this time to say hello.

It wasn't him – or, if it was, he should enter the cross-dressing speed change World Championships!

It must be Louise's Mum.

She walked straight towards me, a big smile beaming like one of Louise's.

"You must be Paul. I'm Pamela - Louise's Mum!"

I smiled back, and just about got away with an awkward split second of indecision about whether to kiss her on the cheek or not.

"Pleased to meet you, too." I said shaking her hand - definitely the right thing to do.

Brother Simon had advised me to greet Louise's Mum continental style, by taking her hand and kissing it gently. He had also advised that I should take her wine, flowers and chocolates and, upon meeting, tell her how lovely she looked.

It was only at the last minute, as I left the house with a bunch of roses in one hand, a bottle of Blue Nun in the other and a box of All Gold under my arm, that I realised he was trying to make me look like a fool.

I should really *always* be more suspicious about any of Brother Simon's advice or actions. There had been a time when he had somehow managed to steam open a Christmas card I had written to send to my, then, 2nd year junior School teacher, Mr Hill.

Before returning it perfectly to my pile of undelivered cards he had written underneath the printed "Merry Xmas", uncannily similar to my writing, the words "I love you, Mr Hill".

I was subjected to a couple of rather harsh counselling sessions after that little stunt!

The last I heard, Mr Hill was still out of work and remained on some child protection register!

"Is there anything you don't like to eat?" Pamela asked.

I think at best I could be described as a "fussy eater", probably, more accurately, a "freaky eater".

I was certainly not very adventurous with food - a fact I solely blame Mum for.

She only owned one 100 page recipe book that she had picked up really cheep because it had a *few* pages missing. (98 to be exact!)

Mum was always one for a good bargain!

Our meals at home mainly consisted of *'tata ash*!

If it wasn't *'tata ash*, it was *'tata pie*!; if it wasn't *'tata pie*, it was *'tata ash*!

Sometimes, for really special occasions, she would maybe make "corned-beef ash" - but not that often!

I wondered how best to answer the question.

"I'm happy to try anything" my mouth spurted out, without the necessary authorisation from my brain.

"Good," said Pamela "I'm doing fillet Angus Aberdeen with a Perigueux sauce, with croustillante frites."

She must have picked up on the blank expression that gripped my face.

"Steak and chips!" she said with a reassuring smile.

"I do put quite a bit of garlic in the sauce, is that ok for you?"

"I don't really like garlic that much!" I said, relieved to find that my brain was back in control of vocal functions.

In reality I had never had garlic, but I didn't really like the sound of it. What if it turned out that I was a vampire! The whole dinner experience could turn out very messy. (I had seen "The Lost Boys" several times, and knew about the dangers of even being near garlic - let alone eating it!)

"That's ok," she said, still smiling "I'll do your sauce without any garlic."

With that she headed back towards the door through which she had entered the room.

Her pleasantness had left me feeling very relaxed, and I sat down gently into the sofa behind me.

Before the door had closed properly behind Pamela, Louise's Dad had slipped through back into the room.

He again walked in almost slow-motion across the room sporting a similar cold expression, this time in the opposite direction to his first saunter.

I again smiled politely which completed the strange moment of reverse déjà-vu!

Had Pamela sent him back into the room as she left?

Were they performing a tag-team good-cop, bad-cop routine?

Again he left the room without making any communication attempt. In fact, he hadn't made any sound at all.

No words, no footsteps, nothing!

From his complete silence, it was even difficult to tell if he was even breathing!

I suddenly realised what was happening. I had seen enough of David

Goodbye B.M.X. Hello S.E.X.

Attenborough to know the danger I was in.

Louise's Dad was a Lion; stealth like, stalking his prey.

I was a baby Antelope, stranded from his Mother; alone and vulnerable.

I knew that at any moment he could pounce from out of the undergrowth (or from behind the sofa) and shake me round like a rag doll until I struggled no more!

My mouth was beginning to feel dryer than an extreme sports edition, Sure for men sprayed armpit!

I was glad to see the door at the far end of the room open again, surely making way for Louise returning with my water. (Which I now assumed she must have needed to collect from a well somewhere – perhaps in Ethiopia!)

But it wasn't Louise. It was her Dad again - entering the room via his *third* different door!

This time he dispensed with his protracted intimidation technique, and instead headed straight for me.

I decided against Brother Simon's advice of a high five greeting! and, instead, offered him my hand for shaking.

He squeezed my hand no less vigorously than you would an orange that you were trying to extract juice from!

I tried to grip back tightly to show that I was not the weak, baby Antelope that he had previously tried to expose me as, but my crimson face and out-of-skull eyeballs gave me away.

He had established the pack order!

He was the alpha male.

I was somewhat further down the order; perhaps only good for grooming duties, or maybe responsible for pooper scooper clean ups!

"I'm Michael, Louise's Dad." he said releasing my hand.

I smiled and nodded as I embraced the sensation of blood returning to my hand.

I decided against speaking at this point, knowing it was very likely that I would sound like I had the voice box of a freshly castrated Eunuch!

Before coming round I had considered asking him how "Kitt" was - in an attempted Michael Knight / Knight Rider joke; but now that seemed about as safe as taking a dozen cyanide pills!

Now firmly in control, Michael appeared more relaxed and even attempted to lighten the mood.

"So, you're Paul. Louise's boyfriend that I've been hearing so much about? Tell me a bit about yourself…….you haven't been married before have you?"

I joined him as he laughed and things felt better straight away.

That was until a thought entered my head.

Would my marriage to Janine Pearson by the side of Mrs White's mobile classroom in 3rd year infant's count?

Could Adam Williams really have been a fully ordained vicar at the age of seven, as he had claimed?

The concern at this thought, that was now obviously showing on my face, began to project itself on Michael's face like a reflected image.

As I wondered whether I would need to divorce Janine, Michael possibly wondered whether I was actually able to *speak*.

Our confused look stare-off was broken by Louise, who entered the sitting room via yet another of the doors.

She still didn't have my water - maybe the well was dry!

"Mum say's dinner's nearly ready. She wants us to sit down in the dining room."

Michael began to head towards the door at the far side of the room - this time walking backwards. He kept his eyes fixed on me all the way - not even blinking as he almost fell backwards over an ill-placed foot stool!

Throughout his journey, he didn't once change the look on his face that somehow conveyed confusion, concern and contempt all at the same time.

Once Michael had gone I was able to spend a couple of seconds alone with Louise. She gave me a smile that asked how everything was going.

Despite my few minutes of discomfort and excruciating hand pain, I gave her a grin that was every bit as positive as a cheesy, double thumbs up.

She looked pleased as she beckoned me towards yet another door - one that led through to the dining room.

She ushered me to a metal framed seat that was at one end of the table, and said "I best see if Mum wants a hand."

Before leaving the room she kissed me on the cheek and left me feeling tingly inside.

The feeling was halted more abruptly than a seat-belted Crash Test Dummy!

From out of nowhere Michael was at the other end of the table staring at me.

It was possible that he had slipped through the door while I was soaking in the warmth of the kiss on my cheek.

It was far more likely though that he had passed up through some secret trapdoor, had just removed an invisibility cloak or had perhaps even teleported!

Whichever way I was in trouble - he wore the expression of a thirsty vampire.

What had I done now?

I realised.

I was sat at the head of the table!

Perhaps even in Michael's seat.

Had I unwittingly challenged for leadership?

I quickly put both hands underneath my bottom - I didn't want to go through the hand clamp contest again.

I also lowered my head and raised my shoulders, making sure that my neck was no longer exposed - just in case!

(Although, as I had considered earlier, if I was *also* a vampire perhaps then he would lighten up on me a little?).

Michael obviously didn't need to explain his movements to *me* but, once again, he rudely left the room without speaking any words.

Goodbye B.M.X. Hello S.E.X.

As I shook my head and pondered the irony of adults bemoaning the lack of manners, "in kids these days!", I couldn't help but speculate about the dining furniture.

Although pretty sure that it was obviously modern, and ridiculously over-priced designer gear, it was the first time I had seen a metal table and chairs and it seemed wrong.

As I looked at my own chair more closely, it began to resemble an electric chair out of a Hollywood movie.

The door opened again, and Michael walked in carrying a jug of water - obviously for wetting the sponge for the top of my head!

I jumped up in a panic, hoping to make an escape before the viewing public arrived to fill the gallery.

"Help yourself to water" said Michael as he put the jug onto the table. He either hadn't noticed me jumping up in panic or maybe thought I was standing as a mark of respect.

Thankfully, at last there was some much needed throat lubrication.

I reached for the jug straight away.

As I pulled it towards my glass, I noticed that Michael was staring intently.

I realised why - there were five cubes of ice bobbing around in the jug, and he was making sure that I didn't pour any into my glass.

I kept myself together and poured the water - steadier than a Des Walker England performance!

No ice in glass - no reason for Michael to reveal his fangs.

As I slowly allowed the cool water to perform its soothing magic, I was struck by an unexpected and sudden sneeze.

You know, one of those weird ones that appears from nowhere without the usual "*haa, haa, haa, haa*'s preceding the explosive "*choo*"!

Oh no!

To go with it being a weird, sudden one, it had also chosen to be a *stringy* one!

I could only imagine the look on Michaels face as I fumbled around in my pocket for a tissue as a line of snot swung from my nose, like a Spider on a web!

It took me, what seemed like, a couple of minutes to pull out a pocket tissue from behind the ball of string I'd jammed in there and wipe my nose clean.

I looked up at Michael and the look on his face was similar to what somewhat must look like if they've just witnessed someone being castrated!

Thankfully, before he could say anything, Louise and Pamela entered the room carrying two plates each.

Pamela passed one plate to Michael and said "*That one's Paul's*" accompanied by a look that said either "*That's the one with no garlic for the freaky eater*" or "*That's the one with extra garlic - ha! ha! ha!*"

By the look on Michael's face, that somehow changed to evil and smug in the time it took to place the plate in front of me, it was fair to assume that it was the latter.

It seems I would be trying garlic for the first time – which would clear up the old am I / aren't I a Vampire conundrum!

Michael was *now* wearing the expression usually reserved for dentists as they gave you the news that you needed root canal treatment!

His face seems to change faster than Superman changes trousers for underpants!

"Don't wait for me; tuck right in." Pamela said and left the room again.

I began to load a couple of chips onto my fork. As I did, I glanced around the room trying to formulate a food hiding back-up plan should my saucy steak require one.

I delivered the chips to my mouth (crispy and very tasty!), realising that if I had my School ruler with me, I would probably be able to flick small pieces of my steak accurately into an empty vase that stood on the nearby fireplace.

That was if I could somehow stop Michael staring at me for *one second!*

I thought perhaps catching his gaze, showing that I had noticed him looking at me, may embarrass him into stopping.

I was wrong!

He took my looking at him as a perfect reason to attempt to engage me in some awkward conversation.

I quickly reached for my water, before the inevitable question, to give my throat the best possible chance of answering in a manly voice.

"So, are you a *good boy* at School? Have you had many detentions this year?"

I ignored the patronising element and narrowed my eyes, because I saw this for what it was - a trick question.

The clue was within the wording: *good boy*.

I needed to be careful.

He was obviously checking to see if I was some kind of "goody two shoes".

I accepted that nobody wants their Daughter going out with the School nerd. On the other hand, I didn't want to make out that I was a total *bad boy* - that would be going too far the other way.

My brain came up with a fool proof formula.

I should take the square root of the actual number of detentions, before doubling it and adding five.

As I fumbled in my pockets wondering if, by chance, I had brought a calculator out with me, I saw the look on Michael's face changing.

The increasing height of his eyebrows informed me that I was taking too long over my answer.

As my brain refused to waver from the formula but didn't have the skill to even attempt the calculation (what the hell was a square root?), I had to pluck a number out of thin air.

"Seventeen!" I said quietly.

"Seventeen!" shouted Michael at a volume that couldn't have been louder, even if he had just produced a microphone and speaker combo from under the table!

"Nineteen?" I said tentatively, wondering whether seventeen was lower or higher than Michael was looking for.

Goodbye B.M.X. Hello S.E.X.

His look of angry bewilderment, not too dissimilar to a pre-fight Mike Tyson!, cleared any confusion right away.

I reached for the jug of water and began to top up my glass again. This time my lack of composure resulted in all five ice cubes ending up in my glass.

My unfortunate pouring did nothing to calm Michael, and I could now see his temperature rising as quickly as the mercury in an ear-inserted thermometer.

I fought against my instinct that told me to reach into my glass of water, pick out the ice cubes and replace them into the jug; as I had no desire to wear the jug like a tight fitting hat!

My peripheral vision caught Pamela re-entering the room.

Her return seemed to calm the atmosphere and was, thankfully, like she had just extinguished the lit fuses that were edging their way towards the explosives.

"Sorry about that," she said calmly "The cat's gone a bit mental in the living room. Ripped up the carpet and the arm chair again………someone must have moved his string!"

After listening intently to his wife, Michael's head turned sharply to face me as if it was spring loaded.

Pamela had relit the fuses about an inch away from the dynamite!

I'm not sure whether I had some string hanging out of my pocket, or whether my face was as easy to read as someone who had "GUILTY" tattooed on his forehead but, from the way Michael was looking at me, it was clear to see that he was *sure* I was to blame.

I'd probably have been better taking my chances with the Minotaur!

He didn't embark on the on-the-spot stoning as I feared; but the way he shuffled in his seat, concentrating his thoughts, I knew some kind of attack was imminent.

He settled for a fully charged Spanish inquisition.

"So Paul, tell me - have you ever *stolen* anything or done any *vandalism*?"
"Michael!"

Pamela's shock resulted in Michael sitting back into his chair and forcing him into a state of semi-calm. It wasn't the end though because, like a scolded lawyer, I could tell that he was just working out a way to re-word his questioning.

As he took his mini-timeout I wondered whether, in addition to my sitting room string lift, he had seen the big oak tree at Tatty Park into which I had carved "*P4L 4EVA*". If he had seen this he would also surely be critical of my neglect of the proper English language.

There was no time to worry too long, as he had finalised the wording of his new attack and was approaching the bench to deliver it.

"What are you going to do when you leave School, Paul?"

Interesting; he had changed his attack method, delivering a non-aggressive question - he was obviously expecting me to hang myself with a misguided answer.

Gary Locke

But he had made a mistake.

This one was easy - I knew what the correct answer was: I was going to *further* my education.

I would get good qualifications, then a good job with good prospects, and be able to look after his Daughter.

"I'm going to go on to College!" I said confidently.

Les Dennis's voice entered my head.

"Our survey says………………"URR! ERRR!"

I wouldn't be going on to play "Big Money"!

"That's all we need," started Michael, "More bloody students! More young layabouts sponging off the taxpayers."

He was well and truly on his soapbox.

"I left School at fourteen. No qualifications, no diplomas, no bits of paper saying what I could or couldn't do. My education was practical, not out of some books. Not done bad though, me. No Schoolin' never done me no harm!"

I contented and amused myself with the fact that Michael's English was, at least, as bad as my vandalised encryption of love.

I tried hard not to let out a little laugh, but only succeeded in deflecting a potential snigger into an unfortunate rather Pig-like snort!

Michael tried to keep his cool aided by a clenched jaw, but his rage erupted like an angry Mount Etna.

"Paul, do you regularly take drugs?"

"MICHAEL! / DAD!"

He had clearly overstepped the line, and the two women at the table had turned on him.

He knew he had gone too far and backed down immediately.

His hackles were lowered, his claws retracted, his fangs blunted - his threat all but extinguished.

Suddenly, through Michael's rejection, I had become alpha male by default!

The way in which I had obtained my new lofty status did not concern me.

I was now Top Dog at this table and Michael knew it.

"Do you follow football?" he asked in a pathetic, deflated voice; more Pasquale-like than I had ever been.

It was a certainty that, with his bad attitude, Michael was a Man United fan.

But this time the truthful answer to a question held no fear.

It was now *me* that was in control.

So much so that before answering I decided to try some of my steak.

It was like nothing I had tasted before.

And I liked it!

It was probably swimming in a sauce made up of 99% garlic (that may, or may not, result in my head exploding!), but I *really* liked it.

After slowly chewing and savouring, I said "Yes. I'm a City fan!"

"Are you?" asked Michael, showing genuine interest. "So am I. Have been since I was five. My Dad used to take me to all the games. We used to stand in the Kippax at exactly the same place every game!"

107

Goodbye B.M.X. Hello S.E.X.

Suddenly things were looking up.
Michael had melted more quickly than a "no-frills" candle!
The rest of the evening went perfectly well.
Michael and I spent the next two hours chatting like long lost pals.
He told me all about his memories of City - the "good old days" and all the *success* and *glory*.
I told him all about my memories of City - the "ongoing bad days" and all the *pain* and *disappointment*!
We laughed and joked, and bonded like potential Father and Son-in-law!
He seemed to relax totally and became like a completely different man.
Although the laid-back Michael Knight behaviour included shamelessly snogging Pamela - right in front of me and Louise.
I couldn't decide whether this was cool, and showed that they were still in love and passionate, or whether it was all a bit sick!
Maybe it was a bit of both.
It was good they still fancied each other – even if it was as stomach turning as watching the latest small intestine operation on *Jimmy's*!
Although I do suppose that it proved that he was becoming relaxed in my company, which must mean he was beginning to accept me as Louise's boyfriend.
Even later, my *pretty empty* offer of assisting with washing the pots was dismissed out of hand by Michael. (They had a dishwasher! Of course they did!)
I also successfully negotiated two trips to and from the bathroom without being lost for more than five minutes or needing to resort to using my "knocked-off" string.
And, before I left for the night, Michael even practically forced me up to Louise's room to "say goodnight properly"!
I walked home under a bright, Moon-lit sky, knowing that the evening could not have gone any better.
It was also the first time ever that I had experienced an up side of being a City fan!
I'm not sure whether this night had totally made up for 15 years of hurt and humiliation, but maybe it was a start!

Chapter Thirteen - *"...work experience..."*

Seventeen minutes and thirty four seconds!

I had timed it on my Casio "Soccer" watch, (a bit flashy for School? Probably!) and found out that it takes exactly seventeen minutes and thirty four seconds, of sitting on a hard plastic chair, for your arse to become numb!

Not just partially numb, for which the stinging edge off a kick up the arse might be nicely taken off.

No, *proper* numb!

The kind of numbness that would mean an entire ship load of frustrated Navy seamen could give you the full-rogering treatment - without you even feeling a thing!

I was waiting outside the School library, yep, sitting on a plastic chair.

I was here with four other unfortunate anaesthetised-bottomed pupils – waiting for our "work experience" interviews.

Why we'd had to wait quite so long was open to debate.

It may be because these were important interviews that lead to important decisions that, in turn, lead to young people having their first taste of working life.

As such the students who had gone before us may have been given the time needed to get such decisions correct.

Of course, it may well just be the School's way of getting us ready for our most likely post-School career, sitting waiting for our weekly interview – at the job centre!

That was certainly the more probable of the two scenarios. You just had to look at the School's choice of "careers advisor" to get a good idea of their attitude towards the whole thing.

Mr Upson!

Mr Upson, (or Mr *Up-yer-bum*! as some of the more immature students called him!) was employed as a *part time* careers advisor.

Part time may seem a little far-pushed for a role that was required to give after-School life advice for over 200 clueless 16 year olds.

But it was even worse than that!

Mr Up-yer..., sorry Upson was also the Schools main supply teacher covering illnesses to other teachers. And seeing as teachers at our School considered a runny nose to be a minimum of a week on the sick, his actual "advising" time was somewhat minimal!

He was what you would best describe as a "veteran teacher".

He wore old-fashioned tweed jackets with leather elbows and always seemed to be limping badly.

You could also say that he had teaching ideals from a different era!

Or Century!

He seemed to have a real problem with the fact that you could no longer throw black board erasers at unsuspecting, slightly mis-behaving kids!

Goodbye B.M.X. Hello S.E.X.

As any kind of physical abuse was, thankfully, frowned upon he, instead, used rudeness and being miserable as his main weapons.

As such Little Si and I, who had Mr Upson covering our P.E. lessons seemingly as much as "regular" teacher Mr Winters, had made it our mission in life (or certainly our mission in P.E.) to try and make him laugh.

In reality, if our "performance" in most of the *sports* of our lessons wasn't enough to make him laugh, then our jokes had no chance!

The results of those jokes had, so far, been *fair to middling* – if *fair to middling* means the same as *disastrous*!

Our combined laugh total = 0.

Our combined detention total as a result of attempted jokes = 12!

It would seem that Mr Upson is not a big fan of *classic* humour.

I, alone, had recited at least a dozen Tommy Cooper lines – without so much as even a hint of a smirk!

There's got to be *something* that would make him laugh?

Obviously today was not a day for attempted jokes as it was almost a dress rehearsal for the inevitable World of work that was one day ahead of me.

Did I know what I wanted to do with my life?

No, of course not!

But wasn't that what careers advisors were for?

Even *part-time*, glorified sickness cover, limping, miserable old fogies!

"Paul Day!"

It seemed it was *finally* my turn.

I looked at the entrance door to the library beyond four disappointed faces – that knew they had even more time for those plastic seats to work their anal-tranquilising magic!

Mr Upson stood at the door; the usual sour look painted on his face.

Beyond him walked David Wilkes wearing a not too dissimilar look – maybe a result of "advice" not quite to his liking?

"Well come on! I haven't got *all day!*" said Mr Upson, almost spitting in my direction as he spoke.

Did he not realise that his pedestrian paced advice had left the chances of me moving quickly more unlikely than seeing a stampede of Unicorns charging down Stoneport high street?

My plastic seat endurance was the equivalent of me putting my arse in a bucket of ice for a couple of hours! It had Japanese game show written all over it!

It certainly meant that moving fast was not an option!

I slowly stood up from my chair in that careful way that you have to when you've got pins and needles in your bum / legs, after sitting on the toilet for way too long!

I then waddled as quickly as was possible and followed Mr Upson as he limped to the corner of the library where he had two (bloody *plastic*!) chairs set up, facing one another.

The library was empty, apart from a couple of the professional "shushing" librarians wandering around.

"Are you taking the mickey out of my hip replacement?" Mr Upson asked angrily as I finally made it to my seat, walking like an arthritic Penguin!

"No!" I said. "I'm just feeling a bit numb after sitting for so long on the plastic chair outside!"

Ironically, now I'd had a few seconds of walking the numbness had all but worn off.

Was honesty the best policy with what I'd just said?

Would he believe that I wasn't taking the mickey out of his artificial joints – but actually think I was having a go at the speed at which he was working instead?

Which I probably was!

Maybe I should have made up something as an excuse?

Like a sore knee or perhaps being distantly related to an Emperor Penguin!

Would *that* of made him laugh?

We looked at each other for a couple of seconds like two cowboys at high noon, waiting to see who would draw first.

Slowly Mr Upson lowered his eyes away from me and down to the floor, from where he then reached out and picked up a file.

As he flicked through the papers within I actually began to feel a little sorry for him.

Maybe his perpetual grumpiness was due to a constant pain that he had to endure because of his history of hip joint problems?

Maybe being forced to cover P.E. lessons, that he didn't really want to cover because of genuine health issues, whilst having to put up with, at least two, students constantly making ridiculous comments, was reason enough to avoid any kind of smiling and laughing?

Maybe I needed a new mission in life?

"Ok" said Mr Upson after about a minute of looking at his papers. "Let me start by asking you this – what does your father do for a living? Is there any kind of family business that you could potentially join after School?"

Hmmm, do I openly admit that Dad is one of those society-sucking Leeches? Probably best not to.

"He's actually *between* jobs at the moment." I said, using Dad's own justification for his bone idol-itis!

I was going to leave it at that but a Christmas Cracker joke popped into my head.

Why is it only the shit, corny cracker gags that I can remember?

I'd watched a full hour-long special of *Dave Allen* very recently that was so funny it had made me wish I was wearing plastic underwear!

Could I remember any of it?

Not one single joke!

But this was maybe a chance to make Mr Upson laugh.

I was going for it!

"He *was* working for a company fitting trapdoors – but, very suddenly, the

Goodbye B.M.X. Hello S.E.X.

bottom fell out of that business!"

Had it worked?

Was there laughing?

No!

Either Mr Upson hadn't found it funny (understandably, I suppose!) or he hadn't even heard it.

Instead he spoke.

"Ok, seeing as there's no particular family connected work to aim you at, I'll start by letting you know what work experience options we have available."

I sat forward in my chair.

Partly because I was interested in what the options may be, but mainly because the new plastic chair was already beginning to bring on some *re-numb!*

"Before I do though, a quick question." Said Mr Upson. "What do you *ideally* want to do when you leave School?"

Ok, was he really assuming I had *any* kind of plan?

"I'm thinking of moving to America!" I said, dangerously setting up a joke that Dad likes to regularly make.

Another attempted joke?

Was I mad?

"Really?" asked Mr Upson. "You have an urge to travel?"

He looked quite intrigued and interested that I appeared to have plans to travel the World.

It was too late; I was committed to the gag. Would this, somehow, *finally* be the moment that I would see him laugh?

"Just America really – it is a lot easier to be successful over there!"

"I don't think that's right," Mr Upson interrupted. "The economy over there is really quite fragile! Why do you think it would be *easier*?"

"Well," I said, preparing to deliver my punch line. "They make you a Colonel over there for coming up with an addictive herbs and spices recipe for coating fried Chicken. And to be a Doctor, you just need to invent a weird-tasting fizzy drink!"

Was he going to laugh?

The answer was clear straight away – any laughter seemed unlikely due to the frowning, shaking head that Mr Upson seemed to be concentrating on!

Did he need the joke *explaining*?

"You know," I said. "KFC – *Colonel* Sanders! And *Doctor* Pepper!"

Nothing!

Not even the decency again to tell me that he didn't think it was funny. (Which I suppose it wasn't really!)

Instead, he carried on talking as if I hadn't even opened my mouth.

"First of all, there is an opportunity to do a week of admin for McMartins Retail on the industrial estate off Newbury Road!" he said.

Boring!

I'm not sure if he wanted me to comment on this but the fact that he was about to say some more, thankfully, meant I could keep my, shall we say, *feedback* to myself.

"Good opportunity that! Working for a good, honest company!"
BORING!
He carried on.

"Next there is a position working at Manchester City Football Club – doing a bit of everything. Seeing how the club runs from a financial point of view. Working one day as an apprentice. Also having the chance to see how the coaching side of things work. Real good opportunity for anyone interested in football!"

He pulled another piece of paper out, as if he was going to talk about another option.

Should I stop him right now?

Save everyone a bit of time?

It would certainly speed things up and come as a big relief to the four poor sods still experiencing their primary stage of numb-bum!

It was too late – he was beginning to read out the third option.

"There is even the chance to work alongside the caretaker here for the week. A good chance to see how the School is maintained on a day to day basis!"

Was he now trying to make *me* laugh?

I'd rather shove a Cactus plant up my arse!

Before he could even contemplate pulling out a fourth piece of paper, I got my interjection in. (I don't use the word *interjection* often, but it seemed appropriate at this point!)

"Sir," I began in an out-of-character kiss ass-ie way. "I think the football club opportunity would be nearly perfect for me!"

I said *nearly perfect* because I felt that if I told him it couldn't be *more perfect*, even if he was also able to give me the next weeks pools results!, then he might be reluctant to let me do it.

My experience with most teachers was that they'd go out of their way to make a students life (particularly mine!) a complete misery!

But this was a job at *Manchester City* – my club.

It was the chance to see behind the scenes, to meet the players, to be a *part* of it.

It would be a dream come true.

"Ok!" said Mr Upson.

Woo Hoo!

It was mine!

The dream job was mine and no one could take it away!

"It's not quite as simple as that though." added Mr Upson. "We need to talk about it first – make sure *you're* right for the job.

Oh shit!

Well it certainly felt good for the half-a-second that it *was* mine!

"Tell me what it is you enjoy *most* about football." said Mr Upson.

Wow!

As I thought about it, I realised that was actually a deep question.

Goodbye B.M.X. Hello S.E.X.

What *was* it I liked about football?
It definitely wasn't the feeling of winning, as I said - I am a Man City fan! The answer came to me.
"It's because it feels so *accessible*. It's an entertainment, but it doesn't have that razzle-dazzle, somehow detached, feel that something born in Hollywood has. It's a chance for working class people to go out together and watch something that's affordable. And it's something that we all love to play – but obviously nowhere near as well as the professionals – which gives us an admiration for them. And then there are the *debates*. Everyone has a different opinion, and yet no-one is 100% right and no-one is 100% wrong – it's all just opinions. But something we all love to have our say on!"
I stopped talking as I realised I'd probably gone on too long.
Mr Upson was nodding.
He hadn't actually cracked open that smile I'd been after, but he seemed to be in agreement.
"Yes, that's good!" he said. "Ok we just have to go through a couple of the routine things about the subject options you took and your long-term career aims – but I'm happy that you should go to the football placement."
Woo Hoo!
It was mine *again*!
"Ok," continued Mr Upson "The subjects you chose were French, P.E., Geography and Music? That's a pretty odd combination! Take me through your thinking there?"
What?
Thinking?
Was he serious?
I did what everyone else did when they chose their subjects – I found out what my best friends were choosing and tried to link that in to what I also thought all the fittest girls would be doing!
But I bet that wasn't the answer he would be looking for, would it?
As I tried to think of something, at least semi-sensible, I couldn't help but notice a slight flickering in Mr Upson's eyes.
Unless I was mistaken, and as well as the hip he'd also had some kind of eye-replacement, he was actually enjoying this.
Maybe *this* was the time to make him laugh?
"When I leave School I'm hoping to move to France where I'll be a football star by day and a rock star by night!"
I'm not sure why I was hoping that, when real classic, funny lines from Tommy Cooper had regularly failed, a statement of pure nonsense would be a success!
There was certainly no laughing.
I *had* succeeded in extinguishing the slight flickering in his eyes however!
Mr Upson looked down at his file again.
"You're in Mr Winters' P.E. class aren't you? You and that *small boy*?"
I sniggered slightly at Mr Upson's description of Little Si, before realising I

may be in a sticky position.

If, when considering me appropriate for the Man City role, Mr Upson hadn't quite recognised me as one of the two annoying students from the class he regularly had to cover, now he did, would that mean he would change his mind?

He started his, potential, re-analysis with a question.

"So you want to be a footballer?" he asked.

"Not necessarily," I started, trying to be cautious. "But if I was lucky enough to be involved in football, then that is surely the dream job?"

I'd answered in a humble way but passed it back to him. For anyone interested in football, who *wouldn't* want to be a footballer?

Mr Upson stroked his chin.

"Of course being a football player would be nice, but there's so much more to the game than the twenty-two men who run around the field. It wouldn't be able to exist without those who organise and officiate – at all levels. Take referees for example – they are needed at all levels from kids' football right up to those first division games. You ever thought of refereeing or anything like that?"

Was he kidding?

My opinions on referees and their lack of married parents were quite clear but I bet Mr Upson wouldn't want to hear them.

Or would he?

They were a bit tongue and cheek and fairly humorous.

This may be a way to save the situation *and* make him laugh at the same time.

I threw out my stone and waited for it to kill its two birds!

"Really referees and linesmen can't win no matter how good they are! Whatever decision they make – 50% of the crowd *always* disagree with them. And, for today's game, what with all the video replays and slow motion and multiple angles even the *slightest* error is really highlighted. How can they be expected to get everything right, seeing things *once* and at *full speed*, when everyone watching on TV gets multiple viewing in *slow motion*?"

I watched as Mr Upson slowly nodded and his lips curled into something nearly approaching a smile.

He was liking what I was saying!

Now for my finale – that would surely expose that elusive laugh!

"So, in all honesty, no one in their right mind would ever *want* to be a referee or linesmen! That's why we can't be surprised that they're all either complete idiots or ego-maniacs who want a stage to blow a whistle or wave a flag!"

I smiled and prepared to join in with Mr Upson as he laughed out loud.

The only problem was the amount of laughter coming from Mr Upson wasn't going to attract any raised eyebrows from the meandering librarians!

There was total silence!

Oh no!

Goodbye B.M.X. Hello S.E.X.

It appeared I had attempted to use my shoe as a toothbrush once again!
"You're a kids' football referee aren't you?" I asked.
"Yes!" he said sternly.
He began to look around, perhaps searching for a black board eraser!
Thankfully for me the library was free of any such implements of punishment!
I couldn't help but wonder – how the hell does a man in his physical condition manage to do any refereeing?
I suppose he did fit my referee criteria though!
Another theory proven beyond doubt!
I bet *his* Dad was not married to his Mum!
It seemed Mr Upson was just actually looking around at his paperwork that he had scattered around his chair.
He picked one piece up and, after taking a pen from the inside of his Moth-eaten jacket, signed it with an extravagant flourish.
He passed it over to me.
"I think we've found the ideal placement for you!" he said.
"I thought we needed to talk about long term career aims?" I asked, hoping that somehow telling him that I was clueless about *all* aspects of my future would somehow make the situation better.
"That won't be necessary." he said. "Your answers have already proven what the best role for you will be!"
I took a look at the paper he had just passed me.
My heart skipped a little.
If Mr Upson was acting on my answers then surely his decision would be based upon my obvious love for football.
Then my eyes shattered my ridiculous sense of reason.

<u>Student</u>: *Paul Day*
<u>Work Experience Placement</u>: *Caretaker Assistant – Holly Grove High School*

Oh shit!
Where can I get a Cactus plant…?
I slowly stood up and walked out of the library as Mr Upson gathered his papers together.
As I reached the door I looked back - and there it was!
He was finally *laughing*!
It was hard to class it as a *complete success*, seeing as it was a sadistic laugh focusing on my misery, but a laugh is a laugh!
My mission in life (or, at least, P.E.) was complete!

Chapter Fourteen - *"...motorbikes and tits..."*

I stared at the wall in front of me, the shabby, dirty bricks all distorted because of the excessive liquid that was forming in my eyes.

I had held my breath for as long as I could (which wasn't really that long – I wasn't a free diver or a Whale!) but I couldn't hold it any longer.

I was going to have to *breathe in* the air that was making me cry more than a yellow-carded Gazza!

When I did, though, I could hardly taste it.

Not because it wasn't as bad as I'd feared, but because the aroma entering my nostrils was well and truly overpowering *everything* else.

The smell was a mix of stagnant water, bleach, body odour, Cat shit, decaying Fish, burst sewers, sweaty feet and wet Dogs! In fact, it was like a cocktail of every foul stench that you could possibly think of.

It was obvious now that my eye glazing was my body's way of trying to protect my eyes from the, potentially disastrous, effects of the poisonous air.

Where were the "hazardous to breath" signs?

Or, more importantly, the "hazardous to be within ten miles of here" signs?

There were no warning signs at all.

Only posters.

Dozens of posters of various modes of transport and naked women. The majority of which mainly focused on motorbikes and tits.

Nice motorbikes and (very) nice tits!

Yes, I was in the caretakers' room waiting to begin my "work experience" week.

Despite a last minute appeal-attempt, Mr Upson had stood by his "professional careers advisor" decision that a week working as a caretakers' assistant was the "perfect role" for me.

The week working for Manchester City Football Club had gone to Stuart Tunnard – a diehard Man Utd fan! (Who'd vowed to have a shit on the hallowed Maine Road turf!)

An absolute piss take!

And all because I'd attempted to tell a couple of harmless little jokes!

Is this maybe a clear sign that I shouldn't ever try to work in comedy in any way shape or form?

My dream of one day becoming the new Bobby Davro may well be beyond me!

After a few seconds of breathing in the air, I now felt like I may be horrendously sick – which, at least, would *improve* the overall smell!

Louise had secured herself a week working at Buckingham's solicitors, one of Stoneports leading agents of legal advice.

It sounded boring as hell to me but she wanted to see whether a career as a solicitor was something she may like to pursue and so was perfect for her.

Little Si was doing a week at Hassledeans butchers – presumably because

Goodbye B.M.X. Hello S.E.X.

Mr Upson couldn't get him a role as a jockey, or a chimney sweep!

Mark had copped for the week as an admin assistant that I had been threatened with – much to *his* displeasure.

John, on the other hand, had been given a role "on the shop floor" at Stoneports newly built B&Q megastore – which we all agreed was probably a fancy term for "slave labour"!

So, all in all, we had each been dealt a bum hand.

I suppose we couldn't expect anything more from a "part time careers advisor" who held grudges against anyone who had the audacity to think they could have a laugh in life!

As I looked around my "office" for the forthcoming week though, I think it was safe to say, that *I* had received the *shortest* of the short straws!

In addition to the numerous posters (that I *eventually* stopped gawping at!) that were a couple of pairs of scruffy, blue overalls hanging up, an uncountable amount of mops, brooms and metal buckets and several bottles of bleach and other radioactive looking, coloured liquids.

What a depressing place!

I looked at my watch.

07.01 a.m.

Yes, it was *seven a.m.* – the middle of the night!

But where was Old Man Hallsworth?

The owner of this whole "caretaker" role thing!

He'd told me to be here at seven a.m., *on the dot*, but where was *he*?

Maybe he'd had to go home because he'd forgotten his gas mask or something!

I began to wonder how long it would be before I inevitably passed out, when I began to hear footsteps approaching me from behind.

Slow footsteps.

The footsteps of someone who was certainly not in a rush.

I looked around and saw "Mr" Hallsworth (no one ever called him anything other than "Old Man" Hallsworth because, well, he was an old man!) walking towards me. Not at the pace of someone who was ridiculously late, (ok – a minute late!) but rather moving like someone who was taking his walk along the Green Mile!

He was a man of average height with deep set, Grand Canyon-esque, lines on his face that cut into his Rhino-like tough looking skin. His hair was completely silvery-grey but in that "little-bit-yellowy" way at the front that excessive smokers often have!

He was the type of guy that easily fitted the phrase – "had a hard life"!

"You Paul Day?" he rasped through a throat that sounded like it was probably painful every time he spoke.

It crossed my mind that I should say "no" and, instead, pretend that I was a connoisseur of fine smells!

"Yes!" I said, deciding that kind of response may get me off on the wrong foot with a guy I had to spend the next week with.

"You got overalls?" he asked.

"No!" I said.

How many sixteen year old boys have their own overalls?

"Take a pair from there!" he said, pointing at the scruffy looking blue rags hanging on the wall.

"Suppose you want the *clean* pair?" he added.

"No! I'll have your dirtiest, shittiest, smelliest pair, please!" I said.

Well, I said it in my mind!

At what age do you need to reach before you can start saying what you actually *want* to say *all the time*, and not give a shit whether you create awkward situations?

"Yes, please!" I *actually* said.

Old Man Hallsworth walked past me and grabbed the pair that was hanging on the right side of the hooks.

"*Clean* pair!" he said, handing them to me.

After looking at the overalls with the confusion of someone looking at their first Rubiks Cube, I realised there was no need to remove my trainers as I just needed to step into them.

As I did, Old Man Hallsworth offered me more information about my new "uniform".

"Only washed last week!"

"*Last week*?" I shrieked in the kind of high-pitched tone usually reserved for those unfortunate "wall" individuals who'd been struck by a ball about "six inches below the belly-button"!

"Beauty of overalls," Old Man Hallsworth continued "You get a good five or six weeks' wear before they need washing!"

Five or six weeks?

I suppose that, at least, partly explained some of the smell!

They fitted ok apart from being a bit baggy around the stomach area – no doubt because they'd been stretched by Old Man Hallsworths *pot belly*.

Maybe *that's* the age that you start to say *exactly* what you want – when your stomach has taken on that unsightly beach-ball-under-your-shirt look and you realise that the only women who may still find you attractive probably badly need cataract operations?

I noticed that the overalls had some initials sewn onto them, just below the left shoulder.

Instead of OMH though, they said SHH.

How strange that "Old Man" weren't actually Hallsworths' first names!

He must have seen me looking at the letters because ~~Old Man~~ Hallsworth decided to tell me what they did stand for.

"Stanley Herbert Hallsworth!" he said, while at the same time pointing to the same SHH letters that were on his own pair of, shabby blue, overalls.

"You could probably do with a pair of these if you worked in the library!" I said, laughing fairly loudly at a joke that had come so quickly, I was immensely proud of myself for it!

Goodbye B.M.X. Hello S.E.X.

"I do wear these when I work in the library!" growled Stanley Herbert totally unaware of what I was meaning.

Does *anyone* in this School have a sense of humour?

Was it worth explaining it to him?

Was any joke funny anymore after the need for explanation?

No!

Instead I looked at my watch – wildly hoping that it may be lunch time!

07.07 a.m.

Not quite then!

Stanley must now have seen me checking on the time.

"We start at seven so we can clean before the dirty little sods come in!" he began. "Good thing is though, *we* get to finish *early. Three o'clock!*"

Three o'clock – *early*?

I finished at 3.15 everyday anyway – without having to start before even the milkman's woken up!

At least getting up early meant there was no *bathroom race* needed, which did mean I could go to sleep without the pressure of that hanging over me!

"Grab a mop and bucket!" Stan the Man began! (the poetry club thing was really working for me!) "We start each morning with the toilet sweep."

"Don't we need a broom then?" I asked, a little more enthusiastically than I intended.

Old Man Hallsworth smiled a mouth-full of badly neglected teeth at me and put, possibly the dirtiest hand I had ever seen, onto my shoulder.

"You've got a lot to learn my young apprentice," he began, making me feel very Luke Skywalker to his Emperor! "There is more than one meaning to the word *sweep*. I don't want to confuse you right from the start, but this meaning of the word, *sweep,* means to have a check around and not actually *sweep*!"

Thank God for that!

I didn't want to be confused by multiple word meanings – how ever would I cope with that!

How stupid did he think I was?

I stepped forward to grab a mop and stood on a broom head which made the handle shoot off the wall where it was leaning before striking me on the head!

Ok, no need for him to answer the *how stupid…*question!

Before I knew it we were in the sanctuary of the boys toilets.

Smelly?

Yes!

But one Hell of an improvement on Herbie's storage / light porn collection room!

"Ok" said Hallsworth, after casually throwing a handful of those pineapple chunk-looking things into the urinal "You check trap two – I'll check one, three and four!"

He was obviously referring to the toilet cubicles of which there were, indeed, four.

Gary Locke

But how was he numbering them?
Left to right?
Right to left?
In ascending order of smelliness?
And what exactly was I meant to be *checking*?

It was too late to ask Stanley because he had entered the first cubicle on the left.

I think it was fair to assume that was "trap number one" and so I went into the next one to the right.

There wasn't a huge amount of checking needed – because my eyes were immediately drawn into the toilet by the thickest, longest turd you have ever seen!

If there hadn't been a logistics issue with the whole thing, then I think it would have been reasonable to believe that an Elephant had popped in to take a shit!

I popped my head back out just in time to see Old Man Hallsworth walking out of "trap four".

"Mine are all clear!" he said. "How about yours?"

"There's actually a really big.......*poo* stuck down there!"

Had I really just used the word *poo* to an old man who openly displays naked young women on his storage room wall?

"Oh bad luck! You'll have to remove that *"poo"* – we can't leave it like that!" he said laughing, no doubt at my juvenile description of the large shit.

I think it was fair to assume now that I had been *deliberately* sent into "trap two"!

In fact thinking about it, I'm pretty sure that Andrew Owen had been boasting to everyone about needing to bring his camera in to record the "monster of all monster shits"! – a week last Wednesday!

Had it been there *all this time*?

Had Hallsworth deliberately left it, knowing that I would have to clear it today?

And how on Earth had it kept in *one piece*?

That really is some mega-turd!

Without even needing to take a look at it!, the scruffy old caretaker gave me advice on how to shift it.

"With something of that size – repeat flushing is no good. You need to get your hand down there and break it up!"

Was he being serious?

"Do you want some gloves?" he added.

Was he being serious?

He had more to say.

"Gloves are only really for *wimps*!"

Was he being serious?

By the look on his face, it seemed so!

"Yes I *do* want gloves!" I said all flustered, after considering that being

Goodbye B.M.X. Hello S.E.X.

thought of as a wimp by a crazy old man was preferable to any quantity of shit under my fingernails!

"Ok, I'll leave you to it." rasped Stan, throwing me a pair of yellow gloves.

I say "yellow" but, probably due to the length of time he'd had them and the usage they'd seen, they were more white than yellow.

Well, the parts that weren't already suspiciously brown!

"You need to mop the floor as well," he added. "You'll be best doing that first."

He must have seen it on my face – I would probably prefer to swim naked with Piranha fish!

He decided to shower me with his *wisdom*.

"I've got some golden advice for you," he started. "You seem like you're ready for it. You're a fast learner and I can tell you're very keen to get to work!"

Keen?

I was about as keen to get to work as an Eskimo who'd had his coat stolen!

"I know mopping isn't the most interesting of things to do, but the way I see things is like this: For anything in life that you have to put your name to – make sure it's the *best* it can possibly be. Make sure you can be proud to say that it's something that *you* have done!"

He looked deep into my eyes as he said it.

It did sound like a good thing to follow in life in general, but I saw straight away what he was doing.

He just wanted me to make a good job of mopping the floor!

This was a man who had left a big shit in a toilet for a week and a half!

So he definitely didn't believe or adhere to his own advice.

He probably hadn't mopped in here for ages; if ever at all!

He hadn't finished with his top rate lessons in life for me.

"And don't think of mops and brooms as cleaning tools. Think of them as *friends*. And don't push them around....*dance* with them!"

What the Hell was he talking about?

And what the Hell was he *on*?

Luckily he didn't have anything else to say as he decided that was the best point at which to leave me alone with the cleaning mountain that lay ahead of me.

I did as he'd advised and did my mopping first.

But I *refused* to dance with it – just in case the crafty old sod had arranged some kind of Candid Camera kind of trap for me.

Imagine if I got filmed doing an intimate little Foxtrot with a Vileda Super Mop? I'd never live it down!

No, just plain and simple hard pushing and scrubbing for *forty-five* minutes!

But would I like to put my name to doing it?

Not really.

I may have cleaned off five or six layers of ground-in dirt but there was probably double that amount left on there!

Next I had to confront the "monster of all monsters"!

Gary Locke

As I squeezed into the yellow / white / brown gloves I realised that this was the same cubicle that had inspired my new motto in life, back at the start of the year.

Sure enough, those fifteen words were still there on the side wall. (And why wouldn't they be? They were in no danger of being cleaned off by Old Man Hallsworth!)

"This could be the best day of your life – don't let it pass you by."

I smiled to myself as I appreciated its sentiments again.

Make the most of every day.

Every situation.

Every second.

Sure, as I stared at the huge shit I was mentally building myself up towards reaching down to and breaking up, I realised that *this* moment wasn't ever going to be the best part of anything, but it didn't mean that this *day* couldn't improve.

I was going to make the most of it.

I gritted my teeth and plunged my right hand into the toilet water.

I reached down and touched the, soon to be broken "waste log", and it felt as thick as a human arm! (Someone should really check whether Andrew Owen is, you know, *normal*!)

SNAP!

For no apparent reason my glove had snapped in two!

I looked down as the fingers section of it floated up to the surface, as my uncovered hand continued to grip the chunky, brown *poo*!

Before I had chance to change my grip, my hand clenched tightly together dispersing the turd into an explosion of brown liquid!

Oh shit!

Literally!

Here I was, nearing the end of my School days, with my naked hand reaching down a toilet and squelching apart an abnormally large shit!

I may be being hasty, but I felt almost certain that this was *not* going to *be the best day of my life*!

I also made a decision.

I was pretty sure that one of those runny noses that keeps teachers off work for at least a week was quickly going to threaten my chances of successfully completing my "work experience" commitments!

And one thing was for *damn sure*.

The role of Caretaker was clearly only for crazy, old, mop-dancing, stinky wacko's who were probably taking some kind of looney-medicine!

No, there was no way that I would ever, *ever* do a job like this....!

Goodbye B.M.X. Hello S.E.X.

May 1992

May arrived in spectacular fashion.
Not only had the Sun decided to make an appearance; but it was beating down with such intensity that it was cutting through the twenty-four hour air chill.
So much so, that you were now able to differentiate between the people who were smoking, and those who were just breathing normally!
Man City had finished the season, again in fifth spot in Division One.
It was the same place as last year and, after a period of yo-yoing between Division One and Division Two, it seemed we had found some stability.
The only disappointment was that Man United had, unlike last year, managed to finish above us. (2nd place - behind Leeds United. Shame - so close, yet so far!)
Next season marks the start of the "Premiership".
I'm not sure what the change will actually mean, if anything.
Some say it is the start of football becoming driven by money, and that players will begin to earn tens of thousands of pounds a week.
Where do these idiots think things like that up from?
Footballers earning that much money!
Because of the improvements both us and United have made recently, I am sure one of us can take a step further and go on to dominate the league for the next ten, maybe even fifteen years.
I'm sure it will be us!
Come on City!
April had ended with a pop charts number one by Right Said Fred of all bands. Their song *"Deeply Dippy"* wasn't the best song ever - but it was certainly an anthem for any other average pub band who dreamed of success!
At least it wasn't there for long and, as May began, it was replaced by *"Please Don't Go"* by K.W.S.! - quite possibly one of those other pub bands dreaming of success!
It seemed 1992 was becoming quite the year for one hit wonders!
At least Louise and I didn't have to worry about the shit on the radio, because we still had our Bryan.
He had a song for every occasion - well every occasion that involved teenage heavy petting.
Heavy petting that was now taking place at either my house *or* Louise's. I had been accepted totally by her parents following the successful meal.
It was like I was part of the family; and as such I was looking forward to the annual, first-class family holiday to Portugal!
All I had to do was survive School for the next few weeks.
That would be easy, because for all my time at School I had lived by Brother Simons strict set of rules on how to get by.
They were like a "School-yard Survival Guide".

Be Cool - but not *so* cool, that it could be construed as *cockiness*.
In lessons, always try to be anonymous - and blend into the background.
If you can't be anonymous, be neutral. If you are too quiet or too loud, then the teacher will turn to you for answers to questions. (Which, in turn, will necessitate the need for actual learning!)
Never queue up for lunch - find a kid with glasses, and push in front of him!
Never eat the canteen "hamburgers" - they are made from Terrapin meat!
Don't go to any after-School clubs - especially the geeky ones. (I suppose I may have broken *that* rule!)
Act Tough - but not *so* tough that it attracts confrontation.
If you do get into a fight, never fight a fat kid - they are almost always freakishly strong. And never fight with your mouth open - the inevitable, encircling crowd likes to spit at the fighters!

I had always followed these rules to the letter.

How could it be then, that after four years and nine months of near-perfect trouble and confrontation avoidance, I had somehow been undone?

How could it be that an innocuous incident had led me to the one place that all students fear…..?

Goodbye B.M.X. Hello S.E.X.

Chapter Fifteen - "...the corridor..."

Probably no more than nine or ten metres long and three metres wide.

Four plastic chairs tightly squeezed together on a side wall opposite two unmarked doors.

No windows, just an overhead fluorescent strip-light, creating a slightly eerie, flickering atmosphere.

And, at the far end of the corridor, a third door with a polished, gold plate sporting, in black capital letters, the words:

C.J. LANGDEN - HEADMASTER.

Yes, here I was, sitting alone in Holly Grove High Schools answer to death row!

I had been sent by C.D.T. teacher Mr Jones for what seemed, at the time, an innocuous crime; but now I wasn't so sure. As the number of minutes I had waited increased, no doubt designed to make me sweat in the grim surroundings, I began to realise I must be in real trouble.

For the first time ever I had been sent to see "Crazy-eyed Langden", who had been headmaster for over twenty years.

His nickname had come from the fact that he was the owner of wild, zany eyes. So much so, that he even made Patrick Moore look normal!

To describe him as being eccentric would be being kind; he was barking mad - crazier than a rabid Camel!

He had the strange habit of, while presenting School assemblies, finishing seemingly mid-sentence and marching out of the hall, as if someone had just set off the fire alarm.

Apart from these hastily ended early morning lectures, it was actually rare to see him inside the School.

However, you would often see him on the School field at lunch times, stealthily moving like a hunting Tiger, looking for students who may be eating their lunch outside.

No eating outside was one of several, obscure rules that he had put into place, no doubt after finding a couple of crisp packets on the football pitch, and he liked to police it himself.

Instead of perhaps just making a rule that no one was allowed to drop litter outside, he had instead chosen to ban every student from being able to enjoy an outside picnic on a glorious Summers afternoon.

But then again just banning litter dropping would spoil his fun.

Crawling around on his hands and knees, binoculars in one hand, loud speaker in the other; popping up out of some long grass, bellowing "everybody freeze" into his megaphone, scaring the shit out of some, poor kid foolish enough to be holding a sandwich - it was probably the highlight of his working week.

This rule was similar to another he had, in which certain main corridors, including one that led to this very interrogation holding area, were "one-way".

Gary Locke

Supposedly designed to "prevent congestion" - !??! - it meant that at times you had to walk halfway round the School, usually in the pouring rain, instead of being able to use the direct, undercover dry route.

Absolutely crazy!

Maybe it was Langden's way of teaching his students a valuable lesson; and that life was often unfair and confusingly unjust.

Yes, maybe he was preparing all students for the minefields ahead - after they'd left School.

More likely that they were the rules of someone who was totally bonkers!

It was like having the Mad Hatter running the School!

I began to wonder what was taking so long.

Was he waiting for me to have my visit from the vicar?

That's what happened on death row wasn't it?

I couldn't help but think that being on the "green mile" would be better than this. At least there's a sense of finality about what is ahead.

For me it was open ended.

For starters there would be the face to face grilling from Langden, and I was convinced he would be a master of advanced torture.

Then there would perhaps be a suspension or, even, expulsion. That would lead to having to find a new School and make new friends.

Even if I wasn't expelled there could be letters home to my parents, and God-knows what repercussions that could lead to. Dad was angry enough with me when I burnt a piece of his toast at the weekend. How would he deal with this?

No, gas or lethal injection appeared quite inviting from where I sat.

As I reassured myself with the fact that I was perhaps looking at worse case scenarios, and that perhaps he may just give me a detention, my mind pulled out a fact that I had first learned as a first year student, four years ago.

Fancy choosing this moment as the time for recalling data!

Not in the middle of a quiz or, more importantly, an exam; but now!

And the piece of information that it decided to recollect was hardly the type of thing I wanted right now.

Langden still uses the *cane!*

As my sweat glands prepared to go into overdrive, I tried to check the validity of my minds shocking recollection.

What was the source of the "Langden practices medieval discipline" stories?

I remembered being told about summons to the heads office, that was more a torture chamber than a place for administration, that often resulted in broken fingers or bottoms that couldn't be sat on for weeks.

How Langden had then terrorised his victims into being too petrified to report him for his brutality; even to their own parents.

I was pretty sure that it was a tale told by one of the fifth year bullies, no doubt designed to scare and upset naïve and delicate first years; and I was perhaps the most naïve and delicate of all the first years!

It was just a scary story!

Goodbye B.M.X. Hello S.E.X.

Nothing more.

There was nothing to fear.

In fact the only "evidence" I remember being given to back up this x-rated Jackanory fable, was that Langden was an insane, psycho nutcase.

It was true!

Unmistakably, 100% authentic!

I began to appreciate my plastic chair; believing it may be the last seat I would even want to *look* at for the next fortnight.

Suddenly there was a mini explosion of noise from behind the door at the end of the corridor. It was clear to make out it was the sound of a man standing from his desk and walking towards his office door.

A man so manic that he couldn't do anything at less than 100 m.p.h.

As quick as a flash the door opened, and there he stood; every bit as crazy-eyed as his nickname suggested.

Dressed in a black suit and black tie, as if attending a funeral (quite possibly mine!) he somehow managed to stare directly at me, while also appearing to look at the floor and ceiling, and all four walls at the same time!

He was like a human fly.

"Ok, Mr Day," he began.

Good, I thought, finally an adult at this School who treats you like a grown up, and shows you some respect.

"Get your skinny little arse into my office!"

Or maybe not!

It was clear what was going to happen behind that door.

He was going to eat me alive, spew me out onto his desk, before sucking me up again. He would then fly up onto the ceiling and rub his legs together!

I resigned myself to my fate.

I slowly stood up and sensibly walked behind Mr Langden into his office; believing that, even though I was right behind him, he could probably still see me with *his* eyes.

"Sit down" he said, pointing at the chair in front of his desk - a chair that looked surprisingly inviting.

It was made of soft, pale red material and was nicely padded like the ones in the library - but without the hardened chewing gum and marker pen graffiti; like *"po-tree club geek sitz ere!"*

I sat down and watched as Langden sped behind his large desk – a desk that actually looked large enough for someone to hide underneath!

I laughed to myself.

I do have some crazy thoughts!

Why would anyone ever have to hide underneath a desk?

Langden's chair was a high-backed, black leather swivel number; the kind only usually used by Mastermind contestants or Bond villains!

As he slowly turned himself from left to right, something I'm pretty sure you had to do by law when you sat in a swivel chair, I glanced around the room.

It was nothing like I expected.

It was just like a normal office.

There was a big bookshelf that covered the left wall and student-catching binoculars and megaphone sat on the large window that stretched across the back of the room. There were a couple of filing cabinets that stood against the right wall, a thin hook-handled bamboo cane that leaned against a grey wastepaper basket, and there was a normally placed phone and paper-tray on the large desk that was bathed in the bright sunlight coming through the window.

I rewound my mind through my office mini-tour.

I wasn't mistaken.

Propped up against the bin - was a *bamboo cane!*

Oh my God!

A bamboo cane in *real life!*

This wasn't the 1800's, or a re-run of Tom Browns Schooldays, this was <u>real life</u>.

Yet there was a cane, out in the open, unsheathed, fully loaded - in a place where there were hundreds of children.

"Who's sent you?" asked Langden, breaking the silence.

"Bamboo Cane!" I answered without thinking.

The puzzled expression on Langden's face, that was actually difficult to make out because of the alignment of his eyes, alerted me to what I had just said.

"Sorry…..I mean Mr Jones." I said quickly and loudly, correcting myself immediately.

Langden looked pensive before chuckling a little and nodding quickly.

"Yes, he does look a little like a thin piece of cane doesn't he; spindly old fool?"

I wasn't sure if his question was aimed at me, or was perhaps rhetorical, so I didn't reply to him.

He continued talking, his words becoming more confused and muttered as he went on.

"Why does he keep sending students to me every five minutes? Senile, old buffoon. Does he think I have nothing better to do with my time?"

Despite the fact that, by the end of his sentence, his words had merged into one, long, deep drawl, almost like he was talking French!, I did understand the gist of his questions.

Again, I was not sure if he was talking to himself or to me; and even whether he was asking real questions or perhaps rhetorical ones.

As the only other thing I could imagine him doing with his time would be his School-field covert surveillance; coupled with the fact I wasn't really sure what rhetorical really meant anyway, I decided, again, to say nothing.

It seemed like a wise choice because, without delay, another Langden question materialised, this time one I was sure he wanted answering.

"Ok, what have you done that was so bad that Mr Jones felt warranted you being sent to crazy-eyed Langden?"

Goodbye B.M.X. Hello S.E.X.

He caught me totally off guard.

I had prepared a concise, only slightly exaggerated version of the truth, that I hoped Langden would show some lenience with. But his choice of words; referring to himself in the third person, as well as using his rather derogatory nickname (which I was now thinking he may have made up for himself!) left me in a state of shock.

It was like I had mentally been struck by a Mike Tyson haymaker, and it took me a couple of seconds, wondering whether I was about to get one of my ears bitten off, before I was ready to answer.

I composed myself and prepared to deliver the rehearsed speech.

But it was too late.

My mouth had decided to take the initiative and answer on my behalf; and not the agreed, edited version, but rather the extended edition.

The truthful "directors cut", with *additional scenes!*

"It was a C.D.T. lesson in the lower School C.D.T. workshop - which you obviously know as Mr Jones is a C.D.T. teacher. Anyway, for today's lesson he asked us to do some hand drawn pictures of tools for the cover of our practical work record books. Just things like hammers, saws and screwdrivers, that type of thing. Why he asked us to do it, I'm not really sure, you would be best asking *him*. Anyway, I was sitting next to Simon Hadden and, about twenty minutes into the lesson, he hadn't drawn anything he was happy with. He had just rubbed out his latest efforts as Mr Jones walked round looking at everyone's work. He shouted at Simon for not starting and then gave him a hand by sketching a wood-plane and hacksaw for him. He then said *"There you go, that's how easy and quick it is to draw lifelike tools; now get on with it!"* When he returned about ten minutes later, to check everyone's work again, Simon hadn't drawn anything else. I think you can assume that Mr Jones had forgotten that he had drawn the plane and saw because, again angry, he shouted *"What the hell do you call that? It is absolutely pathetic. A three year old could have drawn better than that!"* I couldn't help but laugh, which became uncontrollable as Simon said to Mr Jones *"But you drew them, Sir!"* Mr Jones asked me what I was laughing at and, although I thought the humour in the situation was obvious, I said I didn't really know. So he sent me here to you, Mr Langden, to explain to you why I laugh out loud for no apparent reason."

I realised that I had been talking for far too long.

So long, in fact, that I began to think that Langden may have passed out.

It was strange to see his face without the erratic eye movement. Eyes that had formed a slight film of glaze and were now totally frozen - each staring in a different direction.

I was beginning to consider slipping out of the office during his unconsciousness, wondering if this lengthy talking, almost Ronnie Corbett-esque monologue, could be used in the future as a diversionary tactic, when Langden leapt out of his chair.

He began making, what could only be described as a howling noise while, at the same time, banging his fist on his desk.

I wasn't sure what these Neanderthal actions meant; but between the tribal-like noises, the desk banging and his crazier-than-ever eyes, I couldn't help but be reminded of every cannibal movie I had ever seen.

He was definitely going to eat me alive!

He was a human, cannibal fly!

"Oh, that's brilliant," he said, between the howls, that I now realised was eccentric laughing.

"Imbecilic, geriatric half-wit! Oh I need to make a note of this…" he continued, fumbling around for some blank paper. "…that's definitely going into his retirement speech, so everyone can have a good laugh about how shit he was!"

Involuntary, I began to join in the laughing.

Mine too took on the hint of a Canine tone to it; certainly no bark at the moon, but it was definitely more eccentric than my regular laugh.

We were sharing a real moment.

We weren't student and headmaster, we were two regular people enjoying the humour of the situation, and almost encouraging and enhancing each others laughter.

Suddenly it felt like I was in warm, almost familiar surroundings; and as Langden placed his hand written recount of my tale into his desk drawer, I felt sure that he was going to produce two crystal glasses and offer me a vintage whisky.

I couldn't have been more wrong.

Instead, he slammed the drawer shut, and the look on his face changed from playful Sunshine to angry thunder - faster than Superman in a telephone box!

"Of course you will have to be punished!" he said coldly, all traces of humour gone. "I can't have you insulting a member of my staff."

I watched in shock as he rose from his desk and, uncharacteristically slowly, walked towards his waste paper basket.

I subconsciously clenched my buttock cheeks tightly together as he stretched out with his right hand.

He was reaching for the bamboo cane.

He had picked up the bamboo cane.

He had turned to face me, *holding* the bamboo cane.

I was pleased to be already clenching my bottom, or there may have been an accident!

Langden held the cane at the end in his right hand, before stretching it up high……..and hooking its handle into the window blind!

In one sweeping movement, he pulled the blind shut, instantly removing the bright sunlight shining on his desk.

"That's been annoying me all morning" he said, carefully standing the cane back up against his bin.

"Now, as I was saying, I have to find a way to make it *look* like you've been punished."

Relief washed all over me, like a waterfall in a Timotei advert!

Goodbye B.M.X. Hello S.E.X.

It was a fantastic feeling. Similar to how I had felt a couple of years ago at Alton Towers when, after two hours of agonising queuing, I was told I wasn't tall enough to ride the Corkscrew. (It's amazing what subtle hunching can achieve!)

"I think I'll have to send you home for the day" he said winking at me.

At least I think it was a wink; with his eyes it was quite possible that they blinked independently of each other.

"It's a nice day, go and enjoy yourself!" he added.

I couldn't believe it.

This wasn't a punishment. I was actually being rewarded.

Langden spoke again.

"It would be good for my reputation if you come to School tomorrow wearing a bandage on your hand and refusing to talk about what happened in here."

We smiled at each other heartily, sharing another pleasant moment, just as before.

"I will be happy to." I said.

"Ok, what time is it?" he asked, looking at his watch. "Good, it's nearly lunchtime. Come on, I'll walk you out."

He reached for his binoculars and loud hailer and followed me through the death row corridor.

At the end I instinctively turned right; the quickest way towards the main entrance.

"Stop!" came Langden's voice from behind me. "What do you think you're doing?"

It took me a couple of seconds to realise what the problem was.

I was going the wrong way down one of his "one-way" corridors.

My mind prepared a response impressively and surprisingly quickly.

"I just thought that maybe it would be best if I didn't see anyone before I went home. It would make the whole "bandaged hand" seem more realistic if no one had seen that my hand had not actually been injured."

I smugly waited for his response, safe in the knowledge that he would have to agree that I was merely helping to maintain his reputation.

"You thought wrong!" he said, the air of human flesh eater menacingly returning. "I am sick to death of you students continuously showing no regard for the important rules at this School. You better go and sit back down in there!" he said, pointing at the plastic chairs of the green mile.

"I've got some important work to do now, but I'll be back after lunch. We will see then what kind of punishment will be appropriate for your latest misdemeanor."

With that he was off.

100 m.p.h. down the corridor, towards the main entrance – in the wrong direction!

I returned to the spluttering light of the smaller corridor, muttering "crazy hypocrite" as I walked back towards *square one*.

As I sat down, on the same chair as before, I noticed that Langden had left his office door open.

Gazing in, I could clearly see the bamboo cane, resting against the waste paper bin.

Was it just a glorified blind closer? - merely a symbol used to uphold the image of a nutcase.

Or was it a weapon, sometimes used on students who had gone too far with their bad behaviour - like having the audacity to walk down a one-way corridor the wrong way?

(A one-way corridor for students, but obviously not for crazy headmasters!)

As I settled back into my plastic chair, I accepted that I would find out one way or another in about an hour.

I also knew that it would most probably depend on what kind of mood the crazy-eyed, cannibal, human fly was in when he returned - which, no doubt, rested on how successful his lunchtime hunting mission went!

Goodbye B.M.X. Hello S.E.X.

Chapter Sixteen - "...*Science and Sex Education*..."

"Quiet. Quiet! QUIET PLEASE!"
I think the words coming out of Mr Upson's mouth were more out of hope than any thoughts that his instructions may be followed.
Half of the classroom couldn't even have heard him.
How could they when the School had found it acceptable to merge two classes together, meaning sixty-odd kids had to cram in to one small classroom?
Talk about Sardines!
Thank God for truancy, and the unseasonal vomiting bug, or there may have been over seventy in there!
Yep, due to "staff shortages" (again!) my *sex education* class had been merged with a class that should have been focusing on *science*.
Science and Sex Education.
Interesting combination!
As usual, during times of staffing crisis, veteran teacher *Mr Upson* had been called upon to save the day.
Normally this situation would be perfect for, for the want of a better phrase, *messing about!*
For starters, sex education was just an excuse for immature kids to snigger, giggle and chuckle at the mere mention of penis' and vaginas. (Oh we usually have such a laugh!)
Added to that the fact that "careers advisor" Mr Upson would be *teaching* us, which would surely see him further out of his comfort zone than a Scotsman in a heat-wave!, the lesson was sure to be a non-stop laugh fest!
There were, however, a couple of problems.

1...This was the first lesson I'd had with Mr Upson since our disastrous work experience interview that had led to him giving me, what he described as, the "best role for me" – that of *School Caretakers Assistant*! To say there was a touch of hostility between us was like saying there was touch of hostility between Iran and Iraq! There may well be war!

2...The class that we had been fused together with, was <u>Louise's</u> class!

This would be the first time I had shared a classroom with my girlfriend since our visits to her poetry club – for which the first time was very nearly a complete disaster.
Only good-old-Grandad's poem had saved me from something not even worth thinking about.
And, as such, I was *nervous*.
Despite my instincts, I didn't want Louise to see me giggling like a little boy at the first mention of masturbation or menstrual cycles! (The latter of which, today, I'd have to **not** pretend were the two wheeled transportation choice of

medieval bards!)

And, with our blossoming relationship fast approaching a more *physical* level, perhaps actually trying to *learn* something about sex may be a good idea!

My *main* concern though related to what Mark had told me about his very own sex education class from earlier in the week. As we were fast approaching the end of our time at School it seemed that it had been decided that these classes would be more *practical*.

Mark had recited a very embarrassing story about how poor Barry Coope had been made to stand up in front of the class and fit a condom to a large plastic cock!

Imagine being picked out to do that?

In front of your girlfriend as well!

I shuddered at the thought of it!

Mr Upson decided not to bother with any more shouted attempts at bringing some order to the classroom.

Instead he took the two step journey backwards to the blackboard.

Oh no – he wasn't going to do the old scraping-fingernails-down-the-blackboard routine was he?

I prepared my body for wincing mode.

Thankfully it was not needed as Mr Upson instead grabbed a piece of red chalk and wrote, in huge capital letters, the word – *SEX*.

The loud, crowd-like buzz that had been echoing round the room, slowly gave way to some quiet sniggering as each pair of eyes eventually noticed the three lettered, red word that now shone brightly out of the darkness of the black board.

"Good!" said Mr Upson. "Now I've got your attention – BE QUIET PLEASE!"

He walked back to the blackboard and picked up another piece of chalk, this time a white one.

As he did, I glanced over at Louise who was sat on the left hand side of the room on one of the side desks next to Angela Anthon (who everyone referred to as "national"!)

I had considered asking Louise to sit next to me but, because of the nervousness I was feeling, had decided it was best we stayed at opposite sides of the room.

She flashed her beautiful smile at me and shrugged her shoulders up quickly in an almost giddy way.

Was *she* taking this lesson as seriously as she should be?

Mr Upson turned back towards us, revealing that he had written the words, "SCIENCE AND" in front of the already written, "SEX".

"Ok," he started. "Today we will be doing a lesson that will focus on Science *and* Sex!"

"Is it the Science *of* Sex, sir?" asked Phil Broadley, hoping to create the first laugh of the lesson.

Phil was one of those, annoyingly, confident boys who was always casually

Goodbye B.M.X. Hello S.E.X.

chatting to the good looking girls - as if they were just *normal* people!

He had suspiciously blonde, floppy Jason Donovan-esque hair and always seemed to be at the top of every girls' "*Guys I'd most like to snog*" list.

Even now, I could see many of the girls around me staring at him all dewy eyed.

Caroline Gavin, Kerry Kindness and both Lisa and Kim Bell – all looking at him like he was some kind of poster-boy pop star!

Lisa and Kim had the same surname but, despite everyone making out they must be related, looked totally different from each other and were not related in any way.

Unless they were like those twins you see sometimes who look *so* different you have to think that they were lied to by their parents at some stage, and that at least one of them must have been adopted!

In the past I would have felt jealous about all these girls looking at Phil, but not anymore. Not now I had a girlfriend of my own!

I quickly glanced at Louise to make sure that she wasn't staring at him all dewy-eyed!

She wasn't!

Ha!

Well, at least I *think* she wasn't.

She *was* looking at him – but her eyes seemed very *dry*.

Ha!

Well, *dryish*!

"SHUT UP, BROADLEY!" snapped Mr Upson before anyone had the chance to even decide whether Phil's comment was funny or not.

As Mr Upson began to explain further the format of the lesson, I decided *I* would contemplate the humour value of Phil's comment.

Was it funny?

Verdict – No!

No laughing required then!

I realised I was shaking my head in response to my own question as I rejoined Mr Upsons' monologue, thankfully, somewhere near the end.

"....so that's where we will start – the best inventions of all time. And thank you Mr Day for not minding judging for us!"

Shit!

It seemed my bloody involuntary head movements had got me into another fine mess.

If I was Oliver Hardy then my head was Stan Laurel!

It's one of the main reasons that I could never trust myself going to an auction!

Mr Upson walked into the middle of the class before continuing.

"Come on then Broadley, you seem to have a lot to say for yourself. What, in your opinion, is the best invention of all time?"

"Easy sir!" said Phil. "The wheel!"

Everyone waited to see whether there would be an attempted joke to follow.

Gary Locke

It turns out there wasn't.
Was this going to be one of those *serious* lessons?
Boring!
"Ok," said Mr Upson. "Good choice. Good choice!"
He walked back over towards his desk.
Why was he moving around all over the place?
Maybe his bad hip was causing him some grief. Should I have sympathy, cut him some slack and feel sorry for him?
What? The man who sanctioned my week of cleaning shit out of toilets?
Never!
Never! Never! *Never*!
I suppose if this was a *serious* lesson, and I was judging a *serious* debate on the best inventions of all time, then *I* would have to be serious as well.
Was the wheel the best invention of all time?
Clearly *yes*!
How did anyone ever move *anything* before the wheel was invented?
It must have helped the Egyptians build the Pyramids – and then been a big part of *every other* major construction following.
Then there are cars and motorbikes and tractors and busses!
Not to mention roller skates and skateboards!
And, without the wheel, how the Hell would all those Hamsters ever get any exercise?
There was no actual point in asking any one else!
"Philip Jackson?" asked the *stupid old idiot!*, clearly now just wasting everyone's time. "What's your choice of best invention?"
"Erm, probably *sliced bread* I think!" said Philip.
I tried not to look at Philip as he spoke.
I had been quite friendly with him in first year and we had spent the majority of our time in Science lessons writing silly little songs that we would sing out loud to one another.
One of our favourite tunes was a catchy little number that went by the name of "*Kill Mr Smith*"!
Well it *was* one of our favourites until one day our teacher, *Mr Smith*, found it!
As it was written in Phillips exercise book he was promptly dispatched to see the headmaster, Mr Langden, (an event I now realised was worse than death itself!) while I had got away with it, as they say, *Scot Free*!
It had meant that our relationship since that sad day was, understandably, fairly *distant*!
But ooh!
Sliced bread!
That was good.
In fact, it was the new winner!
Sure, the wheel helped mankind achieve many things and to, pretty much, *progress* as a race, but you still have to *eat*!

Goodbye B.M.X. Hello S.E.X.

And what's more convenient than sandwich making material that is pre-cut?
Yep, there was *now* no point in asking anyone else.
"Anyone else?" asked Mr Upson.
Weren't there laws these days *against* flogging a dead Horse?
Unsurprisingly, seeing as the two obvious candidates had been taken, no one put their hand up.
"Come on there must be, at least, *one* more?" asked Mr Upson sounding a bit desperate.
From out of nowhere, amongst the closely packed bodies at the back of the room, a single hand popped up into the air.
"Yes?" said Mr Upson, trying to see through the crowd of bodies. "Andrew Timmins? What do you think?"
Oh, this will be good – an entry from the computer nerd community!
"The internet and World Wide Web, sir! I've read about it a lot in my computer magazine. One day it will connect the whole World together – it will be huge! So that *has* to be the best invention ever!" said Andrew.
"Ok, interesting." said Mr Upson. "And certainly worth considering!"
Really?
Sounds like the type of thing that will only ever be used by three computer nerds and a Dog!
And a *nerd* Dog at that!
I could safely rule that one out straight away.
"Ok, shall we hand things over to our *Caretaker Assistant* judge?" asked Mr Upson, creating the first real laugh in the class himself, and at my expense.
Dickhead!
"Sir!" another voice announced out of the crowd "I've got another one!"
Everyone looked round to see Chris Onyon waiting to give his choice. Chris was Andrew Timmins' best friend and computer nerd co-pilot so I certainly wasn't holding my breath.
"Ok" said Mr Upson. "Off you go!"
"The Microchip!" he said. "The technology created, opened up a whole new World! It was a real turning point in human history!"
"Yes, another good one!" said Mr Upson. "Ok, no more. Over to you, Mr Day!"
Wow!
I thought that sliced bread had it all sewn up, but maybe Chris was on to something.
Maybe the Microchip did represent a huge turning point in human history.
I had made my mind up.
"Ready?" asked Mr Upson, looking at me.
"I'm going to go with Chris!" I said out loud. "The Microchip!"
"Ok," said Mr Upson, as a couple of disgruntled wheel and sliced bread supporters let their disappointment be known! "Give us your reasons – as concisely as you can."
"It's simple!" I said. "Real, hot chips in three minutes! You've got to hand it

to McCain's!"

An avalanche of laughter started at the back and quickly flowed throughout the whole room.

I'm not sure *why*, but everyone was laughing!

Well everyone except Mr Upson.

His face wore the expression of a man who was contemplating making me do another week-long stint of mopping and sweeping!

"Good one, Paul. Well funny!" said Michael Walsh.

"That's funny *Christmas*!" said Russell Langley.

I nodded in acknowledgment to both Michael and Russell who I knew pretty well from my music class.

Michael played the saxophone and Russell was shit-hot on the guitar. They play in their own band – for which I was actually the lead singer for *two whole months*!

That was until my *fairly horrendous* case of Laryngitis "cleared up" and I was actually able to sing – and they were actually able to *hear* me sing!

Of well, who *really* wants to be a Rock Star?!?

I was getting plenty more compliments from the back of the room, although I still wasn't quite sure why.

Chris Onyon cleared things up for me.

"No, I meant the *electronic* microchip. The ones you get from Silicon Valley!"

My brain initially ignored the first part of his comment and tried to tell me that *Silicon Valley* must be somewhere in Ireland where McCain's get their potatoes from!

It eventually dawned on me though why everyone was laughing.

"Oh, *that* kind of Microchip!" I told myself in my mind, sounding very much like Delboy Trotter!

"He knows that, you pleb!" Rick Brown spat at Chris. "He's just having a laugh!"

"OI!" shouted Mr Upson, "No one uses the word pleb in *my* classes – unless *I'm* the one using it!"

I looked around the class and basked in my unintentional moment of comedy success.

Was Louise enjoying it?

It was hard to tell.

She still seemed to be gazing in the direction of Phil Broadley!

"QUIET!" commanded Mr Upson. "Paul Day – to the front of the class, now!"

I slowly stood from my chair and made my way towards Mr Upson, wondering what he was going to do to me.

Would he be sending me off to see Mr Langden?

I could certainly do without *another* visit to that crazy-eyed maniac's office.

By the time I'd reached the front desk, though, any punishment Mr Upson may be planning to dish out seemed like it would have been worth it. The number of pats on the back and whispers of "Nice one, mate!" and "Good joke,

Goodbye B.M.X. Hello S.E.X.

Paul!" made me feel like a celebrity comedian!

"Alright then, Paul!" started Mr Upson as I stood by the side of him. "Seeing as you want to be the centre of attention, you *can* be. You can be my helper as we start the sex education part of this class!"

Oh no!

Was I to be this lessons' Barry Coope?

Should I volunteer to be sent to Langden instead?

Even the thought of him actually *using* that cane on me seemed preferable to having to grope around with a plastic cock – in front of, what now looked like, a million kids!

Including my girlfriend!

Mr Upson reached under his desk into a bag and pulled out a handful of condoms and a banana!

Oh shit!

Ok, come on. It's not *that* bad.

It was only a few minutes ago that I did actually think that I wanted to *learn* something about sex that could be beneficial to mine and Louise's relationship, so what better way to learn than being right here as Mr Upsons' "helper"?

I needed to stop being immature and just take it seriously.

Was Mr Upson taking it seriously though?

Why was he getting part of his lunch out if this was, as it looked, the condom fitting exercise?

I glanced over at Louise who gave me one of her trademark smiles that always made everything feel better.

I could do this!

"Ok Paul," began Mr Upson "Unfortunately I have forgotten to bring the prosthetic penis for todays lesson, so we are going to have to make do without it!"

A slow ripple of laughter began to circulate the room – no doubt due to the use of the word *penis*!

So immature!

I began to think that, because of the way that he said he'd forgotten it, the "prosthetic penis" must actually *belong* to Mr Upson!

Did I feel sorry for him now?

Never! Never! *Never!*

Wait a minute!

Make do without it?

What did he mean by that?

Did he mean I had to do it for *real?*

In front of *everyone?*

"Whenever you're ready Mr Day." Said Mr Upson. "Show us how you would put a condom on - safely!"

With that, he reached for his banana – obviously wanting a mid-morning snack, leaving me to perform this, somewhat weird, *dressing up* in front of everyone.

Ok, come on.

I said I needed to stop being immature and to take things seriously.

We were all here to *learn* – especially me.

So come on!

I grabbed one of the condoms from the desk, and ripped open the foil as if I'd been a regular user for years! (Which, in reality, I had – they work so much better as water bombs than balloons! Most of which are, frankly, too thick!)

Are those the thoughts of someone being *serious*?

I cleared my mind of street-wide impromptu water fights and concentrated on the task at hand – literally!

For I had reached down to my trousers and undone my zip!

I closed my eyes and concentrated as I realised I would need to think only of *sexy thoughts*.

As my mind travelled to my bedroom where Louise was waiting for a full-on snogging session, Mr Upson rather rudely interrupted my attempted focus.

"Here, use this!" he said, handing me his banana.

Oh, *that's* why he'd got a banana out of his bag!

That certainly made more sense than making a School boy get his cock out in front of everyone!

I grabbed the banana in my left hand and squeezed the tip of the condom with the thumb and forefinger of my right hand. I then began an attempt to unroll it quickly down the bendy, yellow fruit.

As I did, I glanced at the round clock on the wall.

It was exactly ten to two – which ironically, according to the classic *Skid Row* song *"Psycho Love"*, is the exact angle female legs should be at during sex!

I sniggered to myself as I carried on my fast unrolling.

A couple of inches down the banana though the condom gave up on life and, for some reason, decided to break in two!

I had been aware of a growing undercurrent of sniggering as I'd been unrolling and it increased to a fairly loud burst of laughter as half of my condom shot up into the air!

"Ok!" said Mr Upson. "Stop right there! If that condom had snapped *during* intercourse there could have been some *dire* consequences. First of all, the sperm is no longer caught in the condom and can leak into the uterus meaning pregnancy is a *real* possibility. Secondly, if the condom is not removed quickly, there can be a real risk of infection. And any infection in the vaginal area can be very serious and can lead to foul discharge, itching and severe pain in the lower abdomen. In extreme cases it can result in potential problems with future reproduction. So, if it happens to anyone, you need to get to the Doctors as quickly as possible!"

There was a stony silence and a lot of horrified looking faces.

Wow – what a way to *kill a room*!

Any hints of giddiness had been well and truly ended with Mr Upsons, quite frankly, terrifying sex-gone-wrong tale of woe.

I looked over at Louise who was staring at me with a look that can only be described as a mixture of horror and bemusement.

What was wrong?

Had Mr Upsons frightening words scared her into thinking that she may now *never* want to have sex?

Was he on a one-man mission to *completely* ruin my life?

I could hear a bit more muttering coming from the back of the room that then led to quite a bit of, fairly loud, laughter.

Adam Hadfield then raised his arm high into the air.

"Hadfield?" said Mr Upson, probably wondering what other gruesome stories he could tell that could completely put us all off wanting any kind of sexual career!

"Could I give Paul a couple of pieces of advice?" said Adam.

"Yes!" said Mr Upson "I encourage *everyone* to participate!"

Adam stood up as if he was about to perform under a spotlight.

"One, unroll the condom more slowly, rather than trying to do it too quickly………and two, your knob's hanging out!"

I instinctively looked down as a nuclear-bomb intensity blast of laughter exploded in the classroom.

There it was, poking out of my unzipped trousers like an inquisitive Worm!

(I'd like to say *big* Worm but, in reality, it looked tiny! Just my luck to be having a *small* day when the whole World was watching!)

I tried to hear what my mind was saying but it was difficult, what with the loudest laughter that the World had ever heard spinning around the room!

Put it away. Put it away. Put it away. Put it away. Put it away. Put it away. Put it away. Put it away. Put it away. Put it away. Put it away. Put it away. Put it away. Put it away. Put it away. Put it away. Put it away………

I think it was telling me to put it away!

I put it away and then Sheepishly looked over to where Louise was.

The horror/bemusement look on her face had not changed at all.

I attempted to give her a little smile but it quickly turned into the nervous laughter of a manic lunatic!

I tried to reassure myself that my Goldfish-like memory probably wouldn't remember much of what had happened, hopefully, within a couple of hours!

Added to that, at least things couldn't get any *worse*.

I felt Mr Upsons hand slapping me on my shoulder.

"Get to Mr Langdens office – *right now!*"

Oh shit!

I'd managed to go four years and nine months without *ever* being sent to see our nut-job headmaster, but this was now the second time in *a week*!

And how the Hell would I explain *this one* to him……?

Chapter Seventeen - *"...sports day..."*

It was the end of May and most lessons were winding down because the Summer holidays were fast approaching. There was not a cloud in the sky; just a perfect lemon-slice Sun beating down underneath a flawless, blue canopy that stretched as far as the eye could see.

And today the School day was finishing at lunch time – because it was the worst day of the year!

Yes, it was *sports day*!

Not only would it be an afternoon full of "sport-themed activities", but it would also be witnessed by competitive parents, demanding their off-springs push for victory *at all costs*. The kind of over-zealous people who could easily be on Kilroy!

Maybe in an episode titled: *"My parents make me train for eight hours each day, so they can live their Olympic dream through me."*!

At least this year there had been proper "trials" to decide who competed in which event, instead of a repeat of last years "random draw".

I remember having nightmares for weeks following the three-legged race, in which I had been paired with a guy in my year called Robert Wilkes.

Although he was better known by his nickname of "*USSR*" - "Unbelievably, Stinky, Sweaty Rob"!

If the up-close blended stench of Body odour and greasy burgers didn't totally humiliate me; then the fact that he had forgotten his games kit and was running in just Y-fronts and a vest sealed the deal!

Being strapped to a 90% naked, foul scented boy, who was prone to profuse sweating, for over an hour in the baking Sun was not good for anyone's image.

Even mine!

Although hating these kinds of days, I was blessed with being a "natural athlete". I was equally comfortable with long-distance, sprinting and power-throwing, so I had decided to try out for a variety of events.

I entered the 100m, 200m, 800m, 1500m, javelin and hammer but, after coming last in each of these trials, I had to settle for either the high jump or the long jump!

There had been no try-outs for these events because,
A - the School had no real high-jumping equipment and,
B - all the sand from the long jump pit had been used on the car-park, during a *particularly* frosty week in February!

The School was expecting to fill the pit again on the morning of the sports day - Headmaster Mr Langden was returning from a weekend away in Blackpool, where he had taken a fair few buckets and spades with him! (Of course the pit would be made up of 50% sand and 50% Donkey shit – but I suppose it would be better than nothing!)

Because Mum had, at some point, heard a rumour about junkies that used to hang around the School, burying their needles in the sandpit, I had no choice

Goodbye B.M.X. Hello S.E.X.

anyway.

It would be the high jump for me!

Which was just as well really, because the other student who hadn't "qualified" for an event was Little Si. You couldn't realistically ask someone of Hobbit height to attempt the high jump!

He would be competing in the long jump.

Luckily enough for me, I had the perfect physique for taking on the high jump. I was tall, athletic and lean, while also being strong and graceful - almost Gazelle-like.

Although some preferred to describe this as "lanky"!

Whatever way, as I watched the jumping frame being constructed; it was to be made from two metre rulers sellotaped together in the middle - resting on books of differing heights, I felt supremely confident.

A small crowd of expectant parents began to gather round, in readiness for us to start the competition.

There were to be ten of us in the high jump, but with me being one of the oldest, I had an excellent chance of taking a medal.

In fact, there were only two others from my year. Rahilah - who I knew from my French class, and my "three-legged partner", the sweaty, stinkster himself – "USSR" Rob. Thankfully, this year, in t-shirt and shorts! (Although, it seemed, the concept of deodorant was still alien to him!)

As I scanned the faces in the growing group of adults, I soon came across four that I recognised. Along with Mum and Dad, who I knew were coming to watch (Dad had said that he could do with a good laugh!), Grandma and Grandad had also come to lend their support.

As I coolly waved at them, thinking it was nice that they could all get out on such a beautiful day, I couldn't help but feel their presence adding some extra pressure on me.

Until I saw the height that the first jump had been set at.

Mr Cartwright and Miss Randall, who were supervising the event, had propped the taped rulers up by what appeared to be just three thin books on each side. The "bar" would only be a couple of inches from the ground.

Was it even worth bothering?

A draw was quickly made to decide the jumping order, and my name came out last. (As it usually did during any kind of prize draw!)

But this time it would work to my advantage. I would be able to get a good look at my competition before I had to jump.

Everything was falling nicely into place.

The competition started and, one by one, my nine opponents easily cleared the bar - a couple of them almost just "stepping" over, it was *so* ridiculously low.

As I waited, I glanced around the field and looked at the multitude of activities that were going on.

There were kids throwing things, running, jumping, even hopping slowly along in over-sized hessian sacks, like injured Kangaroo's.

In the far distance, I could make out tiny figures starting a three-legged race. Although I could tell that all the competitors were appropriately attired, I couldn't stop myself shuddering!

I turned back round in time to be encouraged by Mr Cartwright to take my jump.

It was my turn.

Showtime!

"*Try and keep your knob in your trousers today!*" I heard being shouted from somewhere behind me.

I closed my eyes and tried to imagine that I hadn't heard it.

To say I'd received a bit of flak in the days between my humiliating sex education incident and now was something of an understatement.

I'd been laughed at more than a little boy who'd been covered in Seagull shit on his very first day at School! (Yep, that happened to *me* as well!)

If it wasn't also bad enough having all the School kids laughing at you, it seemed ten times worse having the Headmaster laughing at you. Yep, crazy-eyed Langden had laughed so hard when I explained to him why I had been sent to his office that the threat of being punished in any way was never even discussed.

Talk about *ultra*-embarrassing!

Having a certified lunatic laughing hysterically at *you*!

I think I would have preferred the cane!

To get through these days of humiliation, I'd tried to ignore every single comment (lots and lots of comments!) that had been directed my way.

And so I did the same today – and just focused on what was ahead of me.

I decided to tackle the jump properly and stretch my muscles nicely for the more challenging heights that lay ahead.

I approached at speed and, reaching my target zone, leapt high into the air. The only problem was, I had been too casual and left the take off a little late.

I caught the bar slightly.

Perhaps "slightly" was the wrong word because, the way the rulers flew way over the landing mat, it was almost like I had deliberately rugby kicked them.

Some sniggering broke out from the small crowd but Mr Cartwright, after collecting the bar from about twenty metres away, and taping it back together, said,

"Come on, go again. You get three attempts at each height!"

I returned to my starting point, laughing slightly myself at the ludicrousness of my failure.

I again ran quickly, but this time without the casual disrespect I had shown during the first attempt. I concentrated on beginning my leap at the right point, about 1.5 metres in front of the bar.

As I tried to leave the ground though, I slipped.

And not just a little; it was the kind of *spectacular* skid that you would only usually get from a sloppy Dog turd on a wet day!

Goodbye B.M.X. Hello S.E.X.

I crashed right into the bar and fell face first into the blue landing mat.

At least there was no sniggering this time - but that was only because there was significant, and *loud*, laughter!

I looked towards the front of the jump zone, wondering what it was I had slipped on. But there was nothing there.

The grass was dry and in more perfect condition than Wembley stadium.

In turn I cocked my legs up and looked at the sole of my trusty, old pumps.

The problem was obvious - the grips were somewhat worn.

In fact there was more baldness than a Right Said Fred look-a-like contest!

As I again trudged towards my run-up starting position, it may have just been psychological but, I felt like I was slipping all over the place.

I was suddenly *Bambi on Ice*!

I was in trouble.

I glanced over towards my fan club and looked at each of them, one at a time.

Grandma was smiling and muttering what looked like *"Good luck!"*.

Grandad was clapping and I could hear him saying *"You can do it!"*.

Mum looked embarrassed and was trying not to catch my eye, as if perhaps hoping that no one would realise that she was anything to do with me if she didn't look at me.

And Dad was waving an angry fist at me, which meant either *"Come on!"*, or that he wanted to punch me. (If I had to choose which one he did mean, it would probably be the latter!)

Behind them I could just about make out the stealth-like figure of Mr Langden, crawling in some long grass, his trusty binoculars held tight to the front of his head!

He was, no doubt, trying to catch out any parents reckless enough to be consuming food or drink on the School field!

Incredible!

Especially seeing as the School had set up a stall on the playground - *selling* drinks and snacks!

Well, I suppose Dad was in no danger of being caught, and reprimanded, by the crazy-eyed maniac.

No, Dad made a point of hardly ever carrying any money on him. In fact, he used to say he was *"just like the Queen!"*

Which he was!

He didn't carry money, and he was a lot like a grumpy, old woman!

I looked over towards the food and drink stall on the playground which had a fairly lengthy queue of people – who were all oblivious, potential victims of Langdens beady eyes!

Beyond the playground were the Tennis Courts where I'd played so many lunch-time games of footy and received more dead legs than I could care to remember.

Further over to the right was the long row of bike sheds, behind where I'd spent an uncountable number of hours during my School "career". From them being a good place to conceal yourself during first-year games of hide and seek, to later trying out, and spluttering on, cheap, knocked-off cigarettes, right through to recent and regular snogging sessions with Louise!

They were a place that held many memories.

As I thought about it, I realised that, although those memories would never fade, very soon there would be no new ones to add to them.

For my days at School were coming to an end.

These were now, truly, *the last days of School*!

"Come on, get on with it!"

Another rude shout came out of the crowd, aimed in my direction.

It was probably for the best really because, as I reminisced about old times and contemplated their end, I could almost feel a tear forming in my eye!

I took a deep breath and started again, running as carefully as I could.

I jumped *early* to compensate for any potential slippage.

I was up - soaring perfectly through the air.

But I was up too early.

Way too early!

I crash landed directly onto the rulers, splitting them back in two.

Laughter erupted from the crowd as if I had just told them the funniest joke they had ever heard.

I couldn't believe it. I had failed in all three attempts at this first height.

Even Rahilah had managed to get over the "token gesture" height - wearing a tightly fitting, full-length Sari!

I helplessly looked over at my entourage once more.

Grandma was still smiling and mouthing *"Good luck"* - I think it was clear she had no idea what was going on.

Grandad was clapping sympathetically and saying *"Never mind"*.

Mum was looking slightly shocked and disappointed, a little like the time when her "lucky dabber" ran out mid-game at Mecca bingo!

Dad on the other hand seemed now to be dealing with my failure a little better than before - he had joined in with those who were laughing the loudest.

Actually he appeared to be *leading* the laughter, and was attempting to start a chant of *"You're shit and you know you are!"*

I again felt moisture forming in my eyes which thankfully, at least, was blurring out the hysterical faces in the unforgiving crowd.

A lone voice, barely audible over the heartless Hyenas, shouted,

"Let him have another go!"

It was hard to decipher whether this was a sympathetic soul trying to lend me a hand, or some sarcastic joker just trying to rub my nose in it further.

As Miss Randall tried impatiently to find the end of her sellotape roll in preparation for repairing the high jump bar, Mr Cartwright made a beeline for my fellow competitors.

"Should we give him another chance?" he asked them.

No-one answered at first, all seemingly bemused that I had actually failed this two inch jump - *three times*!

Goodbye B.M.X. Hello S.E.X.

Rob eventually stepped forward and said,
"Yes let him go again."
Bless him!
I would've hugged him, if I couldn't clearly smell his festering armpits!
Mr Cartwright turned towards me,
"Stop messing, and bloody well jump over the thing - *last chance!*"
I blinked hard, trying to clear my eyes.
As I retreated down the run-path once more, I felt embarrassed and humiliated; confidence at an all time low.
"How's it going?" asked a gentle, velvety voice.
It was Louise approaching, obviously finished with her egg and spoon race, and judging by the gold medal around her neck, rather successfully so.
I cleared my throat and squinted my eyes in an attempt to hide any evidence of recent tears.
"It's just the first round," I said, making sure that no one could hear me, before continuing, "It's just my first attempt now."
"Ok, I'll let you get on with it." she said before giving me a kiss on the cheek and walking around to watch me from the side of the landing matt.
Thankfully she went to the opposite side to where my family were standing, because I'm sure that Dad would have revelled in recounting to her what she had just missed.
I focused on my "second chance"; or technically "fourth chance", and attacked the re-positioned bar once again.
This time I mastered the pump-skid and leapt over the bar as if it were just a couple of inches high. (Which, of course, it was!)
As my feet hit the landing mat, the people in the crowd cheered and clapped uncontrollably, as if I had just hit the winning shot at the Wimbledon final.
I looked at Louise who, although clapping gently, looked absolutely bemused by the euphoric reaction to me clearing such a low height.
I shrugged my shoulders at her as if I was equally confused.
I pointed to the medal around her neck and gave her a thumbs up to congratulate her.
She flashed me one of her huge smiles that always made me feel good whatever mood I was in.
I walked to the back of the other nine "jumpers" feeling a lot better about things. I was much more confident about how to jump in my friction free pumps; and was also pleased that Louise had excelled in an event featuring a spoon and an egg - which had to be a good indication of potential kitchen skills!
As the bar got higher something strange happened.
While others began to fail, I was now succeeding, and quite comfortably.
After six of the others had been eliminated, including Rahilah, who had to be lifted off the mat by two people, like a carpet, I was still clearing the bar with ease. (Although there were now increasing crowd mutterings of "*He shouldn't still be in this competition!*" and "*Bloody cheat!*" etc.)
I now realised why I had been given such long, gangly legs.

Gary Locke

It wasn't so that whenever I wore a pair of shorts Dad could say, "That reminds me, when we next go to the supermarket, we need some more spaghetti!", but rather that I was a *natural* at the high jump.

Who needed the Fosbury Flop when you could spring as high and naturally as a Cuban tree Frog!

The bar continued to get higher and, by the time we got to seven Bibles and five hard backed copies of War and Peace, there was just two of us remaining.

Me and USSR!

Both of us cleared the next couple of heights comfortably and, because the event was now threatening to last longer than a Catholic Christening!, Mr Cartwright decided it would be sudden-death.

A couple of Wuthering Heights were added, taking the total height up to around four and a half feet, and Rob prepared himself for his attempt.

As he was about to begin his run, I noticed that the shoelace on his left trainer had become undone.

There was real danger of him tripping on it.

He may injure himself, or perhaps even stumble as he jumped - which could make him knock the bar over.

My mind adjusted to dilemma mode.

To let him attempt the jump, with his lace undone, would seriously affect his chances of being successful - and therefore enhance my chances of winning the competition.

On the other hand, though, he may injure himself if he falls badly.

Could I let him do that?

Especially as his compassion and generosity was the main reason that I had actually stayed in the competition earlier on.

It wasn't a hard decision.

I did the only thing I could in the situation I was in - the decent thing!

Before he started his run I told him that his lace was undone....................as quietly as I possibly could!

I'm not sure even Superman would have heard me!

Rob certainly didn't.

He tripped face first into the bar, sending the rulers and several books flying in various directions.

Miss Randall, after taking a deep intake of air and holding her breath, ran to his side because it was obvious that he had injured his leg.

What had I done to him?

Mr Cartwright turned and shouted,

"Can we have the stretcher over here please?"

I looked round and saw that the stretcher was actually already in use.

At the long jump pit, two parents were carrying Little Si, who suspiciously looked like he had a hypodermic needle hanging from his back side!

As I turned back, Rob was gingerly returning to his feet.

"I'm alright" he said, rubbing his right leg vigorously.

He wasn't too bad - I was ok.

Goodbye B.M.X. Hello S.E.X.

Conscience clear.
The high jump was rebuilt, and I was one leap away from victory.
I took one last look at the people who were willing me on.
Grandma and Grandad standing together, arms around each other.
Mum, at last, looking in my direction.
Dad, attempting to start a slow hand clap, because he obviously felt I was taking too long over my jump!
And opposite them Louise, still smiling more brightly than the unimpeded Sun.
By clearing this one last jump, I could make them *all* proud of me.
At the same time I would be earning myself a shiny, eighteen carat gold-look medal - that would look fantastic in my display cabinet next to my Jim'll Fix It badge! (Which wasn't actually *my* badge, but was one that Dad had picked up cheap at a car boot sale. Despite numerous letters to Jimmy I'd never even had any response, let alone an appearance on his show. I wonder *how* he selected who would be the ones he wanted to "fix" things for?!?)
I took a deep breath and set off; trying to repeat the successful technique from my previous efforts.
Head down, running carefully but fast, concentrating on the approaching bar.
I reached the take off point and put the pressure on my right leg. The smooth underside of my pump held firm, as I flexed my muscles and sprung into the air like a tightly wound jack-in-the-box.
I soared effortlessly, sensing the taped rulers passing several inches beneath me.
As I landed perfectly on my feet, I wondered whether performing a somersault would appear a little cocky!
I decided not to do one as it may frustrate those in the crowd who believed that I should have been out of the competition after those first, disastrous jumps.
Well that and the fact that I didn't know how to even attempt a somersault; and I decided that a roly-poly probably wouldn't be, in any way, nearly as spectacular!
I settled for putting my arms in the air.
I glanced at Louise who was beaming and pointing to her own gold medal, indicating that I would be receiving one to match.
Mum and Grandad were cheering and Dad, next to them, was actually jumping up and down. The only other time I had seen him do this was when he was trying to be noticed in the crowd at the Bulls Head, when they were giving away some free beer!
Grandma was still smiling and mouthing "Good luck"!
I closed my eyes and soaked in the moment.
I was the last man standing.
The winner.
Number one!

I may have arrived at my gold medal via an unusual journey, but it didn't matter.

It was also nice to welcome that another potential career path had opened up for me.

Paul Day, Olympic high jump champion.

That has a nice ring to it…..

Goodbye B.M.X. Hello S.E.X.

June 1992

June rolled in with just one word on everybody's lips and on everybody's minds: *exams*.

It was like there was nothing else going on in the whole World; like everyone had stopped what they were doing to wait for us to sit our GCSE's.

The next few weeks were going to shape the destiny of every fifth year School-student in the country.

Including mine!

Those exam dreads that had been slowly creeping up were now banging on the door!

But I'd had five years of going to High School - which roughly worked out as 950 days, or 4750 hours of the best education that this Country could offer.

So surely after that amount of work, the exams would be a walk in the park?

Why then, did I feel *less* than prepared?

Why, in fact, did I feel like I did the time that I had forgotten my trunks for a Junior School swimming lesson?

The time I was *encouraged* to swim anyway - in my brown Y-fronts!

Brown Y-fronts that were clearly too big for me!

The time when, said Y-fronts would slip off every time I tried to move in the water - and float around like a brown Lilly pad?

Why, if the exams were to be a walk in the park, did I feel as vulnerable and exposed as a naked kid in a swimming pool - with all his class mates laughing, pointing and staring.

Or, unfortunately more accurately, squinting! (The water was *very cold!*)

It took two years to shake off my "Cocktail Sausage" nickname!

Yet, here I was feeling just as inadequate again.

I tried to tell myself that, despite the looming shadow of doubt, I still had a few days before my first exam.

A few days to re-learn 4750 hours of forgotten education!

Chapter Eighteen - *"...exams..."*

The morning alarm sounded, in the unique way that it does on Monday mornings. Somehow louder, more high-pitched and harsher than on the other days of the week.

It was like the alarm was mocking me that the weekend was over!

I reached over and calmly turned it off.

It didn't bother me the way that it usually did, because I didn't need to get up straight away - there was no School for me today.

I was on exam leave.

There was no more School for me – forever!

(I now know what Alice Cooper feels like!)

I heard frantic movement coming from Brother Simon's room, but I wasn't fazed. I didn't need to take part in the bathroom race.

I smiled to myself smugly as I heard him sprint from his room.

It sounded like he stumbled and fell on the landing, (that would have been nice to see!) before entering the bathroom - no doubt revelling in his "non-existent" victory.

No, I could just turn over in my warm bed content that I could get up when I eventually felt like it.

In fact, I had no idea why I had even set my alarm so early.

As I snuggled into the duvet, I realised there was a reason why I had set it for such a time.

My first exam was just two days away.

It was French; and my French vocabulary was about as impressive as Del-boy Trotters!

I fidgeted around.

I should get up.

I had set the alarm so I would be able to get in a full days revision, (or more accurately, a full days *learning*) not waste the morning away in bed.

But my bed was so *warm and comfortable - five more minutes* couldn't do any harm, could it?

But how many times had I done this? When five minutes had turned into two hours in the blink of an eye?

My conscience was having a full blown argument with itself.

I was like a cartoon character with a Devil on one shoulder and an Angel on the other.

I was interested to see which one of them would win, so I snuggled up and listened to them fighting it out.

I had set my alarm fully expecting to get up *early*. My books were ready on the computer desk - I should get up and make a start like I had planned!

Not bad from the Angel!

But the fact I was even thinking this through meant I was still *tired*. We had been told many times by various teachers that you should <u>never</u> try to revise

Goodbye B.M.X. Hello S.E.X.

when tired, because you do not retain the information!

(I think that the advice was probably more aimed at preventing students staying up too late, rather than encouraging them to stay in bed of a morning! - but, nevertheless, it was *real advice*.)

Therefore I should set the alarm for an hour later; doze off in my *lovely, warm, comfortable* bed, and then get up feeling refreshed and ready to work *properly!*

It was hard to see how the Angel could recover from that - it was surely an unchallengeable argument.

It was like the Devil had given a Perry Mason-like court room closing speech!

The Angel played its Joker though.

You get *one chance* at these exams.

If you *don't* pass them, you *don't* go to College.

If you *don't* go to College, then Louise will be there *on her own*.

On her own - with all those guys like *Dave Barlow!*

I was up - quick as a flash!

I was dressed and sitting at my desk, faster than a ferret up a pair of bell bottoms!

As prepared the previous evening - my books were already waiting for me.

The French-English / English-French dictionary, the French GCSE syllabus, my French exercise book and Dads book on the French Revolution. (Which probably would be of no use, but who knows?)

To help me get into the French way of thinking; I had also put a small French flag up on my bedroom wall (cut out of my Panini World Cup 1990 sticker album!), as well as borrowing an old beret Mum used to wear (she was a big fan of Frank Spencer!) and having the first two series of 'Allo 'Allo ready to play through my video.

I also had several bottles of Lucozade on stand by, to ensure that my energy levels were kept high.

All I needed was the desire – check.

The commitment – check.

And, most importantly, the brain power - there was always a snag!

I wondered whether there was anyone who could help me.

There was no point speaking to any of the guys - Mark and Little Si didn't do French, and John was every bit as shit at it as I was.

Mum and Brother Simon couldn't help - they were at work; and Dad had said, on several occasions, the only French he knew well, was the *kissing!* (He was such a cliché at times!)

Unfortunately for me, French was also not a subject that Louise was taking - because, if she was, she definitely would have been able to help.

She was much more organised than me.

She had worked out a revision time-table that factored in every single second over the next two weeks. She had even set aside time for meals and sleeping; and even some (very short) breaks in which I could see or speak to

Gary Locke

her.

I tried to remember some of the revision advice she had given me.

She recommended that you should always start by focussing on your weaknesses.

That wasn't going to narrow things down for me!

I needed a plan.

I began to vaguely remember an episode of Grange Hill in which one of the characters was selling answers to the exam questions. It turned out that he was giving the other students answers to the wrong questions; but something he said had stuck with me.

"If you don't know *everything* - just make sure you know *what you need!*"

I think he was on to something.

There was no way I could learn *everything*, so I had to learn something *that I needed*.

The biggest percentage of marks for the French exam came from the Speaking Examination - the "conversation" that lasted five minutes.

If I knew roughly what my first question would be, and could prepare myself an answer that enabled me to speak for a couple of minutes, using some fancy words, maybe deliberately change tenses a couple of times, throw in a lot of deep sounding "errrrs!" and "eoouugghhhs!", I may be on to a winner.

I wracked my brain.

What did I do in most of the French lessons? (Apart from playing connect four under the desk with John?)

I tried to think about what my French teacher, Mr Martin, used to talk about a lot.

(Well I say "French" teacher - he was actually Scottish; and he sounded like the voice-over guy from the *Irn Bru* adverts. It was hard enough trying to understand what he was saying in English - let alone French!)

My mind pulled something out of its abyss-like memory bank: *holidays*.

He often spoke about holidays, and even said that it was a popular examination subject.

I couldn't be sure whether this was actually true, or if it was just something my brain had made up in an attempt to stop me pushing it so hard!

Either way, I had to give it a go.

I had somewhere to start.

I cracked open the first Lucozade, plonked Mum's beret on my head, and set about scouring my exercise book for everything there was about holidays.

By the end of the day I had come up with something pretty good.

In response to the question

"Ou vas-tu en vacances cette annee?"

(Where are you going on holiday, this year?), I had over two minute's worth of quality response.

About going to Prestatyn with my family; with in depth details about Mum, Dad and Brother Simon. (Not *so* in depth that it would scare the Examiner, mind you!)

Goodbye B.M.X. Hello S.E.X.

About staying in a caravan and all about what we would do while we were there. (Obviously made up. No one wants to hear about four people sitting inside for a week, listening to the rain!)

About where we'd been in the past and where I would like to go in the future. (Anywhere but bloody Prestatyn!)

It was pretty good, if I did say so myself.

If I could coax the Examiner into asking me that question, or something similar, I was in business.

It wasn't actually *cheating*.

It would only be cheating if I handed over some money as I did the "coaxing".

It had been a good day's work.

I may, however, have drunk a bit too much Lucozade while putting the answer together.

It can't be normal to have orange coloured urine can it?

I spent most of Tuesday making sure that I knew my "conversation" off by heart. I did have a five minute phone call "window" in Louise's revision timetable (which didn't last *one* second over!); other than that, it was pure French learning.

Louise had told me that she was really nervous about her first exam, History, which was also on Wednesday.

I couldn't help feeling a little smug, because I now felt reasonably confident. She had all these fancy timetables and schedules to keep to when, all along, all she really needed was a Grange Hill-inspired plan!

I felt so good that I slept perfectly well on Tuesday night.

I got up promptly at the Wednesday morning alarm call - my little devils argument of *"Who the Hell in the World wants to speak to the French?"*, while technically correct, didn't really delay my rise!

I even beat Brother Simon into the bathroom - which is always doubly satisfying when he bangs on the door shouting he's "desperate"!

I made a point of walking to School with John.

We had been through five years of French lessons, sitting side by side - I wasn't going to desert him now.

Besides, Louise's History exam wasn't until the afternoon!

John and I tried to put ourselves at ease as we walked, by reciting commonly used French words to each other.

I was put at ease by the fact that he was as rubbish as I was!

On top of that - I had a plan!

We arrived at the School Hall, where we joined countless numbers of students wearing concerned and nervous looks.

It was a similar scene to the one last year when everyone in my year had to have their BCG injections repeated.

I remember it well, because I had a bad reaction to mine.

After administering my jab, the "sympathetic" doctor laughed and shouted "WE'VE GOT A BLEEDER!", as blood poured from my arm; not too dissimilar

Gary Locke

looking to a punctured carton of Ribena!

At least it helped to cement my tough guy image - walking past a queue of panicking, still-to-be-injected students, with blood trailing down my arm - somehow hiding the fact that my head was feeling fuzzy and my legs were buckling a little!

Within fifteen minutes of arriving; crazy-eyed Langden had explained to us we were taking the "written" part of the French exam, all together in the hall; before being taken separately into classrooms for the all important "speaking" part.

Before I knew it, I was sitting in a queue waiting to be called for my "conversation".

The written exam had passed without a hitch - if that meant the same thing as "passed without a correct answer!"

The fact I was less than confident about the written part, meant there was even more resting on my "plan".

Luckily for me I wasn't the nervous type, and as I waited I felt cooler than a shopping trolley full of cucumbers!

Who was I kidding - I was more jittery than Stuart Pearce and Chris Waddle during a penalty shootout!

I didn't have too long to suffer though.

Within a couple of minutes my name had been called.

At least I think it was my name; the accent that the shout had come from was, although familiar, a little difficult to understand. The voice could have called my name but could also, just as easily, have shouted "Made from Girders!"

At least that recognizable, Scottish drawl meant one thing - my "conversation" would be with Mr Martin.

Surely he would play along with my plan. Surely it had to look good on him, if more of his students passed the exam?

This was a good thing.

Nevertheless, despite this seemingly positive turn of events, I walked into the "classroom of destiny" with my legs feeling like they had been donated to me from a Jelly Baby!

I sat down as Mr Martin took a new tape off a shelf and began to remove the plastic wrapping.

Now was the time to ask him - before he got the tape into the recorder sitting on the desk.

"Mr Martin," I began, with a croaky voice. "If at all possible, could you start by asking me a question about where I'm going on holiday this year? Or about holidays in general?"

I got the words out as quickly as possible, and was almost afraid to watch for his response.

I was right to be apprehensive; the disappointed frown that formed on Mr Martins face was not the reaction that I had hoped for.

He didn't say any words, instead indicated that he was putting the tape into

Goodbye B.M.X. Hello S.E.X.

the machine, and was about to begin recording.

I wondered whether it was worth trying to slip a tenner across the desk, but it was too late, he began talking.

"Paul Day.....French Oral Examination.....Wednesday, June 3rd 1992.....11.07 am."

It was like a police interrogation.

Shouldn't I be allowed a solicitor?

At the very least I should be allowed a phone call.

I DEMAND A PHONE CALL!

Luckily the shout was only in my mind, as Mr Martins words brought me back to the fact that I was in an exam.

Surprisingly, he spoke clearly and I was able to understand every word.

"Ou vas-tu en vacances cette annee?"

I couldn't believe it - it was word for word as I had prepared.

The plan was up and running!

After finishing the question, Mr Martin even winked at me.

And it was quite a good one - maybe, in exceptional circumstances, teachers could be added to my list of those who can pull off winking!

I began my answer - trying to make it sound like it wasn't rehearsed, but rather like I was thinking it through as I went.

Although I probably wasn't quite ready for the French version of "The Archers", I was pleased with how my "acting" for the tape was going.

I was helped along by Mr Martin's encouraging nods but, as I continued, I began to wonder about his "wink".

I assumed that it was just a sign to show he was helping me out - a gesture from the goodness of his heart.

But what if it *didn't* mean that?

What if he did it to show that I now actually owed him something?

And, if so, what?

If it was the tenner I had considered slipping him, then that was fine.

If Mr Martin had something else in mind, perhaps even something physical, I would have to give careful consideration before accepting.

How much did a pass in French mean to me?

Luckily, I didn't have to explore that question; because Mr Martin didn't demand payment of *any* sort following the exam.

Instead he just congratulated me, and said I had given one of the best conversations he had heard this year.

(It seemed sadly ironic that now, when five years of lessons were over, I was finally getting a grip on understanding his accent!)

I thanked him for his "help", but he dismissed it, saying,

"I ooonlee assed ye summit frome m'querston lissed" (He only asked me something from his question list! - I think!)

He wished me good luck for the rest of my exams, and shook my hand.

What a lovely man.

Why does it take the realisation that the teaching is over for teachers to

Gary Locke

become, well, un-teacher like?

The other eight of my exams were spread over the following twelve days - almost like an Olympic Decathlon.

Or perhaps, more accurately, an Olympic Enneathlon - which Daley Thompson always competed at for Britain. (He always pulled out of *one* event injured!)

I approached them with similar tactics - cram in as much information as possible leading in, developing "plans" where possible.

The results were, at best, mixed.

A mix of mini-successes (there was a whole section on William Blake for the written English Literature exam!) and major-failures (everything else!)

At least I didn't have any panic attacks - like the one Daniel Gleaves had during the Maths exam.

He was hyperventilating so much he had to use his brown paper bag. He had his head so far in the bag, he looked like a horse having lunch!

It was almost as though he had written his Maths formulas inside the bag, and was reading them back to himself.

Genius!

Why didn't I come up with a plan like that?

When Geography, my final exam, was over, I was physically and mentally drained.

I did the only thing possible to make me feel like all the effort was worth it - I set off the School fire alarm!

Those "for emergency break glass" boxes are tougher than they look!

I almost had to give up after four "embarrassing" attempts.

Fortunately it was fifth time lucky - I didn't want a failed alarm-set-off attempt to by *my* lasting School legacy!

How had I done, overall, in the exams?

Chances were: Not Great.

But there were two words that kept my spirits up - "multiple choice".

Most of the exams had multiple choice sections, and I think it was reasonable to believe - where there was guessing, there was hope!

It was no use worrying about it anyway.

It was all over.

It would be 69 days before the results came out; which meant there would be 69 days of, perhaps for the final time, freedom.

It would be our very own "Summer of '69", and it was time to live a little.

And it would start on Friday 19th June with a huge, end of exams party.

Appropriately at Tattington Park......

Goodbye B.M.X. Hello S.E.X.

Chapter Nineteen - *"...Father Christmas and the Tooth Fairy..."*

As the end of exams party was going to be at Tatty Park, I decided to stick with tradition.

Although Louise was going to go, I said no to walking with her; because I wanted to go with John, Mark and Little Si.

As such, we met at Marks house.

Not for the usual two reasons but, this night, because of three.

1...As usual, his parents were out.
2...As usual, we could pay his Brother, Daz, extortionate rates for getting us some Diamond White cider.
3...The reason Marks parents were out tonight was, in part, due to the fact that they were getting divorced!

They had waited until Marks exams were over before announcing it, but had apparently both been having affairs for several years!

As we sat in the living room, watching a video of Roy "Chubby" Brown in concert on Marks Dad's huge new TV, the mood was somewhat subdued.

As we cooed about the size of the television (it was like a cinema within the house!), Mark sombrely explained to us that his Dad always had to have the latest technology.

He had said to Mark he was going to get an HD (High Definition) set when they became available.

John, Little Si and I sat there some what perplexed.

We had no idea what he was talking about.

It was like being in an exam all over again!

Mark explained that, apparently, "HD" is *the future,* and is like having the real action within *your room!* You are supposed to be able to see every small detail – like every individual blade of grass on a big field. You actually get to see things *exactly* as they are.

It all sounded very impressive, but I was content enough with my Television – happy that I no longer had my old, fuzzy, black and white set.

Teletext was the height of extravagance for me!

How good is Teletext?

It's one of those genius things that you just *know* will be around forever!

As we took our first few harsh sips of Diamond White, the atmosphere was hardly reflective of the quality of the comedy on show; or indeed the promised *wild night* ahead.

Mark almost seemed suicidal as he contemplated what the future may hold for him.

"I know we're all entering a new chapter in our lives - but why does it have to be one that is so *different?*" he asked.

None of us answered.

Gary Locke

I don't think he wanted us to.

I felt BT's advice was best for this situation - sometimes "It's Good To Talk!", so I let him get on with it.

"No more School. Mum and Dad splitting up. Don't know which one I'll live with." he sighed. "They have both put their cases across for living with them to me and Daz. Neither of them were that convincing - I think they both actually want us to live with the other one!"

I laughed, thinking he was joking.

By the shocked and hurt look on his face - it was obvious he wasn't.

I decided to go back to silence.

"We won't be living in this house anymore - they're going to sell it." Mark continued. "Not sure where we'll end up living. If I end up somewhere far away, it may be difficult to see you all as much - until I can drive next year."

He gave me a sly look that said *"Except perhaps for you, Paul - seeing as you no longer come out with us as much as you used to anyway!"*

He didn't *say* the words.

Presumably because he didn't want an argument.

"Why do things always have to change?" he added.

Nobody spoke for the next few minutes, perhaps because we were all contemplating Marks last question.

Eventually Little Si reached forward and picked up the TV remote control off the coffee table. (Or was it possibly a "cider table" tonight?)

He cranked up the volume and soon the giant screen, surround-sounded comedy had us in a better frame of mind.

A few smutty jokes raised the spirits, and when we were all near the end of our second bottle of Diamond White, a Chubby line about having "a twelve inch tongue, and being able to breath through his ears!" had us all rolling around on the floor.

I'm not really sure what it meant, but it's hard not to laugh when everyone else is!

It marked the sign that *we were ready*.

The cider "haze" was coming, and we were all hyped up - we were ready for the Park.

The walk was pretty much as it always was - slow, a bit staggery, waving at passers by and talking cider-fuelled gibberish that made us laugh.

John, after a thoughtful pause, even said "If things *are* all changing, maybe I'll get to snog Zoë tonight!"

We all took a couple of seconds to think about what he had said - before bursting out laughing; none of us more uncontrollably than John himself.

Everything was just as it always was - we were going to have a great night!

We arrived at the entrance to the Park and could see the main field literally jam-packed with people.

There were at least three times as many faces as on a usual Friday night.

We swaggered down towards the swing area where, as usual, several of the girls we knew from School were hanging out.

Goodbye B.M.X. Hello S.E.X.

"Good evening!" John said loudly; rather similar to an old-fashioned Police Constable.

Zoë Pott and Vicky Starr, not put off by Johns authoritative greeting, made their way towards us.

Because it was a special occasion, we had got five bottles of Diamond White each tonight. Whether that was pushing it too far, only time would tell.

I still had a full bottle in each of my jean pockets. I felt like a Cowboy with a loaded gun on each hip!

As we were chatting to the girls, I noticed Mark sneaking off.

I began to follow him, wondering if he was feeling a bit down again and perhaps needed company.

He quickly sat on a vacant swing, next to Kim Bell - who was also on her own.

I looked back at John and Little Si who were laughing along with Vicky and Zoë. I decided to leave them all to it for a few minutes.

I made my way to the roundabout where I had got to know Louise - all those weeks ago.

I sat down and slowly cracked open one of my "Loaded" Diamond Whites. I took a long, slow sip as I leant back and looked around the Park.

It was fantastic.

There were faces in the crowd that I had never seen here before.

Rob Swain, Jon Dowson, Zoë Cooligan and Emma Hadfield, who had all been in my class in Junior School, but I hadn't really had much contact with at high School. They were all here for the first time ever and seemed to be enjoying themselves, giddily sipping away at, what looked like, Carlsberg Special Brew.

Ouch that will hurt them all come the morning!

I looked further round and noticed Charlie Deighton and Clive Quinn and there was Richard Rowe, no doubt impressing / repulsing people with his "party trick" – a freakishly, scary double jointed finger!

Closer to the stream were two faces who were fairly regular visitors to the park. Andy Blundell, no doubt sipping away at his usual cocktail of mixed spirits, siphoned from his parents' drinks cabinet, for which he always stuck a label on, reading *"Death In A Bottle"*!

Next to him was Matt Garnett, although he looked like his head was placed firmly in a hedge! No doubt a result of him having had too many swigs from Andy's bottle!

I chuckled to myself as I continued looking around.

Over by the tennis courts, quite separated from everyone else, were Johan Tiplady and Anthony Taylor, two guys who I knew from my C.D.T. class.

Although my eyesight wasn't the best, it looked very much like they were holding hands!

What the Hell is *that* all about?

Beyond them I saw Gemma Wilson entering the park, no doubt listening to her walkman.

Gary Locke

She always had her portable music player with her and whenever you asked to listen to it, it always seemed to be *Midnight Oil's "Bed's Are Burning"*!

Great song, but she must have played it to death by now!

Wow all these *new* faces along side the regulars.

It would be great to talk to many of them later - see if they were enjoying themselves; ask them why they hadn't been here before, and why they were here *now*.

As I thought about it though, I realised that I didn't need to ask them any of those questions.

I knew the answers already.

They were here because the exams were over.

They were here because it was the *last party*.

For many, their first time here would also be their last time.

And I realised that there were many, many faces here that I could see, laughing, joking, having fun, that I would probably never see again.

Ever!

In my whole life!

Because there were no more days at School.

No more lessons.

No more exams.

No more detentions.

There would be no more *fun behind the bike sheds*!

There would be no more parties, for us, *here*.

Before long, Tatty Park would be the place for the *next generation*.

No longer us - because our time will have passed.

Mark was right.

Everything *was* going to change; and it was actually beginning *right now*.

The World was turning fast, and there was no way of stopping it.

From my seat on the roundabout, I could see things how they really were!

But I instantly wished that I *couldn't*.

Because it felt like Father Christmas and the Tooth Fairy all over again.

You know, that first time when you are told for sure, despite the rumours and your suspicions, that Father Christmas doesn't actually exist.

And straight away you have, forever, lost a sense of wonder.

There may be a relief that you can stop worrying about magic keys being lost or stolen!, but that relief is drowned in the shadow that is the *loss of innocence*.

I remember clearly the day I realised that the Tooth Fairy wasn't real.

I had lost a tooth, but had not told anyone about it - on purpose.

I wanted to prove that there *was* a Tooth Fairy.

I left it under my pillow as usual - but woke up the next morning to find it was still there.

There was no five pence coin like there had been whenever Mum and Dad had known about one of my previous teeth falling out. (I had known some kids who were left twenty pence - but I had always assumed our Tooth Fairy was

Goodbye B.M.X. Hello S.E.X.

hard up, or was maybe a little tight!)

But the reality was - there was *no reality.*

It wasn't real.

All that was left, apart from a manky baby tooth, was the empty feeling of the truth - and the wish that I hadn't had to see things the way they really were.

Perhaps ignorance *is* bliss.

My deep thoughts were broken by the energetic and excited voice of Little Si.

"I've heard that "USSR" is here. Do you want to come and help us throw him in the stream?"

I pondered for a second.

"Unbelievably, Sweaty, Stinky, Rob" had actually helped me greatly on my way to winning the high jump gold medal during Sports Day. I couldn't realistically throw his help back in his face as I threw him in the stream.

That would just be immature.

Something a care-free, ignorantly blissful, innocent child would do.

"Hell, yes!" I said, and giggled along with Little Si, Mark and John as we raced off towards where "USSR" had been spotted.

Later, as we reflected on a reasonably successful stream dispatch; the only slight problem being that Rob couldn't swim, and he had to be pulled out of the water by a man passing with his Dog, (although he must have smelt *much better* afterwards!) I tried to breathe in the moment.

It was quite possible that these would be the best days of my life.

Carefree; having fun with my friends.

After a while Mark sneaked off and, to everyone's astonishment, began snogging Kim on the roundabout.

My roundabout!

Obviously buoyed on by his success, John and Little Si asked if I minded if they went to find Vicky and Zoë.

"Of course not." I said, although mentally noting the moment for when they next accused me of deserting *them*!

I sat on one of the swings and watched them for a few minutes.

They quickly found Zoë and Vicky and, as they chatted away, from a distance at least, it looked like they were both doing pretty well. Neither of them had been slapped in that time - which was certainly an improvement on past efforts!

It wasn't long before I saw Louise entering the Park with Abbey Trueman and Lisa Bell.

I waved at her but, instead of walking to meet her, I stayed sat in the swing.

I knew I would be with her in about minute; but I wanted those sixty seconds to myself.

I took a swig from my bottle and leaned back, letting the Summer breeze gently caress my face.

I slowly looked around again, scanning the whole Park.

I gazed at my friends, and at everyone else who was there, and I soaked up the wonderful atmosphere that was quietly, but vibrantly buzzing.

But as I did, I had to accept that it wouldn't be so far in the future, that all of this would just be another tainted childhood memory.....

Goodbye B.M.X. Hello S.E.X.

HD

I'm not sure that I'll get HD,
The World I see is o.k. with me,
I don't want to see the dust in this place,
Or a couple of little lines on your face.

Maybe it's not all it's hyped up to be,
The World I see is o.k. with me.

The sky doesn't need to be bluer than blue,
Like it's something that's shiny and newer than new,
No, I want to look up and see the sky,
The way that it has been, for all of my life.

Not sure it's what I want to see,
The World I see is o.k. with me.

Maybe with HD I could see into your eyes,
Zoom so far in, I could tell when you told lies,
But sometimes it's the truth, that pierces your heart,
Sometimes it's much better, to be left in the dark.

Not sure it's for me, this HD,
The World I see is o.k. with me.

We don't need to see a close up of the moon,
If it shows man's never been there, that we have all just been fooled,
I remember when I was told, Father Christmas wasn't real,
It left a hole in my soul, that can never be healed.

No, there's no way that I'll get HD,
The World I see is o.k. with me.

Chapter Twenty - *"...en-suite hostage..."*

His sweaty lower back slowly moved up again before, once more, purposefully thrusting back down.

As it did, she again groaned as he reached deep within her.

"Oh yes!" she panted. "That's it, my lover! That's it!"

His back raised and lowered, raised and lowered, raised and lowered.

Each time slowly and with the precision of a metronome.

"Yes, my lover!" she moaned again. "That's it! Keep going.........keep going my lover!"

She reached up and stabbed her long fingernails into his wild blonde hair.

The dim, bedside lamp began to slowly rattle to the rhythm of the sex, whilst subtly projecting their two interlocked bodies onto the ceiling.

Two sets of hastily removed clothes remained scattered across the wooden bedroom floor, exactly where impatient hands had thrown them.

I continued to watch as his back, once again, raised into the air.

This time though, he stopped.

He was totally still.

She removed her hands from his head, leaving his blonde hair standing up.

"Keep going, my lover!" she whispered. "Keep going!"

"I can't!" he gasped. "It's my bloody asthma! I'm wheezing more than bloody Mutley!"

"Who's Mutley?" she asked.

"You know, that Dog that hangs out with Dick Dastardly!"

"Who's Dick Dastardly?" she asked.

"You know – from the Wacky Races!" he replied, his voice almost disappearing into an inaudible rasp.

"The what, what?" she asked.

"You know, the *Wacky Races* – with Penelope Pitstop, the Anthill Mob and…"

"I don't care!" she said, cutting him off mid-sentence. "What I *do* care about is – you're not stopping now – I'm nearly *there*!"

He leaned over to his left and fumbled around in his jacket that was abandoned at the side of the bed, eventually pulling out a blue inhaler spray.

Two puffs and a deep inhaling breath and then he returned to his upright position, seemingly refreshed and ready to go again.

"*I'm* going on top!" she said, reaching her hands up to his shoulders. "I'm not letting you have a bloody asthma attack while on top of me!"

She rolled him over to his left and, in a fairly impressive wrestling-like maneuver, emerged on top without appearing to *de-engage*! (I've seen a lot of wrestling and most of the time it seems like a big excuse for scantily dressed, over muscled men to fondle each other – also rolling around hoping not to *de-engage*!)

Now she was on top I could see her a bit more clearly.

Goodbye B.M.X. Hello S.E.X.

The first thing I noticed was her tied up dark hair and a picture of a large Dragonfly that was tattooed on her right shoulder.

Damn it was tacky!

Perhaps yet more evidence that the whole tattoo (on me!) idea was probably a none starter. (Especially seeing as they can sometimes last forever and can, apparently, hurt like Hell!)

My right eye began to feel strained after several minutes of squinting through the keyhole, so I swapped to my left eye and waited for the action, in its new position, to start again.

I'm not sure *why* I was even watching.

I suppose because it would feel wrong to pass up the chance of watching a free, live porn show. Even if it was turning into one with health handicaps and obscure references to a 1960's cartoon!

(Albeit a bona fide *classic*!)

The only experience of porn movies I'd had were old films that Neil Jacksons Dad used to keep stored in an old pram in the porch of their house.

The understanding was that you could take what you wanted as long as you left a pound note for each one you did.

Some were ok to watch but, for most of them, the quality of the picture was pretty grainy. Which sometimes was a blessing because a lot of them seemed to involve chains and whips, and all kinds of nasty weapons, that always seemed to be used for causing naked men pain!

It was enough to put you off sex for life!

How the Hell does anyone enjoy *that* kind of thing!

There's no way I'd end up in a relationship where sex was more focused on *pain* rather than pleasure!

She leaned back towards an angle that looked like it must have been, at least, *uncomfortable* for him, before starting to bob up and down.

He didn't make any noise at all. He was either used to having his dick bent right back or was in the early throws of *that* asthma attack!

Her idea of the perfect rhythm was certainly faster than his and, from my vantage point, she didn't look too dissimilar to a naked, tackily-tattooed woman riding a pogo stick!

As she bounced up and down her back rippled loosely like a not-quite-yet-set jelly!

Errghh!

"Oh yes, my lover!" she said, much louder. "That's definitely it!......Oh yes!"

She spoke whilst at the same time throwing her head back and rotating it from left shoulder to right, perhaps readying herself for the full-on Meg Ryan treatment!

And I caught the first real glimpse of her *face*!

I recoiled immediately from the keyhole and scrambled back to the wall behind me, narrowly missing banging my head on the toilet.

Oh my God!

I wanted to rip my eyes out!

Gary Locke

And, as the panting and "Oh yes, my lover!" began again, I would have ripped my ears off if I had a pair of pliers to hand. (Or had Gary Lineker-esque ears that you could get a good hold of with multiple hands!)

It's not because her face was grotesquely ugly that I now wanted to rip out / off my primary sense organs. No, she was very attractive – for an *older* woman.

It's because, after seeing her face, I realised I knew *who* she was.

There seems to be something acceptable, and arousing, about watching two strangers *going for it*. When it's someone you actually *know*, then it's a whole different story.

(I tried to clear my mind before it had chance to horrify me with another replay of, what is shamefully known as, the *Mum-and-Dad-after-pub-night-of-June-'86-kitchen-"bang"-last-time-I-ever-go-for-a-midnight-glass-of-R-Whites* incident!)

This time, thankfully, it wasn't *my* Mum but, perhaps even more problematically, it was Louise's Mum!

Yes, I had just been staring through a door keyhole watching my girlfriends Mum having sex!

What was worse still was the man she was having sex with.

I hadn't seen *his* face but was pretty sure about one thing.

He *wasn't* Louise's Dad!

Michael Knight has *dark* hair!(*Dum, dee, le, le, le, le, le, le, le, le, le, dum, dee, le, le, le, le*.....damn, why does the *Knight Rider* theme tune have to play in my head *every* time Louise's Dad is mentioned?)

The man that Pamela Knight was currently pogo-ing on has *blonde* hair!

I know this didn't take a Sherlock Holmes level of deduction – but Pamela Knight was having sex with someone other than *Michael* Knight!

What would I say to Louise?

How do you break it to your girlfriend that her Mum is having an affair?

"Oh, by the way, I was just upstairs and saw some strange bloke knobbing your Mum?"

Damn it!

Why couldn't I have just queued up at the bathroom toilet with the other two people who were waiting?

Why did my brain have to come up with the *ingenious* thought that a house this size must have, at least, one en-suite bathroom?

Bloody brain!

I suppose it was just my luck that, ten seconds after walking into a strange en-suite, having hardy had time for a good rummage around!, a horny, middle aged couple decide they want to have sex in the adjoining room!

And not just *any* couple.

Or a couple who are *officially* a couple.

No, a horny, middle-aged couple who want to taste the *forbidden* fruit!

One of which was my girlfriends Mum!

All of which meant I was now the Worlds first en-suite hostage!

Wait a minute!

Goodbye B.M.X. Hello S.E.X.

Oh here we go – my brains way of trying to make things look better than they are.

This'll be good!

Maybe it <u>is</u> Michael Knight (dum, dee, le, le..STOP IT!) – maybe he has <u>dyed</u> his hair!

What to *blonde*?

As far as I know he isn't an *actor*, isn't *gay* or isn't a *professional footballer*!

Okay, maybe it's one of <u>those</u> sorts of parties!

Hmm.

I suppose it was possible. The party, which was for Louise's Aunt Violets birthday, was certainly different to any party hosted by any of the Day clan.

For a start there seemed to be a lot of champagne and canopies rather than beer and over-cooked Chicken drumsticks!

For another thing, people were actually *talking* to each other – without even a hint that things may turn into a fight of some description before the end of the night!

But I hadn't seen any car keys being thrown into empty fruit bowls.

No, I'm sorry brain but you're not getting off that lightly. It was a different party than I was used to, but it didn't make it one of *those* parties.

"Oh that was fantastic *my lover!*" I heard Pamela say, before a double thud on the floor suggested that she had dismounted almost immediately.

Thank God for that!

I was worried that I may be stuck in the bathroom for hours.

Hallelujah to sordid affairs and the *wham-bam-thank-you-Mam!* approach those involved have towards to sex!

"Let's have a shower together!" she added.

"It'll have to be quick or people will wonder where we are!" came the wheezy reply, obviously from Blondie.

Good!

The sooner they get out of that room, the sooner I can get back downstairs to Louise.

She was probably beginning to wonder where *I* was.

Wait a minute!

Shower?

I presume they weren't going to go and queue up to use the shower in the main bathroom and would, instead, be planning to use the shower in the en-suite?

This en-suite!

The very en-suite that I was currently a hostage in!

Oh shit!

Footsteps began to sound straight away and were headed in my direction.

I quickly looked around, the state of panic jabbing at me furiously like an early-career Barry McGuigan!

Despite my instinct to jump into the bath and pull the shower curtain across, something told me that particular hiding place wouldn't keep me out of sight for long!

I glanced at the window which was one of those with the tiny flap-like openings right at the top.

Could I squeeze through there?

Not a chance!

Damn me for not being a two foot tall anorexic!

I could smash the main window and make a run for it?

Of course, when I didn't appear back downstairs then it wouldn't be too difficult for people to put two and two together and realise that I was the window-smashing peeping Tom!

And that could, very possibly, bring an end to mine and Louise's relationship.

I looked further round the room.

Was there any way I could fit into that wicker laundry basket?

There wasn't time for any kind of accurate measuring because the door handle was turning.

I leapt across the room, whipped the top off the wicker basket and, without giving a second thought as to whether there may be a Snake inside, jumped in with both feet!

I managed to somehow pull the basket lid over my head just as the bathroom door opened.

Hopefully the whole basket wasn't shaking around too much as the lovers entered the room.

It seemed not, as I could hear their horny footsteps quickly crossing the room and stepping up into the bath. The shower was turned on immediately and, thankfully, the cascading water blocked out the sound of their giggling and flesh slapping!

I let out a big sigh, relieved that I had avoided being caught in a somewhat embarrassing place by the skin of my teeth.

What would I have said if discovered?

How the Hell would I have talked my way out of that one?

There would be some seriously awkward questions that had to be faced!

It wasn't worth thinking about.

What *was* worth thinking about was how long I could actually *survive* in the position I was in. Due to my, somewhat, hasty entrance into the basket, I had left myself curled up more tightly than a cornered Armadillo!

Whilst fairly impressed that I could probably one day become a magicians' assistant, I also had to accept that anyone who spends more than ten minutes in such a position could well end up being stuck like this forever – even without a change in the wind!

It is probably almost a guarantee that you will have a life plagued with constant back pain.

I wonder if Dad found himself in a similar position to this sometime in his early life?

That would certainly explain how he seemed to need to spend most of his life, these days, confined to his bed!

As I contemplated whether there was any call, in any part of society, for a *human wheel*, I couldn't help but wish that I'd taken the deepest breath of air in my life before entering the contortionist's basket.

For I now realised that there was no point in worrying about whether there was a Snake in the basket, waiting for a crazy Indian man with a home made flute!

No self-respecting living creature would, willingly, spend *any* time in this basket.

The smell was *horrendous*!

Obviously caused by the damp towels that I could feel underneath my ridiculously curved spine – damp towels that smelt like they had been used to dry a pack of Dogs that had rolled around in a festering swamp!

Wow – maybe it would be better to face those awkward questions than have to spend another second in here!

I slowly lifted the basket lid, that was balancing on my head like a wicker Fu Manchu hat, to try and let, at least, a sliver of fresh air in.

The atmosphere in the room was steamy and smelt of shower gel and, what must be, sex but anything was better than the wet Dog aroma.

Through the inch wide gap at the top of the basket I could just about see, by the blurry, intertwined silhouettes behind the shower curtain, that their "session" was still ongoing.

Could I make a run for it *now*?

Would they be so engrossed in what they were doing that they wouldn't even hear or notice me?

Could I afford *not* to make a run for it?

How long could I possibly survive in these conditions?

So far it seemed that Pamela and Blondie weren't taking any notice of the Governments "Save Water" campaign – so I could be stuck in here for a while.

As I glanced around the room another factor made the case for running even stronger.

I couldn't see any towels on the towel rail.

It's quite possible that the only drying garments were the ones in *this* basket.

God help them!

But, if that was true, then I would be rumbled anyway when they got out of the shower and began to look for towels.

And what's well known for being worse than being caught in the en-suite – being caught in the smelly laundry basket in the en-suite!

Yep, I was going for it!

As quietly as possible I reached down and placed my Manchu hat onto the floor, before slowly standing up straight.

My back made the kind of noise you get from an antique door that hasn't been oiled for a good couple of decades, but I had no time to worry about that right now.

Once stood upright in the basket, I could clearly see the dark outlines of their bodies behind the white shower curtain.

God knows what they were up to.

Is there such a position as the *Bucking Bronco*?

Maybe the water and shower gel on the bath surface was making it slippery and they were battling to keep upright?

Maybe this was….

What was I doing?

Why the Hell was I staring at the very thing I was, supposedly, in the middle of running away from?

I took a big step out of the basket and, thankfully, landed my foot on the bathroom floor with the quietness and grace of a Butterfly landing on a rose petal.

Unfortunately I wasn't able to repeat the act with my left leg and I caught the top of the basket and kicked it over into a low shelf-full of cleaning equipment and fluids.

CRASH!

"What was that?" I heard Pamela's voice ask over the drone of the shower.

I moved quickly towards the door.

"It was just the Earth moving!" I heard being replied to her just before I left the room.

What a cheese bag!

I didn't wait to see if Pamela wanted to look behind the curtain to see what the *real* noise was caused by or to, perhaps, be quickly sick because of Blondie's cheesiness!

I ran through the bedroom trying my best to avoid the scattered clothes on the floor, before casually walking out onto the landing.

There was still a queue, this time of three people, waiting outside the main bathroom (losers!) and, thankfully, no-one seemed to notice me leaving the bedroom.

I headed towards the stairs my heart beating faster and louder than a policeman knocking on the window of a knocked off Capri!

It seemed I was in the clear….!

Goodbye B.M.X. Hello S.E.X.

Chapter Twenty One - "...the woman with the Dragonfly tattoo..."

Is there anything that feels better than the feeling you get when you survive a *near miss*?

When you drop the bread knife and it spears into the floor – just an inch away from your foot?

Ooohh the relief!

When you hear on the news that an asteroid that was big enough to wipe out all life on Earth missed us by just a couple of miles?

Ooohh the relief!

(Which in reality means a couple of *hundred thousand* miles – but it still gives you that *glad to be alive* feeling!)

When you're out walking the Dog and a bolt of lightening strikes a tree just a couple of fields away?

Ooohh the relief!

When you just about manage to get your ass on the toilet mere milli-seconds before the shit, that you've been racing as fast as you can for, breaks through your clenched butt cheeks?

OOOOOOOOOHHHHHHHHH THE RELIEF!

I'd just survived one of *those* moments.

Stuck in an en-suite bathroom as my girlfriend's mother and her blonde *lover* had performed an asthma-stalling sex show in the next room.

Her *lover* who was *not* Louise's father!

I'd had to sit there for what seemed like forever, entranced by the Dragonfly tattoo on her shoulder, as she panted and he wheezed, and she called him "*my lover*" over and over again!

Imagine if I'd been caught?

Imagine if this whole event had *not* been just another of those near misses?

Oohhh the relief!

I slowly walked down the stairs and the feeling of relief left me faster than a milkman who hears a key entering the front door!

Because, as I walked, I realised that I hadn't even had the piss that was the reason this whole shambolic adventure was started for!

Damn it!

Should I head back up and join the main bathroom queue?

Did I really *still* need to go?

I hadn't felt like I needed to for the previous, God knows how long, while I was subjected to the live sex show from Hell.

But you just know, don't you, that when your minds on it again – you'll *need* to go again!

"Where have you been?"

I looked to the bottom of the stairs and Louise was standing there, her hands on her hips.

Ok, what do I tell her?

That I had popped to the toilet, decided to side-step the queue to the regular bathroom, then, as I snooped around the bedroom en-suite, been trapped in there by a randy tattooed / asthmatic couple, one of which was her Mum, the other of which was *not* her Dad?

"I've just been to the toilet – there's a queue a mile long!"

How could I tell her the truth?

It would break her heart!

"Ok, come on. I want you to meet some more people!" she said, flashing that beautiful smile.

Great!

Not only was I now having to falsely grin at weird relatives, I now couldn't really go to the toilet for at least an hour if I didn't want to look like I had the bladder of an eighty year old!

Or maybe half an hour, if I could convincingly make up some kind of bladder infection story!

As I reached the bottom of the stairs a flash of shocking pink by my foot caught my eye.

Shit – I had a hideously bright thong stuck to the bottom of my right shoe!

I must have accidentally stood on it as I rapidly passed through the "lovers" bedroom, as they showered in the bathroom, giving me the opportunity to make my escape and have that *near miss*!

Without giving too much thought as to why and how it was actually stuck to my foot *(shudder!)* I reached down, grabbed it and stuffed it into my right jeans pocket.

There's no point having a near miss if you're going to walk around with clear evidence that gives *away* that near miss!

I followed Louise as she led me into the living room.

The first two people I had to meet were an *eccentric* couple called Peter and Patricia who lived next door. Their, almost identical, jumpers made them uncannily similar to that *eccentric* couple from *Ever Decreasing Circles*.

Have you ever looked up the word *eccentric* in a thesaurus?

It comes up with words like *unusual* and *unconventional* instead of the words that it should. You know, like *looney* or *nutjob*!

I suppose I would also have looked eccentric / looney / nutjob if I hadn't noticed the bright pink thong stuck to my foot!

"Are you ok?" asked Louise when I had finally steered us away from a conversation about *Butterfly conservation* that was threatening to last *all night*!

"Yeah, I'm alright!" I said, trying hard not to *look* like my right hand was now actually having to squeeze my dick from inside my jeans pocket!

A couple more minutes and I could probably get away with going to the toilet "again"!

Just keep squeezing!

"Ahh!" said Louise excitedly. "I wondered where he'd been all night. Come on I want you to meet my Uncle Tom."

She grabbed my left hand and led me through a crowded kitchen towards a

Goodbye B.M.X. Hello S.E.X.

tallish man with blonde hair.

Slightly *damp* looking blonde hair!

"Uncle Tom!" Louise said, as we got close. "I want you to meet my boyfriend, Paul!"

Although I got that heart-warming tingle, that I usually got when Louise referred to me as her *boyfriend*, I couldn't stop myself changing into detective mode.

It was almost like I had slipped on Columbo's dirty Mac!

We had a very awkward handshake, during which Tom seemed more than a little confused as to why I insisted on leaving my right hand in my pocket and shaking with my left hand!

Following that a couple of, *very wheezy*, "Nice to meet you! You're a lucky man!"-type sentences, meant that I needed no more evidence that Uncle Tom was the man I had just seen upstairs - *acquainting* himself with Louise's Mum!

Damn!

If he was Louise's *real* Uncle that either meant her Mum was having it off with her Sister's husband, her husbands Brother – or her *own* Brother!

Eeeoughh!

The pieces of a sordid jigsaw were all coming together and leaving an image that was more than a little uncomfortable to look at.

Had I missed any other possible options for *Uncle*?

I suppose he could just be someone that Louise referred to as Uncle, rather than an *actual* relative?

Would that make things better?

Is an affair with someone you're *not* related to, better than one with someone that you *are* related to?

Wow that was a deep question!

Far too deep for someone now gripping his penis so tightly it was becoming quite numb!

"Why is your hair wet, Uncle Tom?" asked Louise, now turning Detective herself.

"Erm, I, erm," stumbled and wheezed Tom "I had to pop out to the garage for some more booze and it's raining a bit!"

Louise looked satisfied with his answer, but I knew better.

And just one glance outside would have shown exactly why the local weathermen were describing the current weather as a *heat wave* – we hadn't had any rain for at least the last three hours!

"I best go and find what your Auntie Hilary's up to, I've not seen her for a while. See you later!" said Tom, obviously uncomfortable with the current line of questioning.

With that he lurched off, with his blonde mop bouncing up and down in a very, unfortunately, *familiar* style!

Suddenly there was an orange warning light flashing in my mind.

Something was wrong.

Despite all my instincts saying that I should just ignore it, I thought I better check it out just in case my inside-jean-pocket grip hadn't been as firm as it should have been!

I didn't want somebody else having to tell me that there had been some level of *leakage*!

Straight away though I could see that this wasn't another of those *you've-just-pissed-yourself* warnings!

No, this was a *moral dilemma*!

Shit, I knew I should have ignored it!

It was too late now though, because I had seen it.

Should I tell Louise about what I saw upstairs?

Did she have a right to know?

If she had seen something similar involving one of my parents, would she tell me?

Would I expect her to tell me?

Would I *want* her to tell me?

Damn it!

I should have *definitely* ignored the orange warning light!

Because the more I thought about the questions circling my head, the more the answers were becoming clear.

I *should* tell her.

She *did* have a right to know.

I probably *would* want to know if she had seen my Mum or Dad at it with someone else.

It would most probably make me feel sick picturing it, but I *would* want to know!

"I need to tell you something." I said with serious face mode turned firmly on.

I turned to face her full on.

"Ok." She said, looking slightly worried.

"I'm not exactly sure how to tell you. It's something about your Mum...." I started, before being interrupted by a dark haired woman approaching from behind Louise, quite quickly.

Shit!

It was Louise's Mum, brazenly also walking around with damp hair.

I know those towels in the basket were only really fit for an incinerator, but surely her and Tom could have made a better effort to dry their hair somehow!

Louise noticed that I was staring over her shoulder and so instinctively glanced behind to see what I was looking at.

"Oh, here's someone else I can introduce you to!" she said. "It's my other Auntie – Auntie Hilary!"

Louise could obviously read my shocked face.

"She's my Mum's identical twin Sister," she said. "Uncle Tom's wife!"

Ohhhh!

Thank God for that!

All the jigsaw pieces had rearranged themselves and had now constructed a picture that was far easier to look at.

"This is Paul, my *boyfriend*!" said Louise as Hilary joined us.

Another round of pleasantries and an awkward left-handed handshake followed.

Damn I needed to go to that toilet.

"I'm going to get some more wine" said Hilary. "Do you two want another drink?"

"No thanks!" we both said at exactly the same time, which prompted us to *cutely* look and smile at one another. (Sickening aren't we?)

"You haven't seen your Uncle Tom anywhere have you?" Hilary asked Louise. "I haven't seen him for about an hour! He's probably gone home!"

Ha!

Haven't seen him for about an hour?

What, apart from that little *thing* that was going on upstairs?

"Yeah, we just saw him a minute ago!" said Louise. "He was looking for *you*! He headed off towards the living room, I think."

"I'll probably find him in there, flirting with someone – as usual!" Hilary said laughing. "And I need to do something about this!" she added, pointing at her hair.

"What happened?" asked Louise. "You get caught in the rain outside?"

"Oh there's been no rain!" said Hilary. "One of the kids got me with a water balloon!"

Hmmm.

Not seen him for an hour?

He's probably flirting with someone - as usual?

Water balloon?

It seems someone may have added a little cornflower to this plot!

I suppose the whole *water balloon* thing could just be her excuse for being as wet as someone who'd recently had a shower!

She could even have been hit by a water balloon *after* coming down from the sex shower.

On the other hand she could be telling the *truth*. She may not have been upstairs *at all*!

Maybe it *was* Louise's Mum, Pamela?

Stop it!

Take that bloody Mac off!

The case has already been solved – there's no need for further investigation.

"You don't know whether there are any towels upstairs do you love?" Hilary asked Louise.

Louise turned to me – obviously wanting me to answer.

"Yes there are but...."

WAIT!

I stopped myself.

I was about to say that there were some in the en-suite, but they were a bit damp!

Thank God my brain was on the ball for once because, I have to agree, that sentence may *slightly* insinuate that I had been in the en-suite bathroom at some point in the evening!

Louise and Hilary stared at me obviously waiting to see what my *"but..."* was for.

Shit!

I didn't even know if the main bathroom had any towels anyway – I, unfortunately, hadn't managed to make it inside.

If it was anything like the en-suite then any towels may well have been damp, horrendously stinky, and confined to some, just-about-able-to-fit-in wicker basket!

"I just meant...."

Shit, what *did* I mean?

Louise and Hilary held their stares.

"I meant there *were* some when I was up there!"

Good!

I'd insinuated that there were some towels in the bathroom when I was there but added, in small print, that they *may* have been removed since.

Brilliant!

No one could prove *or* disprove that!

It does seem that, for most circumstances in life, you are best adding small print to every sentence you make, whenever possible!

Hilary left the room, leaving just Louise and me.

And my, possibly soon-to-fall-off, being squeezed-to-death penis!

"So, what were you saying about my Mum?" she asked me straight away.

Oh no!

Me and my big mouth!

It was now evidently irrelevant, but I couldn't *say* that.

The minute you say "oh, it was nothing" is the minute that the other person starts to panic, because they know very well it was as far away from *nothing* as you can get!

Thankfully Hilary re-entered the room before I had to answer.

"Hi Mum" said Louise. "Where've you been? I haven't seen you for ages!"

Damn Pamela and Hilary looked alike!

And Louise hadn't *seen her for ages*?

"Why's your hair wet?" added Louise.

Her hair *was* also wet!

"Erm," said Pamela. "I was looking at the Petunias round the side of the house and the sprinkler system came on and soaked me!"

Really?

Who actually *looks* at flowers?

Round the side of the house?

Sprinkler system?

Did this all seem a bit far-fetched?

Did I need to slip my Mac back on?

Goodbye B.M.X. Hello S.E.X.

"Don't tell anyone," said Pamela, taking a purple looking clump of shrub from her pocket. "But I took some cuttings from Aunt Violet's lavender. We'll be able to grow some from it at home!"

Ok it appears she *had* been looking at flowers – while at the same time *stealing* some!

At least it nipped any thoughts it could have been *her* upstairs with "Uncle Tom" in the bud straight away.

Pamela looked at me.

"Hiya Paul!"

"Hi" I said.

"How are you..........my lover?" Pamela asked.

My lover?

I shuddered so hard that it was impossible to tell whether my skeleton had just jumped right out of my body!

It was possible I would be collapsing to the floor at any second, ready to begin my new life as a Jellyfish!

"I'm ok thanks!" I said whilst in a state of some shock.

Did the case need re-opening in light of this devastating new evidence?

"How is Auntie Hilary's shoulder tattoo now?" Louise asked Pamela.

Shoulder tattoo?

Thank God for that!

Re-opened case now re-closed!

"It's fine, it's fully healed now." said Pamela.

"Is it the same as *yours*?" Louise asked.

Pamela has a tattoo as well?

Damn it!

Re-re-closed case now re-re-opened!

"No, she went for a completely different one!" said Pamela.

Everyone's attention was drawn to the buzzing of noise that was coming from the next room.

I watched as both Louise and Pamela's eyes looked over towards what was happening.

No!

Don't stop the conversation there!

You CAN'T stop the conversation there!

Thankfully Louise looked back at Pamela.

"So what tattoo *did* she get then?"

Pamela smiled.

"Have a guess!"

What was this – a *shitty game show*? (Or a *game show* – they're all actually *shitty*, aren't they?)

Louise looked at her thoughtfully.

Obviously thinking about it.

And thinking about it.

And thinking about it!

COME ON!
"Did she get the Tiger that she was thinking about?" she finally guessed.
"Nope!" said Pamela.
Louise smiled.
"Oh I know – she got that Chinese writing thing!"
Pamela didn't answer.
Instead she was looking into the living room from where more and more noise was emerging.
WELL WAS IT?
She looked back as Louise.
"No, she didn't go for the Chinese symbols!"
Come on, get on with it!
My right hand was squeezing as hard as it possibly could now.
Tell us what tattoo Hilary got so I know which one of you was upstairs with Uncle Tom and then I can get to the toilet before my *floodgates* open!
"Give me a clue!" said Louise.
Jesus Christ, it felt like Lionel Blair might just come in tap-dancing at any minute!
"It's got wings!" said Pamela.
Oooh!
Dragonflies have got wings!
Louise thought about it again.
Just like a good magician, I tried to channel my best *Extra Sensory Perception*.
Dragonfly, Dragonfly, Dragonfly, Dragonfly, Dragonfly, Dragonfly......
"Is it an Eagle?"
I've said it before, I'll say it again – Paul Daniels is full of shit!
"Nope!" said Pamela.
"A Dove?"
"Nope!"
"Humming Bird?"
"Nope!"
"A Parrot?"
"Nope!"
"Oh, I know – a Phoenix?"
"Nope!"
"She probably went for a Pigeon or something like that, didn't she?" said Louise seemingly losing some interest.
Pamela laughed.
"No, she didn't………………do you want me to tell you?"
Yes.
Tell her!
TELL HER NOW!
"Yeah, go on!" said Louise.
"She went for a….."
Clink, clink, clink, clink, clink, clink!

Goodbye B.M.X. Hello S.E.X.

The noise of a glass clinking stopped Pamela mid-sentence.

"Can everyone gather round please!" shouted a voice from the living room. "The birthday girl, Violet, would like to say a few words!"

Pamela and Louise headed straight towards the living room like some programmed robots following orders.

Ever thought about finishing your conversation first?

Especially when that conversation was probably just *one* bloody word away from completion?

I followed them into the living room and joined the other robots who had been summoned in.

Maybe it would be easier to carefully watch Hilary and Pamela walking – and work out which one of them was missing their underwear!

As Violet spoke, thanking everyone for coming and recounting a couple of "humorous" incidents from birthdays gone by, I couldn't help but wonder about a couple of things.

1…Why the Hell do people insist on giving speeches at birthday parties? Surely speeches are only really required by a best man at a wedding and Prime Ministers – preferably *only* at Wartime! Everyone else should do us all a favour and keep a dignified silence!

2…Will I ever actually find out who the woman with the Dragonfly tattoo is? Is it Hilary? Or is it, disturbingly, Pamela?

As I contemplated where this left me in terms of needing to tell Louise or not, thankfully, Violet brought to an end her completely unnecessary speech.

The dozens of people who had gathered in front of her, began to do what polite dozens of people do after enduring pointless speeches.

They began to clap.

And it happened.

I pulled my right hand out of my pocket in preparation for adding my own polite clapping – and I inadvertently threw a shocking pink thong that struck Auntie Violet right on her nose!

And right on queue, as everyone turned their shocked faces in my direction, those floodgates opened!

Oh shit!

July 1992

I entered July realising that the next few weeks would probably be the most carefree and best weeks of my life.

As such, I was determined to make the most of every minute available.

Unfortunately there wasn't going to be a memorable soundtrack of the summer because there was a real lack of quality music on the radio.

Whereas in 1991 we had been treated to Bryans' record breaking number one, and other classics such as The Simpson's - "*Do the Bartman*" and Chesney Hawkes - "*The One and Only*" - this year continued to be very low quality.

To illustrate, the number one spot was now being occupied by Erasure with "*Abba-esque*"! It was an EP made up purely of ABBA songs - performed by Erasure.

It was like two worst nightmares rolled into one!

The poor music, however, was more than balanced out by the glorious weather. We were being treated to day after day of beautiful Sunshine.

As such my "best days" were mainly being made up of days in the Sun, and parties in the dark.

One benefit of Mark's parents' imminent divorce was that they weren't staying at home that often. That coupled with Marks "*I'm not going to be living here much longer*" attitude, made his house the perfect venue for numerous wild parties.

And whereas Marks Mum usually made sure that everyone took their shoes off before entering the house, Mark seemed to be almost encouraging an *anything goes* attitude for anyone attending the parties.

Me, Little Si and John usually hung around the following day to help with any fence panel repairs, sick pile scoop ups or any vases that needed gluing back together!

And those Yellow Pages *French Polishers* were getting plenty of work thrown their way!

I was having a great time; and I was even finding the perfect balance between spending time with Louise, and spending time with the guys.

I was having the best of both Worlds.

I was having my cake and eating it. (Whatever the Hell *that* meant! Why would you want your cake and not eat it?)

I was also trying to put the whole *who is the woman with the Dragonfly tattoo* incident out of my mind.

For one, Louise had somehow forgiven me for throwing a pink thong at her Auntie Violet and pissing myself in front of all of her family!

My *explanation* of my jean-wetting being due to a severe bladder infection and the thong-throwing being a freak accident, and result of a Brother Simon-placed "prank", had somehow been accepted by her.

How many members of her family felt the same, and I would ever be able to face *ever* again, was a different matter – and something I probably didn't want

Goodbye B.M.X. Hello S.E.X.

to know!

As such, I felt it was not my place to try and get to the bottom of whether it was her Mother, Pamela, or Auntie Hilary, who had *that* Dragonfly tattoo and was therefore the one I, unfortunately had to witness, having sex with her Uncle Tom.

Besides, the couple of times I had tentatively enquired about tattoos on relatives had resulted in confused and suspicious questions about *why* I was so interested in a weird subject!

I think, maybe, Louise thinks I have some kind of permanent-ink body-art fetish!

So, for now at least, I thought it was better to let it go.

During many of these sweltering Summer days Louise and I were taking my Dog out quite a lot - walking along many of the semi-rural paths around the Holly Grove area.

I came to realise it really is a beautifully green and colourful place, if you take the time to appreciate it.

Louise liked to make fun of the fact that my Dog was called "Wally".

He was a Springer Spaniel, and Mum had named him when we got him as a puppy, about twelve years earlier.

She still claims that "back then", "Wally" was just a name, and not a term also meaning "idiot".

Whether this was true or not it was ironic because, despite him being a cute and loveable fella; Wally was, without doubt, a "Wally"!

He certainly wouldn't have got very far on a Canine version of Mastermind!

All he really ever did was eat, sleep and shit.

He was like a living example of a digestive system!

And he would eat *anything*.

Anything put in front of him.

Anything accidentally dropped anywhere near him. (in fact, it didn't even have to be *that* near!)

And anything he wound while we were out walking.

I think his personal favourite may have been discarded trays of chips and curry left by the railway line. (Obviously they were stone-cold and had been left the previous night by someone who had rejected them - while they were hot and that someone was pissed out of their head!)

I think it's safe to say he's *not* a fussy eater!

He would clear anything - he was a four-legged version of those orange road sweeper trucks that cleared the gutters!

But Wally also loved to run. He was excited to be let off his lead so he could just chase around a field. (Sometimes with other Dogs that were out; one of which he would usually try to hump!)

But to see the enjoyment he could get from the simply pleasure of just running made me determined to try to enjoy even *my* simple pleasures.

Including Cricket.

During the Summers months, I had been playing Cricket for Holly Grove with Little Si for a number of years, without ever really having a great time.

Mark and John always refused to play, saying it was a boring, and silly, game that no one in their right mind could understand!

John used to ask *"How can they play a Test match for five days and still only draw? Seems like a big waste of everyone's time!"*

This Summer though, even following the bad start we had made, I was determined to embrace it.

In the past I have always been a bit-part player; but from now on I decided I would make it different - I would impose my personality onto games.

It was an under-17's team so this would be my final year.

As such, like everything else in my life, I would make the most of it while it lasted.

Goodbye B.M.X. Hello S.E.X.

Chapter Twenty Two - "...*my moment*..."

It wasn't supposed to come to this.

It should have been the perfect day.

The Sun was beating down and, when Maple Ridge posted a dismally pathetic 47 all out, everyone assumed we would coast to an easy victory.

The fact that we had lost all our six games so far this season, and had actually scored less than 47 in *five* of those outings, should have perhaps been an indication that success may not have been the inevitability everyone was expecting!

Having said that, after our openers had reached a confident 30-0, watching nine batsmen falling faster than a domino rally was a new low - even for us!

We were now 42-9.

What were we doing? We were Holly Grove Cricket Clubs Under 17's - doing another pretty good impression of the England Test Team!

The personal implications were huge - I was next man in.

Our last hope.

Our last chance of somehow saving a game that we all, foolishly, thought we had already won.

The team's fate was in my hands.

Oh shit!

But I wasn't the number eleven batsmen because I was useless at batting, or in Cricketing terms "a rabbit."

No, I had been assured by our coach, Tony, who dressed as if he thought that, now in 1992, Miami Vice was still cool!, that he picked me at number eleven for two reasons.

One, because he saw me as one of his best bowlers. It would be unfair on the other lads if I was high up the batting order as well as being a main bowler.

And two, he said that at number eleven, I was perfectly placed to turn a tight game by surprising the opposition.

Exactly this sort of game!

As I glanced over to where he was sitting on the pavilion balcony, I think I was correct in assuming that he may not have been totally honest with me. He was sitting with his head in his hands, crying his eyes out!

As I stood up, ready to make my walk towards destiny, I also reflected on the fact that, despite Tony's endorsement, he hadn't actually called on me to bowl in this game.

In fact, he hadn't called on me to bowl in any game *all season*!

Instead, I usually occupied the "most important fielding position" in the team - deep, deep, *deep* extra cover!

On most grounds this meant being stuck on the boundary next to a farmer's field - usually closer to Sheep or Cows than any actual Cricket action!

I cleared my mind.

This wasn't the type of positive thinking I needed to assist my situation and impose my *personality*.

Instead, I remembered some lines from a T. Summerfield poem called "This Is The Moment".

Still unbeknown to everyone, I had taken an after School poetry class in an attempt to spend some extra "romantic" time with Louise.

I had even actually found out that not all poems were just over-sentimental words, hap-hazardly put together by sad loners with too much time on their hands. Some were actually quite good, and semi-inspirational.

And *"This Is The Moment"* had actually left me feeling positively motivated. I pumped out my chest and ran some of the words through my mind.

"One last push, reach for the finish line,
Sink or swim, fade or shine…..
Don't rely on fate, don't rely on luck,
This is the moment, Step up."

I put the fact that I couldn't swim very well out of my mind, and felt the inspiration rise inside me.

I was ready.

I picked up my bat and began to stride towards the wicket - as purposefully as I could with the pads I was wearing.

I had been left with the pads that were at the bottom of the kit bag - the ones that no-one else wanted to wear.

They were rock hard and closer to yellow in colour than white - as if they had possibly spent too much time in a Sun-drenched shop window.

It was also an understatement to say that they were too big for me. They would probably have been too big for Courtney Walsh's big Brother!

As I crossed the boundary I received what could best be described as modest encouragement. One voice said meekly,

"Come on Paul!"

Followed by a much louder one that shouted,

"Yeah, come on Poetry geek!"

It seemed that my "secret" after-School class would no longer be so secret anymore. I tried not to speculate on who may have shouted this out - although the voice did seem suspiciously like that of Dads!

I shook my head, clearing my mind as if it was an (almost!) spherical Etch-A-Sketch, and focused on the task in hand. I was going to face the Maple Ridge bowler who had taken all nine of our wickets.

From my vantage point in the changing room his bowling had appeared blindingly fast, but I contented myself with the well known fact that everything appears faster when viewed from a distance.

It was something that I had learnt in a Science lesson.

As I struggled to walk on, the fact that I couldn't remember anything else I had ever learnt in Science (apart from the fact that you should never mix sulphuric acid and ……damn it, some *other* chemical!) I began to question my knowledge.

I decided to test my theory out.

Goodbye B.M.X. Hello S.E.X.

Aeroplanes were really, very fast and when you see them up in the sky, from a distance, they appear……..really, very *slow*!

Oh no!

I'd got my facts mixed up – *again*!

I was in trouble!

"Shit, that guys as fast as a train!"

I had just passed by Little Si, who was the latest to have had his wickets flattened.

I was in *big* trouble!

For a split second I felt pleased that my reasoning had been proven correct. Then I realised that I was voluntarily walking towards this lad, who could bowl a ball like a *speeding bullet*.

And he wasn't throwing something inoffensive and fun like a wet sponge, or even a ping pong ball, he was throwing a Corky ball - the only object on Earth known to be harder than Diamond!

And I was *voluntarily walking towards* this.

What an idiot!

I had no doubt in my mind that if I had been in The First World War, I would have been the first to volunteer to go "over the top"!

I looked up at the ridiculously blue sky and wondered where the Hell all the dark clouds were when you needed them.

Why couldn't it rain *today*?

It rains around here most days.

In fact, I'm pretty sure that it has rained in Holly Grove *everyday – for the whole duration of time!*

It rains here so much that it wouldn't be too far-fetched to believe that *Evolution* was probably working overtime on developing *waterproof skin*!

As I got closer to the square, waddling like an Emperor Penguin with diarrhea!, I saw Maple Ridges' answer to Waqar Younis close up for the first time.

He was only of medium height, but had a build not too dissimilar to a fully grown male Rhinoceros!

Another feature that immediately grabbed my attention was his fully formed six o'clock shadow - and it was only three-thirty!

In fact, he had thicker designer stubble than George Michael! (That's good, manly, stubble isn't it?!?)

Had anyone told him that this was the under 17's league?

Had anyone checked his passport?

One thing was for sure; if he was under 17, he would have no problem getting into Yates' Wine Bar!

He noticed that I was staring at him.

He turned to look directly at me and his mouth morphed from a smirk, as he noticed the pads I was wearing, into a menacing sly grin - as if he was a hungry Fox that had just found his way into a full Chicken coop.

He was looking forward to making some of my feathers fly!

He began to head for his bowling starting point and so I shuffled awkwardly towards the wicket.

"Middle, please." I asked, and the Umpire helped with my guard, before I stood back and had a look round at where the Maple Ridge fielders were positioned.

It was something I always did, as if I was going to caress my shots into any gaps in the field but, in reality, I was just happy (and some what surprised) just to get bat onto ball.

Whilst looking around, I had hoped to catch a glimpse of Louise.

She had told me she would come and watch some of the game if she could. As I couldn't see her, I accepted that she mustn't have been able to make it. Either that or, because I had told her that matches usually lasted three or four hours; she had expected it to last more than the forty-three and a half minutes we had played so far!

As I tried to concentrate, I realised that an eerie silence had descended over the entire ground. It was as if the players and spectators were staring intently at me, waiting to see what sort of damage would befall me.

The mood was similar to what I assumed it would have been like at the Coliseum, as the crowd waited for the Emperor to deliver a thumbs-up or thumbs-down verdict.

If the Umpire was playing the Emperor role, then his seven words couldn't have given me a clearer thumbs down.

"Right arm over, five balls to go."

Five balls to go? I had to survive *five* apple-sized, Diamond plated, speeding bullets fired directly at me.

Could I possibly concede?

It may jeopardise my dignity, but what good was dignity if I couldn't walk back to the pavilion?

In fact, who was I kidding?

How much dignity did a "main bowler" who *never* bowled really have anyway?

Someone who always batted at number eleven; and fielded so far away from the action that he hadn't even noticed the twenty minute spell in last weeks game when the rest of the players left the field because of bad light?

No, there was no point in worrying about dignity.

Now how did you go about conceding a Cricket match?

Did I just mention it to the Umpire, or did I need to shake the hand of the Maple Ridge captain?

I was pretty sure that the captain was the maniac pace bowler but where was he?

Initially, as I glanced around, there was no sign of him. Then, through the low simmering haze, in front of me in the distance, I saw a train of dust growing out of the ground. It was being produced by the smirking captain, who appeared to be attempting a new land speed record as he raced towards the point at which he could hurl his missile at me.

Goodbye B.M.X. Hello S.E.X.

I was suddenly struck by a moment of bravery (more like stupidity), and I gritted my teeth and took my guard in front of the wicket.

If he wasn't polite enough to wait and see if I wanted to concede, then I wouldn't be polite enough not to smash his ball out of the ground.

"...*fade or shine.....this is the moment.*"

He arrived at the crease and, in a blur, his arm rotated over his head.

At first I assumed that he had not released the ball, because I had not seen anything leave his hand, but by the umpires reaction I realised he must have.

The Umpire was standing there as if he was about to feed the five thousand - he must have given a wide!

The ball had been so fast that I had not even seen it. I did console myself with the fact that, maybe because he had tried to bowl too fast, that he had lost some control.

I buoyantly realised that five more wide's would win us the game!

The words that came from the wicket keeper behind me did nothing to maintain my mini-high.

"Don't bowl it *slower* trying to swing the ball - you lose some control. Just bowl it *fast* and *straight*."

Even though the Maple Ridge captains' hand was within shaking distance, I had decided that I was now beyond conceding.

Therefore there would be one of three scenarios.

One, I would hit the winning runs and become the hero of the team. (As my mind laughed out loud, I told myself that it *could* happen!)

Two, I would be bowled out and therefore would have let our best chance of winning a match this year slip away. I would have let the team down badly.

Three, if I could somehow survive for five more balls, then I would be off strike and it would be up to Cameron at the other end!

He was a better batsman than me and had a chance of winning the game for us, and being the team hero. Something I was happy about.

Also, if it was *him* that was out, then it would be *him* that had let the team down badly and not me - something I was equally comfortable with!

So there it was, I had a plan.

I just had to survive.

I didn't have long to think about it, as another dusty mini-tornado approached at high velocity.

At the crease his arm performed its speedy catapult-like motion and released its projectile.

Again I saw nothing, but there was a terrifying buzz in the air which suggested the ball was closer this time. This was instantly confirmed as I felt a pain worse than a hundred of Brother Simon's Chinese burns - the ball had brushed past my forearm.

"HOWZAT?"

The Maple Ridge team appealed in unison for a caught behind, assuming the ball had hit my glove and not my arm.

I held my breath and anxiously waited. My fate was in the hands of the

Gary Locke

Umpire.

I couldn't believe it. He had only given me *not out*!

I had to go through it all again.

The pain in my arm began to subside. It now felt like it was only broken in *four* places!

I realised there was no time to call for Mum because the Maple Ridge Dynamo was coming again.

This time I managed to see the buzzing ball. It flashed past my eyes like a mini red arrow - slightly before the images of my, oh too short, life!

I shook off the scenes of embarrassment and humiliation quickly, I didn't need to witness them for a second time!, and once again stood upright, ready to face the next wave of attacks.

Time was mocking me; because there was no respite, and straight away he was back again, running like Linford Christie, and spinning his arm faster than a helicopter rotor blade.

I reverted back to not seeing a thing, which may have been more pleasant than the red flash inches from my face, had I not had the split-second scent of leather!

There was also an increased intensity to the buzzing in the air and, although I know it hadn't been struck, my nose felt like it was vibrating.

That one must have been really close!

It suddenly occurred to me that, because of the speed of our wickets, I did not have the chance to go to the toilet before I entered the bombardment zone. This now felt like something I should definitely have done.

I was wearing protective pads and gloves, but realised now what a prudent, and equally essential, piece of protective clothing a *nappy* would have been!

"Two balls remaining."

I'm not sure if the Umpire had seen my resolve wavering and wanted to offer me some hope; but his words did offer me some comfort. When I came in I had to face five balls, and now there were only two left.

Therefore I had survived three balls without incident.

Actually, no, there had also been a wide - I had survived *four* balls without incident.

I was positively upbeat.

I gripped my bat with a strength I did not know I had.

As he approached again, I felt more ready than for any of the previous balls.

This was maybe reflected in the fact that I actually saw the ball quite clearly this time. It was as if it was larger than before, and travelling in slow motion - straight towards my head!

An alarm sounded in my mind and the brain pilot (perhaps rather fortunately, because he was rarely at his station!) shouted:

"TAKE EVASIVE ACTION!"

Luckily I had remembered how to fall easily and spectacularly during a trip to Altrincham Ice Rink.

I was on the floor; head first, faster than an Olympic diver!

Goodbye B.M.X. Hello S.E.X.

Again, a close call had been avoided, and there was only *one ball* left to face.

I ignored the laughter that was circulating the ground, especially the loudest laugh that, again, sounded uncannily like Dad's, and instead wiped the dust off my pads.

With them restored to their former majestic yellow, I thought about facing the last ball and prayed that it didn't come as close again.

Now fully upright, I noticed that my mouth was filled with a taste that I had not experienced before. I could only put it down to one thing - it was the taste of pure, undiluted *fear*.

I tried to ignore it and again looked forward towards Maple Ridges' student of Bodyline.

For the first time I actually saw him reach his starting point, possibly as far from the wicket as my usual fielding position!, before he turned and began his approach.

Just behind him, standing tight against the sight screen, I saw a sight for sore eyes.

Louise had turned up.

I had a new focus.

I could stand letting the team down; I could stand letting myself down, but I *couldn't* stand letting Louise down.

I was now determined to win this Cricket match.

Not selfishly for myself, but for Louise.

How good would she feel about herself to be going out with a Cricketing God?

I pumped my chest out and as the bowler slowly got bigger, approaching through the dust, I stared more intently than a Lion focused on a herd of Wildebeest.

I was in the zone.

Unfortunately my new found focus disappeared quicker than a John Major election pledge!

It occurred to me that the Maple Ridge' skipper had been attacking my senses.

His previous deliveries had tested my *touch, smell, sight* and *taste* - the only thing remaining was to attack my *hearing*.

Perhaps the sound I would hear would be my bat on the ball as I smashed him over the boundary for six?

He arrived and released the ball.

Again I saw it, fairly clearly.

I swung my bat with all my might and a sound occurred: wood against leather.

But it wasn't the wood from my bat; it was the sound of my wickets crashing behind me.

I had failed.

In one motion I instinctively swept my bat up under my arm (I was fairly well rehearsed with this move!) and began to walk.

Gary Locke

I stared at the Umpire and wondered why he was indicating that he was turning right!

Wait a minute!

He wasn't turning anywhere - he was signalling a no ball!

I had another chance.

The Maple Ridge captain looked disgusted.

The look on his face said that he was more fired up than ever. He returned to his starting point, revved his engine, and set off even quicker than he had before.

I had a feeling that this delivery would again result in another sound.

Would it be ball against wickets again?

Or perhaps this time ball against bat?

As he neared, my mind foolishly offered me another sound option. This time it may be the sound of the ball crashing against my helmet - leaving my head shaking around like a bell clapper.

I suddenly realised that I *wasn't wearing a helmet*!

The lack of wearing a nappy did, after all, become an issue!

I tried to clear my mind and focused on the approaching, speeding figure.

Another thought gripped me.

It was worse still - I *wasn't wearing a box*!

I had leant mine to Little Si.

I had always been uncomfortable with sharing a box, but right now I felt like if I could wish for anything in the whole World, it would be for my box.

No matter how sweaty it may be!

I realised now that even wearing a nappy wouldn't be enough!

He had arrived, 22 yards away, ready to unleash his final delivery.

His arm once again rotated and let out the speeding corky.

I closed my eyes tight and thrust my bat sideways, almost like a Rounder's shot.

Sorry Baseball, I mean Baseball shot!!

The bat and ball connected and sent a shock wave right through me.

Despite feeling like I had been struck by lightning, I watched clearly as the ball travelled straight up into the air - and high over the pavilion!

I had hit a six!

We had won the game!

I was the hero of the team!

I was uncomfortable with how *quiet* everyone was!

After a couple of seconds of shocked silence, like there was some kind of satellite delay between the centre of the pitch and the spectators, a roar of euphoria erupted.

I could see Tony standing on his chair, dancing up and down in his stone washed jeans and white jacket with the rolled up sleeves. His permed hair bouncing up and down on top of his ridiculously fake-tanned face!

"Not bad for a bowler!" I could hear him shouting.

What a prick!

Goodbye B.M.X. Hello S.E.X.

He wasn't the only one shouting, there were also cries of,
"Well done Roger" and "Way to go Bugs"!

I ignored the "Rabbit" jokes and instead of wading towards my adoring public, I looked over to where Louise was standing.

She smiled and gave me a thumbs up.

I was more pleased for her than for me - I think she had probably always dreamed of being a celebrity's girlfriend!

I closed my eyes and soaked up the glorious sensation of being a winner.

This was the type of moment I knew I had to savour.

I was no longer one of the (many) useless members of the team.

I had *single handedly* won the game for us!

My new found fame and talent was also rewarded in the next game.

I was promoted up to number nine batsman!

Admittedly, two members of the team had not turned up, but I think I would have been number nine anyway.

I was part of the team.

I was *respected* and *important*.

My time as number nine may have been short lived (one ball) but, as I've learned to accept, you can't be the hero every time!

Chapter Twenty Three - "…Love!…"

It was a Friday night and, unusually for the Summer period, I had let the guys down.

I was with Louise, but this time I had a legitimate excuse.

It was the 24th July - Grandma and Grandad's Golden Wedding Anniversary party.

They had hired a room at the Holly Grove Liberal Club.

It wasn't a large room - but it had a cute little bar in the corner and a small dance floor.

It felt cosy and intimate.

Mum had decorated the room with multi-coloured balloons, including a whole section of "gold" ones and tinsel behind the small stage to the right of the room. (The gold balloons looked more yellow than gold - but when you pointed it out, she went a bit mad!)

She had also spent a lot of time putting together a huge collage of photographs that was like a montage of Grandma and Grandad's life.

It almost filled an entire wall, and was a huge point of interest.

She had even hand written a huge sign that read *"Edna and Howard - Happy Golden Wedding Anniversary"*.

It was a relief that she had spelt everything correctly this time. For their "Ruby" anniversary, she had unfortunately written "Happy <u>Rudy</u> Wedding Anniversary"!

Despite her embarrassment, at the time it did prove to be a valuable source of humorous conversation! (What else do distant relatives, who see each other once every five or so years, have to talk about – until they're completely pissed!)

For the early part of the evening things were fairly low key; pretty much how most of our family parties were.

Dad had, though, bought me a pint of lager and Louise a Vodka and Coke - which was better than the shandy or *"Rola Cola"* that I usually had to have at these kind of "do's".

A couple of our "distant" Aunties did try to set an early pace on the dance floor as the DJ threw on an premature rendition of *"Agadoo"*, (It was possible that he had peaked too early!) but there was no mass movement following them.

Mum referred to so many women as being our "Auntie" that it was hard to keep a track of who we were related to, and who we weren't.

I found a reasonable gage was - any "Auntie" who insisted on kissing you, usually by clamping your head in their hands, was more often than not a relative.

How can frail looking, old women suddenly develop Geoff Capes-esque strength when there are vulnerable kids that they feel they have to aggressively kiss?

Goodbye B.M.X. Hello S.E.X.

There was about an hours worth of being re-introduced to people I had forgotten since the last major party - people I would probably have to be re-introduced to again in a few years time.

During their brief chats with me and Louise, most of the females noted *"How much I had grown"* and *"How different I looked."*

Most of the males tried to give me a secret head nod and curled lip - presumably indicating they thought I had done quite well in securing Louise's services as a girlfriend.

Dirty old pervs!

Dad and Uncle Geoff were betting on who would be the first person to make a fool of themselves by falling over on the dance floor.

I heard Dad putting his money on Mum - and then watched him as he promptly went and bought her a double Vodka!

There was always <u>someone</u> who fell flat on their face.

Dad thinks he could make a living out of buying a video camera and sending "trips, slips and falls" into that *"You've Been Framed"* TV show. I'm not so sure - it doesn't seem like the sort of show that will last very long!

It's certainly not in the same league as the great, new BBC soap, *Eldorado!* Now there's instant TV gold!

I wouldn't mind betting that it goes on to run longer than even *Coronation Street*!

I spent much of the early part of the evening grinning smugly at Brother Simon.

I was at the party with Louise, who was pretty much centre of attention, and he was there - on his own.

Even cousin Angus had brought a girl with him - much to Dad's surprise, and expense!

Brother Simon wasn't amused when I pointed at Grandma and said to him "Maybe, your "secret" Valentine will dance with you later!"

It amused Dad though who spent the next ten minutes telling Louise the tale of Brother Simons Valentines Day card humiliation.

Brother Simon just sat there saying nothing; his face the same colour as the *"99 balloons"* *Nena* was singing about on the DJ's latest record!

About 9.30 the DJ lowered the music volume and said he had an announcement to make.

People began jostling for position, assuming he was about to declare the buffet "open"!

Not me, Dad or Brother Simon though - we knew Mum had made much of it herself!

The DJ didn't speak about the buffet though; instead he introduced Grandad - who wanted to say a few words.

Grandad arrived on stage to a rapturous ovation - almost like he was a Rock Star.

It came as a bit of a shock when, arriving at the microphone, he didn't begin singing.

Gary Locke

Spurred on by the cheering he did, however, roll his cap - from one hand, along his shoulders, behind his head, and into the other hand.

It was his party trick, and the crowd went wild.

"HOWARD! HOWARD! HOWARD!" the chant echoed around the room.

Grandad put his flat cap back on, (which, seeing as he was wearing a suit, would have looked silly on anyone else - but not Grandad!) and waited for the applause to die down as he caught his breath.

When the chanting finally died down he began to speak.

"On behalf of me and Eddie…"

I chuckled a little.

I know that "Eddie" was Grandad's pet name for Grandma, but it always amused me - because *Eddie* was such a butch, manly name.

It was also funny to think that Brother Simon had received a Valentines Day card from someone called Eddie!

As Grandad spoke my eyes were drawn to some of the differently coloured balloons that had somehow made their way onto the stage.

Is it just me, or do pink balloons always make you think about tits?

And red balloons make you think about tits in a hot bath?

And green balloons make you think about Alien tits?

And blue balloons make you think about really cold…..

Oh, you see what I'm getting at!

Before I got myself too excited, I re-focused on Grandad.

"We would like to thank you all for coming here tonight to help us celebrate our Golden Wedding Anniversary. It's so nice that, ten years ago, so many of you also helped us celebrate our "Rudy Anniversary"!"

Everyone laughed - even Mum!

She usually got embarrassed about being reminded of her spelling cock-up. The double Vodka was obviously taking its effect - and was possibly pushing her towards that money winning dance floor fall!

"You may want to sit comfortably" continued Grandad,

"I've got quite a few things to say………Eddie and I were both born in 1924. She's a couple of months older, which maybe explains why she bosses me around all the time!

We grew up on the same road, Grafton Street, in Rochdale, Lancashire. We've known each other all our lives.

We were friends as kids and, when the War broke out, and people went away and didn't come back - it makes you realise what is important, and which people are important.

And, for me, it was all about Edna Laurie.

We lived on the same street for a reason - we were *meant* to be together.

We were married on July 24th ……1942 - for those of you who aren't great at maths!

It was a small wedding - we didn't have any money.

I wore a suit that was my Uncle Herbert's. It was too small for me."

"WAS IT THE SAME SUIT YOU'RE WEARING NOW?" someone shouted

Goodbye B.M.X. Hello S.E.X.

from the bar area!

A few laughs echoed around the room.

Grandad smiled but showed by the look on his face that this wasn't the time for heckling. He always had a cool authoritativeness about him.

There would be no more interruptions.

"Eddie wore the dress her Mother had been married in. It was too big for her.

We looked ridiculous.

There is a photo on the wall, of us in our ill-fitting Wedding clothes - if you want to have a good laugh!

But it was a beautiful day.

A *perfect* day.

There was no honeymoon - I was sent to Germany with the Army a couple of weeks later.

I saw some heavy action - lots of good men being killed.

From one day to the next, I didn't know if I would ever see Eddie again.

But the mere possibility I *would*, kept me going every single second.

After the War we said we would treat ourselves to a honeymoon away if we could.

Just a week away - just the two of us.

We never managed to do it.

I don't think we missed out though, because luckily, our whole marriage has been like one long honeymoon!"

I looked at Louise and was about to say "He's laying it on a bit thick, isn't he?", but she was concentrating on Grandad and was all glazy-eyed, so I said nothing.

"Apart from my time in Germany, we have been with each other every single day.

We are lucky enough to have two beautiful daughters - Anita and Lynda - who we want to thank, not only for their help in arranging tonight, but also for being wonderful people, wonderful daughters and wonderful friends.

Along with their husbands David and Melvin, they have brought up our four wonderful Grandchildren - Angus, Violet, Simon and Paul.

Thank you all."

Louise nudged me in the side - maybe just in case I hadn't noticed my name being mentioned!

A small round of applause was stopped by Grandad's outstretched hand - he had more to say!

I wondered whether sneaking off to the toilet would be rude while he was still talking.

It would certainly be less rude than what would happen if he kept talking for much longer!

I squeezed my legs together and gambled that he was nearly finished.

"If you can judge a man's wealth by his family and the friends he keeps, then I am the richest man in the World!

The final words are to Eddie.
Thank you for always being with me.
I've had a Hell of a time!
I know a lot of you were worried that I was going to recite the poem that I wrote for Eddie while I was in Germany - like I did ten years ago. Don't worry - I'm not going to!"

There was a small amount of cheering.

"I've written a *new* one to recite!"

The cheers quickly turned to good-natured boo's!

"It's only a short one.

It's to you, Eddie - it's called "Always"

<u>*Always*</u>

Always in my heart, Always in my Soul,
Always on my Mind, Always - Everywhere I go.

Always by my side, Always, 'til the end of days,
Always destined to be one, You and I - Always!

People started clapping as he walked off stage.

I looked around and saw that lot's of people were wiping tears from their eyes.

How the Hell did he do it?

I looked at Louise and could see my blurred reflection in her moist eyes.

"That was *so* beautiful" she said, staring at me all content and serene.

Her look nicely reflected the mood of the whole room. There was a pleasant calmness as people soaked in the warmth of Grandad's words.

The DJ interrupted the quietness with another announcement.

"What Howard forgot to add, was that the buffet is now OPEN!"

The calmness collapsed like a house of cards.

Chairs were thrown out of the way as most people jumped up off their seats.

A massive tide of people headed towards the buffet area; climbing over the up-turned chairs, knocking children and old people out of the way, like a herd of stampeding Buffalo!

And leading the way, as usual, was Uncle Geoff.

For a slimish guy, he does seem to put away more than his fair share of food. Although Dad says that "*food catches up with everyone, sooner or later!*" – arguing that Cyril Smith was once a slim man "*until the chocolate éclairs eventually caught up with him*"!

Dad does seem to have quite an anthology of sayings that cover pretty much every situation in life.

Most of them are complete nonsense though.

Actually, most of what he says in general is complete nonsense.

For example, he's one of those people who insist that, although everyone

Goodbye B.M.X. Hello S.E.X.

else's smell disgusting, there's quite a nice, fragrant aroma to his own shits!

Luckily for us, at our table at the side of the room, we were not sitting along the dangerous, manic route to the feeding zone.

Mum stayed still in her chair; an almost crazy grin underlining her vacant eyes. She was maybe thinking about Grandad's sentimental words, was well and truly under the influence of the excessive Vodka or was sinisterly anticipating the ravenous mobs' disappointment when they got to her food!

After the human tidal wave had passed, I carefully shuffled my way to the toilet - moving carefully, like my knees were glued together. I certainly didn't want another public display of escaped urine!

The feeding frenzy lasted for about forty-five minutes, after which everybody entered the right frame of mind for the "business-end" of the evening - drinking, dancing and more drinking!

Auntie Miriam turned out to be the first dance floor faller.

Dad refused to pay up to Uncle Geoff though, claiming that Geoff had "carefully positioned" the ash tray that she tripped over!

Well "tripped over" was the wrong description.

After standing on the ash tray, Miriam skidded on it with one leg in the air, not unlike a figure skater on ice, for about five metres before she fell.

Luckily she wasn't injured.

Her fall was somewhat "cushioned" by an innocent by-passer - Brother Simon!

She was almost badly burnt though - by the redness of Brother Simon's face!

It was a brilliant moment!

Damn Dad for being too cheap to follow through with his video camera buying idea!

At the end of the night things slowed right down and the DJ played some soppy, smoochy songs.

I even asked him to play mine and Louise's song - Bryan Adams' *"Heaven"*.

He either didn't hear me properly, or didn't have it and so decided to play the closest thing he did have; because we were soon in a slow embrace dancing to a Showaddywaddy version of *"Three Steps To Heaven"*!

At least it got Dad on to the dance floor.

Although the music wasn't what we were used to; I couldn't help but feel like everything was perfect.

Like everything fitted.

Just like how Grandad had told how Grandma was always with him - Louise was always with me.

She was always at my house, (including, now, at the Sunday night card Schools) she was there at the high jump contest, she was there at my Cricket triumph - she was always around when I was doing anything to be proud of.

She brought the best out of me.

And I loved being with her!

Because......yes, I loved her!

It *was* love!

Gary Locke

This time I didn't need a Doctors opinion - I was sure of it!

Mum had always told me that you knew what *real* love was, because it was something that was worth more than anything else in the whole World.

And Louise was *definitely* worth more than anything else in the whole World.

The following night, away from the hysteria of the party; just the two of us in my room, I told her how much she meant to me.

Not to Showaddy-bloody-waddy, but during *our* song.

I told her I couldn't imagine life without her.

She told me she loved me more than anything in the World.

Suddenly "hands on" kissing was not enough.

And, after her disappearing to the bathroom to "slip into something comfortable", it happened!

Not overly pre-planned, and fitting some cliché sporting analogy!

But spontaneously and naturally.

And it was everything I ever thought it would be.

Awkward, (those condoms *really* are a tricky item!) painful and very fast!

But also beautiful.

There was no doubt at all – it really was love!

Goodbye B.M.X. Hello S.E.X.

<u>*Something Worth*</u>

Something Worth fighting for, Something Worth crying for,
Something Worth cheating and stealing and lying for,

Something Worth believing in, and making a stand for,
Something Worth following, and changing life plans for,

Something Worth the birds, and the Sun in the sky,
Something Worth the air, that is keeping you alive,

Something Worth today, Something Worth tomorrow,
Something Worth loving and losing and sorrow,

Something Worth the Moon, Something Worth the Stars,
Something that's even Worth, changing who you are,

Something Worth your soul, Something Worth your heart,
Something Worth risking, having them torn apart,

Something Worth reaching for, Something Worth trying for,
Something Worth living for, even Worth dying for,

I think you're Something Worth.....

August 1992

Chapter Twenty Four – *"…the day will come…"*

As August arrived, Holly Grove was gripped by a full blown 1970's style heat wave. (Why do people still go on about the "real" Summers of the Seventies?)

It wasn't just the baking Sun that was Hot! Hot! Hot! though; me and Louise had entered a new physical phase in our relationship that could only be described as "inferno"!

(This was more in my head than the actual truth. I was still struggling with understanding how to put a condom on quickly – it was near-impossible to tell if they were inside out or not!)

So, in reality, my fumbling "Johnny" application was somewhat spoiling our momentum!

Whatever stage I was at in my love making career, (it was safe to say I was at least *one or two* steps away from *expert* status) I could certainly hand in my "Virgin Card" – because I wouldn't be needing it anymore.

Louise and I had decided to keep our "progress" to ourselves.

It was something private; just between the two of us.

Therefore we agreed to keep it that way – and not even tell our best friends.

This wasn't a problem for me, because I had always let John, Little Si and Mark believe that me and Louise had already "done it".

Why is it automatically assumed that the phrase *"I can neither confirm nor deny it"* is an open admission to doing something?

I didn't mind though, that they already thought I had earned my "flying stripes".

They were all still employees of Richard Branson, and it kind of made them look up to me.

Explaining to them what it was like had been a bit tricky, but it turns out that what I made up wasn't too far from the reality. (Apart from it being somewhat quicker than the twenty minutes I had optimistically put in my story!)

Louise had said that if, and when, we did tell our friends – we shouldn't say that we'd had sex, because we hadn't.

Although I had established that I wasn't an expert, I thought I would have to disagree.

If there was a Scouts' badge for having sex, then I was now entitled to sow it onto my jumper!

It's good that I hadn't argued this point with her though, because she had meant something else.

"Because it wasn't sex," she had said,

"It was love!"

And she was right – it was!

Goodbye B.M.X. Hello S.E.X.

And we had the *whole* Summer ahead of us – with nothing much else to do. How would we fill the time?

As well as trying to master my condom speed-dressing, (I was buying a lot of large cucumbers! Ok, medium sized cucumbers! Ok, *small!*) Louise and I also spent much of the Summer walking Wally or shopping.

I also found time to see the guys quite often, as well as making sure I was teasing Brother Simon daily. After all I was on holiday, and he was going to work everyday – trying to differentiate between real tasks and wind-ups!

When with Louise, she actually preferred seeing each other at my house rather than hers. She said it felt more comfortable and cosier – more in keeping with a house she would want in the future.

This felt like a waste, because I am sure her Dad would be able to buy her a much grander house than the one we lived in.

I would have to work on her!

Although it's probably best for me not to try and insist that, in general, bigger is better!

But I suppose it made me realise that our house *is* nice – inside and outside.

Perhaps surprisingly, Dad liked to work hard in the garden.

And it showed.

It was a lovely place to sit in the Summer – very colourful and calming.

Dad had recently installed a bird bath and it was beginning to attract a wide range of feathered visitors.

The garden was perhaps a little too exposed for some of mine and Louise's favourite Summer activities – but that's what *indoors* were invented for!

I had lived in the same house all my life.

It was modest, or "cosy" as Louise had commented; but it was certainly adequate for me, Brother Simon, Mum, Dad and Wally.

Mum and Dad weren't big on "mod cons" – they were still trying to get the hang of touch button telephones and video recorders.

It was embarrassing the number of times that Dad had tried to tape "Match of the Day", but had somehow mistakenly ended up with some late night European movie full of naked Swedish women!

Fair play to him though, he wanted to learn from his own mistakes.

No matter how many times he messed it up, he would never allow me or Brother Simon to set the video correctly for him!

My room was different – it was like the technological hub of the house.

I not only had a video (that I could set correctly!) but also a TV with teletext, and a triple decker hi-fi system.

And everything was remote controlled.

From the comfort of my bed, I could turn off the TV / video, and put on a Bryan Adams song – all at the touch of a button.

Very useful in certain circumstances, giving me more valuable time to do other things – like attempt another condom "puzzle"!

Downstairs was a bit more "traditional".

In the living room, there was a colourful, patterned carpet that had laid

Gary Locke

there for as long as I could remember.

Mum loved it.

The rest of the World weren't quite so sure!

Mum said that it had been advertised in the carpet shop as being based on a pattern by the Spanish designer "Gaudi".

Dad always joked that she had read the advertisement wrong, and that it had actually said "Gaudy"!

Mum always answered back by saying "Laugh all you want David – you paid for it!"

It was of oddly shaped and coloured flowers on a blue background.

The strange patterns however, did look a bit like roads, and were therefore good for playing with your matchbox cars on – which worked well because I was never allowed a *real* car matt to play on!

Ok, probably time to let it go now!

And I was never allowed to have a Spiderman outfit!

Ok, probably time to let *all* those childhood frustrations go!

Although the carpet was "eye-catching" the main feature of the living room was the brick built fireplace and mantelpiece that dominated a side wall.

It wasn't *just* a decorative feature though.

Oh no, as Brother Simon and I grew, we weren't measured in feet and inches, or the European-favoured metres and centimetres; *we* were measured in *bricks*!

In fact, I think the fireplace was Mum and Dads main way of scaling our very development.

I remember being at a party once, when one of the other Fathers had asked Dad "What age is Paul now?", to which Dad answered "Six and a half bricks!"

When we were younger Brother Simon was always three or four bricks taller than me.

He was the "Big Brother" and took the role seriously; using this size difference to his advantage.

He used to think I was there so that he had someone to practice on. Things like knuckle rapping, Chinese burns and BMX jumping!

A particular favourite of his was the self-invented "Typewriter".

Because of his extra weight, he could easily pin me to the floor by putting his knees on my shoulders.

In that position he would pretend that I was a typewriter and jab his fingers into my chest. (Or typewriter keyboard!)

When his "typing" had reached the end of each line; he would initiate the carriage return by slapping my face and yelling "BING!"

Whilst having me pinned down, he also liked to "pretend" to spit onto my face. He would draw up something preposterously green from the depths of his throat, and let it slowly drip down towards my face.

Most of the time he would suck it back up just as I thought it was going to drop onto me.

But every now and again he misjudged the "point of no return" and, despite

Goodbye B.M.X. Hello S.E.X.

trying to retrieve it, the green bomb would plummet onto my helpless face!

He would also often try to catch me off guard with the offer of a friendly and innocuous looking handshake. If I was taken by surprise and embraced his hand, he would squeeze so hard that I inevitably ended up on my knees.

"Who is the King?" he would ask repeatedly, until I said it was him and swore my everlasting allegiance to him.

I'm not sure if anyone ever considered Brother Simons actions to be, at least, bordering on "bullying".

Certainly no-one seemed to be over-concerned by my constant bruising, red-raw wrists or scarred knuckles.

Or by the fact that I jumped a mile every time I heard any kind of "bing". (Even the sound of the microwave brought me out in a cold sweat! And not just because it was a sign that Mum had over-radiated another ready meal for tea!)

Brother Simon couldn't be totally blamed for his actions though – Mum and Dad had said, on a number of occasions, that they'd only had me so that he would have someone to play with.

It was just unfortunate for me, that he decided to play with me, the way that other kids played with their "Stretch Armstrong's"!

As time passed by though, this size difference got less and less.

I like to think that it was due to me "willing" myself to grow a bit more each night.

A matter of will-power.

It may well just have been a genetics thing though.

Some people were naturally small, like Ronnie Corbett or perhaps, closer to home, Dad.

Some people were naturally taller, like Bruce Forsyth or perhaps, non celebrity, someone like our Milkman!

I vaguely remember one Sunday evening when Auntie Miriam must have noticed that I was catching up with Brother Simon in size.

After some particularly bad Chinese burns, (Brother Simon was pretending my arm was the throttle for "Street Hawk"!) she said to him,

"Be careful Simon – the day will come when Paul's bigger than you!"

Brother Simon scoffed at the suggestion.

"It will never happen" he had confidently predicated.

He hadn't reckoned on the strength of will-power and/or genetics!

It was a Thursday evening when it happened.

I was preparing to go and meet Louise when Brother Simon challenged me to a game of catch.

We hadn't measured ourselves for months and months – I have no idea what "brick age" Mum and Dad were telling people we were.

A "game of catch" was not really an adequate description for what our contest really was.

We would take it in turns to throw a tennis ball at each other, as hard as was humanly possible.

The loser was either the first one to drop the ball; or the first one to be

Gary Locke

knocked out by a blow to the head!

Brother Simon had a near perfect record; almost all wins coming by knock-out – but recently I was becoming more competitive.

Ten "finger-stinging" catches each and I changed tactics.

I launched a lower aimed throw that reaped a double reward.

Not only did Brother Simon drop it, making me surprisingly victorious, but he was also badly winded.

It was like I had won twice with one throw!

He was a bad loser at the best of times, but this defeat was not helped by an on-looking Mum who commented,

"Paul, I think you're taller than Simon now!"

"No way!" came the cry from Brother Simon as he tried to catch his breath.

We were marched off to the "measuring wall" straight away.

Four comparisons later, Brother Simon had to accept that I was "perhaps, possibly, slightly taller."

He was right; it *was* close, maybe only half a brick in it, but I was definitely taller.

"You may be taller, but I'll always be stronger and better looking!" Brother Simon said, trying to assert some authority.

He was not impressed by my look – which could not have said "whatever – loser" more clearly if I'd have written it on a banner and waved it around!

I checked my watch and realised that it was time for me to set off to meet Louise.

As I moved towards the door, Brother Simon caught me unaware by holding his hand out for me to shake.

I was careless.

Before I Knew it he had me in his "death grip" hold.

It hadn't happened for quite some time, but I followed my usual tactic – try to resist as long as possible, by squeezing hard, before accepting the inevitable "crushing".

I resisted for about five seconds and realised, by the redness of his face, Brother Simon had reached "full thrust".

But I wasn't at *my* limit.

I put all my effort in and watched in amazement as he slowly sank to his knees.

It was like watching a once-mighty Oak being felled. Silent and dignified, but ultimately ending up crashing to the ground.

He was down but I wasn't sure what to do.

It came to me quickly.

"Who is the new King?" I asked standing over him.

He didn't answer.

I didn't ask again. Instead I just maintained my grip at full power.

"You are!" he finally said, like a squealing little Rat begging for mercy. (Pretty much how I had always done!)

"Pardon?" I asked, trying to milk the glorious situation for all that I could.

Goodbye B.M.X. Hello S.E.X.

"You are!" he said again quickly.
I released him.
He slowly rubbed his right hand with his left as he got back to his feet.
"I didn't have a proper grip!" he said.
They were the words out of his mouth, but his eyes betrayed him.
They told a different story.
He was a fallen warrior.
Defeated.
I decided not to offer him a rematch.
Instead I just gave him a knowing smile.
After the recent chinks in his armour, most notably his Valentines Day Card humiliation, I decided not to rub his nose in it further.
But there was no doubt about it – this had been a fatal blow!
I knew there would be no more Chinese burns or knuckle rapping.
And he certainly wouldn't be turning to me the next time he felt like "typing a letter"!
"I'm off to meet Louise" I said, nodding at Brother Simon as I headed for the door.
I walked with a slow swagger – not unlike I was leaving a Wild, West Saloon that I had just cleaned up.
There was a new Sheriff in Town!

Gary Locke

Chapter Twenty Five – *"…exam results…"*

I was beginning to wonder whether I had sold myself short at the start of the year. Not only was I flying through my targets list, but I was achieving things I could not have thought possible in my wildest dreams. (And my dreams could be wilder than Ken Dodd's' hair!)

The latest achievement of succeeding Brother Simon as Alpha (minor) Male in the Day house would have been one I would have taken great pleasure in ticking off.

Maybe I should add a few new targets to go at for the remaining four and a half months of the year.

I suppose turning the tables completely on Brother Simon by performing his "typewriter" on him could be an enjoyable experience.

Watching *him* jump at the tiniest hint of a "bing" would be very satisfying.

Also, was a Merv Hughes-style handle-bar moustache a possibility, or perhaps still beyond me? Given my exceptional year perhaps I should attempt to grow one. (I could always smear some fertiliser above my top lip when I went to bed each night!)

Realistically though it was now time to concentrate my positive thinking towards just one thing.

For a date with destiny was fast approaching.

What started, at the beginning of Summer, like a dot on the horizon was now becoming a skyscraper that was casting a looming shadow over everything.

Exam Results!

They were due on Thursday 27th August.

There were two options available.

You could have the results delivered through the post; but there were was a charge for that, so it wasn't a realistic possibility for me.

Alternatively, you could go to School and collect them by hand.

They would be available from 10am.

There was something more sociable about collecting your results. You could travel with friends, and be there for one another as you discovered your fate.

I suppose there was also something slightly sadistic about it all.

There would no doubt be someone who was overwhelmingly disappointed with their grades, and would make a scene of themselves.

It wouldn't surprise me if one of the more callous teachers was filming the student reactions.

Maybe, some time in the future, these "humorous" videos will be accessible to everyone, if this whole "internet" thing takes does ever take off!

Well accessible to those two nerds and a Dog anyway!

The day before the results were due, several strange things happened.

1…Dad was up before lunch – *"I felt like getting up – no big deal!"* (Very odd!)

Goodbye B.M.X. Hello S.E.X.

2…The postman was late. We didn't get our mail until 10.30am. "Lazy, lanky, late idiot!" Dad moaned as he dropped just one letter off.
3…The one letter we received was an official looking one, sent from Holly Grove High School, addressed to the "Parents / Guardians of Paul Day".

Dad looked confused as he stared at the white envelope.
It turned out he was trying to work out what the letter was before opening it. (Why do people insist on guessing a letters' contents – instead of just opening it and finding out?)
"Looks like your exam results have been sent here" Dad said, after completing his diagnosis.
"Let's see how you've done shall we?" he asked, accompanied by the sort of sinister stare and grin that a butcher gives a Turkey a few weeks before Christmas.
Oh my God!
Dad was holding the blueprint to my future in an envelope in his hands; and was about to open it and reveal all.
"Don't you think I should look at it first?" I asked in a panicky voice; twice the speed at which I normally spoke.
Dad just gave me an irritated "Shhhh!", as if he was one of those old women working in the library.
As his finger slid along the envelope, tearing the paper as it went, the tension was unbearable.
I felt a sudden urge to jump through the front window and run as fast as I could. (In my mind I was momentarily Rocky Balboa running up the steps of the Philadelphia Museum!)
Before jumping though, I stalled wondering how Dad would react to me landing on, and crushing, his prize Geraniums in the front garden.
After the delay, there was no time to think up a new plan, because Dad had the envelope open, and the papers were in his hand.
It was here – the moment of truth!
I stood, more still than a marble statue, as Dad flicked slowly though the pages, with a confused look on his face.
"These aren't your exam results." he finally said.
Relief showered over me, like cool raindrops on a mid-Summers day.
"It's your end of term-two report card," Dad continued,
"And if your exam results are as bad as these predictions – you're in *big trouble!*"
The refreshing relief sensation I had been feeling changed instantly; and now felt like there was a large flock of loose Seagulls hovering overhead!
Dad passed me the report, almost throwing it, like it was a hot potato he had to get out of his hand.
He gave me a disapproving shake of the head, which wasn't unusual – he did more head shaking than a mechanic looking over a car!
I sat down in the arm chair by the window and began to read.

Gary Locke

Dear: Parent / Guardian of: Paul Day

This report was not collected by the above student on the final day of term two, as was instructed.
It has been found during the Summer holiday file clearing exercise.
If you have any comments and / or queries, please do not hesitate to contact the School directly.

Yours faithfully,

Jeanette Sawyer – Schools Secretary Office.

Perhaps my plan, back in February, of *"If I don't collect my report, then my parents will never see it"* had not been so fool-proof after all.
John's plan of *"I'm going to collect mine – then burn it!"*, now seemed to make a lot more sense!
I continued reading.

English Literature / Language – Miss Wilder

? Mistake, student not in my class!
Paul usually likes to keep himself to himself.
He should try to be more actively involved in lessons, rather than sitting at the back of the class, humming children's TV show theme tunes.
I am surprised but pleased about his recent attendance at Poetry Club – and he shows some understanding and flair – especially for contemporary poetry.
Should try to be more "visible" in lessons.

Expected Grade(s) -

English Language – E
English Literature – B/C

French – Mr Martin

Paul is getting to grips with some of the basic principles, but must learn that speaking English in an attempted French accent (like a bad episode of 'Allo 'Allo) does not substitute the need to learn real French words.
He should also resist the temptation of playing games under his desk, and shouting out comments like "Should have shown more backbone in World War Two!"
Learning three new words a day (preferably non-swearing or sexual!) would greatly enhance his vocabulary.
He would also find it helpful to volunteer for more conversation practise – the "conversation" is the most important part of the final exam.
Has the potential – but needs to push himself.

Goodbye B.M.X. Hello S.E.X.

Expected Grade(s) – B/C

<u>Applied Science – Mr Boland</u>

It is easy to see that Paul has some natural flair for many of the Science applications. His knack of being able to mix the most volatile of chemicals, without supervision, is staggering.
Unfortunately he may not be able to take this talent further, as one of the main stipulations from the insurance company, as they paid their cheque, was that Paul should not be allowed to use the Science labs once they have been rebuilt!
Still he will never forget what not to mix sulphuric acid with until his dying day!
With closer guidance (working only on theoretical projects) Paul has made some progress. I'm not sure that he will ever astound us with anything close to "Einstein's theory of relativity", but he has taken steps in the right direction with observations such as "ice is much colder than water" and "the Sun is probably bigger than it actually looks"!
I have been pleased with his telescopic descriptions of the Moon, even if his essays resemble the reference book (sometimes word for word!); and despite when I've checked his telescope position, it not always being focused on the Moons surface – but more often Miss Rathbone's netball class!
A career in a scientific environment may not be an option.

Expected Grade(s) – E/F

<u>Mathematics – Mr Gillard</u>

If Paul spent as much time concentrating as he did throwing exercise books around, I am sure he would benefit greatly.
He has a natural understanding of most topics, but fails to put in the commitment to know them inside out.
This is a big term for Paul and he needs to work much harder to achieve his potential.

Expected Grade(s) – B/C

<u>Geography – Mr Rivers</u>

I think it is safe to say that Geography is not one of Paul's strongest subjects. (I certainly hope so anyway!)
His awareness of where places are is so poor, that it is a mini-triumph if he manages to find the class-room once in a while.
In our recent "mock" exams, Paul stated that the "Watford Gap" was "a clothes shop near Northampton"; that "Ordnance Survey" was an "opinion poll of Military equipment", and that "Gibraltar Rock" was the "earliest form of Heavy Metal".
My advice for the final term is "daily praying". Let's hope someone "upstairs" likes Paul!

It will be an achievement if he finds the School Hall to take his exam.

Expected Grade(s) – N/U

Craft, Design and Technology (C.D.T.) – Mr Jones

Paul is slightly better as making jokes, than he is at making things out of Wood or Metal.
Unfortunately this is not a compliment!
If he spent as much time learning practical techniques as he did trying to entertain the class (especially the female half) he may do much better.
Has a tendency for laughing for no apparent reason – something that is not welcome in any part of society – School or Workplace.
Some of his coursework is ok, but he needs a big improvement in the final term to secure a reasonable grade.

Expected Grade(s) – E/F

Physical Education (P.E.) – Mr Winters

It would be unfair to label Paul as having "two left feet". Unfair to those who do have "two left feet"!
Paul usually performs like he's got "two left flippers!"
But what he lacks in natural ability, he makes up for in enthusiasm.
Not sure about the wisdom of entering the high jump for the forthcoming Sports Day events – with his lack of technique he may even struggle to successfully complete the first height!
There are times, when playing for the School football team that we are waiting for a member of the opposition to foul Paul. His "Vinnie Jones" persona serves the team far greater than his attempted "cultured Glenn Hoddle" prance.
I sometimes feel that his approach to Rugby is more geared towards keeping clean than being actively involved – even though the School Sports Centre has perfectly good showering facilities.
His written coursework is showing some promise, so with hard work he may achieve a good pass grade.

Expected Grade(s) – B/C

Music – Mrs Wright

Things are working much better for Paul now that we have found an instrument that matches his talent.
He may have some small timing and volume control issues, but he is making good progress the more he uses the triangle.
He has even been asked to audition as third triangle reserve for the School Orchestra – in case they ever incorporate a triangle into their set up.

Goodbye B.M.X. Hello S.E.X.

It seems a shame now that several good instruments were damaged on the way to finding "Paul's instrument" – although the Schools "replacement budget" should be able to replace these over the next twenty years or so!
I have been pleased with Paul's willingness to help with some of the musical projects (thankfully in a non-playing sense). In particular he worked well as a "roadie" on the annual "Rock 'n' Roll" evening and, although the band no longer has School guitars, drums or keyboards they can play, the night was a great success.
Paul is not the most naturally gifted musician in the class, but he has certainly (and unfortunately literally at times) given everything a good bash!
Perhaps, with hindsight, Music was not the best choice of subject for Paul.

Expected Grade(s) – N/U

    I finished reading and took a big gulp.
    One of those slow, noisy gulps that you are not sure will make it past your throat!
    The predictions were pretty bad.
    But maybe the teachers weren't that great at predicting results.
    In fact, as I thought about it, I remembered Brother Simon saying the same thing about the exam predictions he was given.
    He had said that the teachers were "about as good as predicting as the weathermen"!
    I remembered something else though – Brother Simon's results had been much <u>worse</u> than predicted.
    I stood up and re-contemplated the window jump. I didn't think that a few squashed Geraniums could make Dad anymore angry than this report had.
    I thought things through.
    Most of these comments had been from the end of the second term.
    I'd had the whole of the last term to improve things – and if I remembered correctly, I had worked really hard that last term.
    I had put every ounce of effort into working as hard as I could.
    For a moment, I was convincing myself everything was going to be alright.
    Good old brain questioned how it really was.
    I wasn't perhaps distracted from my School work by something like the growing feelings for a girlfriend?
    Who needed enemies when your own mind always turns against you?
    After about an hour, which included at least five of Dads disappointed headshakes, and me thinking about my bad results and contemplating life as a potential triangle busker; I thought things through again.
    Maybe this report *wasn't* such a bad thing.
    Perhaps it was actually good timing that it had arrived today.
    Maybe Dad, and later Mum, could get all their disappointment and anger out of the way now.
    Maybe when I got my results the next day – there may be a pleasant little surprise.

Unless, of course, if my results did turn out to be even worse than the predictions.

Bloody brain!

I walked to School the next day with Louise.

It was a fairly quiet walk.

I think Louise was really nervous and anxious. She had put a lot of pressure on herself to do well – and she was about to find out the results of all her efforts.

I was quiet because my mind was split in two.

I was half contemplating not being able to go to College; thinking that potentially this could be one of the final walks I would ever have with Louise.

The other 50% brain capacity was working out songs I could play with a triangle.

There weren't many.

In fact the only thing I could come up with was a high-pitched rendition of the "Bongs" part of the News at Ten theme tune!

I wonder if I could get an orchestra to play the rest of it with me?

Before I knew it we were at the School Hall.

It was a similar scene to the ones I had become used to during the exams themselves.

Worried faces wherever you looked; a blanket of near silence draped over everyone and the unmistakable aroma of nerves festering in the air!

It was ten to ten – and everyone was anxiously waiting outside the locked Hall doors.

I could see several smug looking teachers walking around inside – no doubt basking in the power of their final act of control over us.

After ten tense minutes trying to act cool, alternating my mingling between Louise and the guys (who arrived together, slightly after us) Mr Langden opened the Hall doors – carrying his trusty loud hailer in one hand.

A couple of people eating crisps panicked and instinctively stuffed the packets into their pockets!

Despite the urge to surge forward, everyone actually backed away from the crazy-eyed one; no doubt in an attempt to protect their ears from the imminent, deafening announcement.

"EVERYBODY LISTEN CAREFULLY....."

"HE'S ONLY GOING TO SAY THIS ONCE!" I shouted.

Only one person laughed – me.

Was I the only one who had watched too much 'Allo 'Allo whilst revising for the French exam?

"......THERE ARE SIX TEACHERS INSIDE HANDING OUT YOUR RESULTS. MR RIVERS HAS ALL SURNAMES BETWEEN A AND D,

MISS HOWARTH HAS E TO H,

MR SMITH HAS I TO L,

MRS TAYLOR HAS M TO P,

Goodbye B.M.X. Hello S.E.X.

MR MARTIN HAS Q TO T,
AND MISS RATHBONE HAS U TO Z.
QUEUE UP CALMLY, IN SINGLE FILE, BEHIND THE RELEVANT TEACHER, AND YOU WILL BE GIVEN YOUR RESULTS.
GOOD LUCK EVERYONE."

Mr Langden stepped aside in his usual speedy, flamboyant style; and the crowd of teenagers moved as one, like a shoal of fish, almost swimming towards the open doors.

"Bring your results out here," said Louise. "We'll open them together."

I nodded as she leant in and kissed me on the cheek.

With that she joined the other fish, desperately pushing and fighting for entry into the Hall.

I turned around to where Little Si, John and Mark where standing. I put my hand out and the other three, in Musketeer style, stacked their hands on top.

"Here goes" I said. "Best of luck!"

We joined the mass of bodies and got pulled along by the movement of the crowd. The sensation of moving without really needing to walk felt like it did to be standing in the Kippax stand when City scored a goal. (A feeling that, despite standing in there often, I hadn't experienced that much!)

I was soon in my relevant queue (after spending a couple of minutes mistakenly in the M to P queue – until it was pointed out my surname was *Day* and not *Paul*!) and was just four people away from receiving my "results of destiny".

Mr Rivers was asking for names, finding the correct envelope from the box in front of him, then handing it out with a wish of "Good Luck!"

"Paul Day!" I said when I reached him.

He flicked through the letters, but to no avail.

My results weren't there. I didn't know what to feel.

Should it be relief, should it be panic?

There was no time to wonder, because a second look had proved fruitful.

"Good Luck!" said Mr Rivers.

I didn't thank him, because I didn't appreciate the snigger that accompanied his words as he passed me my envelope.

I looked around to see that Louise was just making her way back out of the Hall doors – towards our planned meeting point.

I also saw that the guys were still queuing for their results.

In fact Mark was being advised by Mrs Taylor that he, also, should not be in the M to P queue, but actually the E to H one.

What a plonker!

It crossed my mind not to follow Louise.

I could easily jump through a side window and make a run for it across the School field.

No I should stick to the plan.

I made my way out to meet Louise, while being concerned about the number of windows I was recently contemplating jumping through!

Louise had a terrified look on her face, but at the same time her eyes were dancing with excitement.

"You go first" I said, seeing that she was dying to open her envelope.

She smiled and then ripped open her letter; with the same intensity that someone who hadn't eaten for a week would rip the leg off a cooked Chicken!

Her eyes lit up as she scanned her grades.

She didn't say any words and instead just passed me the results sheet.

GCSE EXAMINATION RESULTS
Centre Number: B622 – HOLLY GROVE HIGH SCHOOL
Candidate Number: D9749 – KNIGHT, LOUISE

GRADE	SUBJECT
A	German
A	Eng. Lang.
B	Eng. Lit.
B	Mathematics
A	App. Science
A	Technology
B	History
B	C.D.T.
A	Drama

I didn't take it in at first – I could just see that she had achieved a "double ABBA".

It took a couple of sickly seconds of *"Dancing Queen"* in my mind, before I realised she had five A's and four B's.

For a moment she was that annoying, swotty girl that she had been before I had got to know her.

Then I had to smile.

She had worked extremely hard, and had got the reward she deserved.

I was delighted for her.

My secret wish that, if I didn't get enough passes to go to College, then hopefully Louise wouldn't as well, was always going to be a bit of a long shot!

"Brilliant!" I said, giving her a big hug.

"That's absolutely brilliant. Well done, you!"

"Do you want me to open yours?" Louise asked excitedly, pulling out of the embrace.

Even though every inch of me screamed NO!, I nodded.

I felt like I really didn't want to find out my results, and it felt even worse that someone else would find out first.

As she opened the envelope, with the same starving-like intensity that she had for her own, I realised that maybe finding out my fate through the discovery of the one I loved maybe was better than seeing it for myself.

I tried to read her eyes as she pulled out my results sheet.

Goodbye B.M.X. Hello S.E.X.

This time, unlike when she read her own grades, when they found the information her eyes didn't intensify and shine like two blazing Suns.

This time the sparkle died and faded out of sight.

She didn't say a word, but instead slowly passed me my sheet; her face frowning with sorrow.

I took the paper and prepared myself for the worst.

Realities flashed through my mind.

No College.

Angry parents.

Probably no more Louise.

Probably a job ay Uncle Geoff's garage with Brother Simon – as new mickey-taking sitting duck!

I let my eyes meet the words on the sheet.

GCSE EXAMINATION RESULTS
Centre Number: B622 – HOLLY GROVE HIGH SCHOOL
Candidate Number: R5117 – DAY, PAUL

GRADE	SUBJECT
A	French
B	Mathematics
E	App. Science
E	Eng. Lang.
F	C.D.T.
B	P.E.
U	Music
N	Geography
A	Eng. Lit.

All I could think of for a few seconds was curry, until my mind decided to process the data.

I had the four A – C grades I needed!

And two of them were A's!

Poetry Club had obviously been a godsend as far as my English Literature was concerned; and my French "plan" had been an unequivocal triumph.

I had achieved the greatest Anglo-French success story since Concorde!

Louise removed her poker face mask and her smile shone as brightly as ever.

"So this means you can come to Stoneport College?" She asked.

"You try and stop me!" I said hugging her; the euphoria flowing over me like an unstoppable avalanche.

I <u>was</u> going to College.

I <u>wasn't</u> going to be working with Brother Simon – well at least for the next two years anyway.

I <u>was</u> going to be in Mum and Dads good books.

Gary Locke

But first of all I was going to kiss my girlfriend.
"Well done, you!" I said as I pulled her close to me.
"Well done, you!" She said as her lips touched mine.....

Goodbye B.M.X. Hello S.E.X.

September 1992

September started like a whirlwind.
Not literally (Although Holly Grove was no stranger to Hurricane-like Autumnal weather!) but because so much was happening in a short space of time.
I had started College.
I had taken P.E., Maths and English Literature to study at A – Level. I had been encouraged to continue with French following my unexpected GCSE A grade, but I didn't want to push my luck.
I was also pretty concerned that Mr Martin would crack under the pressure of his guilt at some point – and expose my exam "plan" for the *cheating* it probably was!
Despite the fresh feeling of going to College, (including the teachers rather generously "leaving it up to you" how much homework you actually did!), the music blaring out of the radio in September was showing no signs of improvement.
After the disastrous early Summer "anthem", courtesy of that ridiculous Erasure / Abba hybrid, (is it some kind of double-edged irony that the word *Erasure* must mean the act of erasing?) we had to endure number one hits from Jimmy Nail (the curly haired, multi broken-nosed, Geordie *Auf Wiedersehen Pet* actor! – Whatever next? Vinnie Jones *acting*??) and a "dance" tune, called "*Rhythm is a Dancer*" by *Snap!*
It was safe to say a new music charts low had been reached!
The first new song to hit the top of the charts while I was at College, was the unashamedly blatant hard-drug "advert" that was *The Shamen's "Ebenezeer Goode"*!
Let's see how long the controversy surrounding it can keep it at number one!
As well as College to contend with in early September, I also had my birthday. (Which happens around that time every year!)
This year I received the best present ever.
Not the "one day paragliding course" that Louise bought me; (God knows what she was thinking!) but rather the pre-paid driving lessons that Grandma and Grandad had got me.
Apparently, as they had done for Brother Simon and Cousin Angus, they had saved up for the best part of a year to buy them for me. (How lucky we are to have them both!)
As an extra "Brucie Bonus", Mum and Dad's "present" was the promise of a car once I had passed my driving test. (Dad was probably banking on me being some kind of record breaking multi test failer!)
So there was no time to worry about Louise's *strange* present, and certainly no time for too much College work (and *none at all* for homework!) because, after cramming my lessons into a two and a half week period, I had a driving

Gary Locke

test to pass.....

Goodbye B.M.X. Hello S.E.X.

Chapter Twenty Six – *"…the driving test…"*

I sat waiting on a leather chair that looked much more comfortable than it actually felt.

In my mind, before sitting, I saw the seat as a "soft" fireside armchair that had been loved for many years before being donated to the test centre.

I now realised that the leather was probably intended to be made into a saddle but had failed some quality check – because it was much too hard!

I had sat on concrete pavements that were softer!

Brian, my driving instructor, had gone to "check us in" at the front desk, leaving me alone with my thoughts.

He had delivered on his promise to get me to my test by the end of twelve lessons. Although this had included six "double lessons", which therefore adds up to eighteen hours of driving or eighteen "regular" lessons, but I was happy to let this go.

Yes eighteen hours of driving that had slowly got me to the point where I was confident I could pass the test.

That was until the night before.

Oh yes, a half an hour "last minute confidence builder" with Brother Simon and his Peugeot 206 changed all that.

Half an hour of stall after stall after stall, interrupted only by sibling giggling and predictions of (roughly translated and heavily censored) "you've got no chance *whatsoever* of passing your test tomorrow – why don't you phone to say you're ill and save your money".

I managed to put the whole episode out of my mind, convincing myself that Brother Simon's car was completely broken, or, at the very least, was not as finely tuned as Brian's high-spec, Micra supercar!

As I waited, I went through the pre-test check list that Brian had given me.

"Wear a good pair of sensible shoes – definitely not white trainers." – check.

"Do not have some kind of crazy shaved haircut that would make you look like some kind of thug." – check.

"Wear some fairly formal and sensible clothes, without them being too formal and sensible that would make it look obvious that you don't normally wear formal and sensible clothing." – no idea what he meant by that, but he hadn't commented on my clothing choice this morning, so I assume that they were ok.

"Michael Arnold!"

I looked up to see a man in a fluorescent vest had just stepped out of the Examiners office and had shouted for his test subject.

A young man with blondish, maybe gingery, hair stood up at the far side of the waiting room. He was joined in standing by an older man, obviously either his instructor or father, who stood in front of him and grabbed him by both shoulders.

After being given some kind of bizarre, inspirational "pre-match" talk, which involved vigorous shaking, Michael walked towards his Examiner. He confirmed his name and then strode confidently behind the luminous vested man and out of the room.

I didn't know how he could look so confident when I felt like my shaking was about to make me fall right off my, harder than concrete, saddle.

I had been told that waiting for your driving test was as nerve wracking as doing an exam, or maybe going to the dentists. But I felt like I was waiting to do an exam while at the dentists, being seen by a dentist that was doing his dentists exam!

I looked up and noticed Brian taking the last few steps back towards me.

"Ok, we're booked in. We'll be ok as long as we don't get the head Examiner, Frank Carter, he can be a bit of a swine. But there are five other Examiners in today, and thankfully *no* women, so I'm sure we'll be fine."

Brian's Caveman-like view on women driving instructors and, I suppose, women in general had been something I had been subjected to on numerous occasions.

Apparently *"it was bad enough giving women the vote, to let <u>them</u> drive as well is taking the piss!"* and *"to let <u>them</u> decide who is capable of driving is another example of society-gone-mad!"*

And to top his ranting off, he added *"whatever next? A <u>female</u> Prime Minister? Or a <u>female</u> King?"*

You should maybe keep up with current affairs a little more Brian!

God knows what sort of life of slavery his wife has!

Brian's observations about the Examiners did nothing to calm me, and instead blended into the hollow messages of "good luck" from Mark, John and Little Si.

Little Si had already passed his test – at the first attempt, (after producing three forms of id to prove he was actually seventeen!) and I'm sure he would love to gloat if I failed.

If it took me several attempts to pass, it would also certainly lessen the pressure on John and Mark, for when they faced their tests in the New Year.

It almost felt like they were waiting to see which one of us would be the first to fall off the cliff – and here I was, staring over the edge!

I stared at a wall sign that said "Didsly Test Centre" and again questioned in my mind why Brian had actually brought me to *Didsly*.

Like me, he also lived in Holly Grove, that actually had its own test centre, and there were at least three others closer to Holly Grove than Didsly was!

My thoughts were broken as my eyes were drawn back to the Examiners office as the door opened, almost in slow motion.

Something inside told me that this was my time, as I desperately tried to stay on the chair that was feeling more and more like a rock hard, wild rodeo ride by the second.

From behind the door out stepped, quite possibly, the tallest man to have ever walked the Earth. He didn't speak, but rather noise erupted from his mouth.

"PAUL DAY"!

I had never heard my name sound so scary.

Goodbye B.M.X. Hello S.E.X.

As I tried to focus and prepared to stand, Brian's whispered voice crushed my spirit.

"Ok, you've got Frank Carter, but there's an *outside* chance you can still do it!"

I noticed how he said "you" for the first time instead of "we" as he had always done before.

I also noticed how he didn't stand up with me.

He didn't give me any words of wisdom, or even shake my shoulders or anything. He just allowed me to walk towards my new nemesis, alone, uninspired and unmotivated.

I felt numb as I confirmed my name.

I then followed Frank out of the waiting room towards the car park, walking like I was wrapped up tight like an Egyptian Mummy.

"Right," came the booming voice "simple eye test. Can you read for me the number plate on the red car?"

Oh my God!

I couldn't even see a red car!

It was alright, I was facing the wrong way.

I turned around and faced towards the red car. As I focused on the number plate my eyes began to glaze over, making the letters and numbers blur into something that resembled Chinese writing.

I hadn't thought about this pre-test eye check but realised now I should have done. I had always shied away from the routine eye tests at School in the fear of maybe being found to be short sighted and therefore made to wear national health spectacles.

The thought of having to hang around with the kids who wore glasses and/or fixed teeth braces used to keep me awake at night. Imagine the indignity of being the only non super brain in a group of pre-destined rocket scientists and brain surgeons!

I blinked my eyes quickly in an attempt to remove the excess fluid. Before I could focus clearly though, I heard the correct number plate sequence spoken out loud – "B622 VBA".

I instinctively repeated the plate quickly enough, I hoped, so that it wouldn't <u>sound</u> repeated.

I looked around to see another testee and his Examiner standing only about five metres away, looking at the same red car. I didn't dwell on staring at them and instead kept my head moving round until I was facing my Examiner.

From just above the clouds, I could make out the look on his face.

It was suspicion.

He glared at me as if he had caught me cheating in an end of year exam. (Or what I thought such a look would be like – I was never <u>caught</u> cheating in an exam!)

I tried to give him a subtle, innocent look that said that I was only reading the number plate that he had asked for.

At least I thought this was the look I gave him. The way his face morphed from suspicion to shock to anger suggested that perhaps I had been unwittingly betrayed by my sub conscience, and given him a "you are a giant oaf" look.

After a split second that seemed like ten minutes; ten minutes of aggressive eyes that bore two holes right through my forehead, he decided not to test me on another number plate. Instead he said "Take me to your vehicle!"

There was something kind of robotic, almost Schwarzenegger, about his command, although my snigger was regrettably louder than planned.

I decided against attempting any small talk en-route to the car and actually nearly walked straight past the gleaming white Micra.

I was too busy being amused by the image in my mind of me being followed by a giant, leather jacketed, sunglasses wearing Terminator.

"This is it." I said, noticing just in time.

As I said it I noticed that, at times, my voice sounded like a timid little mouse.

"Get in. I need to inspect the vehicle exterior," he said.

"I'll be back!"

I will probably never be sure whether he actually said those last three words or if, more probably, my mischievous mind had added them for my amusement.

Either way, I was amused again.

I tried to curb my sniggering and cleared my throat before replying "Ok", and was very pleased about how much more like Barry White I now sounded!

Brian had told me that the Examiner would check the car number plates, tyres and exhaust etc. before the test, so I opened the door, unconcerned that a giant man was getting to grips with my exhaust pipe! (No, that's not a euphemism!)

I slipped into the drivers' seat that felt like it was actually made for me; as though moulded perfectly for my body. I put my hands up onto the steering wheel and the familiarity made me feel more confident than I had all day.

I closed my eyes and blanked out all sound, including my own breathing that I now realised sounded like a pregnant woman in labour.

I began to think about what Brian had told me about the importance of remembering where the *unmarked crossroads* were. "The Examiners Venus Fly Traps" as he called them.

As I pictured them (there were three of them – which was surely another reason why it was strange that Brian favoured Didsly – perhaps he had actually been barred from test centre's at all other areas?) I could make out a faint tapping emerging out of the silence.

I tried to block it out, instead picturing the unmarked crossroads that in my mind turned green and ate any cars that did not "approach with the necessary caution"!

The tapping didn't go away and instead increased quickly in volume until it reached a firm banging.

I looked up to see Frank Carter standing by the passenger door knocking furiously against the window.

Goodbye B.M.X. Hello S.E.X.

I realised that I hadn't unlocked the passenger side door after getting in the car!

Damn the Nissan Micra for not having central locking!

I quickly leant over and unlocked the door and Frank squeezed himself improbably into the seat next to me.

"Sorry about that!" I said to him, accompanied by ill-timed nervous laughter and grin. He threw me a stare that perfectly fitted the phrase "a face like thunder" that crushed the smile on my face.

Had I failed *already* without even starting the car?

"Alright then, Mr Day, start your ignition and move away from the kerb when you believe it is safe to do so."

Ok here we go.

This is it.

I cleared my mind of what had just happened, turned the ignition key and was instantly comforted by the warm purr of the finely tuned Micra engine.

I fooled myself into thinking that it was just me and Brian during one of our lessons and my confidence, that felt like it had been hibernating, noticeably began to wake.

I checked the rear view mirror – that had been cleverly positioned so that I had to stretch slightly to see out of it. This way it was obvious to the Examiner every time I used the mirror! (Brian hadn't been a driver instructor for over 30 years without knowing all the tricks of the trade!).

Behind was clear.

One quick glance over my shoulder (to show that I had checked the "blind spot" – Brian is a true genius!), and then I moved slowly out into the road – as smooth as a Richard Madeley chat up line!

No bunny hopping.

No stalling.

No problem!

All thoughts of the Peugeot 206 debacle the previous evening were banished to the locked part of my mind usually reserved for unwanted nightmares and the odd bed wetting experience.

The roads were quiet and everything was going perfectly.

Left turns, right turns, hills, roundabouts, traffic lights, even two of the dreaded *unmarked crossroads* – everything Frankie was throwing at me, I was hitting back, right out of the park!

"Ok, Mr Day, pull over to the kerb – just after this next corner."

My heart laughed out loud.

He was going to ask me to reverse around the corner – my specialist manoeuvre.

He was throwing the towel in!

"In your own time reverse around this corner, staying as close to the kerb as you can, until I tell you to stop."

Big Frankie was almost beginning to sound semi-human, and certainly a lot less threatening than he had been.

It almost felt like *Terminator 2 – Judgment Day* now – where the *cold blooded killing machine* was actually reprogrammed to be a "good Terminator"!!??!!

How could such a ridiculous idea, actually turn out to be a real classic movie?

Half way around the corner I pictured myself with a big, fat cigar – everything was all so easy now.

As I continued past the corner, I decided to impress my new best friend further by getting even closer to the kerb.

"Ok, stop please." Said Frank, just at the same time as I heard the most sickening sound in my life – "ccrrrrr" – the rear tyre scraping slightly against the kerb!

Frank bolted upright in his seat like a Mongoose that had just spotted a Cobra!

His eyes were as wide as Homer Simpson dinner plates!

He could clearly smell blood, and the look of menace returned to his face instantly.

I could feel myself physically deflate.

From being like a hot air balloon soaring through the clouds, I suddenly felt as flat as an overused whoopee cushion!

The next ten minutes were hell, but my unswerving concentration just about outfought my hands that were shaking more than geriatric hips at an Elvis convention!

A "turn in the road" (three point turn in old money!) was performed competently enough, and four occasions of "pull over by the next kerb" (a heartless attempt to catch me scraping my tyre again?) thankfully passed without a repeat of that terrible sound.

Before I knew it we were back parked outside the test centre and chatting about car safety, stopping distances and looking at road signs.

After three or four successful sign recognitions (or, more accurately, guesses) I realised that Frank wasn't really checking my answers anymore. So much so that he didn't notice me answering one as "bike jumping over car"; although my snigger that accompanied my "camel on the road" answer was met by that now familiar storm-like frown.

And then came the moment.

Frank clicked his pen closed and slowly slid it into the pocket of his shirt.

He straightened the papers on his clip board, then turned square on and looked me in the eye.

His lips seemed to freeze, before beginning again in slow motion as they puckered into shape to pronounce a "c".

Then came the words.

"Congratulations, Mr Day. You have passed!"

In my mind fireworks exploded, as trumpets played and ticker tape fell.

Frank filled in my pass certificate while saying some random words like "learning", "now" and "starts"; and "weapon", "like", "is", "car", but I wasn't really paying attention.

Goodbye B.M.X. Hello S.E.X.

How could I when *Queen* had just entered the stage in my head and were singing "We are the Champions".

Freddie Mercury began to carry me around on his shoulders as the crowd went wild, and began chanting my name. The vision disappeared as I began to become concerned about how close Freddie's head was to my groin area!, and I was back in the car just in time for Frank to pass me my pass certificate.

"Well done." He said as he left the car and began walking back towards the test centre, ducking under a lamp post on his way!

An uncontrollable sensation formed in my stomach and raced up my windpipe before I released it through my mouth as a euphoric and deafening, triumphant scream.

Frank stopped and looked back at me, and I'm sure I saw a glint of red sparkle in his eyes!

But there was nothing he could do.

It was too late – I had the endorsing paperwork in my hand.

It did cross my mind that he could actually *terminate* me if he so desired, but luckily he decided not to, and continued his robotic stomp back towards his office.

I had passed *first time*.

I pictured the disappointed looks of John, Mark and Little Si's faces when I told them my good news. I think they had all had bets with each other about what aspect(s) I would fail on. Even Brother Simon had joined in – he had placed a tenner on "excessive number of engine stalls".

I remembered Dad's words from the previous week.

"If you pass the test, we will get you a run-around – something small, like Simons Peugeot."

I suppose this ruled out my first choice of either Ferrari or Porsche, but it didn't really matter.

For I had recently decided that, because of my flourishing relationship with Louise, a two-seater would be no good anyway – because we all know what the back seats of cars were invented for!

Yes, I *definitely* needed a car with a back seat!

Imagine Louise's excitement when I told her I had passed.

I could take her for days out; maybe even weekends away.

I'm sure Louise wouldn't be too bothered by what car I would get, but I wanted something *cool*.

Grandad was the coolest driver I knew.

He wore shades when he drove, come rain or shine. I know they were to help his eyesight, but he was like the *Fonz*.

For as long as I could remember, he had always driven a Beetle. Differing colours, but always a curvy, loud-exhausted Beetle.

I'm not convinced that I would want one, but Grandad made Beetles seem cool. Yet he would make even a Skoda seem cool.

I had remembered Dad saying something about Polo's, but I allowed myself to believe he was talking about fresh breaths rather than cars.

Gary Locke

I cleared my mind before it got too involved in flicking through the car section of the imaginary Exchange and Mart that had popped in there.

I focused on the test building, just in time to see Brian emerging, sporting the biggest smile seen on a face since Frank Sidebottom!

"Congratulations!" he said when he reached the car, offering me his hand to shake.

I noticed for the first time that two of his fingers were more yellow than glowing buttercups.

I probably shouldn't have been too surprised, seeing as the majority of our lessons started with five minutes of chat while the smoke-filled air in the Micra cleared enough to allow safe driving.

Nevertheless, I had never seen fingers that extreme in colour in real life well, with the exception of Bananaman!

Brian told me to get into the passenger seat, because he was going to drive us back to Holly Grove. It was the only time I had ever seen him behind the wheel, as he had always told me what to do but had never actually shown me.

What a terrible driver!

As he waffled on, all the way home, saying something about "weapons" and "cars" and "starting now" and "learning", I couldn't help but observe his driving.

He was riding the clutch, over revving the engine, and going so ponderously slow that I'm pretty sure he must not be aware that the car had a fourth gear!

It was on that journey home that I also noticed how many other bad drivers there were out on the road.

As Brian dropped me off and I got out of the car, pass certificate tight in my fist, I wondered whether I should offer him some advice about good driving.

I decided to bite my tongue and accepted that not everyone could be as good at driving as me!

Goodbye B.M.X. Hello S.E.X.

Chapter Twenty Seven – *"…if I could turn back time…"*

"Have you seen my car keys?" I asked Dad as I came down the stairs.
I knew very well where they were, but just liked asking anyway.
It was like, by saying the words, I was confirming the reality.
I had passed my driving test, *and* had my own car!
As promised, Mum and Dad had bought me a car as a belated birthday present.
It was only a little second-hand, maroon coloured Fiesta – but it was *cool!*
Certainly cooler than Brother Simons "stall machine" Peugeot 206.
Now there was a daily battle over parking spaces.
As there was only room (and at a squeeze) for two cars on the drive; and we were now a three car family, someone had to park on the pavement outside the house.
And that was actually the prime position that we now all fought for.
If you were one of the two cars on the drive, you were either blocking someone in, or were being blocked in yourself.
And that was a problem.
If you were first car on the drive, inevitably, when you wanted to rush out, the person blocking you in "couldn't find" their keys or "were just finishing watching this TV program".
The situation had become so bad, with none of us wanting to be first on the drive; that Dad, me and Brother Simon all ended up parking on the pavement, at various points on our road.
This was much to the annoyance of many of the neighbours who, although also being multiple car families, were civil and cooperative enough within their houses to swap and change when needed.
Dad, obviously aware of the emptiness of my question, lazily looked over at the mantelpiece – where I always left my keys.
He was kneeling on the floor, surrounded by photos and pieces of paper that he must have emptied from a couple of boxes that looked like they'd been in the loft.
I walked over to take a closer look.
"Where's Mum?" I asked as I got closer.
"Her and Simon have gone to see your Grandad……….be careful where you're stepping."
Grandad had been in hospital for the last couple of days.
He had a bad chest and sometimes needed to have his lungs cleaned out by a hospital nebuliser.
Me and Louise had been to see him the previous night.
I had picked up Grandma on the way. (I could do things like that now I had my own car!)
Grandad had asked all about the car – and said he was looking forward to me taking him for a "spin". (Hopefully not literally – it always seems a strange

Gary Locke

word to use in that context!)

He was hoping to be home by weekend, so I had said that I would pick up him and Grandma and bring them to Sundays card School.

Mum says I'll get bored of offering to pick everyone up all the time, but I don't think so.

In fact, I love it so much, I'm considering a career as a Taxi Driver.

"What's all this stuff?" I asked Dad, as I looked over his floor-scattered items.

"I was just tidying up the loft – and found these boxes. They were filled with old photos and documents and what have you. Look, here's mine and your Mum's Marriage Certificate, and some of the wedding photo's!"

I glanced down at the certificate.

David Day and Anita Fry were united in Marriage on the 17th day of May, in the year 1968.

It seemed strange to imagine, possibly one of the most special days of Mum and Dad's lives, happening well before I was even born.

My eyes scanned down the rest of the certificate before being drawn to some of the black and white photos. (I still sometimes wonder whether, pre-1970's, the World was actually devoid of all colour!)

Everyone looked so young.

Mum and Dad.

Grandma and Grandad.

Aunties and Uncles.

Even my other Grandparents, Dad's parents, who sadly both died before I was born.

There was a photo that had about 100 people in, stretched across the front of the entire Church. The sort of picture I had been told used a *moving camera*, and took about an hour to take. (Dad had once said that one of his Cousins actually gave birth while being involved in that type of photo – I'm sure he was joking, but sometimes you just can't tell with him!)

There was also a photo of just Mum and Dad, standing by a fancy car that was apparently about to take them to their reception.

It was a near-identical copy of a second picture, one of many that are displayed above the T.V. in the front room.

Pictures that, if anyone walks past the T.V. too heavily or too quickly, end up falling down the back of the video cabinet! (There is then a mad operation to reach over and retrieve them quickly enough so Mum doesn't notice that it has happened *again*!)

"Maybe you and Louise will go through all this one day!" said Dad referring to the Wedding stuff.

I gave him a frown.

"You never know." He said.

"After all, there is that classic love song that was written about the two of

Goodbye B.M.X. Hello S.E.X.

you!"

He began his best Frank Sinatra impression – which always sounded more like Frank Carson!

"Whether near to me, or far,
It's no matter darling, where you are
I think of you
Day and Night….."

"Ok, thank you" I said.

"NIGHT AND DAY….." he continued loudly into the chorus.

"THANK YOU!" I shouted.

Dad had begun making these "Day" and "Night" references.

He had either only just found out that Louise's surname was "Knight", or it had taken him this long to come up with something "humorous" about it.

Whatever the reason, I had started to retaliate.

If he wanted to make surname jokes, then two could play that game.

I innocently picked up a photo of him and Mum when they were younger.

"How did you and Mum meet again?" I asked.

"We met at a bowling alley in Manchester. We were both queuing for a DoozleDog…..you know that!" Dad said.

(I did know that – we had heard the story many times about how they had found love at the "DoozleDog Counter"! It was like a fast-food sponsored Romeo and Juliet!)

"Of course. Yeah, I remember" I said chuckling – the word *DoozleDog* always made me laugh.

"What day was it that you met?" I asked.

Dad thought about it, unaware where I was going.

"It was a bowling league meeting – so it must have been a Sunday night." He said.

"Oh!" I said,

"I always assumed you met the day after Thursday – and that, because it was so special, the day was renamed after the two of you!"

Dad frowned at first, but then began to smile when he realised what I meant.

(Of course the "Fry-Day" joke I'd put out there wasn't going to win any comedy awards, but it was the type of humour Dad liked.)

"Very good!" he said as he continued to smile – perhaps pondering what it would be like to have a day named after you.

Dad reached forward and picked up a photo from another pile.

"Do you remember that?" he asked.

I looked and saw that it was a picture of me some years earlier, in shorts and a T-shirt wearing a sash that said "1st Place".

"That's from on holiday in Prestatyn, isn't it?" I said.

"That's when I won the "Prince of the Week" contest…….was it 1983?"

Dad laughed.

"Prince of the Week! – That was just a fancy title for the kids' "knobbly knees" contest!"

As he chuckled to himself, he casually leant on top of a different photo.

I assumed it was the one of him, from the same year, wearing his sash for when he won the actual "knobbly knees" contest!

As I looked around at the other photos, one in particular stood out.

It was one of Dad, maybe when he was about similar age to me now, looking very smart wearing a fancy suit.

"When is that photo from?" I asked, pointing at it.

"Whose wedding or funeral were you at?"

Dad shot me a look dirtier than a Samantha Fox photo shoot!

"That was from when I worked at the education offices" he said.

"That might even have been my very first day at work!"

"Education offices?" I asked, "What did you do there?"

"I was a trainee accountant. That was my first job."

I had never heard him speak of this before and had a few questions about it.

By the pensive look on his face, that had now turned very serious, I knew I wouldn't have to ask them.

I decided to sit down for the inevitable Shakespeare-length soliloquy that was about to follow.

"1963.....I had just left School. Your Grandad, Francis, my Dad, got me the job. He had worked there for over twenty years – doing exam marking and verification. He pulled a couple of strings to get me an apprenticeship. It was a good opportunity. I would have got professional qualifications."

Dad seemed lost in the moment – as though his mind was lingering on another time.

"What happened?" I asked.

"I left after two months." He said, shaking his head slowly.

"The money was really bad; and I was offered a job in the factory – earning three times as much!

I couldn't see the bigger picture.

I just wanted the money.

I bought myself a little van; went out a lot. I had a good time for a while.

But I threw away a career!

And for what?

Twenty years of lumping stuff around, a laughable redundancy package and a knackered back!"

His voice began to go a little slower and became slightly high-pitched.

"If I could turn back time....." he began.

He paused a little while he thought about what he was saying. I half wondered whether he was still talking or trying a soft-rock impression of Cher!

He soon continued.

"If I could turn back time, I would. I'd do things differently. I'd do it *all* differently.

But I can't.

I failed. *Spectacularly* failed!"

I stared at him as he spoke and, even though he would never admit to it, I

Goodbye B.M.X. Hello S.E.X.

saw some tears forming in his eyes.

"When I was in my last year of School I had three dreams. Well two really – I'd grown out of wanting to be a train driver. You know, a real train – a big steel, steam train, like the flying Scotsman!

No, I wanted to either play for, or manage Manchester City; or to be a professional worker. Wear an expensive suit and have specialist qualifications.

I failed.

I held the dream in my hand and threw it away – because I didn't have the patience.

I could have been a top accountant, or a financial adviser; earning hundreds of thousands of pounds.

I could have lived a life of luxury – jetting off on dream holidays all the time."

He held the thought in his mind for a second – perhaps imagining himself on an unspoilt, paradise-like golden beach somewhere.

He then turned his attention to me.

"Don't waste your time Paul, like I've wasted mine.

You've got so much to be positive about. You've got your own car now, you're at College, you've got a lovely girlfriend, you've got family who love you.

You've got everything you need – to do whatever you want to do.

You find a Star, and you reach for it.

And don't you stop reaching until you grab it!"

I tried not to make it look like I'd noticed, but there was definitely several, fully formed tears coming from Dad's eyes.

It was weird, I had never seen him cry properly before.

Well apart from August 1985, when on the way to a Shawaddywaddy concert in Southport, the car broke down!

But this was different.

I leant over and put my hand on his shoulder.

"Don't talk like that Dad. It's not too late for you." I said. "Well maybe too late to manage City; and certainly too late to play for them! But where's the future in *that* anyway?"

He managed half a smile at my attempt to cheer him up.

I decided to try and find the full smile.

"It's not too late. You're not fifty yet; and I keep seeing in the papers and on the news – people saying that fifty is the new forty!"

I wasn't sure where I was going with this – because even forty seemed "well over the hill" to me; but Dad seemed encouraged.

"You could still go to College and get some qualifications. There's loads of mature students. You could then still have quite a few years of living one of those dreams!"

The smile I had been aiming for emerged; and Dad's face even glowed with a sense of optimism.

"You're right, Paul" he said.

Gary Locke

"I could even come to College with *you*!"

I realised that I hadn't thought this through properly!

"You might be best doing an evening course." I said hastily.

"But once you've got your qualifications – you could be a freelance accountant or independent financial advisor. You could choose your own clients, and even choose your own hours to work!"

Dad looked at me nodding slowly.

"You could get yourself a new suit – a nice one!" I continued.

Dad frowned.

"I've got a nice suit" he protested.

"You could get one that was made within the last two decades!" I said cheekily.

Luckily Dad smiled.

I continued trying to make him feel better about himself.

"You can still do whatever *you* want to do.

You haven't failed anything until you give up trying!"

He gave me a rueful grin.

"I gave up trying *years ago*!"

I shook my head.

"You haven't failed anything until you give up trying – *forever*!"

He smiled at me.

"You've just been on a career break – a long one!"

We both began to laugh.

"Thanks Paul" Dad said, and leant over to hug me.

As he moved, he exposed the photo of himself that he had been leaning on – confirming that he is the World's most knobbly kneed man!

We both looked at it.

"Like Father, like son!" Dad said, and we both laughed some more.

Goodbye B.M.X. Hello S.E.X.

<u>**Mirror, Mirror**</u>

Mirror, Mirror, won't you look me in the eye,
Tell me why and when, did you become so shy.

Once we were brave enough, to take on any fight,
Even the whole wide World, against just you and I.

Where now are those hungry eyes, that used to shine so bright?
The ones that had an appetite, just for living life?

Because now I see an image, that I do not recognise,
Of an aged and broken face, all tired with deep set lines.

Why did you never stop, to check the hands of time?
As all your hopes and dreams, slowly drifted by?

And tell me when it's time, for us to say goodbye,
Could we look at one another, and be the least bit satisfied?

I've watched on as your life, has all but passed you by,
And I've had to feel your pain, as you cried time after time.

But maybe it's never too late, and if both of us can try,
We can face the World, and again reach for the sky.

Mirror, Mirror, won't you look me in the eye,
Mirror, Mirror, let's look each other in the eye.

Chapter Twenty Eight – "…Lynsey…"

I allowed the, pleasantly mild, wind to caress my face as I gazed out over the football field.

As September days went round here, the weather was more than acceptable.

It was one of those days the weather forecasters (or *weather guessers*, as Dad likes to call them!) would describe as *fine*.

But is there really any other word that is more *non-committal*, *bland* or *beige* as *fine*?

You know, apart from *beige* or *bland* or, yes, *non-committal*!

Because fine is really just a way of saying that something is middle of the road. Unfortunately not great but, thankfully, not shit!

So, maybe, most of us are happy to stick with fine rather than roll the dice – hoping for great but risking shit!

And, talking of shit, why was it that my mind was full of it?

Why the Hell was I speculating on the merits and limitations of the word *fine*?

The answer was obvious, and could be summed up neatly in one word.

Weed!

I'd inhaled three mouthfuls of a particularly potent joint that was being passed around and, as such, my mind was mushier than chip shop peas!

Me and Mark had befriended a guy called Steve in our P.E. class because he seemed to be constantly puffing away on the old *exotic tobacco*!

Was there anything *cooler* for College students than smoking pot?

Alcohol was really just for School kids!

Luckily for me and Mark, Steve was more than happy to share!

So much so, that he actively encouraged us to invent false ailments, so that we could avoid the more physical P.E. lessons and, instead, subject our lungs to illegally grown plant extracts and high levels of unfiltered tar!

Today, I had a "bad knee" which was the result of a "fairly horrific BMX accident which needed the fire brigade to cut free my leg that was stuck in the wheel spokes"!

Mark had a "bad cold"! (Who has "bad colds" when the weather is *fine*? Where was his imagination?)

Steve, or *Skids* as he liked to be called (not sure why and don't want to ask!) apparently often suffered from bad "shin splints"!

Whatever the excuse, our P.E. teacher Mr Owen (who, strangely, preferred us to call him by his first name – Anthony!) didn't seem to mind at all.

At School, if you wanted to miss a P.E. lesson you needed written proof that you had only been let out of hospital, because of something life threatening, within the last twenty-four hours!

But not at College!

No parental confirmation was required for *anything*.

At College, the majority of teachers went out of their way to tell you that

Goodbye B.M.X. Hello S.E.X.

they were treating *you* like adults.

Ha!

They now used phrases like, "*It's your life you're throwing away if you don't work hard*", "*I won't be sending a letter home to your parents*" and "*I'm not going to punish you. You're an adult now – you can make your own mind up!*"

Which was good enough for me because I was far too busy with Louise and my car, and this new-found attitude that no-one was going to force you to work hard, to actually work hard!

The teachers still strutted around, over-inflated by their own perceived power, only now they looked at you differently to the teachers at School...

Instead of *disgust*, it was now closer to *contempt*!

They also didn't give out any detentions – presumably because none of them wanted to work late!

It appeared that the progression from School teacher to College teacher was a choice made primarily through laziness!

How lazy must those University "Professors" be?

There were other subtle differences between School and College.

Now, you weren't worked to the bone 24/7 like you were at School (or probably more like 5/5!) because there were *free periods*.

The reason for free periods wasn't obviously clear.

It could be to give the students free time each day to study in the library, as claimed.

Alternatively, it could be on the insistence of the work-shy workforce who, as *College teachers* probably expected, at least, five breaks a day!

It was also a possibility that it was all just a big money making scheme. Whereas at School the canteen would be open for an hour a day – leading to dangerous rushing to the dinner queue and resulting in mass panic and daily multi-child pile ups!, the College canteen was open *all day*.

And what better way was there to make money, than to offer food for teenagers who had plenty of spare time and regular cases of the post-weed munchies?

The free periods also meant that you didn't always have to arrive at College first thing in the morning.

Which was a bonus for anyone who hadn't passed their driving test and/or owned their own car.

Obviously that didn't include me!

And, seeing as the *new driver* novelty hadn't worn off yet, I was happy to pick up anyone who wanted a lift.

Usually it was Louise, but sometimes it could be any of Mark, Little Si or John. (All of whom had, by some equally miraculous event as me, passed enough subjects to *go* to College!)

There was also no uniform that had to be worn at College- which was good and bad.

Good, because now everyone had there own individuality.

Bad, because you needed cool "going out" clothes, not just for weekends but for everyday of the week.

Luckily, Louise was still in control of my wardrobe purchases, so I was okay.

I was also finding that at College it was very difficult to instantly recognise the geeks!

There were certainly no students wearing blazers!

Also, a lot of them seemed to have purchased contact lenses or had dyed their ginger hair!

It was almost *impossible* to see who the *real nerds* were!

It really shouldn't be allowed!

Another thing that was different was that, at School, almost every corner that you turned didn't reveal Dave "Arsehole" Barlow!

That's all I needed, the arrogant dick who fancied my girlfriend somehow managing to be *everywhere, all the time*!

If it wasn't bad enough bumping into *him* all the time, he also hung out with two guys who could easily have been clones of him.

They all wore ridiculously tight T-shirts or vests to show off their hideously pumped physiques. (T-shirts or vests they *must* have co-ordinated – because it was always *all three* of them wearing T-shirts, or *all three* of them wearing vests!)

It was like a new Olympic sport – Synchronised Knob Heads!

They also swaggered around as if they owned the place.

It's like they were constantly having a sponsored "who can look like the biggest prick" contest amongst themselves!

Luckily, I think any encounters Louise was having with Dave were when I was with her; and she seemed less than impressed with his endless cocky, attempted flirting.

Hopefully she was seeing him for what he really was – usual daily winner in the "who can look like the biggest prick" contest!

"Day-ee!"

I looked across to see Skids offering me another drag on his brain-blitzing reefer.

Skids insisted on calling me by a nickname and seemed really offended when I refused to be known, "from now on", as *Spider*!

As it was, I could just about put up with him calling me "Day-ee".

The joint had almost burned right down to the end meaning that another finger burning event was more than a possibility.

I wonder if it would take the edge off me trying to look cool if, for my next ganja session, I wore a couple of Mum's sowing thimbles?

I carefully picked the smoking stick out of his hand and reluctantly raised it to my lips.

In reality, I was starting to question my weed smoking career already.

Sure, it gave you that spaced-out hazy head sensation that was pleasant, but I'd found that those feelings were very soon joined by a headache and the thought that being sick was a very real possibility!

And, although a bit of weed couldn't compare to a heroin addiction, for

Goodbye B.M.X. Hello S.E.X.

some reason I couldn't get Grange Hills' *Zammo* out of my head singing the ludicrously catchy *"Just Say No!"*

As such, I tried to keep Skids in sight of the corner of my eye so I could take a quick mouthful of smoke without inhaling it properly, whilst he wasn't watching.

"Here they come!" shouted Skids standing up and looking over to the left.

I took it as my opportunity to pretend I'd had my turn and pass it over to Mark as quickly as possible.

"Shit!" he muttered as he took it off me and burnt his finger.

Ha!

Thimbles needed all round methinks!

I looked over towards where Skids was staring and shouting.

It was the rest of our *un-ailed* P.E. classmates, who were running towards the football field that was in front of us.

The class was made up of sixteen boys and three girls.

Most of the time I sat next to Mark in classes and had therefore not got to know many of the others (apart from Steve/Skids and one of the girls) that well.

What I did know though, was that the other fifteen guys in the class (including Mark) were, what you could only describe as, *mortified* about the boy/girl ratio.

This was made even worse by the fact that two out of the three girls had presumably taken P.E. at A-Level because they had shown some real *natural talent* for the shot put!

Any further description of their physiques was probably not required!

The third girl was a different matter!

Lynsey!

I had sat next to her a few times when Skids had been too quick for me and grabbed the seat next to Mark.

Lynsey further confused the whole geek/not geek thing for me even further.

She had ginger hair (or auburn as she preferred to call it!), but was, quite possibly, the coolest person I had *ever* met. She was funny, very pretty, very competitive, part rock-chick tomboy, part girly-girl and overall, a whole lot of fun.

And she was a natural at *all* the sports we had done so far.

Maybe it was time to re-evaluate my geek criteria?

Was it possible that, for five years at School, I had been pre-judged many students who were actually really *cool, nice* people?

Of course not – I was being silly!

Lynsey was just a one off!

Skids whistled and *whooped* as our classmates made it on to the football field and began to kick balls to each other and embark on some painful looking stretching exercises.

Mr Owen/Anthony then got the class to jog ten, exhausting-looking, laps of the pitch and do fifty press ups and sit ups to "get warmed up" for the game.

Gary Locke

I'm so glad I had a bad knee!

Lynsey, like the rest of her team wearing a nice Man City-blue-ish football shirt, waved over at us as Mr Owen blew his whistle to signal the games' kick off. It was immediately followed by an intense debate between Mark and Skids as to which one of *them* she was aiming her wave at.

My money was on Skids – he could smoke a joint all the way to the end without burning his fingers!

The next hour or so was incredible.

I was watching closely at Lynsey to see if she was also any good at football.

Imagine a pretty, cool, funny, good-to-be-with girl who also *loved* football and was good at playing it?

Talk about perfect!

But *any good* didn't cover it – she was *fantastic*!

And watching her as she dashed around – hot, sweaty, breasts bouncing around like two mesmerisng mini-Space Hoppers that any man would love to ride!, while she ran circles around everyone else on the pitch, made me begin to worry.

How could *she* be *perfect* when it was *Louise* that was *perfect*?

I spent the few seconds after the final whistle (the game finished 3-0 – Lynsey scoring *all* three goals!) concerned that I was focusing on Lynsey too much.

What was I thinking!

And then it happened.

Jamie O'Neil (who Skids insisted on calling Jimbo-O!) rather cheekily asked Lynsey to swap shirts with him.

To everyone's amazement Lynsey said yes and grabbed her blue football shirt by the collar and began to pull it over her head.

It was hard to know what Mark and Skids' reaction was to all this as my eyes were about three feet outside of my skull!

I was completely spell-bound.

It wasn't right that I should be so transfixed by a girl that wasn't Louise.

Thankfully all illusions, sooner or later, become completely shattered.

And this one was sooner than soon!

I quickly realised that, thankfully, Lynsey was *anything* but perfect.

It's not that under that blue shirt she was the owner of a pair of hideously disappointing tits. No, after seeing them bouncing around as she played, I'm pretty sure that *they* were perfect.

It's because underneath that blue shirt she was wearing *another* football shirt.

Obviously her *own* football shirt.

A red Man Utd shirt!

Illusion, thankfully, shattered…..

Goodbye B.M.X. Hello S.E.X.

October 1992

A new month arrived, bringing with it a couple of new and surprising developments.

1...Dad was not only still talking about "chasing the dream that I thought had slipped away", but had actually signed up to take a computer course at the job centre. It had taken us so much by surprise; that it felt like we were living through a good episode of "Tales of the Unexpected!" (Brother Simon and I had teamed up, though, to bet him £20 that he wouldn't stick at it for longer than a week!)

2...Louise and I had experienced our first real argument. (Which maybe wouldn't have been so bad had it not been quickly followed by our second, third, and fourth!)

I suppose some arguments are inevitable – Mum and Dad seem to have one at least every half an hour!

What made the first one all the more worrying was that it grew from a rather light-hearted debate on whether "Home and Away" had overtaken "Neighbours" as the premier Australian Soap!

Before I knew it, Louise had entered a full blown rant about how I took some "pointless and ridiculous" discussions too far. (I didn't even have time to discuss the merits of "Sons and Daughters" or "The Young Doctors"!)

She went on to say something about me not listening to.....something or another!

She also said that our whole relationship was in danger of becoming "routine and predictable".

Maybe that's why she had bought me the "one day paragliding course" – to try and mix things up a little.

Either that, or perhaps she had somehow managed to take out some life insurance on me!

Whatever way, I had somehow avoided going on the course so far.

But, despite ignorantly hoping otherwise, that wasn't going to be the case forever.....

Chapter Twenty Nine – *"...view from the hill..."*

"I've always fancied something like paragliding or sky diving!"

I remembered it well.

It was an off the cuff, throw away comment; no more than an attempt to be part of a conversation about high octane experiences with bungee ropes and white waters.

Little did I know that it was being noted and would one day be used in evidence against me!

And in manifested itself five months later as a voucher that innocently and quietly sat in my birthday card from Louise. That was until I read it, when it broke its silence and screamed out loud: ***Paragliding – One Day Taster Course.***

It lead me to where I was now.

Hideously orange, oversized jumpsuit covering my trembling body.

Bright red helmet on my head – probably designed to shut out sound and all rational thoughts.

Parachute attached to my back, fully inflated high above me by a "perfect flying breeze".

All I had to do was take a few energetic steps forward, off the side of the hill, and let the parachute do what it's paid to do.

The only problem was; because I was at the top of the hill, I had the perfect view *from* the hill – down to the bottom of the hill!

The bottom that was littered with rocks and was at least one thousand feet down! (In reality it was rock-free and probably less than fifty feet down, but it's strange how your sense of perspective can by distorted in certain situations!)

I couldn't help but imagine myself as Wile E. Coyote on the verge of taking another never-ending plunge out of sight down a canyon, before turning into a small puff of dust at the bottom. To complete my vision, instead of my parachute, I just needed to be sat in a giant rubber band catapult!

"Go on! Couple of big steps, to me, to me, then – Just Jump!"

The words came from Dave, the paragliding instructor standing in front of me, and came with the over-the-top enthusiasm of a Chuckle Brother carrying a door towards the accidentally, but inevitably, to-be-smashed pane of glass!

I decided to try and lighten my mood and provide Dave and the rest of the group with a good laugh. It was a sure-fire thing – everyone loves *Only Fools and Horses*.

"IS THAT OUR CARPHONE I CAN HEAR RODNEY?" I shouted at the top of my voice.

By the look on Dave's face this was not the first time he had heard this line.

Probably not even the first time he had heard it within the last minute!

He was far from amused – there was less laughter than at a screening of Sly Stallone's latest "classic" *Stop! Or My Mom Will Shoot*!

As I stopped myself laughing, (I knew it was funny despite Dave's sour stare!) and looked out to face the leap of faith (or perhaps leap of *death*) my life

Goodbye B.M.X. Hello S.E.X.

began to flash before my eyes.

Or at least my life since last week, when Louise brought up the subject of my "One Day Taster Course" present again.

"When do you fancy doing the paragliding?" she annoyingly slipped into an innocent conversation about Neighbours and Home and Away.

I smiled and coolly said,

"Whenever really – there's no rush though is there?"

Although the words were stutter-free, I had the feeling that my eyes were showing a completely different message.

They were windows that had a perfect view over bowels that suddenly had more movement than a funfair waltzer!

"I was thinking that we could go next Sunday. You've not got anything planned have you?" asked Louise with a twinkle in her eye.

It seemed wrong wanting to throttle someone round the neck who was obviously trying hard to give you a special birthday present, but I couldn't help myself.

I fought the urge through gritted teeth and instead just stared forward into space.

Louise obviously took my silence as an overwhelming: Yes.

"I'll phone the paragliding club now. Try and book you in. We'll soon have you up in those skies!"

As she left her bedroom, headed towards the telephone, I began to feel something trickling around my modest manhood and then down my left leg. I feared the worst until realising it was just my box of tic-tacs leaking through the hole in my trouser pocket!

What a relief!

For a split second I thought I may have to start wearing plastic underpants again!

I picked up the tic-tacs that had undertaken the unpleasant journey and carefully inserted them into Louise's half full box on her bedside table. I comforted myself thinking that watching her eat them later may give me some slight feelings of revenge – for her wanting to put me through the *pleasure/suicide* of attaching a piece of fabric to my back, and hoping it will save my life as I jump off some mountain!

I had to think quickly.

Surely I *could* have had something planned for Sunday?

I know - I had already planned an afternoon out with the lads?

No that wouldn't work, I went out last week. Two weeks in a row could only result in Louise's face *transformation*.

She had begun taking on a look I had often seen in married women; when their husbands mentioned those three words – "with the lads".

The one where they end up looking like the proverbial Bulldog chewing a Wasp – a Wasp that was suffering from a bad case of diarrhea!

I could say that we had promised to have a meal with my parents for the day on Sunday – even that ordeal would be better than having to do the paragliding.

No that wouldn't work – my parents were going away for the weekend.

Maybe I could say that we had promised to have a meal with *her* parents for the day on Sunday – even *that* ordeal would be better than…..I stopped myself.

I was being ridiculous. That ordeal was better than nothing!

Come on brain, I pleaded; you have to come up with something.

It was too late.

Louise had re-emerged into her room wearing a sinister smile that wouldn't have looked out of place on a hangman!

"You're in luck. They *were* fully booked – but someone cancelled just half an hour ago. You've got the *last* place – we're going on Sunday!"

I instinctively smiled.

It was a defence mechanism – something I often did to prevent myself crying.

There was no other choice – I would have to face it like a man.

I took a deep breath and took inspiration from Grandad and all the other heroes who put their lives on the line for this Country.

I would be a British Bulldog.

I would face the fear head on.

I would go on Sunday and I would look out over the hill, and I would leap out into the unknown, without hesitation and without regard for my own safety.

I would do what I had to do.

Or maybe I could emigrate!

"Just to let you know though" said Louise,

"Dave, the instructor I spoke to on the phone, said we would have to call him on Sunday morning. If the weather isn't great, he would have to cancel the course."

As she finished the sentence my left eyebrow raised uncharacteristically high, as if perhaps mistakenly thinking it was part of Roger Moore's face!

There was a loophole!

A possible way out!

An *escape plan*!

As the optimistic part of my brain began to release endorphins in celebration of this thought, the pessimistic side, as was usual, prepared his spanner for throwing.

It reminded me that I had seen the weather forecast for Sunday and, for this part of the World, it was unusually positive.

The optimistic side responded instantly and, as I smugly basked at the brilliance of its failsafe plan, it continued with the endorphin injection that would keep me smiling as ludicrously as a tipsy Aunt at a wedding, right up until Saturday evening.

As I began to execute the "plan" at six-thirty on Saturday, the tightness of my outfit began to make me question the brilliance of it after all.

Would performing a rain dance whilst wearing the costume I had worn for

Goodbye B.M.X. Hello S.E.X.

my year four School play of *The Lone Ranger* really work?

I remembered how the Stoneport Times had reviewed my portrayal of Tonto as "uncomfortably realistic", but looking back I couldn't recall a rain dance being part of my performance.

And how did you actually *do* a rain dance?

You'd think something that useful was something that they'd teach you at School!

They could easily replace something as useless as trigonometry with it!

Or all those useless spelling tests!

Because I needed to be sure of as much rain as possible – a light shower was no good, I needed a good old fashioned old testament style monsoon – I tried to put in elements of every dance that I had ever heard of.

From *Oops Upside Your Head* to the *The Birdy Song*, and from *Break Dancing* to the *Hokey Cokey* (I know, all *classics*!), all was going well until I attempted a fusion of *Russian Dancing* and *Limbo*!

It was then that my painfully tight imitation leather trousers gave way in the rectum area!

It was also at that exact moment that Mum entered the bathroom, obviously concerned about the noise I was making.

As I lay spread-eagled on the floor; bare-chested, two red lipstick stripes under my eyes, wearing a headband with Pigeon feathers sellotaped to it, and my trousers almost ripped in half, she contented herself with throwing me a look that was becoming ever more frequent.

One that roughly said something like – "I would rather not know what you're doing!"

To be honest, it wasn't the worst position she'd ever caught me in!

And at least she wouldn't have to pull her angry face and shout something like – "I hope you're going to throw that sock away when you're finished with it!"

When she'd left the room, despite the slight indignity, I reassured myself that I had done enough.

It was with confidence that I opened up my bedroom curtains on Sunday morning.

Ill advised, misguided, idiotic, bloody confidence!

Because as I pulled back the drapes, there were the skies – bluer than a Chubby Brown/Bernard Manning/Jim Davison triple headed, Blackpool pier comedy special!

(What a great night that was!)

Before I knew it, I had picked Louise up in the Fiesta, the telephone call had been made and we were given confirmation that the day was going ahead.

This was despite me wishing for an overnight illness to have struck Dave the instructor.

Although I have to say that I was relieved that my bad thoughts had caused no harm after Louise starting explaining to me what "karma" was during the car journey.

Gary Locke

Before then I had always thought it was a creamy, mild curry!(The first curry you ever try, but the one you would never dream of having again once you had embraced any other with more "oomph!")

It didn't seem long on the motorway until we had reached the Paragliding School or the "hill of death" as it was better known.

A quick change for me and the seven other "trainees", and then there we were, on the "learning slope", jump suited, our helmets in hand. (Crash helmets, thank you!)

There was not much time to appreciate the (unbelievably Sunny!) morning before Dave had begun his first enthusiastic Chuckle Brother impersonation.

He spoke of *thermals* and *cloud bases*, but also of *parachute collapses* and *crash landings*. For each tale of *wondrous gliding* there was one of *broken bones*.

His tantilising promises of soaring on the breeze was tempered by the threat of a wheelchair-bound conclusion to life!

I couldn't work out at first why he was being so positive and yet so negative at the same time.

And then it struck me.

Dave loved flying but hated *teaching*.

It was a job he had to do so that he could spend as much time as possible in the skies. The thought of having to share those skies with incompetent new recruits like us obviously sickened him to his stomach.

And there it was.

The motivation I needed to see this crazy suicide adventure through.

If Dave didn't want me up in the air, crashing into other flyers before hurtling towards the ground, then that was exactly what I was going to do……..?!?

Besides, Grandad had often told me about "parachuting behind enemy lines" during the war and he had made it sound quite exciting.

Well apart from the time that the wind took him straight into a German military camp!

But I was fairly confident that there were no such camps these days!

Not in Cumbria anyway!

The morning training went well. I perfected my "roll turn landing" before anyone else – although, regrettably on two occasions, a little too closely to some unattended and inexplicably unmarked Sheep droppings!

I mastered how to capture the wind in my 'chute (that is how us flyers refer to our parachutes), and how to create that initial acceleration you need to take off – while having a large dragster braking system attached to your back.

I was ready.

And after our packed lunch I would march on up to the top of the hill with my ten thousand men (or rather the seven other (slower) learners) and prepare to take flight.

Although it turned out that "march" was not the correct adjective.

"Labour", "struggle", "crawl" or even "nearly die" would have been more appropriate!

Goodbye B.M.X. Hello S.E.X.

Because climbing up a seemingly endless hill (which I think technically would easily class as a mountain – perhaps even the highest in the World!), with thighs burning more than a pasty Englishman in Benidorm!, was not something that should be part of any birthday present!

In addition to every painful step, I had to desperately try to stop a ham sandwich, 2 mini pork pies and a melted Kit Kat from making an unwelcome reappearance!

All this, while sweating so much I looked uncannily like a human impression of Niagara Falls!

The only respite from certain dehydration was a bottle of water that was close to boiling point – because of those damn-near perfect weather conditions!

Once everyone was at the top of the hill, and mouth to mouth resuscitation had been performed on all of us needing it, we were ready to fly.

"What a fantastic view down to the car park" boomed Louise, knowing very well that there was no chance of her getting a head-first, two-second zoomed in close up of its concrete surface!

The urge to throttle her again came over me but Louise, being a couple of feet away from me, was in no danger because my legs felt like they may never be able to move ever again.

Now that we were all at the top of the hill, of course someone had to "test" the flying conditions. Dave *manfully* volunteered to take the jump before any of us trainees.

Three times he "tested" the conditions!

For an hour and fifteen minutes we watched him as he took off from the hill, glided around and then down before traipsing back up.

Then off again and *slowly* back up.

Once more launching off the hill, flying around for a while, before ponderously trekking back up to join us.

Finally he begrudgingly acknowledged that he was not alone.

"Ok, I think it's safe enough for you lot to try. Who wants to go first?"

The inspiration that had gripped me before lunch had long gone.

It disappeared during the climb up towards the clouds, around about the same time as I lost my struggle with the melted Kit Kat!

All that remained were thighs that still simmered warmly enough that they threatened to burn right though my jumpsuit. If the Police were flying overhead with their thermal imaging camera, they would surely be blinded by the brightness of my lower limbs!

As I glanced around the group, I began to feel an uncomfortably high number of eyes focusing their stare upon me.

"Come on then, Star student", said Dave after following most of the eye lines to where I lay, prostrate, still wondering whether I would ever move again.

I took a deep breath.

I couldn't keep my audience waiting.

The guys needed a front runner.

A pioneer.

A leader!

I stood upright (as best you can on numb legs) and gave a dignified nod to the applause that exploded.

I couldn't let them down.

They needed inspiration.

An example to follow.

A hero to inspire them!

Nothing was going to stop me.

"I think the wind may have dropped!" said Dave.

Thank God for that I thought and quickly sat back down!

Dave scratched his head

"We can still try, but if the wind is too low, we will have to wait to see if it picks up again."

I was encouraged back to my feet, to try to inflate my 'chute and get it into the air.

But no matter how hard I tried, I could not *get it up*. (My 'chute, thank you!)

And so that was that.

Too little breeze = no fly.

We all relaxed, outstretched on the grass, basking in the beautifully warm Sunshine and perfect tranquility.

It began to feel like I was actually going to end up having a good day.

This perfect moment couldn't even be spoilt by the pile of "mud" close to where my head rested, that again had that unhealthily strong stench of Sheep shit!

After twenty minutes Dave stood up and said,

"It looks like the wind may have blown itself out for the day. We'll give it another hour and, if it hasn't picked up, we'll have to call it a day. Those of you who are back tomorrow – you will be able to fly first thing in the morning.

Those of you who aren't – well you've had all the training you need – so when you come back again, you will be able to fly straight away."

As he sat down something strange happened to my face.

Although I was trying hard to keep it straight, my smiling muscles were beyond my control. So much so that I must have looked like I was auditioning for a role as the Joker in the next Batman movie.

I looked at my watch. It was three-thirty p.m.

A pleasant hour of Sunbathing, I thought, and then we could leisurely make our way home. I even felt relaxed enough to talk to Louise civilly for the first time in the day.

And she suddenly started feeling less like an enemy and more like my girlfriend again.

Then it happened about quarter past four.

Slowly at first, but noticeably increasing – as though someone, somewhere was slowly opening a valve.

There was movement in the air.

Goodbye B.M.X. Hello S.E.X.

It increased at such a rate that by four-thirty, the pre-promised "call it a day" time, I was facing out towards the edge of the hill.

My equipment was on, my 'chute was inflated above my head and Barry Chuckle was in front of me, encouraging me to make the jump.

I'm not sure what ultimately made me do it.

Perhaps it was the fact that I was first and didn't want to look like the first yellow-bellied Chicken.

It was possibly the thought that, if I survived it, I could tell Grandad all about my *own* heroic time in the skies.

Maybe it was the knowledge that, when I left the hill, I would no longer have to listen to Dave reciting the latest episode of Chucklevision!

But, most probably, I think it was the look I saw on Louise's face as I nervously glanced across at her.

There was no sinister sneer.

No wicked look, excitedly anticipating my imminent fall to my death.

Instead there was a genuine sparkle.

It was the look of love from someone who was thrilled to be fulfilling my "lifelong ambition".

I had no anger left.

Only the thought of giving back the gesture that had been given to me.

If jumping from that hill would complete Louise's feeling of satisfaction; then jump I would.

So forgetting my nerves, I controlled my trembling body and pushed my paralysed legs into something resembling a forward movement.

I lurched towards the edge of the hill, with my eyes shut tighter than a pair of 1980s stonewashed jeans!

And then the feeling of the floor disappeared from under my feet.

My 'chute had taken a huge gulp of air and had lifted me right up into the sky.

After a couple of seconds of the most wondrous feeling of weightlessness, I decided to open my eyes.

I was greeted by a sight that matched the way I was feeling.

I was miles up in the air (certainly several feet!); soaring effortlessly alongside two Golden Eagles (possibly two scruffy grey Pigeons!).

It was the greatest moment of my life.

Not even a glance upwards could dampen my spirits, when I could have sworn I saw, written on the underside of my 'chute, the word "ACME"!

After what felt like hours (later I was told it was 37 seconds!) drifting through the sky, at one with the breeze and with nature itself, I was safely touching down at the bottom of the hill.

I took just a second soaking in the marvelous pleasure that I had just experienced. After that I gathered my 'chute together quickly and, using my miraculously re-energised legs, ran up the hill faster than an irritatingly smug Road Runner!

Four more times I ran up that hill, as if now it was nothing more than a little mound made by Ratty's mate from *Wind in the Willows*.

When Dave said we needed to pack our equipment away because it was getting too dark to continue, I couldn't stop myself reacting like a toddler who'd just had his dummy taken off him.

I *needed* to carry on – just one more flight.

I obviously hadn't experienced much adrenalin in my life, but found now that it was a sensation that I quite liked.

It was not until the car journey on the way home that I appreciated what a strange day it had been.

I had arrived, terrified about what my last day alive had in store, searching desperately for elaborate reasons to excuse myself.

I was leaving now feeling that I had been short changed and hadn't had enough time in the sky.

I had to content myself that, before we had left, I had signed up for skydiving and hang gliding courses.

As I drove, I also wondered about what was the best way to contact NASA, to enquire about the possibility of a trip into Space!

Goodbye B.M.X. Hello S.E.X.

Chapter Thirty – "…~~Love~~…"

It would be almost comical if it didn't hurt so much.

Looking back, why would Louise ask me to turn off my bedroom TV, and then try to recite a scene from the "*Sound of Music*" out of the blue?

But that's what I thought she was doing.

"I am Sixteen, just going on Seventeen. You're Seventeen, but some way off Eighteen….."

No wonder she looked confused when I interrupted, and said it may be more realistic if she tried it in an Austrian accent!

I blame Dad really, and his insistence on making me and Brother Simon sit through every bloody musical under the Sun!

On the outside, Dad is the last person you'd expect to like that sort of shit, but you put a rendition of "*I could have danced all night*" in front of him and he's happier than a Dog in a lamppost factory!

As such, I could probably recite any *Rodgers and Hammerstein* work, word for word, without too much effort. As claim-to-fames go, I realise it's probably not going to impress the masses!

Looking back, I think Louise had probably been waffling, trying to cushion the blow.

After my interruption, she came straight to the point.

There were nine words.

Nine words that could have been forged onto a steel brander, heated in the hottest fires of Hell, before being pushed onto my heart; where they would mark me and remain as a scar forever.

"I don't think we should see each other anymore!"

By the distinct lack of even the hint of sparkle in her eyes, I could tell she was deadly serious.

Half an hour later, after a conversation that is a hazy blur, I drove her home.

Although it was the same, quick two-minute drive it always was, it was painfully silent.

I can't even remember if we said goodbye to each other when she got out of the car.

We certainly didn't kiss, as we always had every other time I had dropped her off.

I drove back home in a confused daze.

I'm not sure which way I went – but it took me an hour and a quarter to get back, and I cannot remember a single second of the drive.

Seventy-five minutes to complete a two minute journey – more than thirty times longer than it should have.

It's the sort of thing that only usually happened when we were going on holiday and Mum was in the passenger seat navigating!

It was only the next morning, alone at the breakfast table, that things started to sink in.

Gary Locke

With two pieces of toast on a plate in front of me, I stared at the Valentines Day card that Louise had sent me back in February. I had brought it downstairs with me before breakfast as I had looked at it as I thought about some of the things she had said to me the night before.

Had we been growing apart?

Would it be *best* if we took some time to ourselves?

Had everything between us, become *too routine*?

They were all things that Louise had said; and yet they were all things that my brain still couldn't comprehend.

Was my mind not working because I hadn't had any sleep?

Or, was it because I had been taken so much by surprise?

Was it because Louise had said words that I never even contemplated that I would have to hear her say?

I picked up a piece of toast but, after realising I had no appetite (which felt like it would be permanent condition) quickly put it back down.

Wow, I couldn't eat properly when I first met her, and I can't eat now.

Have any of these diet experts thought that they whole key to losing weight is to either fall in love, or fall out of it?

I stared out of the window into the garden and, for maybe a couple of minutes, watched as four or five Sparrows took it in turns to dunk in and out of the bird bath.

It was a sight that usually enthralled me but, on that morning, it felt like it was something mundane.

An unwanted, and yet perhaps also wanted, distraction.

I asked myself a question I was sure I knew the answer to.

Was this what a *broken heart* felt like?

You don't feel like *eating* anything?

You can't concentrate on *thinking* about anything?

I looked at my watch – it was 09.05.

Mum and Brother Simon were at work, and Dad was at his computer course. (It had been over two weeks now and he was still at it – unless he was just getting up early each day and going out so he could win £20 off me and Brother Simon! That may seem extreme – but it would be totally in character for him!)

I had to be at College by ten o'clock for an English Literature lecture.

As I thought about it, I realised I didn't want to go.

I didn't want to see anyone.

I didn't want to have to tell anyone that I was no longer seeing Louise – because, somehow, I thought that telling someone would make it true.

But it *was* true!

No amount of hiding away could change reality.

But I didn't want to face the comments.

"Life goes on!"

"You'll be o.k.!"

"There's plenty more fish in the sea!"

Goodbye B.M.X. Hello S.E.X.

I know that there are lots of fish in the sea – but I only wanted *one* of them. Louise!

I really wanted to kiss her.

I really wanted to see my reflection in her sparkling eyes, as she leant in to kiss me.

I really wanted to wrap my jacket around her shoulders because she was feeling cold.

I really wanted Dad to shout at me for spending an hour chatting to her on the phone again.

I really wanted to touch her.

I felt a jabbing pain in my chest as I remembered something else she had said the night before.

"It's got nothing to do with Dave Barlow!"

I hadn't even mentioned Dave Barlow; so I can only assume it had <u>every</u>thing to do with Dave "arsehole" Barlow!

The thought of <u>him</u> kissing her, or <u>him</u> chatting to her on the phone, or <u>him</u> *touching* her sickened me to my stomach.

I began to breathe a little faster; and felt anger bubbling inside me, like restless lava.

That arsehole would only be *touching* her – because that was what *she* wanted!

And if that's what she wanted – then I didn't really know her anymore.

I didn't *need* her anyway.

There was more to life than Louise Knight!

I had my friends.

I had my own life.

She isn't the air in the sky; or the water in the streams.

She isn't the fruit on the vines.

I didn't need *her* to survive.

I looked at the Valentines Day card again, and focused on the words inside.

"*Paul, I Love You, x ?*"

I quickly took a pen off the kitchen table and slashed at the word "love".

I put the pen back down and looked at the card again.

"*Paul, I ~~Love~~ You, x ?*"

I immediately wished I hadn't done it.

The rage that had been building inside me, died down instantly.

My mind was calm.

If it turned out that Louise and I were just a moment in time; then it was a perfect moment in time.

I didn't want to spoil it by thinking about what would happen in the future.

Whatever was to come; no-one could take away that moment we had.

I looked back down at my toast.

I still had no appetite.

Despite calming my anger, I didn't want to eat.

The emptiness I felt inside certainly wouldn't be remedied by a simple bit of breakfast.

I pushed the toast to one side – I wouldn't be eating it.

I wasn't sure what I would be doing.

Everything felt strange and confusing – like nothing made any sense anymore.

I stood up and walked out through the kitchen door but, perhaps for the first time in my entire life, I didn't know where I was going.....

Goodbye B.M.X. Hello S.E.X.

Just A Beautiful Dream

Just a beautiful dream, born from the heart,
Broken by the harsh morning light,
Just a shooting Star that shines in the sky,
And then drifts on by, out of sight.

Like two hands that were holding so tightly,
You'd never think they could ever let go,
That have now been put into coat pockets,
Because the Winter air just got too cold.

A cheek-to-cheek waltz on the dance floor,
In a loving embrace, slow and swaying,
That ended as fast as a heartbeat,
Because the band on the stage has stopped playing.

Like a flower that grows in the garden,
With bright colours that bloom in the Sun,
One day it will fade into nothing,
A victim of the frost that has come.

Two hearts you think belong together,
Because they're closer than the salt and the Sea,
Is it a Love that will last forever?
Or perhaps just a beautiful dream?

Gary Locke

November 1992

Chapter Thirty One – *"...box of memories..."*

After the spectacularly explosive previous couple of months, November arrived disappointingly like an old door that needed oiling – quietly and softly squeaking!

This was probably more to do with my down-trodden attitude, than the opening weekend Bonfire night.

Another pathetic number one seemed to be playing wherever I went; obviously to mock the end of my relationship with Louise – Boyz II Men *"End of the Road"*!

Even the election of a new US President had been low key.

Some guy called Bill Clinton won the race to be the new "leader of the Western World". He seems like a good, old-fashioned, honest, loyal family man – so I can't see *him* being involved in any kind of scandal!

As usual at this time of year; the family trudged off to Auntie Lynda's, for her annual "Guy Fawkes Night Extravaganza."

I had been slightly worried about taking Louise – in case she was somehow put off me by seeing another of our bizarre family rituals.

But of course that was no longer a problem – obviously she had already seen something in *me* that she hadn't liked too much!

It had been two weeks since I had spoken to her.

I had seen her at College a couple of times; but I had avoided catching eye contact, and walked away from her quickly.

Anyone watching may have wondered if I was adhering to some kind of court issued restraining order!

The bonfire "party" was the time I had decided to tell the family that I was no longer seeing Louise.

The general reaction coming across was one of disappointment.

There was a lot of sympathy.

"Oh, I am sorry about that!" and *"Oh what a shame – I really liked her!"* were two phrases used on several occasions.

No one had the decency to say something like *"Thank God for that – I thought she was a real bitch!"*

As usual, Grandad found the right reaction.

He didn't say anything.

Instead he gave me a look that said something along the lines of *"That's a shame, because Louise was great.*

But you'll be ok – because you're great as well.

And we will all be here for you, whenever you need us!"

It was amazing how he had the ability to say whatever he wanted, not by having to speak, but by just changing a few little facial muscles.

It made me feel a little better, but I had hoped that someone had said

Goodbye B.M.X. Hello S.E.X.

something a bit negative about her.

Uncle Geoff usually liked to be a bit controversial, so his *"That's a pity!"* comment had been a bit of a let down.

I had been half hoping he would have claimed that Louise had tried to touch him up during Grandma and Grandad's Golden Wedding Anniversary party!

At least at College I had received some more *constructive* support.

The guys had been pretty good.

They were making sure that one of them was always with me during the times they knew I used to spend with Louise.

Free periods, breaks, lunchtimes - there was always one of them with me. They were operating a well co-ordinated "chair-side vigil".

Even Lynsey from my P.E. class was trying to cheer me up.

She was telling me a joke each morning, in an attempt to help me "start the day with a smile!"

Most of them had been ridiculously bad; not much better than my own Christmas Cracker standard, but the effort she was putting in was much appreciated.

The best she had come up with so far was -

"A guy goes into the Chippy and studies the price board.

"What will it be?" asks the man behind the counter.

"Just a fish please." says the guy.

"It won't be long" replies the man.

The guy angrily says "Well, for £1.50, it better be bloody fat then!""

I'm not sure she had a future in stand up, but she was certainly trying to raise my sprits.

It gave some support to Marks theory that she fancied me.

Although his other "evidence" of her "staring at me throughout the whole of lunchtime" one day; was later exposed to be more likely because I had mistakenly put my T-shirt on inside-out that day!

I think she was just being nice, because she was a very happy-go-lucky, friendly person.

Despite not receiving the "Louise slagging" I was hoping for, being at the bonfire "extravaganza" did make me feel a little better.

It felt familiar and somehow that made it also feel safe.

And I wasn't sure if I was beginning to feel a *little bit* better about my break up with Louise because, for the last couple of days, I had begun to kick myself for never getting to the bottom of the whole *Dragonfly tattoo* mystery of the Summer!

Why hadn't I come out straight and asked Louise the relevant questions that would have brought the truth about whether it was her Mother or Auntie that I, unfortunately, witnessed having sex on that fateful night.

At the moment it felt like it would be something that would trouble me for the rest of my life!

As usual for bonfire night, Auntie Lynda had made some jacket potatoes that were probably slightly *overcooked* - by about four or five hours!

She had also baked a tray of treacle toffee that, again as usual, could only be broken once Uncle Melvin had been to his garden shed to retrieve his hammer!

Everything was just how it *always* was.

The first part of the evening was spent mainly watching the neighbours' fireworks and having a surprisingly civil conversation with Brother Simon. He told me of his intention to make a move on a teenage Italian girl, who was part of a new family that had moved in to the house behind ours.

"You can't speak Italian," I warned him,

"Most of the time you struggle with English!"

"You don't need words to make contact with the opposite sex!" he had said.

"You don't need language qualifications, or anything fancy like that. You just need experience and the knowledge of how to effectively *communicate*. I'll find a way to communicate with her!"

Not sure what he meant; but I can't see the Italian girl being interested in him - she's far too attractive!

It will be interesting to see what tactics he tries with her.

When ten o'clock arrived, Uncle Melvin emerged from his fancy garden shed with his biscuit tin of fireworks, some oven gloves and his lighting wick.

It was *Showtime* for his explosives display.

After a couple of "bangers" that sounded less aggressive than damp "party poppers", and a "firework fountain" that must have been out of date (instead of spitting flames, like an angry Volcano, it was rather dribbling them, like an overfed baby!), Melvin turned to his imported "Super Catherine Wheel".

Before he applied his glowing wick, Melvin boasted about how it had cost him £5 off the market and about how you couldn't buy one legally in the shops. (Who needs out-of-control wild youths, when we've got irresponsible parents?)

I'm sure that he wished he had spent as much time checking it was securely nailed to the fence, as he did giving it the pre-lighting build up. Because, after five seconds of impressively bright and dangerously fast spinning and spitting, it leapt from the fence and sped along the ground like a runaway, rider-less unicycle!

"WATCH OUT!" we all screamed as we noticed the rampaging Catherine Wheel heading towards Grandma; who was standing in front of the shed looking at Uncle Melvin's Sundial (even though the sky was pitch black!).

Luckily her reactions were more Caterpillar than Cat; and she stood obliviously still as the fiery wheel shot through her legs and crashed into the shed like an Exocet missile!

Uncle Melvin let out a Homer Simpson-like shriek as his wooden garden getaway burst into flames following a loud explosion.

He ran around for a couple of minutes like a chicken that had just received the Ann Boleyn treatment!

First of all he wasted a valuable forty-five seconds searching for his fire extinguisher. (How many houses actually have a fire extinguisher? - it turned out Uncle Melvin's didn't!)

Next he frantically attached a hose pipe to the kitchen tap, and extended it

Goodbye B.M.X. Hello S.E.X.

out down the garden. We all waited for the water to come through the hose - while the kitchen was slowly flooding due to a big hole in the pipe!

It was like being part of an episode of "*Some Mothers Do 'Ave 'Em*"!

Eventually Grandad organised a "human chain" and, between six of us, we passed two buckets to and from the kitchen, and put out the flames in about ten minutes.

Luckily no real damage was done.

Unless you count the shed and its entire contents!

Everything was burnt to a cinder - nearly as badly as Auntie Lynda's treacle toffee!

I don't suppose that the night turned out as Lynda and Melvin had planned, but I suppose it's events like those that make the strongest memories.

When we got home later, I wrote on a piece of paper what had happened during "The Catherine Wheel Incident". It culminated with Uncle Melvin putting the last of the flames out and saying; with perfect comedy timing, "I think we just about got it in time", a split-second before the shed collapsed behind him!

I found an old shoe box and put my evenings account into it.

At the same time I thought about putting some other bits of "memorabilia" into it - it could be a kind of "box of memories".

I scoured the bottom of my wardrobe and began to find numerous items that I had saved over the years. (The kind of things that most people call *rubbish* and just throw away!)

I picked up my Valentines Day Card from Louise and opened it.

I focused on the word "love" that I had crossed out in a rage a couple of weeks earlier.

I suppose my defacing had become part of the memory too. The card would symbolise and remind me of, not only the great pleasure of the relationship, but also the shock and the pain that followed.

I put it into the box.

I rummaged further into the wardrobe and found various bus and train tickets and School exercise books.

There was my "driving lessons progress card", with Brian's scrawled hand writing, and the odd yellow stain where his fingers had tightly held the paper.

I found a couple of marbles; impressive shiny, silver ones I had probably won and refused to play with again in case I lost them.

There were packets of "Top Trumps", a glow in the dark Yo-Yo, and even a couple of "knives", that were wooden ice cream sticks that had been sharpened at the ends - no doubt from when me and Paul Dale were Roman Soldiers or Musketeers.

A strong smell of vinegar emerged as I disturbed half a dozen conkers that had probably been stored there for many years.

I found a small, gold trophy that I had won from being "Pentathlete of the Week" one year at Prestatyn.

I smiled as I remembered my victory.

There had only been four of us competing, and the other three were considerably younger than me; but a win is a win!

The trophy used to be displayed on the bookshelf in the living room - until one day Uncle Geoff noticed that the tiny gold running figure on the trophy was actually a *woman*. The holiday camp must have run out of "male" trophies.

For a few weeks after Eagle Eyed Geoff's discovery, Dad had made a point of showing everyone, saying I won it around the time I was "taking some of Mum's hormone replacement tablets by mistake"!

(Which had "amused" Mum just as much as it amused me!)

I even think I am correct in remembering that it was Mum, bored with Dad's take on events, who "helped" the trophy make its way from the bookshelf and into my wardrobe.

Along with most of the other things I had come across, I put it into the shoe box - it was still an interesting memory.

With the trophy, I found a picture of me running in shorts and a T-shirt - quite possibly even competing in that very pentathlon.

I looked at it closely; Dad was right - I did have knobbly knees!

I found an old BMX handle; that I remembered taking off my bike at the last minute as Dad took it to the local tip. It was no longer needed because it had been replaced by a brand new Raleigh racing cycle - but it felt right to keep a little part of it.

The next item I found confused me.

It was a very discoloured looking cinema ticket stub, from a screening of *"Return of the Jedi"*, on June 18th 1983, at The Futurist Cinema in Birmingham.

It came to me quickly.

I had seen a film with Paul Dale and his family when I had visited him once, after he had moved away.

The film was brilliant - and I remember *loving* the Ewoks. (They were cuddly, cute and funny - and saved the Universe from the Empire!)

It's another example about how time changes things because, as I got older, I realised the Ewoks were the *worst* thing about the film.

Paul Dale and I loved Star Wars and, before he moved away, he was often Luke Skywalker to my Han Solo.

(I was secretly jealous because I wanted to be Luke as well, but am now relieved - because Han is *so much* cooler!)

I wondered whether the stub in my hand actually represented the last time I ever saw Paul Dale.

I wonder what he is doing now?

I put it into the box; quickly followed by a plastic mask of "Face" from the A-Team, (I thought I might need it one day if I was badly struck by a changing wind!) and a 7" of Bon Jovi - *Bad Medicine*.

It was the first music single I ever bought.

It was proper Rock - none of that Bryan Adams shit!

I then came across several posters of Gloria Estefan.

Where the Hell were they from?

Goodbye B.M.X. Hello S.E.X.

I then remembered that Brother Simon used to have them on his bedroom wall.

I wasn't sure why it was in my wardrobe - perhaps the whole family were now using it to store the junk they didn't want to throw away!

I suppose she was kind of hot.

Pity about the nose!

I threw them to one side - I wasn't safeguarding Brother Simon's memories.

Next I found a bottle top from a bottle of Diamond White.

It was from the first time I met and kissed Louise at Tatty Park. It was from the bottle that she had drunk from.

I quickly put it into the box, before I got lost in that particular memory again. There would maybe be times in the future that I would want to revisit it; but certainly not now.

I smiled as I looked at the assortment of items that were in the box.

No matter what happened in the future, no-one could ever take away these memories.

They were *my* memories, and it was up to me to choose which ones I wanted to remember - when I wanted to; and why I wanted to.

Just as I was putting the lid on the shoe box, satisfied that I had everything I wanted and happy that my wardrobe had undergone it's first real clear out in the best part of a decade!, I noticed a scrap of newspaper amongst the "large-nosed poster pile"!

I picked it up and read the headline.

"Stoneport Times - Wednesday, December 17th 1986

The Lone Ranger - The Musical Review."

I smiled again as I remembered the play in which I had co-starred as Tonto. This was definitely going into the box - after I had read it again, of course.

Stoneport Times - Wednesday, December 17th 1986.
The Lone Ranger - The Musical.
Review.
By Gary Clarke.

Wednesday nights in the Clarke household usually revolve around a remote control tussle which dictates whether the T.V. shows a procession of second rate soap operas, or European Cup football. (How Mrs Clarke loves her football!)
Not this last Wednesday though, because I was asked to attend the premiere night of Mountfield, Year Two's production of that well known Christmas-time classic - The Lone Ranger: The Musical!
Just walking into the School hall felt like being transported instantly to the Wild, Wild West. Chairs were almost unrecognisably decorated as cactuses, teachers walked around dressed as Cowboys and Indians and there was the perfect humming atmosphere of spaghetti western breeze effects. (Although I was later informed that this was caused by a boys' toilet fan that was jammed on by an unfortunate first year students' gym bag.)
From the instant the curtain was raised, to the second it fell (or regrettably didn't, due

Gary Locke

to a faulty string-pulley system) there was a real buzz of electricity that gripped the entire (at least half-full) audience.

The commitment and enthusiasm of the cast created an energy to the show that rarely dropped throughout the entire performance. Perhaps the only real dip on the night was during a strangely miscast scene in which an angry fire-wielding lynch mob stormed the Sheriff's office - played out rather stiffly by the School dinner ladies!

Apart from this small oversight, the rest of the cast fitted their roles perfectly. Russell Garnett in the lead role showed a good range of emotion; convincing equally in the action scenes and in the, surprisingly moving, more tender moments.

At times his thick Geordie accent made it difficult to pick up any words other than "pet", yet he always managed to convey his emotions.

A particular highlight was his one handed BMX wheelie (just about passable for a white horse) while shouting

"Hi - Ho Silver....H'Away.....The Lads!"

This was well received by the engaged audience, especially Russell's personal entourage - who were recognisable by their Newcastle United shirts, and later by their large, bare-chested torso's!

Paul Day's portrayal of Tonto was also impressive; in fact, at times uncomfortably realistic. The first meeting of his Tonto and The Lone Ranger was, I'm sure, supposed to be a tense moment, but the vigour into which he put into an attempted scalping (thankfully interrupted by an onrushing teacher) displayed a savagery that I assume was not conveyed in the script. (Maybe the legacy of an unsettled playground dispute?)

A special mention needs to go to Miss Adshead, who was both director and musical choreographer of the show.

Despite a nervous night behind the piano, (and for the member of the audience behind me who rather loudly questioned; I can confirm that it <u>wasn't</u> Les Dawson playing!) she should be proud of the mixture of "re-worked" classics and her own original compositions.

From the melancholy of the solo, lead performed "It's Lonely Being A Ranger On Your Own"; to the recognisable tune of the cleverly re-written "Ranger In Paradise", the music always flowed nicely.

The unmistakable musical highlight came as the whole audience joined in and sang along to the original, instantly classic deluge song "Tonto, Tonto, Get Your Poncho!"

Being ultra critical there were a couple of small details that prevented the show receiving a perfect score of 5/5.

There did appear to be a few costumes and sets recycled from last years Star Wars musical "The Empire Sings Back".

Most of the time this didn't matter, but it did seem a bit strange when The Lone Ranger and Tonto toasted marshmallows on an open fire - on the bridge of The Death Star! Also the Sheriff; possibly the smallest law man I've ever seen, played by Simon Haddon, looked uncannily like Boba Fett.

My other small gripe revolves around political correctness gone mad. A bar-room fight scene, in which The Lone Ranger captures a bank robber with a well-aimed lasso, lost a little realism when it was deemed that using real rope could be dangerous. Despite the performers' best attempts; something was lost - probably due to the decision to replace the rope with silly string!

Goodbye B.M.X. Hello S.E.X.

(Although I was told that, for tomorrow night, the whole scene is in jeopardy because tonight the barkeeper (an excellent Phillip Holbrook) was struck close to an eye by some cross-fire string.)

These are minor quibbles though on an other-wise well polished show that thoroughly deserves a score of 4/5.

It was impossible to take your eyes off the stage all evening, and if the heart warming finale of "Rangers In The Night" didn't make you smile, then nothing would.

So one more time.

"The rain is coming down,
Crashing all around,
Before you get too wet,
There's something you should get,
Tonto, Tonto, best be pronto,
Tonto, Tonto, get your poncho,
Tonto, Tonto, best be pronto,
Tonto, Tonto, get your poncho….."

Gary Locke

Chapter Thirty Two - "*...the Birds, the Bees and Snooker...*"

It was a Wednesday night and, now that I had nothing to do in the evenings, I was doing what I seemed to be doing a lot of - I was aimlessly wandering around the house.

It was probably an exercise in killing time, but as I had vowed this year to make every second count, I like to think I was just seeking some company and conversation.

Anything - so I didn't feel like a total loser!

Even if that company had to be Mum and Dad, which meant the conversation was usually mindlessly boring about computer courses or Lollipop "adventures"!

In reality I did have things to do.

College work; and lots and lots of it.

It was a perfect opportunity to get up to date, and build a good understanding of the syllabuses so far - because it was more than likely that they would throw some exams at us some stage!

Bloody teachers!

But the vast amounts of free time I had meant I also had the opportunity to learn how to play the bagpipes, or to knit a Doctor Who-like scarf - but I had no intention of doing those things either!

So aimless wandering it would continue to be.

I entered the living room and slowly walked over to the mantelpiece.

Mum was on her own watching TV.

I began to randomly pick up and put things down.

Firstly, a glass vase.

A vase that I'm not sure was even there for because, as far as I could recall, it had never had any flowers in it.

In fact, as I picked it up, it also appeared like it had never been cleaned - it had a layer of dust thicker than Pat Butchers make up!

I picked up a pack of cards that I recognised as Dads "lucky deck"; that we sometimes used on a Sunday night.

As I flicked through, it was odd to see that there appeared to be six aces!

There were sets of keys that jangled as I picked them up and put them down.

There were several letters which, as I flicked through, turned out to be a gas bill, a credit card advert, a car tax reminder and a rather interesting looking one for Mum I could see was from the "*Crossing Patrol Review Panel*".

Before I got the chance to read what she had done this time (the "Panel" had investigated her before - the time her lollipop had been "run over by a bus"!), Mum interrupted me.

"Paul, what are you doing?"

I quickly put the letter down, held my hands up and stepped away from the mantelpiece.

Goodbye B.M.X. Hello S.E.X.

"Nothing." I said, acting more guilty than someone who had been caught shoplifting.

"If you're bored," Mum said "Then go and be bored *somewhere else!*"

Mum had been remarkably patient with me in the four weeks since my break up with Louise, but it didn't extend to me irritating her while *Coronation Street* was on.

"Where's Dad?" I asked, finding it strange that he wasn't also watching "Corrie". He had a bit of a soft spot for the new barmaid - Raquel. (His description of her - "*Rough as a Badgers arse; but heart of gold!*")

Mum gave me a look that may it clear she wouldn't tolerate any further questions following this one.

"He's in the Snooker room; go and mither him!"

As I began walking, Mum added,

"And while you're in there, ask him what he's set the video for. I've checked the T.V. guide and "Match of the Day" isn't on tonight!"

I reached the door to the Snooker room and prepared to go in.

We called it the Snooker room, which maybe made it sound like we lived in a grand, stately house.

In reality it was a room with a small Snooker table in.

In fact, it was a small room that was too small for the small Snooker table!

If the cue ball landed close to one of the cushions, you either had to play your shot vertically, or play with the custom made mini Snooker cue. (*Custom made* by Dad taking his circular saw to a previously six foot long cue!)

It wasn't the perfect environment for Snooker but me, Dad and Brother Simon got hours of entertainment from it.

It was like our own mini "Crucible Theatre".

Dad was "Steady Eddie" Charlton.

He would not be rushed into choosing and playing any shot - even if someone shouted from the living room that Raquel was pulling a pint!

Sometimes our "hours of fun" could be whilst waiting for Dad to take a shot!

Brother Simon was like Steve Davis.

Annoyingly good, annoyingly consistent, annoyingly usually winning, and just as annoyingly arrogant and boring!

I was Jimmy White.

Exciting, flamboyant and adventurous - but ultimately reckless, and destined to never win anything!

I entered the room and saw Dad staring out of the back window.

On hearing me, he jumped and quickly grabbed a cue, before leaning into a "shot pose" next to the table, as if he was practising a shot - only there were no balls on the table!

"Oh, it's you!" he said straightening up again.

He watched suspiciously as I closed the door behind me, as if he was checking that I hadn't brought the Police with me.

"Are you alright?" I asked slowly.

Dad nodded.

He beckoned me over to the window.

"Come and look at this." he said.

I approached cautiously, wondering what he had been staring at, as it was pitch black outside.

Maybe he had spotted a UFO!

I quickly thought about it, and accepted that now I wasn't busy with Louise anymore, it was ok for aliens to visit us!

As I looked out of the window though, there was no flying saucer.

Something immediately grabbed my attention, but it wasn't unidentified, or flying, and it wasn't one object that I was focussing on, but rather two.

In plain view, standing at her bedroom window, was the Italian girl who lived in the house behind us.

She was stripped to the waist doing, what could only be justifiably described as, "shaking her melons!"

My face entered cartoon mode, and my eyes popped right out of my head into the window, as my chin crashed into the floor.

What a hypnotic pair of melons they were!

Me and Dad stared, transfixed; we couldn't have been in a deeper trance even if Paul McKenna had given us the full treatment!

My eyes bounced along to the rhythm and, although everything was totally silent, I could hear the seductive tune she was swaying to.

The moment was broken by the sound of a door opening and Mum's voice asking "Did you ask him about the video?"

Me and Dad jumped and quickly grabbed a cue each, before leaning into "shot poses" next to the table, pretending to be practising shots - even though there were still no balls on the table!

For a split second I thought we had been quick enough, but the fact that Dad was holding his cue back-to-front didn't go unnoticed by Mum.

"What are you two up to?" she asked in her Police interrogation voice.

"We're practising a trick shot!" said Dad, impressively quickly.

Mum looked at the table.

"What, with no balls?" she asked.

"It's a *magic* trick shot!" I added, my brain successfully joining the quick fire, attempted deceit.

Dad and I looked at each other, both suitably impressed by each others speedy deception endeavours.

It didn't wash with Police Inspector Mum, though.

She had noticed the half open curtains and was walking towards them.

After a couple of seconds, during which she looked like she was watching someone on a trampoline, Mum asked "What's going on out there?"

Dad and I both did impressions of surprised and innocent by-standers as we looked out of the window.

My attempt wasn't great, but Dad's was appalling - he was almost like an actor from "The Bill"!

Goodbye B.M.X. Hello S.E.X.

I think it's safe to say that neither of us should be expecting a phone call any time soon from Steve Spielberg!

"Is Simon upstairs?" asked Mum pointing up to the ceiling, beyond where Brother Simon's bedroom was.

"I think so." said Dad.

"I wonder if *he* knows what's going on?" asked Mum.

"Paul, go and see if he knows what's going on!"

With that she opened the Snooker room door and pushed me into the garden.

I reluctantly walked towards the point where I knew I would be able to turn around and look up to see Brother Simon's window.

My submarine-like mind alarm began to siren as I remembered eight words that he had said to me a couple of weeks earlier when we had spoken about the Italian girl.

"I'll find a way to communicate with her!"

I didn't want to turn around.

When I did, my worst fears came true.

Brother Simon was standing at his window; illuminated by his bedroom light, so the whole street could clearly see him (perhaps even the whole World!), half naked and, strangely, holding our mini-Snooker cue in front of him.

He was blissfully unaware I was there.

Suddenly he reached his arms up into a "Y" shape and then put both hands behind his head and began gyrating his hips!

Weirdly, the mini Snooker cue remained where it was.

Somehow floating in mid air!

The truth hit me.

Brother Simon wasn't *half* naked - he was *full Monty*!

And that was *not* the mini Snooker cue!

The image was instantly burnt onto my eye balls *forever*!

My Brother, for all to see, was doing a full blown, totally naked Elvis impersonation!

I felt a movement of sick in my stomach that could only be compared to an unstoppable spewing oil geyser!

I ran into the house, past a bemused Mum and Dad and headed for the kitchen sink - the nearest acceptable sick-dispensing point.

I was soon joined there by Mum and Dad, who had both now also obviously witnessed the vomit inducing sight!

After a couple of minutes of silent, dry retching, Mum stood up straight.

"You'll have to do something, David" she said to Dad.

"It may be time for…..you know…..the *talk!*"

"I know" said Dad, stroking his chin.

"I'll have to think about what to say to him."

He paused for a moment, and you could tell from his eyes that he was working something out.

Gary Locke

"I always think best while I'm practising my Snooker. So you two go in the Lounge, and I'll work out what to say to him in the Snooker room!"

With that, he sped off.

Mum shook her head.

"Come on" she said to me,

"I want to ask your advice on something anyway."

In the living room I reassured Mum that she probably wouldn't lose her job for "accidentally turning around quickly and catching a man in the face with her lollipop - breaking his nose"!

A man who had been, "coincidently", taking the mickey out of the uniform and hat she was wearing.

A bad temper and a lollipop can be a lethal combination!

In the meantime Dad was practising his Snooker at, judging by the noise coming from the Snooker room, a rate of about one shot every six minutes!

He was obviously taking his "talk" with Brother Simon seriously though because, before he was ready, he was in the Snooker room practising and thinking every night for a *whole week*!

It was the following Thursday evening when he was ready.

Not long after we had finished our tea (I think it was 'tata ash night, not 'tata pie night!) Dad rather formally said.

"Simon, would it be possible to have a word with you in the Snooker room?"

I couldn't stop myself smirking as I watched Brother Simon squirming with embarrassment. I had pre-warned him that Dad was planning this "talk", and he had been somewhat dreading it.

The smirk turned into an audible snigger, as Brother Simon helplessly looked at me as he followed Dad towards our "Crucible Theatre".

Before they got to the room, Mum caught Dad's attention with a very unsubtle clearing of the throat. As Dad looked at her, she slowly moved her eyes towards me, in a rather creepy fashion.

It made her look like the Action Man figure with the switch in his neck that moved his eyes!

"Oh, right, yes!" said Dad. "Paul, would it be possible for you to also join us in the Snooker room?"

It was an instant role reversal.

I wore Brother Simon's embarrassed squirm, and he took on my sniggering smirk.

Once in the room, there was an awkward period of silence.

As there was no room for any chairs, Brother Simon and I stood at one side of the table as Dad slowly paced up and down on the other side.

After what seemed like a whole new age of time, (perhaps the Snooker room age?) he finally began to talk.

"I just wanted to quickly speak to you both about a few things - just little things like life, and girls, the Birds, the Bees and Snooker.

Because a lot of things in life; for example meeting and dating girls, are a lot

Goodbye B.M.X. Hello S.E.X.

like "Snooker"."

He looked a bit annoyed at himself for inverting his fingers as he said "Snooker" One of his pet hates was people who excessively used their hands as they talked, and the "inverted coma's" was his particularly most hated gesture.

After possibly telling himself internally that it was necessary for this <u>one</u> occasion, he shook his head and continued.

"Now, if you're invited to enter a "Snooker tournament", it's always a lot safer to take your cue in its case - if you know what I mean?

It can be very easy to "damage" your cue, so that added protection is essential! It can also help to ensure that it doesn't lead to some "unwanted", younger players in the future!"

I looked at Brother Simon who, thankfully, looked as confused as I was.

Dad carried on, still pacing as he quickly spoke.

"Now, when deciding what shot to take - it's safe to say that it's better to go for the *pink,* rather than the *brown.* You get more points for the pink and, well let's face it, the brown is at the *wrong end of the table,* isn't it?

Also, during a game, don't be scared to try different "shots" that may appear more difficult. Learning good techniques like stun shots, a lot of side or "deep screw" shots - can make you an all round better player. And that will give you more chance to impress during each match!

Also, don't be afraid to use some accessories. There's the rest, and the spider; even the "cue extension" if you need it - they can all make the game that much more enjoyable!"

Dad stopped waffling and came to a stand still right in front of us.

"So let's re-cap" he said, this time looking straight at us.

"*Accessories* can help. Learn as *many* shots as possible. *Pink* and <u>*not*</u> *Brown.* And, most importantly, *always* use your *cue case*!

Do you understand, or do I need to go through it again?"

"No, no, we understand!" said Brother Simon quickly.

Dad looked at me.

I nodded to him.

"Ok, good." Dad said, and quickly left the room.

"That was weird!" said Brother Simon, after Dad had left the room.

I again nodded in agreement.

It *was* weird.

What had started out feeling like it was going to be embarrassingly awkward, quickly fizzled out, and became quite informative.

I had no idea Dad knew so much about Snooker!

I certainly felt quite prepared should I ever decide to enter any Snooker tournaments - which it sounded like it was something Dad wanted us to do!

"Do you fancy a quick game?" I asked, picking up one of the queues. (Not the mini Snooker cue - that I was having a lot of trouble *looking* at, let alone *touching,* recently!)

Brother Simon took an age over deciding whether to play or not.

"Ok, then, yes!" he finally said, in an annoying and boring voice.

I realised the time had been needed to warm up his Steve Davis persona!

"You set them up." he said before performing a very dull yawn and stretch.

After reaching his arms out in a big "Y" shape, he turned to face me, about to say something, while putting his hands on his head.

I have no idea what he was going to say; because an unwanted image flashed before my eyes again, causing another uncontrollable stomach uprising, which meant I had to dash for the kitchen sink!

Goodbye B.M.X. Hello S.E.X.

December 1992

So here it was - the last month of the year.
The home straight in the dash towards Christmas and the New Year.
Would there be snow?
Would the Queen give a speech that doesn't instantly send the overfed nation straight off to sleep?
Would the pop charts ever stop mocking me?
The ludicrous *"Would I Lie To You?"* by *Charles and Eddie* which, every time I heard it reminded of the "lies" Louise had told me.
"I love you", and "it's got nothing to do with Dave Barlow". (Which was still actually neither officially confirmed or unconfirmed - but the fact he was prancing around College with a bigger, cheesier grin than usual or appeared humanly possible, was enough evidence for me)
This was followed by *Whitney Houston's* cover of the "classic" *Dolly Parton* hit *"I Will Always Love You"* - surely something she only did to inflict further pain on to my broken and bleeding heart that *already* felt terminal without her interference!
But the start of December brought with it an event that I had not experienced before.
Something that was new to me.
Something unwanted and unwelcome.
Something that put my break up with Louise into perspective; and exposed my "broken" and "bleeding" heart for what it really was - nothing more than a tiny pin-prick…..

Chapter Thirty Three - *"...when Angels scream out loud..."*

A whispered voice emerged through the silence and calmness of the sleep.
Quiet at first but slowly becoming loud enough to catch my attention and bring me out of my slumber.
"Paul.....Paul....Paul....Paul...."
I opened my eyes tentatively and, through my half open bedroom door, silhouetted in the orange glow of the landing light, I could make out the outline figures of both Mum and Dad.
As my mind made sense of the time and place; it must be middle of the night and I was in my own bed, the faces of my parents slowly developed into focus.
My eyes adjusted to the discomfort of receiving light after several hours of darkness, and I began to notice that Mum's eyes were red, and her face was blemished.
She had been crying.
I also noticed that both she and Dad were fully clothed, and wearing their Winter coats.
I suddenly felt the strangling sensation of panic gripping me.
My breathing speeded up and I began to feel my temperature rising quickly.
In the couple of seconds it took before Mum spoke again, my mind went into overdrive.
What was going on?
Why were they waking me up in the middle of the night? - It must be for something important.
Why were they both wearing their coats? - They must be going out, or had maybe already been out.
If so where had they been? - They must have been to the hospital to see Grandad, who was poorly.
But why in the middle of the night? - Was he ok?
Why had Mum been crying?
Oh no!
Oh no, please!
A seconds worth of thinking had prepared me for the words that were coming. But it was not enough to protect me from the crushing feeling that came with them.
"It's Grandad," Mum stuttered with a breaking voice,
"He's died."
It felt like on her last word, someone had placed a huge, concrete block on top of my chest.
It was pinning me to my bed, crushing the air out of my lungs, and I was quite sure that I would never be able to move again.
There was no pain.
Just an overwhelming numbness.

Goodbye B.M.X. Hello S.E.X.

Mum pushed my bedroom door fully open and turned the light on, and she and Dad sat down on the edge of my bed.

They both began talking slowly; no doubt measured words to gently explain what had happened on this night as I obliviously slept.

But I could not hear a word - there was only silence.

They were sitting close enough to touch me, brightly lit by my bedroom light that was directly above their heads.

But I could not see anything - there was only darkness.

It was as if the whole World had stopped.

I realised that, as Grandad himself had explained to me many years ago, this was how it must be - when Angels scream out loud.

The rest of the night is a blur.

No doubt there were tears and hugs and words of consolation, designed to calm and somehow soothe.

But I don't remember anything.

My first memories, after Mum's devastating four words, were from later.

It was after they had gone to bed and I was again alone in my room.

I felt tired but wide awake.

As I stared blankly into the darkness, my eyes were stinging and felt like they had cried an entire lifetime's worth of tears.

I began to maybe think that this shouldn't have come as such a shock to me. Grandad had been in and out of hospital several times in the last year.

On each occasion he had been struggling badly to breath; affected by bronchitis, that was no doubt brought on by an addiction to strong cigarettes. A habit that he had begun during his younger days in the army. An environment where everyone smoked - in a time when the consequences to health were not appreciated.

He had given up some years ago when advised by his doctor, but no doubt the damage had already been done.

Each time he had gone into hospital, he had spent a couple of days taking medication and much of the time wearing an oxygen mask, but he had always returned home seemingly "as good as new".

I suppose it was naïve to assume this, because obviously each visit to the hospital was taking a toll.

But I had just seen him yesterday and, although wearing his oxygen mask, he was bright eyed and in good spirits.

And yet, this was probably because he was always in good spirits.

That was the way that he was.

He was never in anything but a good mood.

Even times when he may have been angry or in a bad frame of mind you would never notice.

He always had the playful sparkle in his eyes - even during the rare occasions he was disagreeing or arguing with someone.

And, on these occasions, he had a unique ability to stay very cool while, with dignity and humour, calmly putting people firmly in their place.

I couldn't believe I would never see him again.
Never talk to him again.
Never play or laugh with him again.
For a while I began to refuse to believe it.
It couldn't be true.
Mum and Dad must be wrong.
Or maybe the Doctors and Nurses at the hospital were wrong - and if they weren't wrong, then how could they have let it happen?
Then, as some light began to faintly glow around the edges of my curtains, the cold reality of the truth began to hit me.
Everything suddenly felt very real.
Grandad had been very ill; something I had not known, or had not wanted to accept. He would not be returning home this time.
I would never see him again.
I closed my eyes, and to my horror, no matter how hard I tried, I couldn't picture Grandad in my mind.
Tears began to meander down my face again as I noticed the exuberant sound of Birds in song, beginning to build outside.
Another day was starting.
Did they not realise what had happened?
How could a new day be starting?
Just as casually as any other?
Everything was wrong.
Before much longer the light entering my room was enough that I could clearly see everything inside.
The computer desk, the TV, chair and wardrobe - everything was present and correct.
Yet everything looked different.
Yet everything was the same.
It was *my eyes* that were different.
Maybe it was a filter of innocence that had been removed.
Perhaps I could be considered lucky that, at the age of seventeen, I had never known anyone really close to me that had died before.
I had therefore been protected and hadn't had to face up to the inevitability of life that was *mortality*.
But any theoretical thoughts or conversations about death were no preparation for *this* reality.
It now felt like nothing else that had happened in my life meant anything. Like every other day I had lived had some how been pretend - because compared to this one, they didn't seem real.
In my mind I recited the well known saying: "Time is a great healer", and allowed myself to believe that I would begin to feel better at some point; that perhaps I couldn't continue to feel this bad.
I was wrong.
There were to be numerous occasions ahead when those initial, crushing

feelings would have to be re-lived.

The breakfast table, just a few hours later; to see Mum and Dad, and maybe more significantly, Brother Simon, in the harsh daylight for the first time.

Their tired faces and sore eyes looked every bit the way that mine felt, and unlike I had ever seen them before.

There was a strange quietness around the table as we attempted to eat something.

No squabbling or jokes or mickey taking.

There was almost a quiet respect for each others feelings.

But it felt different, and unnatural.

And everything was surrounded by a, never before felt, air of vulnerability.

It made the dreadful feelings as clear as they were the night before - like a still bleeding wound being freshly slashed at.

Later that day we all went round to visit Grandma.

I realised that, unlike me, she had experienced the loss of close people in her life before, perhaps several times. Her own grandparents, mother and father, perhaps even close friends.

But also unlike me, her loss was of the man she had been married to for fifty years.

The father of her children.

Her life partner.

Soul mate.

She conducted herself with dignity, giving me and Brother Simon the support and comfort she knew we needed - her own tears kept to a minimum.

But she was evidently hurting the same as us, and for the first time ever she looked different.

She looked old and frail.

Also, like never before, I saw Grandma and Grandad's house for what it was: a small, one bed roomed flat.

It felt tiny, almost claustrophobic.

Yet I could safely say that, the hundreds, possibly thousands, of times I had been there before this day, it had always felt like the most comfortable and luxurious house I had ever been in.

I couldn't even picture Grandad clearly here - not even in his favourite chair directly in front of the TV.

I began to imagine what the future held.

There would be birthday parties - without the balloon animals that Grandad would always make.

There would be Sunday card nights - with an empty chair where Grandad always sat.

There would be football matches - without Grandad watching from the sidelines.

Every occasion would be a brand new cut, on a wound that would possibly never heal.

The next week Grandma asked me and Brother Simon to help carry

Gary Locke

Grandad into the church for his funeral service.

Although there were four of us to carry him, he was heavy.

Extremely heavy.

It was obviously the weight of the wooden casket; but I couldn't help but believe that the heaviness came from Grandad himself.

His memories, his dreams, his personality, his smiles and sparkle, his sheer love for life and his family - it all added up to something huge and heavy.

Dad had told me to be brave and show respect - by not crying uncontrollably and making a scene.

So as others wept gently, I gritted my teeth tightly and tried to listen to every word that the Vicar said.

Although I'm sure that he had never met Grandad, and the majority of his phrases were general and probably used at every service, I managed to put Grandad into every scenario he spoke of; even if I could not see him clearly.

"His great love for his children and Grandchildren" - I pictured us all on numerous random-weathered holidays in Prestatyn: laughing, smiling, having the great time that a years worth of saving had earned us.

"His great love for his wife" - I pictured him side by side with Grandma.

At their flat, at our house, on holiday; everywhere - always together, always happy.

"His love for all sport; especially football, and Manchester United!"

The slight sniggers and groans made the Vicar quickly check his notes, before he corrected himself with "Manchester City!"

I pictured Grandad at, pretty much, every sporting event I had been involved in.

Whether he be watching me from the sidelines, or standing beside me as we watched Brother Simon, he was always there - enjoying being able to share the moments with us.

I pictured me, Mum and Brother Simon waving Grandad, Dad and Uncle Melvin off from the train station as they travelled to London for the 1981 cup final.

I pictured their long, disappointed faces as they returned!

(A face I would come to associate with watching City over the years!)

And yet I remember Grandad, later, speaking enthusiastically about the final anyway.

The atmosphere, the sense of occasion, actually being there and soaking it all up.

And I realised *that* was Grandad.

He found the positive in everything.

He lived his life.

He took in the journey.

And he savoured the view when he reached the destination.

Later at the crematorium, there was the harsh sense of finality as the curtains closed and his casket disappeared from sight.

Everybody was standing up, and beginning to leave.

Goodbye B.M.X. Hello S.E.X.

Were we really going to be leaving him behind?

Again, I felt the wound as fresh as when it had first been created.

I tried to be strong and remembered what Grandad had said about the sound of the screaming Angels passing with time - when you find a way to transform the pain of mourning into a euphoric celebration of life.

I closed my eyes as I walked, trying hard to hold back the tears that I had promised Dad, and myself, that I would not produce.

And there he was.

Grandad - in my mind, clear as day.

And I realised that I would never be leaving him behind.

He would always be with me.

In my mind, in my memories, in my heart.

Always.

Gary Locke

Now

The days seem a little bit longer now,
Like maybe there's a 25th hour somehow,
I never noticed the clock, before days like this,
Now it sounds like thunder, as it slowly ticks.

The wind seems to blow, a lot more cold,
When I'm walking now, without your hand to hold
But now I don't like to wear, my coat, because,
There's one on the hook, that's never taken off.

To have meals together, was one of your rules,
So the family ate, in the dining room,
We still always go, to eat in there,
But now the table has, an empty chair.

The house seems to groan, and creak in despair,
Without you here to paper, and paint and repair,
Even the small cosy bed, where we'd sleep safe and sound,
Feels like a vast wasteland, now you're not around.

We loved how we promised: for better or worse,
But knew one of us would, have to go first,
To carry on living, we both made the vow,
But life is so different; so meaningless now

Goodbye B.M.X. Hello S.E.X.

Chapter Thirty Four - *"…the great tapestry…"*

Dark mornings, dark evenings, dark days.
Was it just the usual December conditions, or a metaphor for how I was feeling?
It was as if all the light had gone from the World.
All the vivid colours replaced by grainy black and white.
Christmas had come and gone.
But not like usual - flashing past; all singing and dancing and non-stop entertainment.
It had *dragged*.
Forced smiles and empty attempts at merriment was the result of one simple fact.
There was an empty chair at the table.
Grandad's chair!
For as long as I could remember, Christmas dinner had been held at our house. There were various visitors throughout the day, dropping off and collecting presents, but the table line up at Turkey-time never changed.
There was Auntie Miriam and Uncle Geoff, me, Brother Simon, Mum and Dad, and Grandma and Grandad.
Mum had extended the table as usual but, despite her trying to subtly move the place settings slightly further apart, there was an obvious gap.
Not only literally, to the left of Grandma, but also atmospherically.
Without Grandad's voice in the conversation, everything felt wrong.
The paper, party hats seemed too small, and ripped as you tried to put them on.
The non-alcoholic wine that Grandma insisted on bringing each year, tasted more like vinegar than ever.
The jokes from the (disappointingly quiet opening) crackers weren't funny. (They obviously never were - but when everyone was in the party mood, they seemed cheesily amusing!)
The only thing that was remotely familiar was Mum's overcooked Turkey and watery Gravy!
She also insisted on me having a couple of *Sprouts*.
(I may as well have had the full pans worth - the Sprout taste ruins your meal whether you eat two, or two hundred!)
During the dark days that followed Christmas, I decided I would not go out on Thursday the 31st - New Years Eve.
Mark, John and Little Si had tried to change my mind.
They had bought tickets for the "*Yates' New Year Fancy Dress Knees Up*".
But I had made my mind up.
I had no appetite or enthusiasm for it.
I also convinced myself that the guys would have a better time without me moping around beside them.

Gary Locke

On Tuesday the 29th, a conversation with Dad changed a lot of things for me. He had actually started *working*!

The job centre had been so impressed with his commitment towards his computer course, they had offered him a part time administration position.

He had taken it, saying that it was his "first little step towards his global domination as a Financial Advisor"!

(Perhaps a little optimistic, or more accurately *delusional*, but it was good to see him giving it a real go.)

I think his new sense of purpose had also resulted in a feeling of pride that, perhaps, he had been without for some time.

It all added up to him becoming more friendly and accessible.

He also, somehow, seemed to be wiser - maybe because he was no longer speaking to Father Christmas on the phone, or talking about "early birds and early worms"!

He was certainly cooler.

"So where are you going out on New Years Eve?" he casually inserted as we chatted about Man City's respectable 1-1 draw at Liverpool the previous evening.

"I'm not going out" I replied,

"I'll just stay in and watch Clive James or something. He's usually pretty funny."

Dad didn't say anything at first.

I don't think he really liked Clive James.

But then again, his opinion on most Australians depended on whether England had won the last Ashes series or not.

So, invariably, he spent most of the time disliking Australians!

Including Rolf Harris.

For years, Dad used to ask "Why is *he* in this country, making money off us, with his "can you tell what it is yet?" or "two little, bloody boys" and his "phone pest-like heavy breathing?"

How can anyone *not* like Rolf Harris?

"I thought you'd be going out with your friends!" he finally said.

"I don't really fancy it." I said, as matter-of-factly as I could.

"Everything's not as dark and gloomy as you think it is!" said Dad.

"I know it's hard at the moment - we all miss Grandad. And I know that you are still upset about Louise as well."

I didn't say anything, and instead put my head down.

I didn't really want to talk about feeling "dark and gloomy".

I was also wondering whether Dad wasn't really working in administration, but was actually perhaps a trainee Psychologist!

"But this is what life is about" he continued. "It can't always be Sunshine - otherwise how would Sunshine be special?

There's got to be some rainy days. Here have a look at this."

He took a piece of paper from out of his pocket and handed it to me.

"You like poetry don't you?" he said rhetorically. "It's not Keats or Kipling;

Goodbye B.M.X. Hello S.E.X.

but I like it."

I looked at the top of what was obviously a poem.

The title read *"To Really Have It All by David Day - aged 18"*.

I looked up in amazement at Dad, who realised that I had seen his name.

"I liked to be a bit creative, as well, at your age." he said. "I wrote some songs and some poems - I was just a bit better at keeping it secret than you" he added smiling.

I laughed a little, before returning my eyes to the paper and reading.

<u>To Really Have It All</u>

If it was only ever sunshine, and there was never any rain,
And feelings only of pure joy, and there was never any pain,
If each and every day was perfect, time and time again,
Could you really feel the pleasure, if it was always just the same?

Is the spring morning so special, because the Sun cuts through the frost?
Or the real joy of being found, in the thoughts that all was lost?
Is the fulfilment in your buying, that before you couldn't meet the cost?
Or excitement in the unknown, as the coin is being tossed?

Can you really savour victory, if you can't compare to when you'd lose?
Is the luxury in variety, born from times when you could not choose?
A scar is there to remind, of a time when you were cut and bruised,
A symbol that you healed, to show that you got through.

You must climb the steps to the stage yourself, to earn the right to sing,
And someone's heart must wear your name, before you deserve to wear their ring,
To really have it all, you've got to know what it's like to have nothing,
Before you truly bask in the Sunshine, you have to live through the thunder and lightning.

I looked up at Dad, as the words and their meanings slowly filtered into my mind.

"That's pretty good!" I said.

"I realised back then, that life is a balance." Dad said. "To really appreciate the Summer, you need to have lived through the harshest Winter. I know it's hard to accept right now, but you'll look back at this year with fond memories. I can't remember ever seeing you happier and smiling more than you have over these last twelve months.

Because of the hard times, like these, you'll be able to look back one day soon and realise how *great* things were. And you'll also realise how great things *can*, and *will*, be in the future."

I smiled at Dad.

Gary Locke

His words made sense and they were making me feel a bit better.

But he was in no mood to stop.

He was talking like a man possessed - he was like Eddie Murphy on Speed!

"There will always be a big hole where Grandad was. Also one where Louise was as well - a different one, but still a hole.

But you'll learn to deal with it differently.

You'll begin to notice just how beautiful the blue sky is, and how amazing it is when the colour fades to black at night-time, and is replaced by those endless, sparkling Stars.

And the Birds - now that you've heard them sound like they're out of tune, they'll sound twice as good when you hear them like they *really are* again.

And you'll see each Season for what it is - an ongoing circle of Mother Nature's miracle, keeping everything fresh; helping us all to stay alive.

There will always be holes in the great tapestry.

Most of the time you'll want to keep them out your mind, but there will also be times when you'll want to look at them closely.

To remember why they are there; why there are holes that can never be filled.

But you'll also see how much else there is to marvel at.

And that will include other girls….."

I interrupted.

Partly because I thought Dad may pass out if he didn't take a breath, but also partly because I didn't want him to talk about "fishes" and "seas".

"You're not going to tell me that there are plenty more Fish in the sea are you?" I asked.

After taking a few gulps of air, Dad laughed.

"No, I'm not. I don't like the saying either. There are *numerous* Fish in the sea, but not all of them will be special for you.

But there *will* be more than *one* special one!

I had quite a few girlfriends before I met your Mother. Some not so great, but some that were special.

I wouldn't say that your Mum was my *first love*.

That was probably a girl who lived on the street next to mine when I was growing up. A girl called Patsy Lomas.

It was certainly love as I knew it back then. When we split up, I thought I would never get over it.

But I did.

Because there were *others*.

Including your Mother.

And, with your Mother, love was suddenly something different.

Something more.

Something that could last forever!

But it doesn't mean that I can't think about Pat now and again.

Because what we had was something to cherish.

It's one of the holes in *my* tapestry."

Goodbye B.M.X. Hello S.E.X.

He turned to me and placed his hands on my shoulders.

"You've still got most of *your* tapestry ahead of you.

You just have to go and watch it weaving.

That's the best part - the journey.

The making of the memories.

The living!"

He took his hands off my shoulders, and the way the intense look on his face faded, I assumed he was finished.

I was wrong!

"I think you should go out with your friends on Thursday. Those guys are lost without you to guide them." he said, a little calmer than before.

To make sure that he didn't start off again I agreed with him.

Also, because he was right.

Despite a bad few weeks that would, no doubt, stay with me forever, I *had* lived a year to remember.

Maybe there would be times in the future when I would choose to reflect on the feelings of emptiness and hurt, but New Years Eve shouldn't be one of them.

Dad was right - without me, Little Si, Mark and John were lost.

They were a rudderless ship.

Sheep without a Collie.

Take That without Gary Barlow!

(To liken myself to Gary Barlow made me realise I had reached a brand new low!)

But the good thing about lows is, as *Yazz* so astutely observed back in 1988, *the only way is up*!

And New Years Eve was surely the perfect time to begin reaching up again...

Chapter Thirty Five - *"...New Years Eve..."*

I had spent the days following Christmas convincing myself that I didn't want to go out on New Years Eve.

Partly because I was feeling depressed.

And partly because I felt going out would somehow be disrespectful to Grandad.

How could I pretend that the World hadn't ended?

It was those words of wisdom from Dad (yep, still surprises me too!) that had put everything into perspective.

The World *hadn't* ended.

Although, it *had* changed forever.

But we would all have to get used to the change – sooner or later.

And maybe Dad was right. Maybe one day those feelings of pain and sorrow, or the *holes in the tapestry* as he'd put it, will be things that can be looked upon as happy memories.

But that was for the future.

For now, it felt like going out on New Years Eve would be a good way to start to try and face up to the change.

Luckily for me, Mark had bought me a ticket for the Yates' party or, to give it its full title, - the *Yates' New Year Fancy Dress Knees Up*!

Apparently he'd got the ticket for me on Dad insistence - perhaps a little over confident about his own powers of persuasion?

Unluckily for me though, John had also hired me a "costume" to wear.

For reasons only known to himself, John thought us four musketeers should go dressed in colourful suits.

"We'll be like the "literal version" of the film Reservoir Dogs" he had said. "It will be hilarious!"

John and his Brother had seen the film in America, during a short break there in October.

The fact that it hadn't been released in England, and next to no-one had even heard of it (I certainly hadn't) seemed to have by-passed Johns thought process.

John was "Mr Pink", and so wore a pink suit.

Little Si was "Mr Blue", and so wore a blue suit.

I was "Mr White", and so wore a white suit.

Mark was "Mr Orange", and so wore a *red* suit! (According to John, the closest colour to orange available at the suit hire shop!)

If we looked like a "version" of *anything*, it was the "gay version"!

Despite the other three of us moaning and threatening not to wear our "costumes", John had insisted that fancy dress was "compulsory".

And with it being so close to New Years Eve it was too late to change costumes, therefore too late to worry about them.

As we entered Stoneport, on New Years Eve itself; after an uncomfortable 192 journey, during which every other passenger stared at us, I realised it

Goodbye B.M.X. Hello S.E.X.

wasn't too late to worry about Little Si!

He had still never been allowed into a pub!

It had been nearly twelve months ago that he was refused entry into Yates' itself (and every other pub within a ten mile radius!), and possible that he had grown since then; but from where I was looking, you would need a ruler with a millimetre scale to notice the change!

If he did look any different than the times he was turned away, then realistically it would only be because he now looked about *thirteen* instead of *twelve*!

As we walked towards the pub, I tried to reassure myself that they wouldn't turn him away tonight - we had already bought tickets.

Even so, I suggested that we should approach in a definite order.

I would go first, and would hand over all four tickets.

Surely my "non-virgin" aura would make me appear oldest.

John would go next. Hopefully the bouncers would be distracted by his pink suit enough for Little Si to sneak through third.

Finally Mark would enter. He was now showing signs of having a moustache that looked like it was being grown through his skin, as opposed to John's that still looked more like several eye lashes that had fallen out and landed above his top lip!

With the door in sight, I confidently walked slightly ahead, as the other three took the order I had planned.

It was like I was leading my troops into battle.

As I closed in on the bouncers, who were the same two freakish Hulks that were usually there (and had previously, and numerously, rejected Little Si's entry), I noticed that the people I had seen already entering hadn't put as much effort into their "fancy dress" outfits as we had.

I then noticed the sign on the chalkboard next to the door.

Yates' New Year Fancy Dress* Knees Up - Thursday 31st December
(*Fancy Dress - Optional)

There was no time to yell the obvious question to John - "WHO THE HELL WEARS FANCY DRESS IF IT'S ONLY *OPTIONAL*?" - so I contented myself with throwing him a quick dirty look over my shoulder.

As I reached the doormen, one held out his large hand like a Policeman halting traffic.

"Nice suit, Romeo!" he said, causing the second bouncer to snigger. "You got tickets?"

I nodded my head and passed him the four tickets.

"Is it these three behind you as well?" he asked.

I resisted the urge to say *"well counted – knob head!"* and instead said, "Yes it is!"

"My, my" began the second bouncer. "You are *all* brightly dressed. Are you afraid you may lose each other once you're inside?"

They both began laughing, but stepped aside to let us in.

I started walking and, disguised with a cough, tried to shout to the others - "QUICK!"

Unfortunately my cough distorted it more than I intended, and it sounded rather like I had shouted "DICK!" in the direction of the bouncer.

A split second of panic, accompanied by a vision of one of the pumped-up door comedians picking me up by my ear and launching me into a head first swallow dive towards the pavement, soon passed.

Neither of the bouncers heard as they were both still too busy laughing.

I looked back at Little Si, and urged him through.

He wasn't going to make it.

How could he; he had a face that gave you an urge to pinch and shake his little cheek.

I began to wish that we had dressed up like "The Krankies".

Little Si could have been Jimmy Krankie, the Schoolboy! (Who in *real life* was a *woman* who was married to the *man* who played Jimmy's *father* - more than a little weird and *scary* when you think about it!)

At least if he was dressed as a Schoolboy, it would explain why he looked so young.

But Little Si was determined.

He kept his head down, and walked like he was one of those hip-wiggling Olympic walkers!

He made it.

Once out of sight of the two giggling gargantuan we congratulated Little Si like he was the first man to break the four minute mile!

It was a magical moment for him - the first time in a pub.

I watched as he breathed in that unique aroma of sweat and stale beer. As the heavy bass in the music shook the floor, I remembered my first time - at this very same place.

John also noticed the excitement in Little Si's eyes.

"Come on" he said to him. "Wait 'til you see the whole pub!"

He began to walk around the corner into the main room, and we all followed.

I laughed to myself as I remembered our first time here, when the DJ made fun of us as we entered the room.

It seemed like such a long time ago.

Suddenly the music stopped and that very same, amplified voice announced itself again.

"HERE COMES THE PINK PANTHER!"

We all laughed out loud at the DJ's reference to John who was a few yards ahead of us.

There wasn't time for John to be embarrassed on his own, though, because the DJ noticed Little Si, me and Mark standing in a row, behind him.

"CLOSELY FOLLOWED BY THE FLAG OF FRANCE!"

There was no need for me to debate with myself whether there was much laughter this time, because people were nearly falling over themselves laughing.

But the DJ wasn't finished.

"OR ARE THEY ALL TOGETHER - MAYBE MIGHTY MORPHIN POWER RANGERS HERE TO RESCUE US!"

I quickly indicated to my troops that we should head for the bar; and we excited the sitting duck target zone.

At the bar, I had a quick glance around and worked out that at least 90% of the people in the bar were *not* wearing fancy dress.

"Did you know that fancy dress was optional?" I asked John.

"Yeah," he said conceding that he had lied. "But I thought it would be good to stand out!"

"Yeah," said Mark. "We do standout - we look like four Dickheads!"

"Here we go!"

We looked round to see that Little Si had already been served.

He'd used his "height advantage" to slip past everyone to the front of the bar.

He passed us a bottle of Diamond White each.

"Not too badly priced - I thought they'd be well expensive" Little Si said.

"Well, there'll be no D.A.T. in here, will there!" said John.

We all laughed and "chinked" our bottles together.

We found a "normal" table (not one hidden under the stairs, in darkness and where things were constantly thrown down on you!), where we drunk and talked and laughed - a lot.

I began to feel glad that I'd make the effort to come out.

I realised that it was nights like this, that needed to be savoured.

After a couple of hours, and four bottles each, we began to contemplate "hitting the dance floor".

Just like everyone else, we all thought, after a few drinks, we could dance just like Michael Jackson!

But before I got chance to head off for a "Moonwalk", I felt a tap on my shoulder.

I looked round and saw Lynsey - the girl from my P.E. class at College.

"Hiya!" she said.

"Hello." I said, turning my head right round, almost Owl-like, to look at her.

She looked fantastic.

Her long, "auburn" hair was sparkling as it reflected the disco lights, and her deep green eyes were warm and friendly.

She was wearing a figure-hugging, short, black dress.

She was red hot!

"Fancy a dance?" she asked.

"Yes I do!" I said, standing up so quickly it was like I had just been called to attention.

"I've got to warn you, though" I said. "I'm quite a mover! - Do you think you can keep up?"

"I'll give it a try" she said smiling and grabbing my hand.

I glanced at Mark as I headed towards the dance floor.

He nodded and gave me a smug *"I told you so!"* type grin.

As we began dancing, Lynsey looked at my white suit and asked,

"Are you supposed to be John Travolta?"

It sounded more reasonable than Johns "literal" Reservoir Dogs thing, so I said "Yes."

"Who are you friends supposed to be then?" she asked.

"Mighty Morphin Power Rangers!" I said. "They love them! They're like little kids!"

By some strange quirk of fate, *"Stayin' Alive"* from Saturday Night Fever began to play, so I gave my dancing the full *Travolta Treatment*!

It probably looked more like I was randomly pointing at the ceiling rather than dancing, but Lynsey seemed to find it entertaining, and I was certainly enjoying myself.

The next couple of songs were slower, and Lynsey and I danced closer until, finally, *Wet Wet Wet's "Goodnight Girl"* played and we were almost in a slow embrace.

"No corny joke for me today?" I asked as we moved slowly.

Lynsey thought about it, before saying

"I'll do you a deal - I'll tell you a joke on one condition."

"What's that?" I asked.

"If I can make you laugh - you have to kiss me!"

"Ok" I said smiling. "But you know that I don't laugh at any old rubbish jokes!"

Lynsey closed her eyes for a couple of seconds, as she thought up her "witty" line.

I stared at her as I waited - she really was *extremely* attractive.

"Ok" she said opening her eyes. "What do "Jack the Ripper" and "Winnie the Pooh" have in common?"

"I don't know" I said.

"They've got the same middle name!" she said smiling.

"That's probably the *worst joke* I've ever heard" I said, keeping a deadpan face.

Lynsey's smile began to fade and a hint of disappointment emerged onto her face.

I held my serious look for a couple of seconds before beginning to laugh gently.

Lynsey began to smile as I leant in, putting one hand behind her head, and softly connecting my lips with hers.

It was the first kiss I'd had since breaking up with Louise.

It felt strange.

It was different.

But it felt nice.

It was good.

Goodbye B.M.X. Hello S.E.X.

We danced for about another half an hour; and enjoyed two more tender, but fairly passionate, "smooches", before Lynsey went off to find her friends.

She said she would come to find my later; adding "I could hardly miss you in that suit!"

I returned to where the guys were sitting but barely had any time to boast about my unmistakeably attractive dancing partner, before I had another female visitor.

"Hi Paul!"

I looked round again, and this time saw Louise standing behind me.

"Hi!" I said, somewhat surprised.

Little Si made a noise that I can only assume meant he didn't approve of Louise talking to me.

It was the sort of sound that a Cat makes when you force it into a travel basket before a visit to the vets!

It was almost an angry "hiss" that took everyone within ten metres by surprise.

After a couple of seconds staring at Little Si, who rightly had lowered his head in embarrassment, I looked back at Louise.

"Could I talk to you for a couple of minutes?" she asked.

I quickly glanced at Mark and John to gage their opinions, and they both gave similar *"it's up to you"* shrugs of the shoulders.

I didn't look at Little Si - his outburst had forfeited his right to an opinion!

I looked back at Louise, who was gently smiling at me.

"Ok" I said, standing up.

I followed her, as she walked towards somewhere a bit quieter where we could talk.

She, too, was wearing a short, tight black dress and looked fantastic.

I noticed a couple of guys staring at me, probably because they'd seen me with Lynsey a few minutes earlier. I assumed they thought I was some kind of super stud, so I gave them a cocky acknowledging nod - which actually made me feel a bit dirty and Peter Stringfellow-like!

Louise was heading towards the "darkened" table under the stairs and, although it was tempting to maybe see her bombarded with ice and straws, I steered her over to the side wall - where it would surely be safer.

When we got there Louise started talking straight away.

"I wanted to tell you how sorry I am about your Grandad. I only heard a couple of days ago - I'm *really sorry*. I was going to phone you, but thought it would be better to talk face to face. Abbey knew John was coming here tonight - he'd been boasting to her about how great your costumes were."

She stared at my white suit as she spoke, but obviously decided not to comment on it.

"Your Grandad was such a lovely man. So welcoming and kind and so friendly and funny. So very cool. I'm so very sorry."

She gently stroked my arm, as I looked down trying hard not to add to the moisture that was forming in my eyes.

She waited for a few seconds, just tenderly stroking my arm, before talking again.

"How have you been?" she asked.

"You know me, I'm always good." I said, keeping my head down.

Louise just continued to caress my arm, saying nothing.

I looked up at her, no longer concerned about the tears in my eyes.

"I've been better." I said.

I stared into her sparkling eyes, and watched as they also slightly glazed over.

"I've missed you!" she said.

"I've missed you, too!" I said.

"It might be nice if we could go out some time. Just the two of us" she said. "Maybe a drink; or just a walk somewhere, or maybe a night in at your house - like we used to?"

I stared into her eyes, helplessly, as she slowly leaned into me; watching my reflection getting clearer.

It was something I thought I wouldn't experience again, and it made me feel warm and comfortable.

We kissed.

It felt the same as it used to - and yet, somehow, different.

I pulled away.

"Sorry" said Louise. "I don't want to put any pressure on you."

"It's ok" I said, smiling at her.

"I said I'd get Abbey a drink, can I get you one; maybe a Diamond White?"

I laughed a little.

"You do owe me one!" I said, thinking about how much of my cider she drank when we first met.

She looked confused.

"I'm just joking" I said. "I'm ok, thanks. I've got a drink at our table."

"Is it ok if I come and see you later?" Louise asked.

"Of course, yes." I said.

We smiled at each other before she headed for the bar.

I stood for a minute, thinking things over.

Louise wanted us to see each other again!

It was everything I had hoped and wished for since we had split up; but was it something that I really *wanted*?

I think so.

But I wasn't sure.

As usual with this type of dilemma, the Angel and Devil of my subconscious appeared to argue it out.

After both not being able to decide which way they should arguing, they agreed a surprise truce and headed off towards the bar together!

What did *I* think about all this?

And, damn, why didn't I ask her about her Mum's tattoo and clear up, once and for all, the whole, is she / isn't she the owner of the shoulder Dragonfly!

Goodbye B.M.X. Hello S.E.X.

Was this really important right now?
I suppose not!
I walked back to our table in a state of confusion.
"What's going on?" John asked as I sat back down.
The answer struck me straight away.
Everything was clear.
"It's New Years Eve; I'm with my three best mates, and we're going to have a hell of a night!"
The four of us raised our bottles, and we all chinked them together again.
We drank and danced right through into the New Year.
Just the four of us - causing a real spectacle, and much laughter on the dance floor, as we boogied away in our multi-coloured garments.
We weren't alone in our eccentricity though.
We were joined by Superman, Spiderman and Captain America, a rather attractive female Gladiator, and a whole group of dangerous looking Samurai Warriors.
We were even briefly joined by a man wearing a Maggie Thatcher mask - but he was quickly knocked out by a hefty blow from Captain Americas Shield!
I spoke to Louise and Lynsey briefly after midnight.
Louise wanted me to walk her home, and Lynsey asked if I wanted to go back to a party at her friend's house.
I said no to both of them.
I was going home the same way I started the night; in fact the same way I started the year - with my best friends.
As we queued for the bus, I remembered some of Dads words.
I looked up to the clear skies and watched the Stars as they twinkled brightly from millions of miles away.
I breathed in the crisp, but fresh air.
I glanced at John, Mark and Little Si, who were standing close together; their ridiculous suits making them look like a circus tent!
I smiled and realised how pleased I was to be sharing this with them.
It <u>was</u> good to be alive.
My mind quickly flicked back to the start of the year when I had made my optimistic aims.
I hadn't done too badly!
Most importantly I had lived my motto.
Despite the dubious setting in which I had stumbled across it, I hadn't let any day pass me by, and there were numerous contenders for the best day of my life.
This day was one of them.
More importantly, I realised that every single day in the future also had the potential to be the best day of my life.
The night wasn't just marking the end of a year; it was marking the beginning of a new one.
And 1993 was starting much differently to 1992.

I now had girls chasing after *me*. (I even heard Brother Simon's potential one word solution as to which of Louise or Lynsey I should go for – *threesome*!)

I had been into pubs (albeit the same one) several times.

I had passed my driving test.

I had experienced extreme adrenalin sports.

I had met and charmed over-protective parents.

I had even made love to a woman.

All these things hadn't perhaps gone completely smoothly! (In fact none had gone smoothly at all - especially the last one!)

But I had done them all.

Life *was* pretty good.

So bring on 1993 - it may just get even better…..

Goodbye B.M.X. Hello S.E.X.

<u>*To Be Alive*</u>

To wake to the blackbird symphony, as a brand new day is dawning,
To breath in the clean, cool air, on a perfect fresh Spring morning.

To gaze at the unspoilt beauty, of an endless clear blue sky,
To make shapes out of cotton clouds, as they slowly drift on by.

To plant a seed into the ground, and watch as life begins to grow,
To reach for heights undiscovered, and embrace the thrill of unknown.

To run as fast as you can, to be as free as the wildest wind,
To feel the Sunshine on your skin, as Summer emerges from Spring.

To taste a fresh, moist grape, that has just been picked from the vine,
To experience a rose, in the perfect scent of its prime.

To climb a hill or a mountain, to look out for miles and miles,
To be alone with just your thoughts, busy doing nothing for a while.

To watching a shooting Star, as it blazes by, burning bright,
To catch a falling leaf, on an orange skied Autumn night.

To imagine a special place, that exists beyond the Stars,
To fit snugly in your skin, content with who you are.

To hear leaves like a tambourine, rattling away in the breeze,
To touch the heart of another, to know what love can be.

To rest your eyes and drift off to sleep, enchanted within a dream,
To see the white sheet of Winter snow, natures very own deep clean.

To Be Alive.....
To Be Alive....

By Gary Locke:

The complete days of 1992 –
Paul Day Chronicles – Goodbye B.M.X., *Hello* **S.E.X.**

Short Stories from 1992 –
Paul Day Chronicles – Love for the Very First Time.
Paul Day Chronicles – Dead Legs, Exam Dreads and Fun Behind the Bike Sheds.

The complete days of 2006 –
Paul Day Chronicles – Happily After *Ever!*

Short Stories from 2006 –
Paul Day Chronicles – Love Is Like Fireworks!
Paul Day Chronicles – The Stag Do.
Paul Day Chronicles – Football Is Like Sex!
Paul Day Chronicles – Fate… Bloody Fate!

Cling and Grow Publishing

Copyright © Gary Locke 2013

Cover Design by Andy Tiplady – Freelance Graphic Designer

www.pauldaychronicles.com

Goodbye B.M.X. Hello S.E.X.

Acknowledgements

Cover Design by Andy Tiplady – Freelance Graphic Designer

The following cover pictures were taken from **flickr.com** under agreement of the Creative Commons license.

Bonfire by Aidan Jones
Cricket by andy_carter
Graveyard by Martin Pettitt
L Plate by tgraham
Paragliding by Snappa2006
Snooker by Ben Sutherland
Yates by Terry Wha
Roundabout by alastairb
1st Love by Muffet
BMX by soycamo
Tree Heart by alykat
Valentine by cambodia4kidsorg
Banana by Sean MacEntee
Exams by comedy_nose
High Jump by Tim Wilson
Santa by mark.groves
Number Ten by The Prime Minister's Office
Binoculars by Joanna Bourne
Mop by Nottinghack

Copyright © Gary Locke 2013

Made in the USA
Charleston, SC
06 January 2014